Fighting
Peace

Jezriah Ray

This book is dedicated to my sweetheart, Jedediah, and my good friend, Curtiss, who made this book ridiculously easy to write through observation of their good humor, coupled with a little creativity.

Special thanks to Soheil Toosi for the amazing cover art.

Chapter 1: Our Childhood.

I am not one who's good with words. I don't claim to be smart or wise; but I have a story to tell about love, loss, anger, resentment, and resolve–or lack thereof. I should probably start way back, so that you can understand my personality and beliefs.

Our childhood was nearly perfect. We were raised in a loving Christian family with a stay-at-home mom and a very involved dad. Evelyn is my older sister by three years. My favorite childhood memories are that of camping, hangin' with pets, and playing sports. During our camping trips, Dad would take Evie and me fishing, tubing down the river, and canoeing. We were all so close. Evie and I played together by making up stories and acting them out. We would enchant Dad and Mom with pre-supper entertainment. In fact, that's the way we played most of the time. We had few toys because money was tight. In those days, we really didn't need much because we had each other.

I realize now that things were tight financially because of my parents' lifestyle choices. We always had horses, and that required a good deal of penny-pinching in other areas. I was thankful to have had this type of childhood rather than one with more money for things such as nicer clothes needed for popularity, for example. Dad worked as a mechanic in a car shop and was the assistant pastor of our church. Mom was a housewife and a Sunday school teacher. She took a job as a secretary of a local school after Evie and I graduated high school.

God and church were always a big part of our lives. We grew up with Dad reading Bible stories to us before bed–not nursery rhymes or Dr. Seuss stories. We prayed together daily and talked about the goodness of God. I learned how to play the piano at a young age, and when I got good enough, I started playing piano specials at church. As my talent progressed, I assisted during church services, alternating with the other pianists. Evie sang specials angelically. I guess you could say we were a musically talented family in that often Dad would play the guitar, I would play the piano, and Mom and Evie would sing.

As we forged into our teens, Evie and I grew apart. I believe that's because of our strikingly different personalities. In fact, if it wasn't for our pronounced physical similarities, one might even guess that we were from different families. Evie was a momma's girl and a girlie-girl. She was a cheerleader, a heartthrob, and quite popular. Dad had his hands full with Evie, trying to keep the boys at bay. I was a Daddy's girl and a tomboy, so much so that I claimed the nickname Rick. Mom hated that, but Dad found it to be charming and agreed to call me Ricky as a compromise. Mom, however, insisted on calling me by my given name, Ericka.

I took pride in being as close to a boy as Dad could have. When I was a kid, I even liked to pretend and look the part. My face was never very feminine, so I'd put my hair up in a hat and could pass as a boy easily. I found that to be quite funny. I remember when some of Dad's closest friends would act like they didn't know who the strange boy was hanging around Dad, just to get me to smile. Even though Dad loved both of us girls very much, I believe that he especially loved all of time we'd spent together doing more masculine activities. I played every sport offered, and Dad coached most of the sports that I was in. I also loved to ride our horses and shoot guns with Dad, but my favorite pastime was riding on the back of Dad's Indian motorcycle. What a thrill. I never got tired of riding on his bike. All of the other kids were envious when my cool dad would pick me up from ball practice on his bike. Dad got me a dirt bike for my twelfth birthday. I was so excited! But we both knew that Mom wasn't going to be happy with this.

"Don't worry, Mom," I urged. "I'll wear my elbow and knee pads that are in the closet with my roller-skates. I already have a helmet and gloves!" Mom sighed as I ran around the house looking for all of the gear.

"It's the safest way for her to learn, dear," Dad reinforced.

"I know," Mom said as she continued to do dishes without looking up.

Shortly after getting the dirt bike, I made a goal to get a job and start saving for a real motorcycle. I was really motivated and self-driven. I would often use charts to obtain my goals, whether it was a financial goal of saving for a motorcycle or a sport-related goal such as improving my free throws in basketball. My first job was pet-sitting. The neighbors readily employed me with caring for their pets, knowing how goal-driven I was to save for my first motorcycle.

After all that's been said, I suppose it wouldn't surprise you that I wasn't really into my looks so much. Evie, however, put quite of bit of time into her appearance daily. She wore lots of eye makeup and her clothes were always in style. I, on the other hand, used just a little makeup and wore all of her hand-me-downs. I didn't mind the hand-me-downs so much except that some of the schoolkids would notice and a make fun of me. "Hey, isn't that your *sister's old sweater?"* they'd say sarcastically. I didn't understand what the big deal was. All of the clothes were in good enough shape.

Despite our differences in personality and style, Evie and I sure did look alike, and we both looked more like Dad. We had ivory skin, long black hair, and blue eyes. Evie's eyes were brighter and just more beautiful than mine. My blue eyes were softer, and on some days, I'd swear they even looked gray. I did enjoy that my eyes looked a bit more like Dad's. Evie and I were both quite thin. I was 5'6" and 103 pounds. Evie was 5'7" and about 106 pounds. Evie liked to flaunt her attractive figure, but I found joy in wearing comfortable, loose-fitting clothing. The only reason I had loose-fitting clothing is because Dad would occasionally have pity on me when I'd complain about having to wear Evie's old, form-fitting clothing that left me feeling vulnerable and naked somehow. He'd take me shopping and let me pick out my own clothes. Then we'd suffer the wrath of Mom's disappointment regarding my appearance. Actually, I hated being so thin! It was always the topic of conversation, not my good grades or how good I was in sports.

Evie's long black hair was especially radiant. Her hair had a medium natural wave to it, whereas mine had just enough wave to look unbrushed all of the time. Her wavy hair was so beautiful that there was no sense in straightening it, even though that was the style. I'd walk by the bathroom in the mornings and roll my eyes as I glanced in to see her spending so much time on her already perfect hair; and she used all that Aqua Net! It was *so* annoying.

Evie didn't really need to spend all that time on her looks because she was a natural beauty. Mom really thrived on how beautiful she was. I tried not to let on that it bothered me when I'd overhear Mom tell her so every morning as she got ready for school. She'd even kiss her on the forehead. I never got that kind of attention from Mom. I'd block out my jealousy and cope by spending more time with Dad and by trying *not* to be like my sister.

Mom persistently tried to get me to change the way I looked. She'd say, "Why don't you try to do something with your hair?" or "You should try a little more makeup." The answer was always, "No, Mom! I look fine!" Giving into that would make me more like Evie. The only real thing I had on my older sis, as far as appearance goes, was a larger rump and bust. So I secretly took pride in that. And why not? Everyone treated me as if I were inferior to her. Yes, even family, except for Dad. He treated us equally.

Evie was *completely* boy crazy. I knew of Evie's loose reputation with the boys, but I didn't tell Dad or Mom. I'm not sure how they would've reacted, well, except it'd be bad. Evie and I didn't talk about anything important like that. No, that's not how I knew. I knew this because a number of the older classmen would harass me by saying horrible things like, "I bet you're a whore just like your sister." This was about the time that I realized I had nearly supersonic hearing. If I concentrated, I could hear guys talk about me in a crowded, loud hallway from quite a ways away. One guy said, "Look at those tits and ass. Those long legs just go on forever. Too bad she's so hard to get." Then the other replied, "I bet *I* could get in her pants. My cousin did her sister and said she was wild."

One jerk in particular who had a locker near mine, would not only verbally sexually harass me, but he'd also try to touch me during room changes. I'd clench my teeth and push him away, ready to fight. This jerk got a thrill out of my reaction with so many observers. He'd respond by holding his hands up, as if it was just a big misunderstanding or something. Then he'd leave me alone just for a couple days, only to start this treachery all over again. Get this: students and teachers alike saw this and *did nothing!* I hated high school and prayed daily for God to help me get through.

Like I said, no one helped me, not even Evie. This made me so mad because I felt like it was mostly her fault that I was a target. Clearly, Evie was too self-absorbed to even notice my dismay, but others noticed and just ignored it. I thought that it would've been really cool to have a brother–someone to look out for me when I was growing up. I imagined him helping me out with these scenarios. "Stop picking on my sister!" he would say, or "The next time you touch my sister, I'm gonna break your face!"

I hated these perverts, and I didn't really have any friends to confide in. I decided that not having friends was for the best because the friends that I had in the past, eventually hurt me and left me. I became a closed door. I deciphered that these former friends' disinterest in me arose because they had become more popular than me, and I guess it wasn't cool to hang around me anymore. By this time in life, I had a sense of worthlessness. I wasn't worth standing up for. I wasn't worth anyone's time. I tended to gravitate toward those who were labeled as nerds because I felt safe around them, and I found them fascinating. Even so, I was afraid to call *them* friends or let them get too close because I feared they, too, would dump me like a piece of trash sooner or later.

Evie, on the other hand, had too many friends to count. It got to the point where I didn't even bother trying to remember their names. I marveled at how many people loved her. She had a great personality and was a teacher's pet. I suppose it's natural for teachers to associate younger siblings with the older ones, but it didn't make it any less annoying. Because all of the teachers liked Evie, there was no predisposed bad attitude toward me, but it was *so* tiring to hear them say with a smile, "Oh, you're *Evie's* sister!" I don't think I would've minded so much except that

Evie was nice to everyone *but me!* She ignored me mostly, but when she did talk to me, she was just plain mean. So, I'm sure you can see why I came to admire her *and* despise her.

This time in my life was bleak because I didn't have anyone to share my burdens with all throughout high school. Regardless, I was pretty good at making lemonade out of lemons, so I bottled up these emotions and used them like fuel. Fuel to motivate myself to do well in sports and school, to have enormous responsibility with saving money, and to be a good person. I *never* had to be told to clean my room, to clean the stalls, or to do *anything* really. I just did it. This was all good and well, but I especially had a fire in my soul that burned as a reminder to not waste my time on dating losers, like everyone in my high school; and not to be promiscuous, like my sister.

Even though this fire burned bright in my soul, it was still a little hard to maintain Christian values growing up in this rural high school. You just weren't cool if you didn't date. I didn't date at all, ergo, many people just assumed that I was a lesbian. So, there was that to deal with as well.

Dad taught both of us girls the qualities to look for in a man, and he *showed* us how a lady is supposed to be treated by the way he treated Mom. Part of the reason that I didn't date was because I didn't know anyone who had those upstanding qualities that Dad told us we should look for in a man.

Evie and I weren't raised with just a regular Christian upbringing; it was more intense than that. Dad and Mom were blessed with the Holy Spirit, and they operated with it to an advanced degree. Part of having this gift with their profound understanding meant that they'd know things that there was no way of knowing. Often Evie would get caught red-handed doing something stupid that God informed Dad or Mom about. There was a blowout about every six to eight months while we were in high school because of this, yet God didn't tell my parents *everything* she did wrong. I knew this because she did get away with some stuff that was huge. I'm not sure how that worked exactly. Where did God draw the line with sharing information about Evie's wrongdoing? I never did anything wrong so, you guessed it, there was no need for God to tattle on me.

My faith was strong because I'd seen so many miracles in my own family. How could I not have faith? One of my favorite testimonies was about Grandma June, who would tell the story of how she fell and broke her femur. Grandma refused to have surgery right away, against the doctor's advice, because she was dealing with a chronic disease and didn't think she could handle it. She went home and prayed for healing, and she had so many people agree with her in prayer. She had to use a wheelchair for a week because of the pain. The next week when she went for a checkup, the doctor was amazed that there was no clinical evidence of a fracture, nor was there a fracture evident in her follow-up X-ray! He couldn't believe it, so he sent her to get a bone scan, which also came up negative! Of course, by then Grandma was pain free and told the doctor, "Jesus healed me!" She told that story to everyone, and she would often show the X-rays to prove it. I never got tired of that story because it was so awesome and because it annoyed Evie so much.

I would often say to Grandma, "Tell me my favorite story again, Grams."

Evie would moan, roll her eyes, and say, "Ohhh, we've heard that story a thousand times." I'd snicker at the fact that it annoyed Evie to hear it so often, but then I'd quickly turn my attention to Grandma and listen to her words intently. Sometimes, I'd recite her tale in my head as she spoke it allowed.

That's not the only miracle that encompassed our family. Dad's vision was healed when he was going blind as a young man, and Grandpa was delivered of alcoholism. I missed hearing Grandpa's story about how he was delivered. I treasured the moonshine bottle that he left me after he passed. Shortly after his funeral, I wrote down Grandpa's story on paper, just the way he told it, and I put it in the moonshine bottle so I'd never forget. When I'd get to missing Grandpa or just needed a pick-me-up, I would pull it out and read it, even though I had it memorized.

Evie and I remained so different into early adulthood. Evie got married to an idiot and a moocher, despite everyone's disapproval. At first impression, Johnny seemed very outgoing and likable. Those who knew Johnny best, recognized that he was legitimately crazy. I guess they called it Bipolar, but I knew that it had to be more than that. I've known many other people who were Bipolar that didn't act unpredictable, hot-tempered, and irrational–*completely irrational!* Oh, Johnny could fool anyone for several months with his phony sweetness. He loved to talk about God, too, but his fictitious pretty painting would eventually become unmistakably sullied like blood on white fabric. That's why he couldn't keep a job for more than a couple months. That's why he mooched off of so many women before he conned Evie into marrying him. How unfortunate. After they'd been married for about six months, Johnny jumped from job to job and began spending more time with his delinquent friends and less time with Evie. She essentially supported him. She put on a good show, hiding her unhappiness. But I knew. Dad and Mom did too.

After high school, I immersed myself in college and became an X-ray technician and a massage therapist by the age of twenty-two. The former degree could have possibly been because of my fascination with Grandma June's story, but also it was desirable because it was a quick degree. I swiftly became independent: renting a small house in the country, maintaining a cheap car, and keeping my treasured motorcycle in great condition. I kept that dirt bike Dad got me in good condition as well. What great memories it kept alive.

I lived close to my parents at this time, so I'd often go over in the evenings to have supper with them or to help Dad take care of the horses. If no one was home, I'd make myself useful by cleaning hooves or stalls. I was kind of spoiled in that Mom would often make supper for me when I'd come over, and I'd get off easy by occasionally bringing desert. I'm sure they found it to be a fair trade because of all of the time I spent helping out. I was very close with my parents, and I quite enjoyed their company. Dad would often explain revelations to me that he received during his weekly Bible studies and prayer.

I stayed rock steady with waiting for the right man. No one made it past a first date with me after high school. As a matter of fact, I got tired of the first date scenario, so very few even made it to the first date. I found it funny to refer to myself as the "female Seinfeld" of dating. Seinfeld would always come up with absurd reasons to stop dating someone, on the hit TV series *Seinfeld*. His logic for dumping undesirables was laughable, such as ditching someone who eats peas one at a time; whereas mine were deep, like not agreeing to date someone who couldn't find the time to hold the door open for the elderly. Someone who spent too much time on a cell phone was also a turn-off. Don't get me wrong, I wasn't unhappy, just disappointed in all of the young men of my generation.

I was still young and didn't feel pressured to find the right man. But it did perplex me when I thought about why men grow up so much slower than woman. I'd wonder as I watched local young men act so immature and ungrateful. Actually, I was quite the people-watcher. You can really get to know a person well by watching them interact with their environment and with others. I'd label people as I watched: overconfident, rude, and absent to name a few. Rarely did I find good qualities in men of my generation. I'd watch older men, too, with different results: intellectual, kind, helpful, and of course, married.

Chapter 2: Mid-Ohio Swap Meet.

Dad and I always went to the Mid-Ohio Swap Meet together, but he couldn't go with me this year. He was sad about it, but he had a great reason for missing it. Whenever he missed something, he always had a great reason. This time he was ministering to those incarcerated. He totally spaced the swap meet and couldn't find a replacement in time. He felt bad, but he would never cancel something so important that could possibly result in someone giving their life to the Lord. That's really the most important thing in life. He was indeed the best role model I ever had. He was my closest friend too.

If Dad wasn't accompanying me somewhere, I'd often go places by myself. Despite my standoffish personality with stupid boys, I was quite outgoing. I would often just jump into conversations with strangers. I had few rejections with this, but I could take a hint very well if there was someone who didn't appreciate my unreserved manner. Most of the time, I was content with going places solo, but occasionally it would strike a nerve when I would see friends hanging out and having a blast. I admit that I would get a little angry. Why couldn't I have that? Oh yeah, because *every* friend I've *ever* had just discarded me like a piece of trash. It still hurt a little. It sounds crazy but when I would need to "change the channel" in my head, I would jolt my head to the side once very quickly. That would help me reset my mind and free me from perseverating on depressing things. I'd try to hide this quirk, but it seemed to fit with the stigma that followed me throughout high school: "Ricky is weird."

Motorcycle rides were at the top of my list of favorite things to do alone. Riding offered so much. The time alone was peaceful. It was adventurous, too, as I'd often ride to a place to hike or hang out. But mostly, it was spiritual. I'd often thank God for the ability to see His great works. "How beautiful this world is," I'd think as the wind soothed around my body. "Heaven must be so wonderful if earth has so much to offer."

A Honda NC700X was my bike of choice. Of course, I got a deal because Dad knew a guy, but it still was a pretty penny. I saved for it, and it was the first real purchase I ever made. My car, well, that was just how I got around when the weather wasn't good for riding. It was a junker, but I never called it that in front of my parents because it was gift for me on my sixteenth birthday. My choice of bike was largely related to how much I loved my dirt bike, which I still used often in the woods behind my home. I respected that motorcycle riding can be dangerous because of the many X-rays I performed on people who had been in accidents. I thought that my chances of wrecking were slimmer if I got ran off the road while on this adventure bike, compared to riding a typical cruiser.

When I arrived at the Mid-Ohio Swap Meet, I felt both excited and guarded. Large masses of people gathered in one place always made me nervous, so I was especially careful in crowded areas. The thought of the tragic incident on the east coast involving the man who was trampled at Walmart on Black Friday just terrified me. Staying in town at a hotel was the answer for my safety that evening. Camping at the Swap Meet alone just was not a smart option.

I smiled as I walked through the parking lot, snapping photos of all of the bikes before I had even gotten to the main event. After entering, I kept to my system of methodically walking up and down every aisle so that I wouldn't miss anything. I missed Dad, but I also enjoyed the independence of moving freely without having a consensus on everything. That's something we all do when we're with company.

The atmosphere was awesome and so were the good eats. A hot dog, chips, and a Coke never tasted so good. Maybe that's because it was so expensive.

I found a booth selling shirts that had different types of motorcycles on them with a trail of flames that followed. I bought one with an adventure motorcycle on it for myself and one with a cruiser on it for Dad. "How cute we'd look," I thought as I smiled to myself. One of the raffle motorcycles caught my eye. Just one ticket for me and one for Dad; that's all we needed. If we were meant to win, we'd win with just one ticket.

Early in the afternoon, I noticed a group of friends standing at a booth near me. They were smiling big and laughing hard at their friend who just reenacted a situation where he popped a wheelie on a motorcycle and landed fishtailing. His dramatization was quite comical. His blond friend assisted with the story by calling out, "Mistakes were made!" To which the storyteller bellowed, "I regret nothing!"

"Nice sound effects," I thought as I smiled at them. The storyteller continued on by leaning backward and flailing his arms around in a circle. Clearly, he meant that he fell off the back of the motorcycle. They were all laughing so hard. The storyteller was bent over a little and holding his stomach for a couple of seconds. I couldn't help but burst into laughter with them. This caught their attention, and they looked toward me as they tried to stifle their laughs.

I approached them without hesitation and with a big smile. "I couldn't help but overhear the end of your story, which was quite entertaining," I said with a big grin. "Hi, I'm Rick," I said as I stuck my hand out.

The blond who assisted with the story reacted first because he was the closest. "I'm Mike," he said with a big smile as he shook my hand.

"Nice to meet you, Mike," I said.

Mike was tall and had a slim muscular build. He had dirty-blond hair and blue eyes. He wore slim-fitting clothes to show off his attractive physique.

I finished my introductions to Ben, the storyteller; and Aaron and Michelle, his audience. They were all so nice and didn't act like I was intruding at all.

"Your name is Rick?" Ben asked with his brow raised while I shook his hand.

"Yeah, it's short for Ericka," I said.

"That's awesome," Ben said with a smile.

Ben was a bit taller than Mike and very thin. He had light brown hair with eyes that nearly matched, but his eyebrows and eyelashes were very dark brown, almost black. I found this trait to be quite distinguishing.

I went on, "Do you guys ride?"

"Oh yeah. I ride a Victory Gunner," Mike said with a smile.

I raised my eyebrows and nodded, indicating approval. "Sweet," I said.

I turned to Ben, whose eyes were still bright from storytelling. "I have a KTM Super Duke," he said.

I snapped my fingers and motioned my hand into a pistol pointing at Ben as I said, "Wow!" I marveled at this because he really didn't look like the crotch rocket type.

"What about you?" I asked Michelle.

"I ride with my husband," she said as she tilted her head toward Aaron, whose arm she was hanging on. Michelle had shoulder-length, bobbed auburn hair and hazel eyes. Her size was larger than average, but she was very attractive. She wore gold hoop earrings.

"We ride a Honda ST 1300," Aaron said. Aaron had brown hair and black eyes. He was the shortest of the guys, but he and Michelle were still taller than me. Michelle was about 5'7", so that made Aaron about 5'8", Mike about 5'11", and Ben 6' even, I supposed.

"Wow. Very cool bikes. I ride a Honda NC 700X," I said.

The guys begin to marvel. "What!?" questions Mike while he's half way laughing.

"Really!" exclaims Aaron. I guessed my size made it seem so funny. Well, the fact that I rode at all could seem kind of funny because I was so thin. I guess I was getting some of my own medicine. I just thought that a crotch rocket seemed unusual for Ben because he was so tall and lanky. Now I was glad I hadn't said anything to him about it.

"Well, all right," Ben said with a smile. "Have you ever seen *Long Way Around* or *Long Way Down?*"

"Of course!" I said with a large smile, an eye roll, and a shoulder shrug, as if seeing those documentaries were a prescription for a happy life. "Numerous times!" I emphasized. I beamed with excitement because each one there had obviously seen it and loved it.

We all reminisced about our favorite parts of the around the world motorcycle trip documentaries starring Ewan McGregor and Charley Boorman. The motorcycles they rode for their trip were BMW GS R1200S.

"I love the part when Charley goes mental about not getting the KTM 900," laughs Mike.

"Remember when Charley couldn't eat the goat testicles," Aaron chuckles as he looks up to the sky.

Ben added, "That was awesome when Ewan ran from the elephants and was like, 'Holy Shit! I thought I was gonna die!'" That's not exactly what Ewan said, but it was close enough.

"That *was* awesome," I said as we laughed together. I chimed in, "I *love* how emotional Ewan is. He reminds me of...me, actually." We all continued smiling like big goofs.

Michelle interjects excitedly with her hand held, palm out, as if to stop us from talking because she had the most important thing to say. With her eyes closed, she started with, "Ewan's sexiest role, that he's *ever* played," she said with dramatic pauses, "was himself in *Long Way Round* and *Down.*" She finished that sentence with her eyes open and with a great big smile.

"I know, right!" I exclaimed and clapped twice. She was dead-on. How many times have I thought that myself!? "Speaking of celebrities, did you know that Keanu Reeves cofounded a motorcycle company called Arch? I mean, I've never been star-struck, but when I found out how passionate he is about motorcycling, I felt connected to him somehow." I told his story with so much passion myself. "During an interview, he compared soaring on a motorcycle to that moment when you hear 'action' on the set. He said something like," I took a deep breath before I continued, "'Everything that you are, everything that you feel or think becomes alive at that moment.'" When I quoted him, I held my hands in front of my body, palms facing me, with my fingers spread wide open as if I were gesturing to an aura that surrounded me. That's not what I was suggesting, but that's how it looked I'm sure. I looked up to see that I had totally lost Michelle. She looked at me like I was a weirdo. I exposed too much zeal for her liking. I get that. She's just a passenger, whereas *I* took life by the horns. I looked at Aaron and then to Mike, expecting a better response. They both looked mildly amused noted by their polite smiles. Then I looked over to Ben and saw him just gleaming.

"You know those bikes are like eighty grand, right?" Ben asked, amused at my spirit.

I shrugged my shoulders and made a funny face. "Meh. That's just one more obstacle in life to parkour." Mike expelled a blasé scoff. Aaron gave me a one-syllable laugh.

"Of course," Ben replied with a hint of sarcasm, as if he knew that I didn't make enough money for something like that.

"Well, if that plan falls through, I'll just have to woo Keanu and get him to give me a ride on *his* bike," I said as a matter of fact.

Ben laughed and held his stomach. "You know those are single seat bikes, right?" he said.

"Well, I'm just going to have to sit in front of him, *facing him*," I said roguishly.

Ben folded his arms across his body and narrowed his eyes. "That sounds like an accident waiting to happen," he replied seriously, as if this scenario had any chance of ever existing.

I lavishly grinned at the thought of him amusing me further with this nonsensical conversation. "That wouldn't happen," I said in a snarky tone, proclaiming his ignorance. "Haven't you seen *The Matrix?* He is the Chosen One and can do *anything.*"

"Well, I can't argue with that logic," Ben said as he cracked a smile.

At about that time, Aaron looked at his watch and said, "The sidecar races start in twenty minutes, so we best be heading over."

"That's where I'm going. Do you mind if I tag along?" I inquired.

"Not at all, Rick," Ben said. "Did you come alone?"

Wow, it was nice to hear someone call me Rick. I was mesmerized for a couple seconds, smiling as I walked next to Ben. I was used to everyone calling me Ricky because that's what Dad calls me, and because it makes them more comfortable. I refocused and said, "Uh, yeah. My dad couldn't make it this year. It's the first one we've missed together in nine years."

"That's too bad," he said.

As we walked along, I said to Ben, "I *did* know that Arch bikes are single-seaters. That was a test, and you passed." He discerned from my sincere smile that I was telling the truth, and he laughed.

Judging by the few wrinkles on their faces and just a hint of gray hairs, my new friends appeared to be in their mid-thirties. I welcomed that because all of my other friends were too young and immature. Wait, what friends? Never mind. None of them seemed to mind that I was younger. That made my heart smile.

We continued with chit chat while we walked to the track. I was still kind of shocked that I met such a nice group of people who had so much in common with me. I listened to the guys reminisce about last year's race and how crazy it was that the side car guys lean so far during the turns. I added to the conversation by pointing out the fact that sometimes I'd hold my breath when I watched because it's so dangerous that anything could happen. Walking along, I felt like I was floating a little. I was so happy.

During the sidecar races, we watched intently but made some time for chit chat as well. I rather enjoyed Mike and Ben's commentaries. They were both very funny. I laughed readily at their wit.

"You guys remind me of Hawkeye and Honeycutt," I said, smiling at them. They both looked at me with a serious, upset expression.

"Whoa, whoa. Don't you mean Hawkeye and *McIntyre?*" Mike swiftly corrected me. I giggled. Apparently, they were *M.A.S.H.* fans too.

"Yeah, I can see that," Ben said before I could reply. "I'm very quick witted like Hawkeye, and McIntyre over here follows me around with his eyes crossed, honking a clown's horn." I laughed so, so hard. Obviously, I remembered that episode.

"No, no," Mike said to Ben, "If anyone's walking around acting like a clown, it's you." I continued to burst with laughter at their banter.

Ben quoted Hawkeye with a British accent saying, "'I'm Dr. Jekyll, actually, and this is my friend, Mr. Hyde.'" He motioned toward Mike with a head tilt. I laughed even louder, remembering that episode as well.

"I think he might be right, Mike," I antagonized. Mike silently rolled his eyes in defeat. Ben raised his eyebrows quickly twice in a row, claiming his victory. I let out a very unattractive snort-laugh. I quickly put my hand over my mouth to muffle the awfulness.

"You okay there?" Ben said with a bright-eyed smile. I nodded with my hand still over my mouth as I giggled. Ben laughed a little too.

Toward the end of the race, I politely tried to break away from the group, only because I didn't want to be a bother any longer. I had already crashed several hours of their day. Surprisingly, they insisted that I stay. "It'll be more fun with friends," Ben said. I hesitantly agreed instead of refusing their offer because he was right. My heart cantered at the thought of someone calling me a friend so soon.

After the race, we walked around some more and talked about where we all lived as well as where we liked to ride. What a small world. I learned that they all lived fairly close to me, that they were regulars at the Mid-Ohio Swap Meet, and that they've even rode to some of the same places that I have! It was really exciting to find out that we lived within forty-five minutes of each other.

"We should plan a trip together sometime!" I said. They seemed open to the idea.

As we continued to stroll the grounds, I learned that Aaron and Michelle had two children. Mike divulged that he was seeing someone on and off, but Ben didn't offer any personal information. That was good because I didn't want to go there either.

I was floored when the guys told me that they all had worked together in an IT department of a medium-sized corporation. Ben and Aaron still worked there, but Mike had recently moved on. I found it funny that they all were a bunch of IT nerds. I let out a quick, short noise, similar to a train piston:

"Pschh." And I had a weird expression on my face as they talked about work.

Ben turned to look at me after I made that noise. "What's going on here?" he said as he motioned his finger around my face.

"Of course you'd be a bunch of nerds because I tend to gravitate toward your kind." This may have sounded harsh, but it was clearly a compliment, noted by the big smile on my face. Fortunately, they got that. "So, have any of you seen *The IT Crowd* by chance?" I asked.

"Funniest show ever!" Mike exclaims.

"Unbelievable," Ben shakes his head and laughs at the fact that I've seen it too.

"That show's dope," Aaron says.

"What on earth?" Michelle asked as she looked at me like I was some sort of freak. We all burst out into laughter and reminisced over our favorite parts and episodes.

"Aw, man. 'The Work Outing' episode was hysterical!" Ben mimics Roy's high-pitched voice and says, "'I'm disabled.'"

I laughed and egged him on with a quote from Jen. "'And how did that happen? If that's not a *rude* question.'"

"'Acid,'" he replied with a crinkle in his nose.

"'And what are the chances of that happening?'" I continued her quote.

"'A hundred to one,'" he replied in a squeaky high-pitched voice. We all start laughing hysterically.

I could hardly catch my breath when I tried to say, "Wouldn't, wouldn't it be more like, a couple thousand to one!?" My sentence was so choppy because I was still laughing boisterously.

"What about the episode where Moss pushes Roy up against the wall and kisses him as cop car after cop car sped by!?" Mike exclaims.

"'Couldn't we have just hid behind those bins?'" I quoted Roy.

"'Suppose,'" Aaron chimes in with a shoulder shrug as he quotes Moss. Then we all burst into laughter again. Michelle rolled her eyes and was likely laughing *at us.*

"I was so sad that Denholm Reynholm's character was written off after season one. He was genius!" I said. "I loved the one where Jen supposedly died, and he said at her memorial, 'She reminded me of me at her age. I mean, when I was her age, she reminded me of her age. She was reminded of my age at her age. When I was her age, she was reminded of...me?'" I could barely get it all out before busting up laughing. Everyone was laughing so hard with me.

I couldn't believe that I had three strong connections with this group. The first being motorcycle riding itself, and the other two were awesome shows that hardly anyone I knew had seen. It was such a beautiful warm and sunny day. I thoroughly enjoyed the company of my new friends. I didn't want this day to end.

We came across a vendor selling light, long-sleeve shirts with padding in the elbow. Ben was checking them out and the price tag was pleasing. "Oh, that's happening," he said as he reached for his wallet. I smiled at his cute comment.

Later in the day, I saw something that I needed: full length pants that zipped off at the thigh. "No way!" I said after I checked out the price. Mike turned to see what I was thrilled with. "These are normally $80 full price, but they're marked half-off here!" I found my size, which was pretty amazing considering how small I was. I jumped up and down twice and grabbed them off of the rack. Then I started quickly sifting through the other pants, looking for my dad's size. No dice. "Aw, they don't have my dad's size," I said to myself. Michelle, Aaron, and Ben turned to see what all of the commotion was about.

"Who are those for?" Michelle asked.

"Me," I replied.

"Those are guy's pants," Mike said as if I didn't know that.

"I wear guy's pants," I said. Mike scoffed like that was weird or something. "If you think about it, it's quite time consuming to try on lady's pants because they are never the same size. Like size 2. What is that? No one knows what that means! Petite, tall, regular. It's all nonsense. Now 26x32, for example, says something. This saves me a lot of time."

"Size 2 means you're pretty damn thin," Mike said. I stood there with my mouth hanging wide open. I was self-conscious about my small size, and I was flabbergasted at his comment. I also didn't mean to give my size away, which was more like 24x32" by the way, but 26x32" was as small as I could find guy's pants usually. And that was a rare treat without specially ordering them.

"So, you're close with your dad?" Ben asked me. I was slow to respond.

"Um, yeah. Closer than any friend I have," I confided for some dumb reason. I put my hand on my face hoping to stop the inevitable change-the-channel head jolt that doubles as a nervous tick.

"Too bad they didn't have his size," he said.

"Yeah. I seem to shop for *us* whenever I go shopping." I smiled at the thought of it. "I like to spoil him." It's then that I realized I had revealed too much about myself. I became self-conscious. "Weird, huh?" I said shyly.

"No. That sounds nice," he replied. You know what was nice? Ben had intentionally diverted from that upsetting conversation about how thin I was and essentially fished me out of that awkward moment. I really appreciated that. You know why? Because I've done that for people repeatedly, and no one has ever done that for me.

Evening sneaked up on us, and I decided it was time for me to say my goodbyes. I needed to see this gang again, and I wasn't going to leave it up to chance. "I have to see you all again," I said with no regard as to how forward that sounded. "Can I have your numbers?"

"Of course," Ben was the first to reply.

"I have a trip planned in a couple weeks if any of you are interested in going to Maggie Marsh," I said to the gang. Mike and Ben looked at each other as if having and unspoken conference. I interrupted their telepathic communication by saying, "I usually picnic there and walk the shoreline a bit."

Then Mike said, "That sounds fun. I'll check my schedule and get back to you."

"Yeah. Me too," Ben added. Aaron and Michelle nodded in agreement.

"Cool," I said. We exchanged phone numbers before we departed.

Chapter 3: New Friends.

After I got home, I found my new friends on social media. I wasn't really sure if they were just being nice by saying that they were interested in the trip or if they really did need to check their schedules. So, I thought if I chatted with them a bit before the trip, then maybe they wouldn't feel uncomfortable riding with me. I tagged the gang in a meme about motorcycling. The one that's titled, "There's no such thing as your pipes being too loud!" It goes like this.

The one man says, "It's windy today!"
The man in the middle replies, "No, it's Thursday!"
Then the man on the other end says, "So am I. Let's get a beer."

I laughed out loud while posting this, even though I've read it several times before. That one always cracked me up. They liked my status, and they did actually get back to me about the trip. Aaron and Michelle couldn't go because of a function with the kids; however, Ben and Mike were in. "How exciting," I thought, "but would it be weird without Aaron and Michelle? Nah, Ben wouldn't let it get too weird. He'd already rescued me once."

On the day of the Maggie Marsh trip, Ben and Mike stopped by my place and followed me since my house was on the way and I knew the route like the back of my hand. It was such a beautiful day.

After we parked, I hopped off my bike and zipped off the lower portion of my new pants that I just bought at the Mid-Ohio Swap Meet.

"Whoa!" Mike exclaimed.

"What?" I snapped. "Are you referring to my white legs or my awesome style?" I posed with my hand on my hip and motioned down my leg as if I were a model, spotlighting my unique style of long shorts combined with my motorcycle boots.

They both laughed. "Your blindingly white, vampire legs," Mike insulted.

"You'll be all right, as long as you don't take off your shades," I said. They both laughed again.

I was making an effort to get used to Mike's personality. I liked Michelle, Aaron, and Ben. But Mike? Not so much. I was used to hearing all sorts of comments about how white I was, but that didn't mean I liked it. And I didn't like his comment about me being so thin either. I decided that I would have to get used to Mike if they were going to let me keep hanging around, and snarking back at him seemed like a feasible coping strategy. This also added to the dynamic group banter.

The trip was amazing. My sandwiches and snacks were a big hit, and the guys surprisingly enjoyed walking the shoreline of Lake Erie just as much as I did. As we walked the beach, we talked about other fun things besides riding. Ben and Mike reminisced about a Rock Band party they had with the gang that was so much fun. Between the four of them, they had two guitars, a drum set, a keyboard, and a microphone. I loved listening to the two of them reminisce and laugh.

"Wow! That sounds super fun!" I said. "Next time, invite me to one of those. I'm pretty good on the bass, guitar, and mic."

"Sounds like a plan," Mike said. "You could even bring a friend if you wanted."

I felt a pit in my stomach when he said that. I didn't want to reveal the severe degree of my social ineptness on our second encounter by letting them know that I didn't really have any friends. Well, I mean, more than the slip of tongue that revealed a little too much to Ben at the swap meet. I averted my eyes after Mike said this, and I unconsciously slowed down as I thought about how to reply. Ben caught onto this and slowed down with me. He said, "You don't have to bring anyone if you don't want to. Just come yourself. Aaron and Michelle are usually there, and they bring their kids sometimes. We'll have a blast." He smiled coyly and whispered, "It might be too soon in our relationship for us to meet your dad." I smirked at his wit. He smiled back at me.

How did he do that? He was able to read my body language and smooth things over. Granted, I felt like my mannerism was discernible just then, but that doesn't matter a lot of times. Certainly, Mike didn't notice. Like I said before, *I've* always been good at smoothing things over for other people, but no one has ever done that for me. I felt warm and weird because this was the second life preserver that Ben had thrown me, and it was only our second encounter. I nervously tucked my hair behind my ear as I dealt with how I was feeling. Finally, I replied softly, "Yeah. That sounds good." We caught back up with Mike.

I love to notice things about people and imagine what those things imply. That's more than saying, "I'm a people-watcher." I realize that it often seems like I'm rudely staring at times, so I perfected my art by monitoring and adjusting how much time I spend studying my subjects. I watched Mike walk with perfect posture. He was attractive: blond hair, blue eyes, tall, slender and muscular build. He wore form-fitting jeans and a tighter shirt to show off his arms. He paid no mind to anything around him. He didn't even notice that we slowed down. He walked with his head held high. I concluded that he was confident and arrogant–probably a ladies' man. I, not being shy, began questioning Mike in order to get to know him better.

"You look really fit, Mike. Do you lift weights?"

"Yeah," he said. "I teach a kickboxing class a couple times a week too."

"Nice," I replied. "I go through periods of exercise and slacking off regularly," I said, laughing. "I work out at home mostly with exercise videos like *Sweatin' to the Oldies.*" I laughed even harder, but the guys had no reply. "Richard Simmons?" I said. "Anyone? No?" I paused a second and then went on, "That was a joke because Richard Simmons isn't around anymore."

"No, I got it," Mike said with a straight face. Ben smiled a little at my constant awkwardness.

"Soooo, I'm not as funny as I think I am," I thought. "That's okay, I'm very entertaining to myself." I've always been my biggest fan.

I moved on to sizing Ben up. He reminded me of a combination of the two actors Jay Baruchel and Paul Wesley. He was tall and lanky like Jay but more muscular, and his light brown hair reminded me of Paul's because of the similar short-cut, combed-back style. Despite his thin frame, he was quite handsome. I was intrigued that his light brown hair nearly matched his light brown eyes, yet his eyelashes and eyebrows were so dark. He had nice laugh lines and just a few gray hairs, which I considered to be distinguishing. At the swap meet, I remembered thinking that his smile and his quirky personality were the things I liked most about him. He had the biggest, most genuine smile I've ever seen, and his eyes lit up every time he smiled. He was also very polite and always seemed interested in what I had to say. I concluded that he was a catch, ergo, he was probably in a relationship. Next, it was time to learn a little more about Ben.

"What hobbies do you have, Ben?" I asked.

"I like watching movies, riding motorcycles, and walking along the beach with the wind blowing in my hair," he said with a distant look and in a voice lighter than his own. I wildly laughed at him. Actually, I laughed so hard that I began coughing a little. I tried to regain my composure, but it was a little difficult considering that we were still walking along the beach and the wind was blowing through our hair. His eyes gleamed at me, letting me know that he liked that I liked how funny he was.

"That sounds more like a profile on Matchmaker," I teased.

"Well, my Matchmaker profile also says that all of my Juliettes must bring me boxed chocolates on every date," he said as a matter of fact. I laughed some more. I could feel my nose crinkle as I smiled, which was about as big of a smile as I could get. I always thought I looked stupid when I did that, so I turned my head away.

"You really *are* Hawkeye!" I said to Ben. Mike scoffed and rolled his eyes. I snickered at Mike's reaction. Ben seemed perfect. He was attractive, had a great sense of humor, and had a smile that could knock you off your feet. You couldn't slap the smile off of my face that day.

We walked a little more and talked about Cedar Point trips and Hocking Hills. The guys had never been ziplining before, and I swore to them that Hocking Hills had the best around. That would be a fun trip in the future, I mentioned.

Ben and Mike reminisced about the time when they worked together at Ben's current place of employment in the IT department. Mike asked a few questions about the old team to see how they were all doing. Ben mentioned numerous departmental problems that would arise without any resolution due to lack of leadership. They talked about how feasible solutions that were suggested regarding various work-related problems always seemed to get blown-off. "It's like they don't want anything to get better," Ben said. I sympathized with them.

"Well, you know what they say," I started. "You can beat a dead horse to water, but you can't make him drink." I made a funny face to myself because that didn't sound right. The guys stopped dead in their tracks with the most amused looks on their faces. "Wait," I started, but Ben had already interrupted me.

"That's *not* what they say," Ben said seriously as he raised his eyebrows. Mike burst into laughter right after Ben said that, but Ben remained composed. "You combined the expressions 'it's like beating a dead horse' and 'you can lead a horse to water, but you can't make it drink,'" Ben explained. By this time, Mike was laughing so hard that he was gasping for air, but Ben was still unruffled.

I laughed nervously, and my face flushed with embarrassment. "I've never been good with expressions. I rarely use them," I said timidly. Actually, I was the *queen* of messing up expressions.

"You should probably *never* use them," Ben went on with a smirk on his face. Mike was now holding his stomach while he laughed obnoxiously.

I tucked my hair behind my ear, folded my arms across my chest, and looked down at the sand, fully unveiling my discomposure. "That's good advice that I'll probably not take," I said, smiling shyly, still looking down.

Ben tilted his head sideways a little to try to get me to look back up. His eyes, powered with a light tractor beam, lifted my head slowly, and my eyes met his. "Well," Ben said, "You can beat a dead horse to water, but you can't make her drink." He winked at me and stole my breath. I masked my light gasp with a small smile and by giving him a little shove on his shoulder. He smiled at me and laughed.

After we walked the shoreline a bit, we decided to head back to the bikes. It was a perfect day for riding with the sun feeling so warm and the wind blew just enough to keep us cool–light leather jacket weather.

During the ride back, I couldn't get Ben off of my mind. "There's no way he's single," I thought, so I fought to keep him out of my mind. Instead, I aimed to focus on my motorcycle riding ritual of thanking God for another beautiful day, for my health, and for our safety during our travels.

I was in such a great mood the rest of the week. I was high, thinking about Ben and his great personality and how much he made me laugh. I'll admit, I'm usually in a good mood, but this was over the top. I could hardly wait for the next adventure. I checked my texts and social media regularly, looking for any posting about upcoming trips, but there wasn't anything that week. In general, guys don't seem to get on social media as much as girls, so I tried not to sweat it. I kept busy after work, as usual, with some dirt bike action as well as riding the horses at Dad's house.

Thursday had come and no word from the guys or Michelle, so I thought I'd give the gang a holla. I sent them a group text saying, "Anyone interested in a ride this weekend? I was thinking of going to Marblehead Lighthouse."

Mike replied, "That sounds fun."

Ben reports, "I'm in."

Aaron and Michelle again declined due to their son having a ball game that weekend, but they said it sounded like fun and they were interested. I made a motion to reschedule for a different weekend so that they could come. I texted that I would go to Oak Openings that weekend and reserve Marblehead for a different weekend. I also nonchalantly announced that I planned on going to Oak Openings whether or not anyone was coming with me. I guess I did that because I didn't want company out of pity. I assumed that no one would be able to come since there was a last-minute change in plans, but Mike and Ben surprised me by saying they were still in.

I'm kind of detail oriented. I know how annoying this can be for some people, but I still went ahead and asked the guys if they wanted me to bring food again or if they would rather go out to eat. They didn't seem to mind my need for planning, and they opted to go out to eat. I suggested Shucker's Restaurant.

"Sounds good," Mike posted.

"Yep," Ben added. We agreed to meet at my house since it was along the way.

All I could think about Friday at work was how much I was looking forward to seeing Hawkeye and McIntyre the next day, but Ben had some bad news for me. He texted me early Saturday morning, "Mike can't make it. Something came up. Do you still want to go?"

"Rock yeah!" I texted him back. "Oh my gosh," I internally scrutinized as I hit my hand to my head. "That was so lame-o." I cringed as I waited for Ben's reply.

"LOL, see you at 10 then," Ben replied. Okay, that didn't go too bad.

I was outside finishing up packing when Ben arrived. "Nice place you got here," Ben said after he dismounted.

"It's quaint but nice," I replied with a smile. "I ride my dirt bike in the woods back there. It's peaceful here, but also exciting." Ben smiled and nodded. That was too much. I was being weird. I planned on making sure that this wasn't going to be an awkward trip with just the two of us, yet I was already crapping things up. What was I supposed to do? Not be myself? I sighed. Maybe Ben would be okay with weird.

I offered Ben some water before our trip, but he declined. "I brought some Gatorade in case we get thirsty," I said as I lifted a bottle from my bag. Ben smirked and pulled one out of his pocket to show me that he already had one. "Ha!" I said; it was the same flavor I had.

Ben and I discussed the route, and then we were off. I considered asking him if he wanted to use a staggered formation while we were riding, but I refrained. That would surely reveal a little too much of my OCD. When Dad and I rode together, I would always be second in the staggered formation. That way when we pulled up to a stop sign, we'd be able to take off at the same time and not get separated by traffic. Instead of asking, I started myself out in the first position of the formation, and then it was up to him to decide what he wanted to do. He decided to keep about five seconds behind me, as if he were in a car. "That's cool," I thought. I was just careful not to lose him.

During the drive, I perseverated on the warm feelings I had for Ben. We had a lot in common. He was so funny and I loved that. And that smile…God, I'm a sucker for a genuine smile. Never mind that he was attractive. I've never been a shallow person. It was everything else that I liked. It's true that he was quite a bit older than me, but that didn't faze me at all. "Stay cool," I warned myself. "You're not one to make relationship mistakes, Rick." If it was not meant to be, then I was convinced that I'd see something in him that would turn me off, and that would be the end of it.

That particular weekend was cooler, so I had my heavier leather jacket on, along with my chaps. I tended to get cooler than most. It gave me comfort seeing that Ben was into safety almost as much as I was in that he wore a helmet, leather jacket, and gloves. I was a little more hard-core in that I *always* wore boots. This was partly because my Honda was a tad too tall for me, and I needed the extra height from my shoes for safety. Ben's choice in footwear seemed to depend on the weather. That day, Ben just wore tennis shoes. I noticed that his feet easily touched the ground, so he wouldn't need boots for that, but I still disagreed with his decision. As I stewed, I remembered the X-ray I did on the guy who had broken his ankle completely sideways after being involved in a motorcycle accident. The doctor said that he may have broken it totally off if he hadn't been wearing his boots.

The cool air brought me back down from the clouds, and I was able to think about being in the moment and put my fascination with Ben on the back burner. Again, I thanked God for the beautiful day, for my new friends, for our physical abilities that allowed us to enjoy such a lifestyle, and for keeping us safe on our journey.

We parked our bikes and dismounted–me with a big, stupid smile on my face. I had to explain that smile to Ben. "It's beautiful out today!" I said.

"Yes, it is," he said as he smiled back. We started to stow our jackets.

"I just didn't figure you for a crotch rocket rider," I said with an intrigued look on my face.

"No?" Ben tilted his head and smiled at me. He left it at that. I smiled back. He was obviously going to leave that a mystery. I had planned on not bringing that up because of how uncomfortable Mike made me feel at the swap meet, but I was glad that I did because it got Ben to grace me with one of his beautiful smiles. Clearly, he didn't seem to mind me asking.

I showed Ben my favorite trail, and I talked a little bit about how the path had changed since the last time I'd been there. I also shared my stories of how Dad and I would ride Priscilla and Diamond, our horses, there often. Energetically and with many gestures, I shared the anecdote of how jumpy Priscilla was, especially that one time when a squirrel ran down the tree in front of her. She did a combination of walking backward, jumping, and turning in an unpredictable manner. Ben laughed as I imitated Priscilla's movements. I went on to say that she nearly bumped my head on a branch, but I ducked just in time and didn't get knocked off. "As a matter of fact, I've never fallen off of a horse," I boasted. I don't know why I was so proud of that. Maybe because I know so many people who have.

I noticed that Ben seemed quite a bit shyer when it was just the two of us, compared to when we were with Mike or the whole gang. I decided that it was natural for most people to feel that way at first, so I didn't sweat it. I just tried to make him feel as comfortable as I could. I'd just keep talking. Really, I never run out of things to say.

Ben warmed up more when we talked about music. I was surprised at his diverse taste. Thank God he didn't love country music. That could've been a deal breaker right there. So he made it past the music test, Miss Seinfeld. Haha.

It was a little more difficult for me to feel relaxed at Shucker's. Now it was starting to feel more like a date. I didn't want Ben to be uncomfortable, so when the waitress arrived for our drink order, I ordered first and told her that it would be two separate checks. Hopefully, that was a relief for him. I also tried not to give him unwavering eye contact, which I'm known for. That's something they drilled into our heads during college: active listening skills. It's polite and lets the audience know that they have your full attention. I gave him about 80% eye contact during our conversations, and I made sure not to look at anything so distant from me that it was obvious I was looking away on purpose. I was a master.

I talked a little about my dad and mom, but Ben didn't reciprocate much about himself. "There must be a reason for that," I analyzed internally, so I tried to keep my questions careful and considerate.

"Do you have any family in the area?" I asked.

"Yeah, my dad and my brother," he said.

"That's nice," I said. "It's always nice to have family nearby." He didn't offer any more information. I started to twinge at the awkward silence that I knew was about to hover over us, so I just kept talking. I made the next one simple too. "Do any of your family members ride motorcycles?" That was pretty safe. I'll admit, I was pretty proud of myself.

"My dad and my brother do some, but not very much." He sipped on his Coke.

Ugh, he was giving such short answers. I thought I'd share a little about myself: "It's just me and my sister, as far as siblings go."

Ben didn't share anything about his mom, and I didn't dare ask him. Not right then anyway. My mind drifted as I wondered about his mom. I wondered about his brother too. Were they close, or did they have a distant relationship like Evie and I?

Because I allowed my attention to drift, I let a silence befall us–the one that I painstakingly intended to avoid. Instead of spinning my wheels on what to say next, I just took a deep breath...and relaxed. I listened to the distant conversations of the diner and the clinking of silverware against plates. I found this to be surprisingly soothing. We sat there just eating. I observed Ben's mannerisms, but tried not to stare. Ben, too, had perfect posture, just like Mike. He had a habit of rubbing his left thumb against the side of his left index finger while he ate right-handed. It didn't seem to be a nervous habit, just a habit. He didn't seem anxious at all with the silence. "This isn't so bad," I thought. I smiled a little. Normally, a silent moment would cause me to squirm in my chair; but right then, in that moment, I felt comfortable.

When we arrived back to my place, I jumped off my bike and bounced over to Ben. "Did you see those bicyclers we passed a while back!?" I asked. I went on before Ben had a chance to reply. "They were pedaling uphill in the wind and getting nowhere!" I held my stomach while I laughed.

Ben chimed in without missing a beat. "Heh! Heh! Heh! Heh!" he said as he imitated their exertion while cycling with his arms.

His quick reply and ridiculous gesture made me laugh even harder. Finally, I said while still holding my stomach, "I laughed for like five minutes after we passed them!" I gasped for air and continued, "I stopped laughing for like thirty seconds, then I laughed *another* five minutes!!" I doubled-over, still laughing hard.

"They would've gone faster if they would've got off and walked their bikes up that hill," he said with a smirk. I shrieked louder into laughter at his funny comment and tears streamed down my face. He was amused with my reaction and went on with a straight-face, "Yeah, I think they were going backwards actually." I laughed even harder. He cracked another smile and finally joined in my laughter.

I continued to talk exuberantly. "Have you, have you ever had that moment where you thought," I stopped and changed my voice to a nasally mocking tone, "'my pastime is *so* much better than your pastime!?' Well that was me today!" He laughed at the stupid voice I used. After a while, our laughs died down, but our smiles remained. "This was fun," I said, smiling at Ben. "We should do this again."

"Definitely," he replied.

Chapter 4: Close Friends.

It seemed like I was able to stumble into some alone time with Ben pretty regularly. It would usually amount to us planning a group gathering and the others not being able to make it, but I was able to trick him into meeting me alone a couple of times. As long as it was an excuse to ride our motorcycles, Ben was in. After he warmed up to the idea of spending time alone with me, he was quite the talker and, of course, very funny too. I loved to laugh, and he sure could make that happen. During one of our encounters, he told me about the woes of his job, including how his coworkers thought that it was his job to walk clear across the building to replace the ink jets and paper when they ran out, just because he was in the IT department. "Would you like me to take your car to the gas station and fill it up for you too!?" he reenacted for me as we both laughed. I felt blessed to finally have such a close friend.

The whole gang finally made it to Marblehead as planned. I took a lot of pictures of my friends and the scenery. I definitely was not a selfie-girl. I preferred action shots. It was a clear day and we could see Cedar Point across Lake Erie. We sat along the rocks and just talked and laughed about everything it seemed. We made fun of our crazy relatives and talked about dream vacations. I told them about my desire to drive Highway 101 in California along the Pacific coastline from Bodega Bay north to Eureka where the Redwood groves are. I got vacation ideas from websites like Motorcyclerides.com. It describes riding in and out of mountains and along cliffs with "hairpin turns." Ben talked about a train ride across Canada. Mike dreamed of surfing on the Hawaiian coast. Aaron and Michelle would take anywhere with solitude, a beach, and booze, so long as their parents were babysitting the boys. We marveled at each other's choices because they were all from the heart.

On the way home, we stopped at a local cafe to grab some coffee and snacks. I was the first in line, and I ordered rose petal coffee. I stepped out of the way so that Aaron and Michelle could order next. I took a sip of the coffee.

"Oh my gosh you guys! This is...so different! You should try this!" I said with excitement.

Ben took my cup from me and took a sip. "That *is* different. You know what'd be good in this? Whiskey," he said with a smile.

Mike sipped it next and said, "Nope." Then he handed it to Michelle.

"Interesting," Michelle said after she took a sip.

Aaron was next. "Eh, I don't like it," he said as he handed it back to me.

This moment was of great significance to me. It nearly made me tear up. They had all just drank from my cup with no regard for germs. No one had wiped the rim. No one had turned the cup to make sure their lips didn't touch where mine were. I didn't grow up this way! My own parents would wipe my germs away from a rim before taking a sip from my cup. I didn't have close friends before these guys, and I didn't know if what they had done was common, or not so much. Regardless, I was moved very deeply about something so simple. I don't know what kind of expression I had on my face, but Ben noticed it immediately.

"You got something on your mind?" he asked.

His words were like being slapped out of a dream. "Um, yeah." I laughed nervously. "But this one's just for me. It's too corny to share with you guys."

"When you're with good friends, nothing's too corny," he said.

Mike pulled his shades down over his eyes, crossed his arms, and leaned up against Ben's shoulder in a gangster pose. He looked at me while talking to Ben. "Don't tell chicks it's okay to be corny. That's a cardinal sin. If a girl says, 'it's too corny,' you say, 'you're probably right,' and leave it at that."

I made a disgusted-childish face at Mike. He smiled at me. Then he stood up and put his shades back on top of his head. Aaron and Michelle were preoccupied, so they didn't hear our conversation.

"You're kind of a tool," I said to Mike.

He shrugged his shoulders and said, "It is what it is."

"Don't listen to him," Ben warned.

"I try not to, but I have to, to hang around you," I said with an uncontrolled laugh. Ben joined in a little with me. Mike childishly mocked me, which just made us laugh even more.

"Me me me, poo poo," I said melodically to Mike as I bobbled my head side-to-side.

Ben produced an exuberant laugh and offered me a high five. Mid high five, I said, *"Emperor's New Groove,"* to let him know where that quote came from.

"Nice," he said, still laughing. Mike scoffed and rolled his eyes.

Chapter 5: Rock Band Party.

The guys made good on their promise to have me over for a few Rock Band parties. Ben's house seemed to be the chosen place of entertainment since it was centrally located for the most part. Sometimes Michelle would bring her boys, and other times they would stay at their grandparents' house. Whether the kids were there or not, we always had such a great time. The kids seemed to like it, too, which I thought was cool. I didn't know of too many kids who liked to hang out with adults, but then we were way cooler than most adults.

This time the boys were not present. We all brought food and our choice of drinks. Michelle made margaritas and Mike brought beer, both of which I wasn't too fond of. Ben furnished several different types of whiskey, and I brought white and red wine. We started unloading the goods on the table with everyone in high spirits. When I saw the drinks that Ben supplied, my eyes got real wide, and I began dancing around the table. I just knew that we were going to have a good time, but my dance was cut short by the understanding that I would have to be careful with how much I drank because of my long drive home. My smile turned into a pouty-face as I leaned over the whiskey, which I had hoped to become good friends with.

"Ooowwah! I can't drink too much because of my long drive home," I whined.

Ben said, "You can stay here tonight. I have a spare bedroom."

"Really!?" I asked excitedly. I pondered this for a few seconds and decided that it was a good idea. "Yay!" I replied in place of saying yes. They laughed at me as I began dancing again. Well everyone except Mike, who rolled his eyes.

As I danced, I talked to the drinks about how many of them I was going to have. I even replied for them using my French accent about how it would be their privilege to be consumed by me. Yep, here's where the age difference between us became remarkably pronounced. I was very high-energy and animated. Using excessive gestures and facial expressions was pretty much my norm. A sudden break into dance also was not uncommon. Fortunately, no one frowned at this. Actually, I think they found it to be quite entertaining.

I took advantage of the fact that they were amused with my dancing. I started crunking up in everyone's personal space while making stupid faces. I started with crunk-hoping toward Ben using a duck face. Believe me when I tell you that it was just as obnoxious as Will Ferrell and Chris Katan in *A Night at the Roxbury*–with my arms flailing and all. "Ben! You are in the splash zone of shenanigans and malarkey!" I said as I crunk-hopped toward him.

"I'm not afraid to get wet," Ben said as a matter of fact while he smiled. I moved on to Mike.

"Get away from me!" Mike said as grabbed his drink and dodged me in a smooth spin. Then I switched to a booty-hop toward Michelle. I bounced in her direction: butt first, looking over my shoulder at her, and making a stupid face–all while I was shakin' it.

"Make her stop!" she said to Aaron. She grabbed him and thrusted him in front of her as means of evading me.

"Don't hide behind me!" Aaron said, startled at his new position closer to me.

I finally stopped and laughed. I had successfully made everyone uncomfortable, except for Ben, who didn't even flinch.

Later in the evening, Ben found a spider on the kitchen floor while he, Mike and I were refreshing our drinks. He retrieved it with a paper towel and started walking it toward the door.

"Awwwwe-wuh!" I said, moved by his gentleness. Ben smiled at my reaction.

"Just kill the damn thing!" Mike said, irritated by my how moved I was.

"It's not hurting anybody," Ben said plainly to Mike.

"Don't encourage him to do heartless things! It's *not nice!"* I snapped at Mike, sort of jokingly.

"Well, it makes me sick when you encourage him to do girlie things," Mike sneered back.

"Saving a spider isn't *girlie*. It's sweet and," I started, but Mike interrupted me.

"Sweet *is girlie!*" he barked.

"It's sweet *and* environmentally conscious!" I mirrored back at him. "Spiders eat insects and control the pest population." I contended.

"So, what are you, like some angel on his shoulder and I'm the devil?" Mike delivered.

I evaluated this for a couple of seconds and replied, "Yeah. That sounds like an accurate assessment." Mike did not like my answer.

"Well, I know this guy much better than you, and believe me when I say, he's no angel." I was astonished by his persistence and speechless for the moment. "Stop trying to turn him into a puss!" Mike added.

"I'll be in the other room when you guys are done fighting," Ben said as he moseyed passed us toward the living room.

"I don't know what's going on here, Mike! Are we still even talking about a spider!?" That seemed to snap Mike out of the aggressive moment.

"*You're* a spider," he replied immaturely.

"What!?" I asked exasperated at his stupid reply. I heard snickering in the other room. Mike smiled at my flabbergasted reaction. Later I learned that this tactic was a Mike-ism. He'd change the conversation at will, especially when in an argument of some sort, by saying "You're a..." and then he'd fill in the blank with whatever nonsense he fancied at the time.

I walked up to him and pointed my finger at his face and said, "Stop the spider-hating." Then I turned my serious face into a partial smile. Mike grabbed at my finger with fire in his eyes, but I pulled it back quickly and jumped back just in time. "Ahh!" I shrieked. He smiled at how seriously I took his threat. "Help," I said as I trotted into the living room. I plopped on the couch next to Ben and said, "This is base and I'm safe."

Mike walked up behind me and menacingly shoved my head forward. "There's no base here, ya infant."

"Is so too cuz I called it," I replied. Mike went over to the recliner and sat down. I was amazed that Mike thought I was being infantile after his stupid comment about me being a spider. Ben looked at me and shook his head side-to-side in whimsical disapproval of our behavior. "Mike tried to break my finger," I whined to Ben.

Ben replied kindly and informatively, "Did you stick your finger in his face? Because he doesn't like that, ya know." I scoffed at the fact that he took Mike's side regarding *any* part of this encounter. Mike leaned back in the recliner and put his hands behind his head. He had the smuggest smile on his face, knowing that his friend had his back.

Since I didn't have to drive that night, I drank and drank that fun-filled evening, more than I had ever done before. I had a low tolerance for alcohol, and it wasn't long before I was completely intoxicated. I warned myself to try not to go overboard because I didn't want to hurl in Ben's house. Honestly, I didn't know how many drinks it would take for me to do that.

My favorite Rock Band songs of the night were "Tribute" by Tenacious D, "Bring Me to Life" by Evanescence, and "Wicked Garden" by STP, all of which I rocked the mic. I even sat a few songs out, just so I could dance to them and play my air guitar. Did I mention how much I loved to dance?

After a while, the guys decided to take a break from Rock Band and do a few rounds of Halo, so Michelle and I excused ourselves to the kitchen to fashion up some more drinks. As we were mixing drinks, Michelle began a conversation almost in a whisper. I strained to hear her because, apparently, alcohol affects my supersonic hearing.

"You and Ben have been spending a lot of time together. Are you two an item?" She raised her eyebrows, eagerly awaiting my reply.

I smirked and giggled a little. "No, we're just friends." Michelle jumped at this perfect opportunity to squeeze more information out of me.

She leaned forward and put her hands on the table to get closer to me and said, "Would you like to be more than friends?" Her beautiful auburn hair fell around her neck as she leaned forward; and her silver, dangling earrings jostled to and fro. Her hazel eyes gleamed with anticipation with what I was going to say next.

"Well, I don't even know if he's single."

"He is," she said with a smile. I sort of knew that without having that conversation with him because of how much time we had been spending together.

There was often a gentle roar from the guys in the other room that would sometimes escalate. Our conversation was interrupted by Ben exclaiming, "Nuts to that, Mike! I'm going this way!" I dreamily looked down from Michelle to my drink as I listened to the mayhem coming from the living room. I smiled for a few warm seconds, but then my smile slowly started to fade away. I sighed softly.

"Is it your age difference?" she said a little softer. She thought she had hit the hammer with the nail. "You're twenty-two and he's thirty-five. That makes thirteen years difference. That's pretty heavy, right?"

"Absolutely not!" I replied just a little too loud. I loved the idea of possibly dating an older man who was more mature. I took another sip of Pendleton straight up, made a face, and restored myself to a normal volume. "It's just that, I was taught my whole life to…" I stopped there because I really wasn't sure how to continue. I just knew that Michelle wouldn't understand what I was about to say, but I had already started. Finally, I continued with, "…date men who have the same faith I do: who are Christians." These words came out so choppy because I was concentrating hard, so as to not say this the wrong way. I hesitantly looked up at her to see that she had a serious face. I was so thankful that she wasn't laughing or scoffing at me. She remained quiet, still looking at me, ready to listen. So I went on, "And I'm known for not making wrong decisions." I sounded confident with that last part. I swallowed the rest of my whiskey in one big gulp, which was the biggest mistake I made that night.

I coughed a little, swayed, and then decided it was time to sit down at the table.

It's true that Ben and I had many times looked into each other's eyes a little too long, and a time or two we'd been closer in proximity than friends should be, but I wondered if Michelle had actually seen this or if Ben asked her to ask me this. Michelle sat down beside me.

She said, "Well, how do you know he's not a Christian?" Her response kind of surprised me.

"He doesn't go to church and he doesn't talk about God," I said.

"That doesn't mean he's not a Christian." I knew what she was trying to say, but I also knew she didn't understand the depth of what I was saying.

"That's true," I conceded.

She continued with a coy smile, "So you're *not* saying that you *aren't* attracted to him?" I smiled at her persistence and at the thought of her question, which only made her smile bigger.

"That's correct. I did *not* say that."

The guy's gentle roar became more boisterous as I was taking another sip of my drink.

"What the Smurf, Mike!?" I heard Aaron yell. I got most of the drink down, but some of it came out through my nose. I started coughing and gasping for air.

"Are you okay!?" Michelle asked.

"Smurf-off ya Smurf-hole! I got stuck with the janky controller this time!" Mike yelled back. I was still coughing, but I started laughing a little too. Michelle stood up and started patting my back as she tried to stifle her laugh.

"Shut your Smurf-holes ya Smurf-tards!" Ben reprimanded.

"It burns. It burns!" I said, fanning my nose and intermittently laughing. Tears gushed from my eyes.

"What the Smurf is going on in there!?" Ben hollered.

I laughed even harder. "I'm gonna, I'm gonna pee my pants! Help me to the bathroom!" I said to Michelle in between laughs.

"Oh, my Smurf!" Michelle said. "Coming through!" she bellowed as she escorted me through the living room, past the guys, and to the bathroom. I was doubled over laughing, coughing, and staggering to boot. "Rick had a whiskey explosion through her nose!" Michelle explained. The guys all laughed.

"I have to," I said between laughs, "I have to pee like a sieve!"

Michelle stopped at the door and said to me sternly, "Don't lock the door, honey." She turned to the guys and gave them a what-on-earth look.

Aaron paused the game and said, "What did she just say?"

"She said she has to 'pee like a sieve.'" Mike said as a matter of fact.

Aaron burst into laughter. "Was she for real just now!?" he asked.

"Yee-ep," Ben said.

"'Fraid so," Mike added.

"Hey, uh, Rick!" Ben yelled. "It's 'pee like a racehorse' and 'leak like a sieve!'" Everyone burst into a round of laughter. "But whichever you decide to do, make sure it's in the toilet!" I heard another uproar.

"And don't forget to wash your hands!" Mike blared.

When I came out of the bathroom, everyone was staring at me with big, stupid grins on their faces. A few snickers escaped their mouths.

"Are you okay, honey?" Michelle asked as she met me at the door. "Did you make it okay?"

I braced my hand along the doorway. "Yes, and yes," I replied. "I barfed a little whiskey, but at least it came through my mouth and not my nose." They all laughed. "And yes, it was in the toilet. And yes, I washed my hands." Their laughs echoed throughout the house. I let Michelle guide me to the recliner chair.

"Here. Sit down, honey, before you hurt yourself," she said patronizingly.

After I sat down, I demanded, "Someone tell me what the *Smurf* is going on here!" Another outburst occurred from the guys on the couch. Aaron had tears streaming down his face.

Michelle said, "It's something Aaron started around the boys so that we don't cuss. The guys thought it was funny and so they've kept the pandemonium alive."

"It is *so* Smurfin' funny," I said. They all laughed again.

We had an absolute blast that day. It was late into the evening, excuse me, early in the morning when the gang had departed. After they had left, Ben offered me his arm as we walked to the kitchen.

"Ya know, I'm surprised at how much I like whiskey. Every sip tasted just a little better than the one before."

Ben laughed and said, "Yeah, that's kind of how that works." I looked at him with an inquisitive expression. I didn't drink enough to realize that this was a common occurrence. Apparently, that's what happens as you get intoxicated.

I went on, "I'm embarrassed to ask you this, but do you have a bucket in case I get sick tonight? I don't want to puke on your floor," I said in a serious tone as I looked at Ben with big puppy eyes.

He laughed heartily, "Yeah, I can hook you up." I let out a small pitiful laugh because I thought that was a funny way to answer my question, and because too much laughing could have made me sick right then.

The next morning, I awoke to hear Ben stirring in the kitchen. I got up cautiously and walked to the bathroom with my bucket in one hand and my other hand on the wall for guidance. I looked in the mirror, and fortunately, I looked a little better than I felt. I changed my clothes, using my emergency stash that I kept in my bag in case I got stranded somewhere. (It's something you learn to do growing up in colder states.) Once I made myself presentable, I meandered to the kitchen where Ben was pouring himself some coffee.

"Good morning, sunshine!" He was obviously mocking me. I stood next to him and let out a small scoff as I leaned on the counter. "Would you like some coffee?" he asked.

"Mmmhmm," I said with a nod. I rubbed my eyes and around my forehead because it ached a little. He snickered again, this time because I hadn't said any intelligible words yet. I stood up straight and looked him in the eyes. "He is so beautiful," I thought. "I could definitely get used to waking up to his smile daily." This notion made me smile at him. He smiled back. Then he leaned over me to reach into the cupboard behind me to get me a cup. I instinctively tensed up because I didn't know what he was doing at first. I'm not sure if he noticed. If he did, he didn't acknowledge it. My heart fluttered at how close he was to me. I held my breath until he backed away. He poured my coffee and put it on the table, and then he turned to help me to the chair. I let out a little giggle.

"Do I look that bad?" I asked.

"No, but I do know that this is your first hangover." He was right. We had talked about how I didn't drink much because it seemed like I always had a ways to drive, or I just didn't want to drink. He grabbed a Gatorade, ibuprofen, and a breakfast bar for me and said, "Here, this will help."

"Thanks," I replied. "It probably won't be the last time either, as good as that whiskey was." He gave me an unrestrained smile–that beautiful smile. And yes, his eyes did sparkle.

We watched a bit of TV while I worked out my hangover. After that, Ben decided to put in a scary movie. "I don't really watch scary movies," I informed him.

"You'll be fine," he said. "Here, sit next to me. Try it for a while. If you've tried it and you don't like it, just say the word and I'll turn it off."

I grabbed his throw pillows and blankets and scooted over next to him. We watched *Thirteen Ghosts;* it was so scary. It wasn't long before I was hanging onto Ben's arm very tightly. At one point, I jumped and pulled on his arm hard. I looked at him and said, "If this bothers you, then you are free to turn this off at any time."

"I didn't say anything," Ben said with a smirk.

I continued to watch the movie through my barely open fingers during the scary parts. I jumped and pulled on Ben's shirt countless times. By the end of the movie, I had a bad tension headache. I wanted to tell Ben to turn it off during the movie, but I didn't because it gave me an excuse to cling to him. I wondered if that was the idea all along. Regardless of the fact that I loved to be able to hang onto Ben for a while, I was truly upset about the headache. I hit Ben with the throw pillow and told him how I was in pain and that it was all his fault. I had just gotten over my hangover, only to replace it with a different type of headache.

Ben put one of the throw pillows down next to his leg and said, "Here. Put your head here and I'll give you a massage. That'll make you feel better."

I mulled over his proposal for several seconds. The pillow was by his lap and not on his lap, so I didn't think I'd be up in his personal space too much. I did hurt so, and I already took ibuprofen earlier. I made the face that Beeker from *The Muppets* is known for as I finished contemplating his offer. Then I gave him a single nod. I lay down on the pillow and let him run his fingers through my hair and massage my head. It felt wonderful, and it was working to relieve my headache. I soon fell asleep.

When I awoke, I did so with a start, and I sat up quickly. "How long was I out for?" I asked Ben as I nonchalantly checked my chin for drool.

"Just a half hour," he replied.

I rubbed my neck and said, "Gosh, I feel so much better. Thank you."

"You bet."

"I suppose I best be leavin'," I said as I stood up. "Thank you for your hospitality," I added.

"Of course," he replied. He stood up and said, "Come on. I'll walk you out." I followed Ben through the kitchen and down the garage steps. That wasn't the way I came in the previous night; I came through the front door. Ben continued through the garage, but I had stopped dead in my tracks to gaze at his cobalt Subaru STI. This was the first I'd seen of it. I let out a quick exhale and walked toward it in a trance-like state. I glanced at Ben's crotch rocket, and then back to the STI.

I walked around the car slowly, studying it. I ran my fingers along the car as I walked, as if it were communicating with me. I had made my assessment: "You sure do have a disease," I finally said to Ben as I continued to saunter around the car. I stopped for a moment and looked up at Ben, who had a perplexed expression on his face. "The need for speed, I mean." Ben had his arms folded and relaxed across his chest as he stood there. He doubled over quick and hard as he laughed at what I had just said. He stood back up just as quick and continued to laugh. It looked somewhat like a convulsion. He laughed so hard that he had a vein showing in his forehead. I smiled at his convulsive laugh. I guess we both had a weird way about our laughs. Mine was like an explosion of noise, and his was like a short-lived seizure.

I went back to studying the car, listening to its story. "It courses through your veins like a disease," I said eerily. I glanced up to see him smiling wildly in amusement with my conclusion. I looked back down at the car and soberly went on, engrossed in my own translation, "Or maybe it's an antidote...to some...some sort of...pain." After several more moments, I looked up from the car to see Ben's smile slowly fade from his face. This was the first moment that I had realized how creepy I was being. It was amusing at first, but it turned sour. Or maybe I was dead-on with my conclusion. "Not a bad pain killer," I said, smiling at him. He smiled back. Thankfully, the weird moment then passed.

I looked at his crotch rocket, and then back at his car again. A huge smile came across my face at my next thought. "I gotta admit..." I said, taking it all in with a deep breath. I exhaled with, "...your need for speed is just a little bit sexy." Ben flashed me his gorgeous smile. Now it was my turn to have my smile start to fade when I realized how forward that just sounded. "I'm sorry. I guess it's too late to disclose that I don't have much of a filter." I let out a nervous laugh. "When it comes to nice things anyway. If it were something like 'your dress is hideous' or 'those heels make you look like a hooker,' *then* I have a filter." I was rambling in my embarrassment. My awkwardness just made Ben smile all the more.

I thought for sure he was going to attest that he didn't have any dresses or hooker shoes, but instead he said, "I like that you don't have a filter. It makes things interesting. I look forward to hearing some more of your uncensored comments."

I *exploded* into laughter. "I'm gonna make you regret you ever said that!" I said way too loud.

"I hope you do," Ben said with a smile.

I wasn't really sure, but I think we were flirting. I had never flirted before, so I didn't really know what it felt like.

Whatever that was, it was fun and exhilarating. We looked into each other's eyes a little too long once again.

"Do you want to take it for a spin?" Ben asked, breaking our trance. I pressed my lips together as I entertained the idea of his offer. I beamed with excitement as I looked down at the car. "Do it," he dared me. "You know you want to."

I laughed. "Yeah, let's go!"

"I'll take you to a place where you can let her rip." We hopped in the car and off we went. Ben drove several miles outside of town. We spent quite a bit of time together in his car that day, and we talked and laughed the whole time. Ben liked it when I said that I enjoyed the sound of his scoop engine. Finally, he pulled over on a back road, and we traded seats.

"Have you ever driven a stick?" he asked me.

"Yeah."

"Of course you have," he said with a smirk. "I don't feel like I need to give you any instructions or advice, except let's see how fast you can get it to 70 a few times." I smiled at him one last time. He smiled back. "Let her rip!" And I tore it up–several times!

We laughed and talked the entire way back to Ben's house. I felt as high as a kite. I was totally wired from having so much fun with Ben and from getting a little wild behind the wheel.

Ben pulled back into the garage and parked. After he turned off the engine, I said, "I misjudged you when we first met. I said that I couldn't figure you for riding a crotch rocket. I was wrong. I get it now." We were already both smiling from all the mayhem in the car that was our conversation. I went on, "That just goes to show ya, you can't judge a book by its color."

You should've seen Ben's face. He raised his eyebrows in full amusement and opened his lips slightly. Finally, he said, "You mean *cover*. You can't judge a book by its *cover*."

I shrugged my shoulders and smiled. "Meh, I've heard it both ways."

"No you haven't," he said without hesitation.

I burst into laughter. It was a deep belly-laugh. Like, "heh heh heh heh heh," deep gasp, "heh heh ha ha ha! Ha ha haaa ha ha ha!!" Ben chimed in with me. I laughed a bit longer and then tried to force my mouth shut, only to have the laughs expel through my pursed lips.

"Whoa! Whoa! You're spruh, sprayin' my car!" Ben said as he chuckled. I laughed so hard that I choked on one of my gasps for air. I started coughing and tears flowed down my face. Ben couldn't make any more sarcastic comments because he couldn't stop laughing either.

At last, I composed myself barely long enough to say, "No! No, I haven't!" Then I went on laughing again. I wanted to explain to Ben that this is how I got, to a degree, when I saw the bicyclers on our ride back from Oak Openings. All I got out was, "Remember, remember the bicyclers!?" I said between bouts of laughter.

"Heh! Heh! Heh! Heh!" Ben said as he imitated their exertion and cycled with his arms, just as he'd done before. I doubled over with laughter, nearly hitting my head on the dashboard.

Ben's laugh turned crazy. It sounded like, "A-heal heal heal heal heal!!" Then he went into a silent laugh while he held his stomach. We were both incapacitated for a while. Finally, he was able to reach over across the car, put his hand on my forehead, and hold my head back. "You're going to hurt yourself!" he said as he laughed. His comment only made me laugh harder. I slouched down in the seat as I laughed.

"My face hurts! My face hurts so bad! I can't remember the last time my face hurt like this!" I said in between laughs.

"Me too!" Ben said. He released my head.

I wiped my mouth with my wrist as I tried to calm down. I was leaking from every facial orifice. Ben reached for some tissues in his middle compartment. He quickly pulled out three. "Here. I suggest you start with your nose." I shrieked in laughter and took the tissue. He laughed too. "Then I have one for your mouth." I reached for that too as I held the other tissue over my nose. So I had both of my hands full of tissues: one over my nose and one over my mouth. "When you stop snottin' and drooling everywhere, you can have this one for your eyes," he teased. I laughed some more into the tissues, which muffled my sounds.

Ben composed himself long enough to say with the most serious tone, "I gotta say, the way snot and drool flows from your face when you're laughing, is just a little bit sexy." I convulsed forward into a hard, silent laugh. I rested my shoulder on his car door as my whole body shook. Ben broke into laughter as well. I gasped for air and several snorts escaped me. "Oh my God! We are on a whole new level here! I hope this isn't the level just before your head explodes!" Ben trumpeted.

I turned to face him and hit his arm three times as I said, "Shut up! Shut up! Shut up! I can't take anymore!" I collapsed my forehead onto his shoulder in the most unnatural way–with my neck extended. Out of pure exhaustion, my laugh fizzled down to a giggle.

"That's right," he said as he caressed my head with his hand, "Wipe all your boogers on my shirt." I giggled some more.

When our laughter finally ceased, I snatched the final tissue from Ben's hand and wiped my tears as he suggested. He snickered and said, "Hold on, hold on." He jumped out of the car and jogged around to my side to open the door. "I don't want you to *hurt* yourself getting out," he said, chuckling. He offered his hand to me to assist me to standing, and I took it. I got lost in his eyes one more time as we smiled at each other.

"This has been so much fun. I don't want to go," I said.

"Then don't go," he replied.

"I don't want to keep you all day. Besides, I have to get my music ready for church tomorrow."

"Well, ya gotta do what ya gotta do," he said. He walked me out of the garage door to my car. We were still smiling like idiots.

"I can't wait to do something like this again," I said.

"Me too," he replied.

When I drove off, all I could think about was how I was going to make him mine.

Chapter 6: Hocking Hills.

After our magical encounter, I started texting Ben more regularly. I eased him in gradually by texting him every couple of days. Then I progressed to texting him daily. Just silly stuff really, like something funny that I heard or saw that reminded me of him. He readily texted me back, and that was a good sign.

During this time, it seemed like I became cognizant all at once about how bland I looked. I wore boyish clothing, but I'm not speaking to that exactly. I'm referring to the fact that I tended to wear baggy clothing. I went binge shopping to remedy the situation. It was awful. I hated shopping. After twenty minutes of wandering around feeling helpless, I approached an attendant for some help. She was young, beautiful, and dressed trendy. I told her how much I hated shopping because it was nearly impossible to find the right size due to my thin frame, and that I had a new boyfriend I was trying to impress. That wasn't entirely true, yet, but my story ignited a flame inside of her. She accepted the mission of helping me transform my style into a fabulous one that was unique and my own. She did an excellent job, and I spent a pretty penny. Ben was worth it, but so was I, quite frankly. I was finally ready to emerge from my shell and look pretty.

As the days went on, all I could think about was Ben and how I was just wild about him. It didn't seem healthy that I was completely captive to my thoughts of him. I determined that maybe another bike trip, either solo or with the *entire* gang, was the prescription for changing my mindset, so I began planning a weekend to Hocking Hills. I invited the gang along and told them how I was looking forward to going there before the weather got too hot. This was one of my favorite local places. I started trip planning before anyone had the chance to get back to me because, even if no one could go with me, I was planning to go myself. It was only about a two-and-a-half-hour drive, but I decided that I would rent a cabin and stay overnight so that I could do as much hiking and sightseeing as possible. I just needed to know how big of a cabin to get.

After I invited the gang, I had mixed feelings about whether I really wanted them to accompany me or not. I felt ashamed about how much I was thinking about Ben lately because that meant that I was concentrating less on God. It would be good for me to go solo and do some spiritual reflection in solitude. Nature had a fantastic way of reminding me of the awesomeness of God. I liked to call Him a "Magnificent Composer" because I believed that the world He created came together and flowed as perfectly as a well-written song.

When the gang finally replied, I learned that the total count for the trip was going to be two, Ben and me! I suspected that Michelle had something to do with this. She probably told Mike not to go so that Ben and I could be alone. My heart alternated between dancing at envisioning us having a weekend alone together, to feeling nearly frantic. I fought hard to refocus my mind. I could already imagine the beauty of the green canopies, the caves, and the waterfalls that we were going to see.

That glorious day finally arrived. I materialized at a screeching halt in front of Ben's house after I came screaming down his road on my lightning bolt. I ran up the stairs and pounded on his door. He answered the door quickly with a smile that matched my own. Before he could even say anything, I blurted out, "Are you ready!? I'm so excited! Are you excited!? I love Hocking Hills!" His amusement with my enthusiasm was undisguised because of his big, goofy grin.

"Yeah, I'm ready," he said. And we were off.

We left pretty early, so I had my leather jacket and liner on as well as my chaps. Despite all the warm gear, I was just a little cool and that was perfect.

Our first stop was Ash Cave. We climbed up the cold cave shelves to sit and relax a bit. We watched the waterfall as we talked. The sound of the water was hypnotizing.

I learned more about Ben's family, which was a heart-wrenching story. His mom abandoned the family for another man when Ben was eleven and his brother, Scott, was thirteen. That left his dad to raise the both of them alone. He said that his dad had to work two jobs and that they weren't supervised very much as a result. This allowed him and his brother to act out through avenues of alcohol, reckless driving and in "other ways." He went on to say that he and Scott bonded together during this time, and that he hadn't gone to church since his Mom left.

"Religion was her thing," he said, "and her religion didn't work out very well for the entire family."

I was shocked and truly heartbroken to hear this story. I successfully fought back my tears. I gave him my sincerest empathy and told him that God had been good to my family.

"Maybe when your heart fully heals, you could give Him another try," I said. He pacified me with a small smile.

I confided in him that my sister was married to an idiot, that I was destined to not follow in her footsteps, and how it made me sad that we weren't close. He sympathized with me.

Even though Michelle had told me that Ben was not seeing anyone, I decided to ask him myself. "No," he replied. It was a closed-ended answer, but I don't know what I really expected him to say.

"Me neither," I said. I fidgeted to fill the silence. After several very long seconds, I couldn't stand the stillness any longer, so I blurted out like a blundering idiot, "I'm kind of picky. I stopped dating actually." I closed my eyes and shook my head to the side in one quick jolt, wondering why I had just told him that. I held my eyes closed for a few seconds too long. When I looked up, I realized that Ben was no longer looking ahead from the cave shelf like he was a moment ago, but instead he was looking at me. I quickly became aware of how ridiculous I looked at that moment. I just exposed one of my nervous ticks! He was still looking at me quietly. I let out a nervous, quick exhale. "I mean, there's criteria one would have to meet to date me and most people fail. It's a precursor to a date so that there's not the 'this isn't going to work out' conversation at the end of the date that I've become so accustomed to giving." He paused a moment, taking in all I had just said, and then he laughed. After a couple seconds, I joined in with him, and the awkward moment shattered. "That sounded crazy, right?" I said timidly.

"Yep," he said. However, his smile told me that it was okay that I sounded kooky. That warmed my heart. "What kind of criteria?" he asked.

"Oh, just like the way one treats other people: general kindness or caring acts such as holding the door for an elderly person." My voice faded off as I mumbled, "Or something like that."

"That indeed sounds like a noble criteria," he said.

"You're making fun of me," I said, not sure if I was questioning him or confirming that I knew this.

"Absolutely," he said, smiling. I scoffed and rolled my eyes.

"Well, from what I can figure, your previous girlfriends really messed up when they let you go," I said, smiling at him. I guess I was flirting a little. He smiled back but gave no reply.

Ben decided that it was time to move on to the next destination, so he turned around and laid stomach-down on the cave shelf and then lowered himself down to the ground. It was a bit of a drop, even for him. That was the quick way down, and not the way we came up. He reached his arms up toward me and said, "Come on. I'll help you down." This seemed like a crazy notion. I could've just crawled down the way I came and there would be no chance of him or myself getting hurt, but he looked confident enough.

"Just like this?" I said as I scooted toward the edge of the shelf.

"Yeah," he replied. I lowered myself down enough to where he could reach my waist and lower me down the rest of the way. I gasped and clutched to his arms as soon as he had my full body weight. Once my feet were on the ground, he said to me, "You have trust issues."

"Duh, Mr. Obvious," I said with a smirk. He laughed.

"Ow. Burn. Well, you can trust me," he said, smiling at me.

We hiked back to our motorcycles and were off to the next destination of Cedar Falls. The trail to the waterfall was wet and full of small wildlife. When we got there, I took a deep breath and looked around at all of the beauty and splendor before me. It was mid-day, and the sun began to shine through the trees, warming me. The sun rays glittered and danced off of the water, making me feel like a fairy on the edge of heaven. Ben had a bewildered expression as he watched me beam like a child who had just been let outside for the first time. I was captivated by my wonderland. All of the sights, smells and sounds whirled around me like a gentle wind tunnel.

I gasped and said, "Isn't it so beautiful here!?" I worked to control my breathing and continued with, "How could anyone not believe in God when He is in every drop of water and every ray of sunshine?" Remember when I said I was an emotional person earlier? I wasn't kidding. I turned to Ben, widened my eyes, and whispered, "I love waterfalls." I grabbed his hand and pulled him behind me down to the pool where the waterfall splashed. "Come on!" I shouted as he lagged behind me. The soft wet sand made it hard not to stumble. I dropped my bag and stripped down to my bathing suit. Ben did the same. I got in the water up to my ankles and screamed, "Ah! It's cold!" I ran back out.

Ben touched the water with his toe and said, "Whoa! Yeah it is."

"This is how you do it," I said as I ran by him. My laughs turned into screams that were necessary to build up my courage for what I was about to do. I belly-flopped into the shallow water and shrieked, "Ahh!" I got up shivering and turned around just in time to see Ben doubled over in his convulsive laugh. This time he stayed down with his hands on his knees for several moments. When he stood up, he was holding his stomach laughing.

He tried to compose himself enough to get this sentence out: "Nope, it's all, it's all you."

"I feel so alive," I said unconvincingly as I shivered. That only caused Ben to double over again. Finally, he walked over to my bag and grabbed my towel as I shivered on the edge of the water.

"Get over here, you goof," he said. He wrapped the towel around me as he smiled wildly. His smile made me smile. You know, that crinkle-nose smile that I hated so much, but I didn't turn away from him this time. He grabbed his towel, too, intending to bundle me up in it.

"I didn't realize we were going to church," he said, looking at my bathing suit as he wrapped me in the second towel. He rubbed my shoulders to help warm me.

I was wearing a very conservative suit: a one-piece with built in shorts and a halter top. "Nothing is wrong with my swim wear," I said defensively as I shivered. "It's vintage, a classic forties look. And it keeps everything in place. There's no question whether it will stay on or not with horse-play. That's important when picking out swim wear."

"I didn't realize there was going to be horse-play!" He laughed heartily.

"Well, you never know. There's *always* a possibility of horse-play," I said, laughing.

We hiked back to the bikes and headed out to grab a quick bite to eat at a local eatery. We talked and laughed uninhibitedly. Ben was so funny and charming.

At one point during lunch, a good portion of my meal drifted from my mouth and hit the table. He always took every opportunity to make fun of me. "Is this your first time?" he asked me. There were several seconds of silence, denoting how long it took for me to get that joke. I covered my mouth to refrain from outright laughing. I smiled and giggled instead. "Actually, what's supposed to happen is the food goes down your throat into your stomach." I let out a hard, silent laugh as I tried not to choke on my food. Amused at my response, he decided to persist. "It's a necessary process in order to survive." I laughed some more with my lips pursed shut and the food still in my mouth. I breathed in and out of my nose rapidly and my face flushed. I tried to stop laughing so that I could swallow. "You should probably just spit it out and start all over." Now he was just being mean because I was bound to choke, and he would be responsible! Finally, I looked away from him and produced a hard swallow. This was immediately followed by an outburst of laughter. It was the worst, most unattractive laugh that I've ever heard come from my mouth. I sounded and looked like an idiot. I was definitely causing a scene, but Ben didn't seem to mind. "Do you want some applesauce?" he asked. "It might go down easier." He was just starting to laugh. I can't believe he refrained from laughing until then.

"What are you, trying to kill me!?" I spouted.

"I'm trying to save your life, actually. I wouldn't want you to *starve* to death." I convulsed forward at my trunk and grabbed his forearm, which was resting on the table. I was back to my silent, hard laugh. "Whoa, whoa. Don't hurt me," he said, laughing. "Who will save you if I'm gone?" I was still laughing hard, but I was cognizant enough to wonder if I had overstepped by touching his arm. I started to remove my hand from his arm, but he put his hand on mine and held it there for a few seconds longer as we both laughed. I was, of course, laughing at how funny he was, but he was clearly laughing at how hard I was laughing.

After our meal, Ben went outside and waited there for me as I used the Ladies Room. When I came out, I overheard a man talking to him. "Nice catch, man," he said to Ben.

"Oh, we're just friends," Ben replied.

"Not for long though, right?" he said with an impish smile as he walked away. Ben gave him a polite smile. I smiled too. Ben didn't notice that I had overheard this because I approached him from behind. I walked up to Ben and watched him tilt his head to the side while he rubbed his neck. He also moved his shoulder in a circular motion a couple of times.

"What's the matter?" I asked as I approached.

"Oh, I'm old."

I laughed at him. I motioned my head toward his motorcycle and said, "That's not a bike of an old man." He gave me a wide, closed-mouth smile with his head still tilted and his hand on his neck. He was trying *not* to smile. This only made me want to give him a hard time.

I skipped over to his bike obnoxiously and swung my hair around as I got down on one knee. I clasped my hands together as if to give him a boost up to his crotch rocket. "Here old man, I'll help you up."

His face was priceless. His lips were pursed together as he tried even harder not to smile, but oh how his eyes did gleam. He walked toward me slowly, trying to look irritated. I laughed at him for a bit before I got up. Then I walked behind him, grabbed his shoulder muscles, and gave him a few good squeezes.

"I'll work it out tonight. You do know that I'm a massage therapist, right?"

"I did *not* know that," he said with interest as he raised his eyebrows.

"It's true. It's more of a side job. X-ray tech is my full-time job."

After we ate, we were off to the Upper Falls at Old Man's Cave. The water was a little warmer with it being later in the day, so I was able to talk Ben into getting in the water with me. We swam around a bit and even went under the falls.

I was feeling ornery, so I started splashing Ben. "Don't start what you can't finish," Ben warned. This didn't deter me, so he decided to teach me a lesson. He grabbed me and picked me up, twirled me around, and released me into the deeper part of the water. I let out a scream just before I landed on my butt. Smack! It was a harsh landing.

When I recovered into standing, I said, "Oh, it's on!" I dove under the water near his legs, grabbed both of his ankles, and lifted with full force. He went crashing down onto his butt and hands. I emerged between his legs laughing.

"Hope I didn't mess up your perfect hair," I said with a nasally tone and a pouty lip.

"Not even a tornado could mess up *this* hair," he said. Then he grabbed my arms, pulled me forward, put his foot on my stomach, and flipped me over the top of him. I went crashing down again on my butt behind him, facing the other direction.

I was completely shocked that he just used a UFC move on me. I whimpered, "Uncle," cuz I did not want the full wrath of Ben. He laughed at me and then helped me up.

"I told you not to start what you can't finish."

"He's impossible," I thought as I tried not to smile at him.

The trip felt magical so far. With each smile, laugh, and exchange of glances; we became more enchanted with each other. I could tell that he felt something too. I know this sounds crazy, but I knew right then, as I stood in front of him dripping wet, still sore from the foot he put into my stomach and from landing on my butt, that I loved him and that he was the one I was going to marry. I just knew this.

We made it to the cabin early in the evening. We had a charming two-bedroom cabin that was nestled deep into the woods. I was happy with this place, because of the rustic location and the fact that there was a hot tub on the deck.

I had nearly two glasses of wine during supper. I planned on taking the rest of my second glass with me to the hot tub. Ben and I changed into our swimming suits and headed toward the door, glasses in hand.

"Where's your church suit?" Ben asked me, looking at my two-piece bathing suit.

"This is my hot tub suit, duh," I said with snark. Naturally, he's supposed to know that women can have different suits for different occasions.

"Sooo, you're saying if something falls out of place in the hot tub because of horse-play, that you're okay with that?" he asked, trying to assess the situation.

I exploded into laughter. My God, he's funny. "No! I *didn't* say that!" I knew what he was getting at though.

"No. What you said was that your church suit keeps everything in place. And that 'there's *always* a possibility of horse-play.' So, what you're saying now by wearing *that* suit is that there's a possibility of horse-play, which may make something fall out of place. *And* you're okay with that. Because if you weren't, you'd be wearing your church suit." I don't know how he said all of that with a semi-serious face, but it made it all the more humorous.

"You're impossible!" I said, smiling wildly at him. I couldn't help but smile.

"No, I'm just trying to understand," he said with a small grin.

"I'm wearing this suit because it will allow the jets to more effectively target my back. So, I guess, yes, I'm taking a gamble as to whether or not everything will stay in place for the sake of the jet massage I'm about to get," I said to him with my eyebrows raised, my head turned slightly, and full of sass.

"I just wanted to know where you stood," he said defensively with his hands in the air.

We turned to head toward the deck door. Ben moseyed along ahead of me. I got a clear view of his back muscles. I was amazed at his definition.

"I thought you said you didn't work out," I said to him as I walked–no stomped–behind him. My legs were feeling sluggish from the wine.

"I don't," Ben said. He stopped and turned to look at me with a confused expression. I stopped quickly, too, nearly spilling some of my wine. I took a sip to keep the wine level down.

Then I said, "I can see your Teres Major and Minor though." I walked around behind him and felt along his back and shoulder muscles to let him know what I meant. "It's just very unusual to have those muscles so defined if you don't exercise."

"I don't know what to tell ya," he said. After a moment's thought, he added, "I do woodwork sometimes."

"Fascinating. That's probably it. Mystery solved!" I said. I raised my glass in a toastful manner, declaring how I masterfully solved the mystery. Then I took another drink.

"Okay, Mister Spock," he said. I exploded into laughter again. "Oh, you got that, did you?" His smile was ear-to-ear. "I'm impressed that a young lady like you is a bit of a Trekkie."

"That's highly illogical, Ben, that you'd assume that I wasn't a Trekkie because of my age." He laughed heartily at that. Since he thought that was funny, I planned to wow him a little more. "'Captain's Log Star date 4525.6. A,'" I said with a long pause, "'small disturbance between the Klingon crew and members of the *Enterprise* crew has,'" I paused again, "'broken out aboard Space Station K7. I am,'" brief pause, "'forced to cancel shore leave for, '" I paused again, "'both ships.'" I was obviously quoting Captain Kirk from the original *Star Trek* series. This dramatization caused Ben to double over laughing, just like he was when we first met. He put his wine glass down on the kitchen island where we stood near the door. I laughed just as hard as he did because of his beautiful, crazy laugh. I followed suit with putting my wine glass down because I was more likely to spill it or drop it while laughing. After he stood up, I placed my hand on his forearm. "This is," I paused and laughed again. "This is perfect. This is how we first met," I said barely able to talk from laughing so hard. "You were doubled over when you and Mike were telling that story about popping a wheelie!"

We laughed quite a long time about this. After our laughter died down, we had a long, enchanting gaze into each other's eyes. Ben felt insecure first. He motioned toward the door and said, "Shall we?" He finished his wine and left the glass on the counter before reaching for the door. I reached for mine and took another sip.

I stumbled a little as we continued toward the door. "I would like to see your woodwork sometime," I said. Then I went on without a second's hesitation, "I bet you don't have an inch of fat on you." He stopped in the doorway and turned around. I almost ran into the back of him. My wine swished around in the glass. This time he gave me an annoyed look. "You're pretty skinny yourself," he said accusingly.

I didn't mean to upset him. I tried to explain. "No no. What I mean is that one can be skinny and still have fat. Like with a caliper test where they pinch your fat and measure it." I was wildly using gestures and facial expressions such as my C-clamp hand and crinkle-nose when I said "pinch." Ben was thin, and there was no way you could pinch an inch on him. I was thin too, but you could pinch an inch on me. That was my whole point. I went on to illustrate. "Like this," I said as I pinched my stomach. I had a very small roll of fat in my hand.

"Ugh! That's disgusting! Put that away!" Ben said as he dramatically held his arms out to obstruct his view. It wasn't disgusting. He was just being ridiculous. I jack-knifed over into a crazy laugh that had no sound. I was trying so hard to not spill my wine. I gasped a few times for air and expelled some noises that most wouldn't recognize as laughing. My stomach really hurt from all the laughing.

Ben steadied my hand and then snatched my drink from me. In one big gulp, he finished my wine. I was shocked. "What the hell!" I said. He didn't even look fazed by this guzzle. I was a little shocked and embarrassed by my language. I didn't normally talk like that. That also didn't faze Ben. I blamed that slip on the alcohol that I consumed and made a mental note to not let that happen again.

"You don't need any more to drink before getting in a hot tub. You can have some more later when we get out," he said as a matter of fact.

I scoffed. "I have a baby-sitter now?" I mumbled.

"Only because you need one," he replied. I scoffed again.

I followed him onto the deck and marveled at how much motor control he had. He had more to drink than I, but you wouldn't have known it.

We chatted about our fun-filled day while we were in the hot tub. The drive was actually smooth coming from the north with not too many hills. I compared this drive to the trip Dad and I took to Mohican, Michigan, where I first comprehended what it meant to use the engine to brake.

"I thought I was gonna die!" I laughed excitedly. "I didn't really know what it meant to use the engine to brake until I hit the clutch in and went from *speeding* to *barreling* downhill, like a bat out of a well, toward the 90-degree turn before me!"

Ben leaned forward as if he were going to say something to me, so I stopped to listen. Instead he smiled, sat back against the hot tub wall, and said, "Go on."

"And when I downshifted," I paused, leaned forward, and widened my eyes to emphasize the importance of this, "my bike slowed just enough as I neared the corner, and I thought 'I'm going to live, to live!' I tell you!" Anyone who knew me, wouldn't deny that I was a great storyteller because of my facial expressions, gestures, and theatrics. He laughed and assured me that he knew exactly what I meant.

Ben and I also reminisced about what brilliance our eyes did see that day. "It was perfect today," I said. I leaned my head back against the hot tub and shook it side to side with my eyes closed as I envisioned its glory. I was then feeling the full, delayed force of the wine. I elaborated with my eyes still closed and in an intoxicated trance, "I love motorcycle rides. I love sun beams. I love green canopies." I opened my eyes and leaned forward to ask Ben, almost in a whisper, "Have you ever seen such a green green?"

"It *was* pretty amazing," he said with a smile. He looked so sexy the way he had his arms resting wide open on the hot tub frame. I marveled at his unique features: brown hair with his eyes nearly matching; distinguishing dark brown eyebrows, eye lashes, and stubble from his unshaven face. He had always been clean shaven before this trip, so this was the first time that I'd seen him like that.

I fell back to the hot tub and let it hold me up as I slowly bicycled my legs around in the jets. Not missing a beat, I persisted with, "I love waterfalls," I said with my arms in the air and my fingers simulating a trickling motion as I narrated. "And I love spending time with you." I finished my sentence by smoothly transitioning my hands from trickling into a pistol formation pointing at Ben. Just then I let out a small squeak as I slipped down into the hot tub as far as my eyes. The slip came about because I was still bicycling with my legs when I lifted my hands off of the seat, and the jets just took me away.

Ben rushed across the water to save me. He sandwiched me by grasping my shoulders together and pulled me into standing. I stepped on the filter in the floor as I tried to get my footing, and I turned my ankle over. It wasn't painful, but I lost my balance. "Ah!" I squeaked as I began to fall. Ben pulled me close to him and I came crashing into his chest. He quickly moved his hands from my shoulders to around my back. Success: I hadn't fallen. My chest was against his, and my hands were on his waist. He started laughing heartily as he held me up; his whole body shook. The annoyed look on my face made him laugh all the more. He backed up from me and put his hands on my shoulders to steady me.

"Are you," he unsuccessfully tried to stifle his laughs, "are you good?" He laughed some more. I took a step back from him, irritated from his laughter.

"Stop laughing at me," I said as I punched him in the chest. When I started to pull my fist away from him, he grabbed my wrist and pulled me forward. I gasped so incredibly loud. In one smooth motion, he spun me around by my wrist so that my back crash-landed into his chest. He had his arm around me, holding my arm across my body, restraining me in a fashion. The force of my back hitting him in the chest caused us to lose our balance back into the hot tub, but Ben controlled our descent onto the hot tub seat. He continued to hold my arm firmly against my chest, subduing me as I sat next to him. He started snickering again. The room spun several turns more than I did. I'm surprised I didn't vomit I was so drunk.

Ben smugly said to me, "What did you learn this weekend?" Oh, I was *so* mad. I knew *exactly* what he meant. I figured that he wasn't going to let me go until I said it.

"That I shouldn't start what I can't finish," I muttered angrily. He laughed even harder and then patted me on my head with his free hand, as if I were a little child. I cringed as he did so. He burst even louder into laughter and let go of my arm, releasing me from the lock. I think my cringe sent him over the top. He'd gasp for air and laugh, and then he'd gasp and laugh some more. He was holding his stomach and laughing so hard that his shoulders shook. He was so out of control. He couldn't even look at me for fear that he'd never stop laughing. As I watched him laugh, I soon realized he wasn't going to be able to wrap this up any time soon. He turned his head away from me and put his hand over his mouth a little: index finger relaxed above his lips, and his thumb rested against his jaw. Even with his head turned away from me a little, his laugh was barely muffled. I started to crack a smile. He did look so sexy like this.

After watching him laugh a few moments longer, I said, "It's hard to stay mad at you when you smile and laugh like that." Again, I was flirting a little.

"Mad about what!?" he asked. "You're the one who fell in the water!" He totally ruined his sexy moment!

"For laughing at me!" I bugled back at him.

"Stop falling in the water and I won't laugh at you!" He snickered some more. "It's a simple concept really." He closed his eyes, leaned his head back onto the wall of the tub, and stretched his arms out along the border. His laugh died down into a smug smile. I scoffed at him because of his non-apologetic attitude. It was then that I realized that I had my "non-restrained" hand on his upper thigh this whole time–since he grabbed me and spun me around, I mean. "Just sit back here and I'll make sure you don't fall in again," he said with his eyes closed, his head resting back on tub, and his arms still outstretched. So, I leaned back and rested my head on his arm with my shoulder against his side. He didn't seem to mind my hand on this thigh, so I left that there too.

"I charge thee with my protection," I said, and then I closed my eyes.

The next morning, I awoke to the smell of coffee and jazz playing in the other room. I strolled into the kitchen to see Ben making coffee while playing the *air piano* and sidestepping back and forth to the jazz music! My mouth hung wide open as I observed him. Finally, I started to laugh. He didn't shy away from his solo when he noticed my presence. Instead, he smiled and continued jammin'. I decided to join in on the fun by dancing along with him. I giggled at his silliness as we danced. When the song ended, we both laughed together.

"I had no idea that you were such an accomplished air musician," I said to him with a smile.

"I've always been a natural," he replied while he ran his fingers through his combed back hair, as if he were a heart-throb. I laughed at his confidence because, clearly, he wasn't that coordinated. I think he knew that and he owned it. I read that in his return smile. "Would you like some coffee?" he asked.

"Mmm," I said, breathing it in. "That smells glorious. Yes, I would love some." Ben was still smiling as he poured me a cup.

"Thanks," I said graciously. I couldn't stop smiling either.

"My pleasure," he replied. He's always smiling, that's why I love him. I wanted so bad to kiss him the previous night but I refrained. What would I have done if he didn't feel the same? We had one more day together and it would've been unbearably awkward if he rejected me. Also, I didn't want to be drunk for our first kiss. He might not take me seriously then.

We sat down together at the table. "You take your coffee black too," I noticed.

"Black...like my soul," he chided with an eyebrow raise that turned into a serious expression. I smiled at the irony.

"There's nothing black about your soul," I replied. He smiled back at me.

After I got up for a second cup of coffee, Ben got on his phone. I walked behind him and noticed he was doing something technical, not texting anyone or being social. I pulled up a chair and sat down next to him and slightly behind him, so that I could look over his shoulder. "What are you doing?" I asked.

"I'm turning up the heat in my house," he replied. I didn't even realize that was a thing! I laughed liberally.

"You are *thee biggest* nerd I know!" I laughed even harder.

He turned around toward me and flashed me his gorgeous smile. He was only about a foot from my face because I had sat so close behind him in order to look over his shoulder. I was startled that he was in my personal space, but I held my composure. "Does that mean you're spiraling out of control toward this black hole?" he chided cockily. My smile fell from my face straight to the floor. Ben looked like he was starting to feel alarmed by my abrupt change in facial expression. He was either about to explain to me what he meant, or he was about to backpedal heavily out of this situation. There was no need to explain. Believe it or not, I knew *exactly* what he meant. He was referring to the comment I made at the Mid-Ohio Swap Meet. The one where I said that I tended to *gravitate* toward nerds.

Before he could explain further, I said most seriously, "Yes, that's exactly right." There was a long, tense silence as we looked into each other's eyes. Finally, I said with a straight face, "I told you that you'd regret saying you wanted to hear some more of my uncensored comments."

"No," he replied without hesitation. "I don't regret that. Not even a little bit," he replied just as serious. I gasped at his reply and fully blushed. This felt different than our previous episodes of lighthearted flirting. This felt hardcore. My heart raced. This was the first time I had lost my composure in front of him. I stayed close to him several moments longer, expecting him to kiss me, but he didn't. Finally, I sat back in my chair some and averted my eyes from him and tried to regain control of my facial color and heart rate. I stewed a little bit about him missing the perfect opportunity to kiss me. I decided that I was going to have to take matters into my own hands, later.

I changed the subject inconspicuously by saying, "Let me work on your neck. I was too drunk to do it last night."

He replied, "No, I think it's a little better. It'll be fine."

"I insist. I'm really good with necks. Come here and lie down." I had Ben lie on his back with his head at the foot of the bed, and I sat on a chair near his head. I massaged his neck and shoulders, and did some cervical traction and stretching. He winced as I went over a couple trigger points, but for the most part, he had the soft tissue mobility of a twenty-year-old. I focused on the troubled areas and got them to relax a little. When I was finished, he sat up and moved his head around with his hand on his neck, assessing his range of motion and pain. Then he looked up at me with a serious, semi-surprised expression and nodded several times, as if he liked how he felt. I giggled at his cute reaction.

"Better?" I asked, still giggling.

"So much better. Thanks." He gave me a closed-mouth smile.

"Anytime."

We stopped at Cantwell Cliffs on our way home. It was so beautiful, but what I remember most was how phenomenal it felt just being around Ben. And how I didn't want our weekend to end. Too soon, we were on our way home. Once we reached his house, he offered to make me some coffee to help with my ride home, and I gladly accepted. We both loved coffee; any time of the day was a good time for coffee.

While the coffee was brewing, I said, "Ben, can I talk to you about something?"

"Yeah, sure."

I turned two kitchen chairs around. Ben sat in one of them. My heart raced at what I was about to do. Ben had forced my hand by not making the first move. I'd never done anything so bold in my life. Instead of sitting down in the chair next to him, as I nonverbally implied that I would, I sat down on his lap, facing him. He instinctively leaned back in the chair and gasped lightly. I loved the shocked look on his face.

"I have a question for you," I whispered as I leaned in to kiss him softly and sweetly on his lips. It was my first kiss and it was simply incredible. I pulled away slowly, not knowing how long a kiss should be, or if he was enjoying it or not.

Ben smiled and playfully said to me, "The answer is, 'Yes, I liked that.'" I giggled. He smiled even bigger and had a gleam in his eyes. "The answer is, 'Yes, you can be my girlfriend.'" I laughed even harder. He reached for my long black hair and pulled several locks over the front of my shoulder and twisted them lightly around his hand. Then he said seriously, "The answer is, 'Yes, I want you to do that again.'" This time *he* pulled *me* close and kissed me. The longer he kissed me, the more it became apparent that he was a good kisser and that I wasn't keeping up with him. I pulled away embarrassed and fully flushed in the face.

"I'm sorry, I don't know what I'm doing. I never done this before." I looked down briefly away from his longing gaze that turned into a shocked expression at what I had just revealed. Before he could reassure me, I added, "But I'll get better with practice." I moved back in for another kiss.

This kiss ended up being a very long kiss. I would guess that I was on his lap for about an hour. I didn't want to stop, and he gave me no indication that he wanted me to either. My kissing skills improved rather quickly. He was a good teacher. As my technique sharpened, Ben started using his tongue. I felt the hairs stand up on the back of my neck. His kiss felt like a touch of heaven. I unintentionally squeezed him with my legs slightly. He responded by sliding his hands up my shirt and onto my back. I let out a light "uh" as he did so. It was the first break from our lips touching. I slid my hands from his shoulders to his neck and then cradled his head as we continued to kiss.

At one point, my lips accidentally brushed against his coarse stubble of a beard that he let grow only because we packed light for our trip. I flinched at the sharp feeling it inflicted on my lips. I rubbed my lips together and made a quick assessment. I decided that I liked that, so I began kissing and brushing my lips against his jaw and down to his neck. Ben made a pleasurable noise that indicated he liked what I was doing.

Ben kissed with his eyes closed, but I wanted to see everything: his skin, his changes in breathing, his facial expression. I'm glad he didn't notice. I'm pretty sure that looking at someone while you're kissing them isn't normal. I've not heard of people doing that anyway. Bruno Mars says it's a bad thing. After a while, I kissed my way back up his prickly beard to his lips. I didn't realize until then just how sexy an unshaven man could be.

After I returned to his lips, he pulled my hips closer to his. I gasped because *he* shocked *me* this time. (I was no longer just sitting on him, rather my legs were snuggly wrapped around him. Also, my breasts were firmly pressed against his chest.) He seized this opportunity and started kissing my neck. I moaned lightly and squirmed as he did so, but he contained me with his strong arms. It felt so different being on the receiving end of this. I unconsciously squeezed him with my legs again. I let out another "uh, uh" as I clutched his shoulders with my talons. He slid one of his hands from my back to my butt as a reply. It seemed like such a simple caress, but it felt so tantalizing. I started to have trouble controlling my breathing. The more he kissed my neck, the stronger I squeezed him. Everything I was doing conveyed that I didn't want him to stop. Everything except my hands on his shoulders that were pushing him away at times, but he held me unyieldingly. I focused on how my legs fit around Ben so perfectly, and I concentrated on how it would feel to have him inside me. I had never thought such things before, not about anyone. I squeezed him with my legs again and started to perspire. More sounds of pleasure escaped my lips and gradually became louder. I began rocking my body up and down against his. I was so overwhelmed and self-absorbed that I hardly noticed Ben let out a few soft sounds of pleasure when I squirmed my neck away from his lips momentarily. I started to feel an intense tingling sensation down below. All of these new sensations perplexed me. I was embarrassed by the way I was acting. I couldn't take it anymore! I pushed Ben away hard enough to break his grasp, and I staggered back several steps. I stood there breathless and lightheaded. He was already standing in front of me by the time my vision returned to full focus. I'm sure he didn't know what to say.

"I'm sorry," I started as I tugged at my collar to cool myself. I looked at him and then quickly looked away. "I didn't know something so simple could feel so good." He smiled at me understandingly.

He stepped close to me and reached for my hands. I swallowed hard before I looked up at him. He was smiling at me more with his eyes, and I finally smiled back. "You should probably get going before it gets dark," he said.

"Of course," I replied.

"Would you like some coffee before you go?" he said sarcastically because what started off as a planned cup of coffee ended up being totally different.

"Well…" I laughed. "I think I have enough adrenaline pumping through my body to get me home okay without a cup of coffee." He graced me with a smile.

"I'll walk you to the door." He did so while we held hands. When we got to the door, he turned to me and said, "I'm not gonna lie, the only reason I didn't kiss you first is because you're quite a bit younger than me, and it didn't seem right to pursue you. But…" He paused and his look transformed to playful. Then he enlightened me, "…now that I know you want me, game on." He put his arms around my back and pulled me up to his level for another kiss. I clung to the front of his shirt while I stood on my toes. It was a long, sexy good-bye kiss.

"When can I see you again?" I asked in desperation after he lowered me back to the floor.

"Can you come over after work sometime this week?" Clearly waiting until the next weekend to see each other was not an option for either of us. I smiled.

"Yes. Thursday I get off early. I'll be here around 4:30."

"That'd be great." He walked me to my motorcycle and he gave me one more kiss before I left. He watched me wrap my legs around my machine with lust in his eyes. My heart began to race.

"See you Thursday," he said.

"I can't wait," I whispered back to him.

I caught a glimpse of him in the rear-view mirror as I drove off. He ran his hand from his forehead back through his thick, short hair with his lips slightly open. It was sexy enough to be on a poster. I caught myself squeezing my bike with my legs as he faded from my view with distance.

On the way home, I beamed with excitement at knowing that Ben had mutual feelings for me. How hard I fought the attraction I felt toward him. And why? It only made me want him more. I reminisced at how perfectly our bodies fit together when we were kissing. I was no longer self-conscious of how thin I was because I was just his size.

Chapter 7: Evie and Movies; Nursing home.

I started calling and spending more time with Evie to keep her mind busy because Johnny seemed to be away more. Mom suspected that Johnny was having an affair, but I figured that he was just an inattentive asshole. When I visited Evie, I would often see him arrive or leave with a group of guys that were all tatted and pierced up. They'd blare their music, smoke their weed, bounce their cars, and God only knows what else. It didn't ease my mind any knowing that there were a lot of drugs in the city that Evie lived in.

Every moment I spent alone with Evie felt awkward because we were just so different, but I didn't let that stop me because I felt that she actually needed me for once. I wondered if she, too, felt awkward when I was around. After I thought about it in detail, assessing several recent and past encounters we had together, I concluded that she felt indifferent towards me. At least that was a step up from when we were in high school. Likewise, she and Johnny were so different. She was too good for him. I couldn't comprehend why she didn't see that. I thought, "One day, she'll come to her senses and leave him, and I'll be there to support her."

I called Evie up Tuesday evening to see what she was up to. "Did you eat yet?" I asked her.

"No, not yet."

"Okay, I'll be over with a pizza and a movie in a half an hour. What do you want to watch?"

"I don't care." That was her typical reply, so I told her I'd bring several movies over for her to pick from. When I arrived, she let me pick anyway. I chose *Deep Blue Sea*, which I've seen a dozen times. She rolled her eyes at my choice, and I snickered at her.

"Shark movies are always a go," I said. "You're just lucky I didn't bring over *Sharknado* 1, 2 3, or 4," I said with a laugh. She shook her head at me.

The conversation was scarce. I didn't want to ask about her stupid husband, so we talked about work and church a little. I told her about my motorcycle travel adventures and about my new friends. She didn't have much to offer me conversationally, so after careful consideration, I told her that I had a boyfriend. Her eyes got real wide.

"You have a boyfriend!?" Yeah, I mean, that was some real news. I was twenty-two, and he was my first boyfriend.

I smiled coyly and said in a teasing voice, "I had a feeling that you thought I was gay this whole time." It made sense to me. I had such a powerful stand-off attitude with the boys in high school, but we all know that was for a different reason.

"Well," she started. "I just didn't know *what* to think." That was okay by me. It'd be terribly rude and judgmental for me to tell her the real reason behind my non-dating philosophy.

I had her full attention as the movie flickered in the distance. She beckoned me to tell her more about him. I started to describe him: funny, charming, tall, thin, light brown hair and eyes that almost matched; eye brows, eyelashes, and facial hair that's dark brown and distinguishing; and a knock-you-off-your-feet smile! I'm sure I was swooning as I described him. I stopped myself and said, "Oh! I have a picture on my phone!" I pulled it out and showed her some pictures.

"Oh my God! How old is he!?"

"He's thirty-five," I said, smiling widely.

"Why are you dating someone," she paused to calculate, "thirteen years older!?" She paused dramatically and repeated, "He's thirteen years older than you, Ericka!" She used my given name with lots of snark to emphasize how much she disapproved.

"I know, Evie, and he's perfect." I still smiled despite her concerned frown. I knew I was in for it now. She was obviously going to nark to Mom and Dad, but I'd be ready for a rebuttal. I figured that an argument was bound to come from them sooner or later. "You know that guys my age aren't mature enough. I wasn't looking for someone older, but now I know that maybe I should have been all along. It's amazing how you can stumble onto a gem when you are not looking." Her look of disdain affirmed that I was going to get nowhere with her. I sighed silently and decided that another topic was in order.

"Are you coming with us Wednesday to the nursing home?" I asked. The third Wednesday of the month, our family would go to the local nursing home and lead the residents in praise and worship. Evie and Mom would sing, Dad would play the guitar, and I'd play the piano. Evie had trouble making it lately, so I'd sing when she couldn't make it. She was still frowning at me.

"It depends if I get off work in time," she said after a long stare-down. I knew that was going to be her answer, but it successfully changed the topic of conversation. The stare-down let me know that she knew I had purposefully altered the subject, and that she was letting me do so.

"Okay. I'll call you a half-hour before I leave. If you want, I can pick you up on the way."

"If I get off work on time," she replied.

We finished the movie mostly in silence with the occasional commentary from myself such as, "See, smart sharks can swim *backwards*. You don't wanna mess with *smart* sharks." As if an attack from a great white wasn't, in and of itself, certain peril. My favorite wise cracks of the night were, "Don't stand too close to the water, fool! Buh-bye, Samuel," and "That's why you always wear a cross necklace. Jussayin." I was only entertaining myself, but in the end, that's all I really seemed to do. It was enough, I supposed.

Evie and Mom weren't able to make it Wednesday, so Dad and I went without them to the nursing home. It was nice to see all of their smiling faces. Susan passed us in her wheelchair as we walked down the hallway, and she said, "I just have to go to the bathroom. Don't start without me!"

"Here, I'll give you a ride back to your room," I said, diverting my path opposite of Dad's. I heard Don loudly talking to Dad as I walked the other way.

"It's you. It's Rod! Rod's here!!" he shrieked. Don really didn't have volume control because of his head injury. He could control it for a few seconds if you reminded him, but after that, he'd already forgotten and was back to yelling. He continued, "I knew you would come! It's Wednesday. Rod comes on Wednesdays! Haha! Hahahaha!" He shook Dad's hand vigorously. I smiled at Don's boisterous greeting as I continued to push Susan in her wheelchair.

I passed Tommy in the hallway who said, "R-Ric-Ricky, are you h-hear to puh-play the pee-piano?" He had some trouble talking because of the stroke he suffered. He wasn't able to walk, but he was able to slowly wheel himself around the nursing home without help. What a blessing. Some people aren't able to do even that after a stroke.

"Yep. Dad is setting up now. We'll probably start in ten minutes. I'll give you a ride down on my way back," I said as Susan and I passed by.

"Okuh-kay," he said.

We had quite a big crowd that day. We sang old-time hymns that most of them knew. They clapped, rocked in their wheelchairs, or sang along with us. Others slept, but I like to think that they had heavenly dreams while we played. My favorite songs were "Mansion Over the Hilltop" and "Jesus Lead Me." It felt so good to play for these people. Most of them appreciated the music more than the congregation who attended church weekly. I always looked forward to playing there. It was one of the most rewarding things for me at this time in my life. We always played longer than our one-hour time slot. We'd have those who would say, "Play 'What a Friend We Have in Jesus' one more time." Or we'd end up playing a song twice because someone was running late and they missed their favorite song the first time.

Don came up to me after the music and said, "That's nice! That was nice!! I love Jesus! He helps me every day! I'm sorry, what's your name again!?" He weight shifted back and forth and swung his arms excessively while conversing. His posture was that of having his head always tilted to one side because his neck muscles were too tight to allow for straight neck posture. I concluded that his constant need for movement was not a nervous problem. He was just sensory deprived, like me. It was a self-soothing technique. I hated it when people asked me if I was nervous when I'd fidget. Some people fidget just because they need sensory input; they need to feel their bodies moving. I could relate to that. I liked Don, even though he could never remember my name. He always remembered Dad's name because, "That's my friend's name!" he would say. "Except he goes by Rodney!"

I always felt really good after playing at the nursing home. The residents there liked it so much, and it just felt good singing about the goodness of God. I also liked spending quality time with Dad alone. We'd usually go somewhere to grab a bite to eat afterwards, just so we could chat. It didn't matter where we went.

Chapter 8: Confrontation with Scott.

Finally, Thursday evening rolled around, and I was off to see Ben. I wondered how I was supposed to act when we met up. I'd never been in this situation before. Was I supposed to play it cool or be really excited to see him? My mind raced. I didn't want to blow things. How could I blow things this early on!? Was that even possible? I turned the radio on loudly to drown out my thoughts. Oh good, Toby Mac was on.

I parked alongside of the road and rushed out of my car without even checking to see how I looked in the mirror. As I jogged up the stairs, I tried to smooth out my hair. Ben opened the screen door as I approached and noticed me fussing with my hair. His smile induced a trance-like state to come over me that caused me to slow down as I advanced. We didn't break eye contact; we both still smiled at each other as I entered. I didn't know what to say.

"Hi," I simply said as I entered.

"Hi," he replied. After a moment's pause, he reached for my arm to pull me closer. He kissed me so sweetly. "I missed you," he said, and then he kissed me again. I couldn't help but feeling like I was floating as he held me tight and kissed me. After he kissed me, he said to me with his lips still close to mine, "What do you want to do tonight?"

"This," I said softly. "Lots and lots of this."

I gathered that's what he wanted to do, too, noted by his devilish grin. He quickly swooped me up and wrapped my legs around him. The surprise of it took my breath away. Then he carried me over to the couch and sat down. Once again, I was sitting on top of him. I could hardly stop smiling enough to receive his kisses. It excited me that he was strong enough to lift me like that. His deep kissing again made the hairs on the back of my neck stand up. That and the way he caressed my back made me just short of crazy.

Ben had a new move for me. He put his lips around my bottom lip and sucked on it ever so lightly. My breathing became erratic and my heart rate rocketed. I didn't know what he was doing. He slowly and smoothly pulled my bottom lip forward as he released my lip from his. I inhaled quickly from the shock of what just happened. I wasn't really sure if he did this on purpose or if it was an accident. It seemed so weird. He looked into my eyes longingly and then repeated this move. It was definitely on purpose. It only took a couple of times for me to realize that I liked this *soooo* much. By the third time he did this, I understood that I could kiss him back while he did this. My paralyzed lips slowly came to life, but my coordination was faulty. This was partly because I just couldn't control my breathing. I tried, but it was no use. I squeezed him tight with my hands and legs, and I made soft shameful noises as he continued this maneuver. A lightheaded sensation overran my body. I didn't like how crazy he made me feel, and I got embarrassed about how I was acting, so I decided to cover up by taking a little more control. I pulled away from him as I held him back against the couch. I delivered, "I really like that. Let me try." Then I did the same to him. Ben loved the way I took the initiative. He responded by caressing my back firmly. The way he held me sent shivers up my spine, and I was unable keep my lips touching his. "Uh," I uttered softly. Seconds after I removed my lips from his, he grabbed my chin firmly and pulled my mouth back to his. He held it there while we kissed as a reminder for me to keep my lips on his despite the dizzying effect it had on me. The lightheaded and dizzying sensations combined to form a hot and claustrophobic feeling. It felt like I was wearing three turtle necks. I finally pulled away from Ben and breathed in deeply several times as I held my shirt collar down away from my neck.

"Are you ok?" Ben asked.

"Yeah. I'm just hot. And I need a break." I smiled at him shyly. He returned my smile.

After indulging me with his kisses for a good while, Ben started talking enthusiastically about weekend motorcycle plans. I'll admit, I wasn't listening intently because it was difficult to avoid staring at his luscious lips and beautiful brown eyes. I've never felt so transparent. I just knew that he knew how bad he swept me off of my feet, but I decided that was okay.

Ben wanted to take me to the local café for supper that evening. On our drive there, he let me pick the radio station. He didn't seem to mind that I picked K-Love, nor that I sang along. "You have a great voice," he said with a look of surprise.

"Thanks," I said. I snickered at his cute reaction.

We really hadn't talked about religion much except that Ben knew that I played the piano for our church. Also, there was that one moment at Hocking Hills when we talked about his mom. I had really hoped to meet a Christian man, but it's more complicated than it sounds. Some who claim to be Christian act in worse ways than others who don't claim any religion at all. Johnny was a perfect example. I guess I let Ben's love for life and his genuine smile sweep me off my feet. I was as high as a kite, knowing that he felt the same way about me.

The next couple of weeks flew by. We spent every available opportunity together. I had only known him for just less than two months when we started dating. We had been together for only one beautiful month when I decided to invite him to church. I asked him very casually when we were cuddling on the couch while watching TV.

"You're invited to come with me to church anytime you want," I said.

"Thanks," he said politely after a brief hesitation. "I'll consider it."

Fair enough. I changed the subject. "I w-would like you to meet my family," I laughed uncomfortably and looked up at him. "If it's not too soon for that." I immediately regretted saying that. I thought that I was going to freak him out. My mind raced as I wondered how to backpedal out of what I had just said.

He kissed my forehead, ran his fingers through my hair and said, "No, it's not too soon for that." I exhaled deeply and relaxed my head back onto his chest. I didn't realize I was holding my breath as I awaited his answer. I just knew that my family would love him, despite our age difference, once they really got to know him. After all, he was pretty amazing. I often thought, "What were his exes thinking? He's not getting away from me."

Occasionally, I would innocently stay the night in Ben's spare bedroom on Friday night so that I could spend a full day with him Saturday. I hid this from my parents because I knew they would disapprove.

Ben's brother, Scott, stopped over unexpectedly early one Saturday morning after I had spent the night. Consequently, I met some of Ben's family before he had the opportunity to meet mine. It was clear to Scott that I had stayed the night, and he made our first encounter terribly unpleasant.

Ben and I were in the kitchen brewing some coffee. The mood was light as we laughed and wrestled about. The knock at the back door startled me. Ben jogged over to let his brother in. "Hey, man, good to see you," Ben said to Scott as he entered. Scott's smile was erased when he looked at me. "Scott, I want you to meet my girlfriend, Erika. Rick for short." Wow, it felt good to hear him say "my girlfriend," but the moment was quickly extinguished by Scott's heavy mood.

I walked up to Scott and extended my hand. "Hi, Scott. Good to meet you," I said cordially. Scott was a couple inches shorter then Ben, stockier, and had dark brown hair and eyes. He had a five o'clock shadow and wore glasses. He was attractive but looked nothing like Ben.

Scott didn't offer his hand back to me. Instead, he turned to Ben and said, "Is this a joke?" I knew where this was going. "She's like half your age!" Clearly he was exaggerating, but he went on, "Is this what you're doing now? You have a few relationships crash and you go after young blood!? She's just a little girl!" I'll admit, I could pass for seventeen, but my blood boiled at how rude he was being to Ben. I lowered my hand into a clenched fist and gnashed my teeth at about the same time Ben grabbed Scott's arm.

"Can we talk outside?" Ben said in a very irritated manner.

Before they could turn to leave, I stopped them by saying, "Scott, let's get something straight. I pursued Ben because I know a good thing when I see one. As for those other *girls*, I'm glad they screwed up and let him go, because I wouldn't be here if they didn't." I let out a small laugh, shrugged my shoulders, and shook my head when I said, "Believe me, he's not going to get away from me so easily." I surprised myself at how assertive and cool I was. I usually avoid confrontations for fear of not being able to control my temper. Then I'd secretly stew about what I should've said.

Ben, still with a coarse look on his face and still having Scott's arm, led him outside. I meandered toward the living room. I'd never seen Ben so upset before, and that upset me just as much as Scott's behavior. I heard their loud, muffled voices outside, but I tried to block them out to save on my nerves. Their conversation was over shortly. I could hear Scott's car door shut just as Ben entered the kitchen.

Ben had a very serious look on his face and was walking swiftly in my direction. I couldn't read that look, and I had no idea what was going to happen next. I was a little afraid, so I took one step back as he got closer. Ben picked me up and flopped me down on my back kind of hard on the couch. He pressed his body heavily against mine as he kissed me aggressively. My neurons were all out of whack because of the adrenaline rush from the fear of what he was going to do and from the new way he was touching me. This was the first time we kissed with him lying on top of me. He started groping my back and butt. My heart pumped out of control.

He paused for a second to explain. "That was so sexy," he said through partially clenched teeth. His breath on my lips made me quiver. He continued kissing me hard and deep as he moved his hand under my shirt and up to my breast. I gasped lightly and pulled my mouth away from his, so he started kissing my neck. My breathing got heavier and heavier. I could hardly move with his full body weight pressed against mine. I became lightheaded and faint.

Prior to this, Ben had let me be in control of how fast we were moving physically, which basically amounted to kissing and light petting. He had never touched my breasts before. I think he just got swept up in the moment and was now taking charge. Even though his hand was over my bra, I instinctively grabbed Ben's wrist and resisted him. This was an unintentional message for Ben to back off.

He paused for a moment, lifted his body weight off of me and said, "I'm so sorry. I got carried away. I'm so sorry, Rick."

He looked really upset. We were moving entirely too fast. I should've told him that, but what I said to him was very different.

"Don't be sorry. I was just a little shocked at first." I paused for a moment and then added, "And don't stop what you're doing." He looked at me with the devil in his eyes. His mouth was slightly open with his incisors showing. He breathed heavily just once, as if he were a vampire about to devour his prey. That look of untamable desire still echoes in my mind. He resumed kissing and groping me relentlessly. Why did I say that? What had I done? I still resisted him at first, but I gradually let my body relax when I realized that he wasn't going to hurt me, and that he wasn't going to go further than this. I was glad that he didn't slide his hand under my bra. I'm sure that would've been too much for me. The noises I made and how I writhed in pleasure underneath him surprised me. I couldn't believe how good this felt, with us being fully clothed, I mean. I had planned on talking to Ben about waiting to have sex until we were married, but I was now aware of how hard that was going to be. After this encounter, I decided to start taking birth control. I struggled with this decision initially. I rationalized it by asserting that it was there just in case and that I really wouldn't need it.

Chapter 9: Fast cars.

The next weekend, Ben asked me if I wanted to go on a picnic with him. I swooned at the idea. He knew from our trip to Maggie Marsh how much I loved picnics. He wanted to go in his STI rather than with the bikes. I thought that was odd because the weather was so nice, but it really didn't matter. I just wanted to be with him. I was okay with whatever he wanted.

He just beamed with excitement when we got into his car. "I have a very special place I want to show you. It's kind of a secret." His unreserved smile sent a chill up my spine.

I giggled at his enthusiasm. "That sounds great."

It was kind of out of the way: a forty-five-minute drive. When we turned onto a bumpy, dirt road, I started to get a little suspicious. I hadn't seen a house in miles. "We're not going to sacrifice any animals, are we?" I asked Ben sarcastically.

He laughed heartily and said, "No!" He continued to laugh some more.

"No cults either? Cuz I'm not okay with that." I was just egging him on to see him laugh some more.

"No cults," he said, lavishly grinning.

I loved to see him this way. I had no idea where we were going, but I couldn't wait to see what had Ben so excited.

The dirt road literally just stopped. It was as if someone thought, "This was a mistake," and decided not to continue on with it. Ben slowed down just a little, and then we were off-roading! I gasped with surprise and grabbed the dash board and the door in order to brace myself. He looked at me with a smile, and then redirected his attention to the path ahead.

We pulled through a wooded area onto a barren plot of land with two trees opposite of each other. It was surrounded by the woods and reminded me of an arena somehow. We came to a halt. I looked at the surroundings in wonderment. What was so special about this place?

Ben looked at me with a smile from ear to ear and said, "Are you ready?"

"Ready for what?" I asked perplexed.

"Keep your seat belt on." He peeled out, and soon we were sailing down the dirt plot. I gasped and braced myself again. "Hold on!" he yelled as we headed toward one of the two trees that had large areas of missing bark. He made a 360-degree turn as we drifted around the tree. We raced toward the other tree as Ben shifted smoothly through the gears. We drifted around that too. We were doing figure eights! I was in complete shock at what Ben was putting me through without having my consent. I was scared initially, but I didn't think he was out of control by any means. Actually, Ben's skill level impressed me. We sped into the middle of the field, and then he drifted into a 180-degree stop. I felt a little motion sick.

"What did you think about that!?" he asked as the car came to a halt.

I hesitated. With my arms still braced, I said, "I feel like...I should be angry with you...but I'm not." I paused as I spoke because I was still breathless from the excitement. "I think...I kind of liked that a little." My huge smile told a different story: that maybe I liked it a lot.

He let out a low-pitched crazy laugh, "Awww-huh-ha-haw." He bit his bottom lip as he took his seat belt off. He leaned over, grabbed me by my shirt and kissed me. He was so wild and alive. "Do you wanna go some more!?" he asked exuberantly.

"Yeah, let's go!"

We tore up the arena, turning and drifting in all directions. He clearly loved to drift. I squealed as he did so. My favorite maneuver was when he did a 360 in between the trees and then kept going in the figure 8. For the finale, Ben did several circles in the middle of the arena.

When we finally stopped, Ben clenched his teeth, pounded the steering wheel with his fists and said, "This feels fucking amazing! Driving fast in my car with my girl!" He was so uninhibited. He'd never used that kind of language in front of me before.

I stared at him for several seconds and said, "You're dangerous. I'm so turned on by you right now." And I was! There was just something about the way that he took the bull by the tail.

Ben let out another crazy, low-pitched laugh. He ran his fingers through his hair, still smiling wildly. He leaned his head back on the seat and then looked at me with that vivacious smile for several moments. It was a good thing I was sitting down. I'm sure I would've crumpled to the ground from being weak in the knees if I were standing.

Ben drove up to the edge of the forest and parked. He swiftly got out of the car, grabbed the blanket and the cooler from the back, and set up quickly. "Where's the fire?" I wondered. He was obviously still lit up about the drifting. I just watched him instead of offering to assist because I would've just been in the way of his lightning movements. After he was done setting up, he grabbed me and started kissing me wildly. Then he put his foot behind mine and knocked me off balance backward. I gasped loudly. He just used a take-down move to put me on my back on the blanket, but he caught me on the way down and ended up lying me down smoothly. He did not have food on his mind. After he lowered me safely to the blanket, I proclaimed, "You're insane!"

He smiled and said, "Finally, somebody *gets* that and is *okay* with it." He started kissing me again passionately, but then he stopped so abruptly that it startled me. "I'm so, *so* glad you liked it," he said referring to the arena extravaganza. Then he continued to kiss me.

We finally did have a picnic. It was sweet and innocent mostly. We talked and laughed a lot. After we ate, we walked through the trees holding hands as we chatted. Ben talked a lot about cars and his former racing days. I hung on his every word. He would occasionally stop to kiss or caress me during our stroll. He was so talkative that I hardly got a word in edgewise. I quite enjoyed it. It was a bonding moment for us, but especially for him. I was already smitten, obviously.

Chapter 10: I'm not fancy.

Ben wanted to take me out somewhere upscale. I tried to talk him out of it, but he practically insisted. "I'm anything but fancy," I discerned, but I agreed to go to make him happy. I wore a black spaghetti strap dress with silver designs throughout. The top was cut straight across, conservative, and very classy looking. I also wore a black shawl and black nylons, and I bought the highest black platform heels that I could walk in–closed toe of course. I styled my hair in an up-do with several curls hanging down in strategic places.

I loved Ben's reaction when I answered the door upon his arrival. He was speechless for several seconds as he looked me up and down. I'd never felt so sexy in my life. Finally, Ben said, "You look," he paused and took a breath, "amazing."

"Thank you," I said with a smile. "You look dashing yourself." He had a gray blazer over his black shirt, and he wore black slacks and shoes. His hair was perfect as usual: short, neat, and combed back. He even left his face unshaven, just for me. I took advantage of me being on a higher step by leaning forward and kissing him on the cheek. I ran my fingers across his face as I did so, letting him know I approved his unshaven look.

"These are for you," he said, handing me flowers that he had behind his back.

"Thank you," I said graciously. "Please, come in." It felt great to get flowers. I instinctively inhaled their wonderful fragrance with my eyes closed. Then I kissed him on the cheek again. He touched me lightly on both of my arms as I did so, similar to an embrace. I placed the flowers in a glass of water because I didn't have a vase. I never needed one before.

"And these are for you," I said as I pulled a box of chocolates off of my table and handed it to him. He smiled kindly, but then a realization hit him. Yes, I remembered what he said about getting "chocolates from (his) Juliettes" when we were at Maggie Marsh.

"I, I've never actually gotten chocolates on a date," he disclosed with a small smile.

"What a crime," I said flirtatiously. "This is the first time I've gotten flowers."

"Oh, it won't be the last time, my fair lady," he flirted back.

I turned around after fussing with the flowers to see Ben holding out a box for me. "What is this?" I asked, so that I wouldn't misinterpret anything.

"This is a gift for you," he replied. I'd never gotten a gift from a man before who wasn't family. Well, obviously, because I'd never had a boyfriend before. I slowly removed it from his hand, still careful not to misunderstand anything. I looked at him one more time before I opened it. It was a beautiful gold necklace with a gold key on it. It had diamonds throughout the inside of the key. I gasped; it was so beautiful. I bet he spent a pretty penny on it.

"Oh my God!" was my first reaction. "It's beautiful. Thank you." I leaned forward to kiss his lips. I looked at it again and then couldn't control how big I was grinning. I looked back at Ben. It seemed like he needed an explanation. "I really like that it's a key." A key to his heart of course! He graced me with a full-face smile.

"Let me help you with that." He put the necklace around my neck and then kissed me very passionately. He didn't have to bend so far to reach my lips, and I didn't have to strain to reach his; my high-heeled shoes were already paying off. He took my hand and led me toward the door. He even held my hand and escorted me down the stairs as if I were a princess. I giggled and smiled at him. I felt like I was about to have the best night of my life.

"I'm sorry I doubted you," I said to him after we got into the car. "This feels really right so far." I realized that this sounded corny because the date just started.

He looked over at me, smiled coyly and said, "Never doubt me, Rick." What a smart aleck. I was loving it already.

On the way up to Toledo, we talked mostly about music and motorcycles. We listened to each other's top picks and thoroughly enjoyed each other's company. By the time we had arrived, my face hurt from smiling so hard.

The place we pulled up to was so fancy, even to the point of having valet parking. I got a pit in my stomach. I was going to somehow make a fool out of myself; I just knew it.

Ben assisted me out of the car and gave me his arm to escort me up the stairs. He looked at my face and said, "Relax, relax. Tonight is going to be amazing." His words and smile reassured me, and I did seem to relax a little. I took his arm and walked up the stairs with him.

When we were seated, Ben began to check out the wine list. "I'm going to order a red wine that's a little sweet. I know you don't like dry red wine, but I think you'll like this one."

"That sounds good," I said timidly with a polite smile.

I was so talkative in the car, but I had gotten really quiet and shy in the restaurant. After we ordered our food, Ben said to me, "I love how you didn't order a salad, and that you didn't order what I ordered." I smiled at him as I rubbed the stem of my wine glass. I took another sip.

"This wine is really good," I said to him. He said that he was pleased that I liked it. There was a little bit of an awkward silence that followed.

"You know, Rick, it's nice to see a different side of you. Not that you being quiet and nervous is what I want you to be, but it's a side I haven't seen before." He smiled again at me with that spark in his eyes. I wondered if anyone else saw that in him. I wondered if he knew that I was already all-in.

After another short silence, I said to Ben out of the blue, "You have such a beautiful smile. I'm sorry that I haven't told you sooner." He looked down for a minute. He was quiet and as close to blushing as I'd ever seen him. After he looked back up at me, I laughed heartily at his disposition. He smiled wider, knowing what I was thinking, but I said it anyway. "Who's quiet and shy now?" I asked. We laughed together.

That seemed to slacken the tension I was feeling. We talked and laughed a lot during dinner. At one point, when we were coming down from another outburst of laughter, I said, "My face hurts so bad from smiling so much." I put my hands on my cheeks and tried not to smile just for a second in order to get a little relief.

"Yeah, me too," Ben said as he laughed.

We finished off the bottle of wine later in the meal. I was clearly intoxicated, as evidenced by my lost motor control. I set my glass down hard and uneven on the table. I made a funny face that indicated to Ben that I knew I was drunk, and that I was a little embarrassed about it. Ben didn't appear intoxicated, although he had more to drink than I did. He smiled at me, but soon his smile slowly faded. Just then, Ben got serious on me.

He said, "What are you thinking, Rick, going out with someone as old as me?" He took me by surprise. His words were like a punch to the chest, knocking the wind out of me. My mind raced. I thought we were having a great time together. As a matter of fact, I was totally in love with him. He didn't know that!? Well, I hadn't told him that yet. I guess I thought he could tell. Why would he ask me something like that!? It had to be because of Scott. No wait, that was a while back. Maybe he asked this because of how many heads we turned that evening. The employees were not especially discreet as they checked out our table. Did they stare because of our age difference or because we were really having a good time?

I felt like I was on the verge of a panic attack. Maybe I was going to burst into tears. "I fucking love you, you idiot!" That's what I wanted to say. "I'm not going out with someone *like* you!" I internalized. "I'm going out with *you*!" I nervously tucked a piece of my hair behind my ear as I considered how to reply. I tried hard to focus and think clearly. I took a deep breath and realized that he really didn't know how special he was. That must've been it.

"I, uh, have always been an old soul. Guys my age are, aren't mature enough for me. I have turned down so many guys." That last sentence was graceless. I pursed my lips together and wondered how he was receiving me so far. I continued, "I got tired of rejecting guys, so I developed a standoffish type personality, with regards to dating anyway." I was really enunciating my words here, trying to look more sober than I was. "My sister was prom-promiscuous in high school, and she developed a reputation as a result. Consequently, I was expected to do the same, and I was constantly harassed. That only made me more defensive." I paused a second. That's not what he asked me. I was getting off track. My heart raced as I tried to refocus. He was still listening intently. "You and I ju-just have so much in common." There was no denying that. I smiled at him. This helped restore my heart rate to near normal. I went on, "I just knew that I wanted you, and I had to be quick about it before someone else beat me to it." I blushed at my words after I had finished that last statement. I just told him that I wanted him. Well, duh. He knew that when I sat on his lap and kissed him after returning from Hocking Hills, but I hadn't told him that directly until then. That felt like a slip, like it wasn't supposed to happen. I started to lose my composure. Ben leaned forward and rested his elbows on the table as he observed my flushed face. I nervously looked away from him toward the dancefloor that I had just made fun of twenty minutes ago. It was dimly lit with strings of Christmas lights. I joked about how I would love to do the Running Man to the slow music that was playing. I swallowed kind of hard and took a slow, deep breath, trying to control my anxiety. Then I looked back to see Ben smiling. He stood up and offered his hand to me.

"Dance with me, Rick." I could only muster up a small return smile because of the flashes of emotions I suffered galloping alongside of my intoxication. I took his hand and stood up. He escorted me to the dancefloor as no other gentleman could do. He held me in all of the right places so that I moved fluently with him, hiding my intoxication.

This felt like the prom I never had. Even better, I felt like a princess in a way. We danced chest to chest, so I just knew that he could feel my heart pounding. I tried to distract his attention from that by saying, "You shouldn't put me on the spot like that, Ben. You know I don't have a filter. I just say what's there."

He leaned closer and kissed my cheek. Then he said softly, "You shouldn't tell me what I shouldn't do, because that just makes me want to do it more." His breath on my neck caused me to tremble in his arms. I squeezed him tight and breathed heavily. My reactions were so amplified. There was no hiding *anything* from him.

Ben thought he'd maximize on the moment. "Tell me, Rick, what are you thinking right now?" He kissed my cheek again and then softly brushed his lips on my neck. I let out the lightest "uh" as he did so.

I was still breathing so heavily, but I said with full confidence, "I love you, Ben. I know it sounds crazy, but it's not. I know it seems too soon to know, but I know."

At the time, I didn't think about how telling him that could've freaked him out. Then we'd have a long, awkward drive home. I didn't consider that he could've possibly gotten upset at me for saying that when I was drunk because he might've wondered if I really meant it. I also didn't think about how heartbreaking it would be for me if he didn't reciprocate my feelings.

His eyes gave me a long cross-examination. Then he kissed me passionately–so passionately. The dancefloor was dark, but we were too involved to wonder if it was dark enough to hide our PDA. He slowly removed his lips from mine. Then he longingly looked into my eyes and caressed my face with his hand. I closed my eyes and let out another soft "uh." I opened my eyes to see that his expression hadn't changed. He was silent and frozen. He pierced my soul with his eyes. It was the longest we had ever looked into each other's eyes. I was pulled between feeling uncomfortable and empowered. These emotions amplified the longer he gazed into my eyes. "What was he looking for?" I wondered. "I hope he finds it." I started to feel a quiver come across my chest, almost like a localized chill. My heart rate rocketed another time, rebounding off of his chest. I decided that I was going to be the one to break the soul gazing this time. I looked down and stole a few deep breaths in order to control my heart, hoping Ben didn't notice. Ben put his hand on my chin and gently lifted my head to look at me again.

"You're so," I stopped and gasped a little as he brushed his thumb across my lips, "ama-amazing." I finished that sentence with my eyes closed. I continued on just as breathless as before, "I feel like your previous relationship fallouts were destined to happen, so that *I* could have you." He remained quiet. He moved his thumb from across my lips to my face, and then he slid his hand behind my neck. I think he was partially holding me up at this point. I started to feel a little nauseous from the wine. I forced my eyes come back into focus so that I could look into his eyes and tell him, "You're mine. You're all mine. I ne–I need you."

I was morphing through so many phases of inebriation. I momentarily reached a point of improved situational awareness. Even though Ben's body language told me that he was so into me, he hadn't really reciprocated my feelings verbally. I had a brief moment of panic. I nervously grabbed the collar of his blazer and said, "Listen to me yammering on about love and destiny. I'm not trying to scare you away." My dismay was undisguised. He pulled me up to his lips and gave me a long, sensual kiss. My high heels paid off exceptionally that night.

"No chance of that," he said after he kissed me. "I love when you say what you're thinking, Rick. You make me *feel* amazing." I smiled. That was enough for me for now.

We were silent as we continued to dance. I eventually rested my head against his chest and enjoyed hearing his heart beat as he held me. It was more like an embrace than a dance. It was magical. After a couple of songs, he said to me, "Do you want to go back to your place? Or to my place? We can continue our dance in private."

"Yes, that sounds amazing."

The drive home was interesting for Ben, I'm sure. I warped through several phases of insobriety during this date. On the drive home, I stroked his upper thigh often. I'm not sure, but I may have fondled his genitals as well. I was also doing some weird things. I crossed my legs and ran my hand down one leg, amazed at the partly numb sensation. Then I'd sit back abruptly into the bucket seat. I brushed my lips with my fingertips several times and said, "My lips are, my lips are tingling." I also rested my head back on the seat several times and closed my eyes during the ride. I noticed Ben watching me as often as he could spare looking away from the road. I was unintentionally turning him on. Ben asked me several times if I was okay, and I told him yes.

I wasn't planning on having sex with him that night, and I didn't mean to convey the wrong message. I trusted that Ben knew this because we really hadn't even seen each other naked yet, and more importantly, because I was a virgin. Fortunately, as we neared my house, I felt like I was sobering up.

I invited Ben in and offered him some coffee. He politely declined and asked for some water instead. By the time I had brought him some water, he had "Just What I Needed" by the Cars playing through my speakers. I handed him the glass, smiled, and nodded in rhythm with the beat at his choice in music.

He sipped his water and set his glass down on the coffee table. Then he abruptly grabbed me and yanked me close to him. He started dancing with me around the room in an uncoordinated manner. He dipped me and spun me around in jerky motions until I laughed uncontrollably. I became a wet noodle in his arms. He held me up as we both laughed together and until I regained my footing. I thought that he was done being goofy, but I was wrong. Next, he interlaced our fingers, put his forehead against mine, and started moving my arms around in a circular, alternating motion. He had to stop his nonsense quickly to catch me once more because my whole body became limp as I laughed in his arms. I began to shake as my laugh progressed to a hard, silent one. I made horrible noises as I gasped for air in between my convulsive laughs. The harder I laughed, the harder Ben laughed. Oh, but he wasn't done yet. He let go of me a couple of times as if he were going to drop me to the floor, but then he'd quickly catch me. I squealed as he did so and laughed some more.

After he helped me back to my feet, he slowly became more serious. He held me close to his chest and rocked me side to side. My laughs died down as his body warmth relaxed me. Finally, he started to kiss me. He walked me back over to the couch with his lips still gently touching mine. He lowered me down on the couch and seductively removed my shoes. A dizzying effect washed over me as he slid his hand from my ankle up to my thigh. Then he resumed kissing my lips as he lay nestled between my legs. His lips stayed in perfect contact with mine as he smoothly untied my shaw.

I was already wet from my hormones being out of control earlier, starting with dancing at the restaurant and progressing during the car ride back home as I had unclean thoughts about Ben. This wasn't helping matters. I feared that my underwear was now completely saturated, and that Ben would notice. I'd be so embarrassed if he noticed and misinterpreted this.

Ben slid his hand up my dress and pulled on the waistband of my nylons and said to me, "Can you take these off?" I gasped at his tugging at them and instinctively grabbed his hand. He looked a little hurt by my reaction. "Rick, I'm not going to make you do anything you don't want to. I just want to touch your legs."

I paused for a moment and then said, "That does sound nice." I took them off as Ben removed his dress shirt. He then nestled himself back in between my legs and leaned in for another kiss. I felt like I needed to explain my reaction because of the hurt look on his face just moments ago. I stopped him right before his lips were to touch mine by saying, "Ben, I'm not afraid of what you might do to me. I'm afraid of what I want you to do to me." This actually stunned him to the point of being motionless for several seconds. It was quite a feat to stun him. He soon became breathless and emotional from my words. He looked like he was fighting for control of himself. After several moments, he grabbed my waist and pulled me down the couch and off of the throw pillows. My dress slid up, exposing my underwear. He pressed his bare chest against my body and kissed my lips. *My God, he is a good kisser.* Just as he promised, he caressed my naked leg with his hand. I was completely intoxicated with passion.

He kissed me for quite a while before he came up for a little air. He looked at me cravingly and said, "I love you too, Rick." I really wasn't expecting to hear him say that. I thought he needed more time to figure things out. I wrestled with my emotions, barely in control of my tears. My breathing became erratic. I was completely speechless.

I caressed his face and lips with my fingers. Time froze when he turned his head to kiss my hand: seconds felt like life-prolonging minutes. When he finally turned back to me, I was able to form words again. At last, I said, "Ben, I've never thought about *anyone* the way I do you. Sometimes I wake up at night, out of breath and perspiring from having very vivid dreams about you." I had so much passion in my voice that I was almost whispering. "I don't know what's going on with my body. My panties are so wet right now, I could literally wring them out." I didn't hold back because he made it clear earlier that he wanted to hear what I was thinking. This also made me feel a little better about being so wet. If he did notice, then he would know why.

This drove Ben mad. After he processed this for several seconds, he pulled my spaghetti straps off of my shoulders and started kissing my lips, ear, neck, shoulder, and collar bone zealously. I tensed up at first and gasped because I wasn't expecting this change in momentum. He grabbed my butt and rocked my body back and forth toward him. I was so confused. This felt like fully clothed sex to me. I gradually relaxed as he moved on me. This was the first time that we kissed and petted with his shirt off. Something that simple made me delirious with desire. I ran my hands down his sides, squeezed him toward me, and slid my hands down the back of his pants, feeling his butt. Strange sounds of pleasure escaped my lips, and they weren't soft this time. There was no more resisting. I became warm putty in his hands and let him move my body however he pleased. There was no way I was going to ask him to slow down because I really didn't want him to. After several minutes of pleasure, it was Ben who freaked out and pushed me away.

"No, no!" he cried. He was off of me and standing in a flash. He ran his fingers through his hair, pulling at it as he breathed heavily. I sat up, pulled my dress down to my knees, and quickly put my straps back on. After Ben took a few deep breaths, he noticed my shocked and confused expression as well as the way I was shyly holding onto my clothing. He folded onto his knees in front of me and enclosed my hands with his. "I'm sorry, Rick. I'm sorry. Every time you say sexy shit like that, I feel like I'm more out of control and more likely to rip your clothes off. I should probably go now so that doesn't happen." I was conflicted about his words. I thought he was in more control than that. I loved that I drove him wild, but I was counting on him to make sure we progressed slowly. Envisioning him ripping my clothes off both thrilled me and terrified me.

I smiled and let out one small laugh. "I get that. Believe me I do."

"Tonight was so amazing. I hope I didn't ruin it just now."

"No. No, you didn't. Tonight has been…" I paused for a second, searching for the most accurate word, "…perfect."

I readjusted myself on the couch as my wet panties were starting to gross me out. Ben watched me with his X-ray vision and knew why I had done this. He closed his eyes for a second with his eyebrows furrowed, and he swallowed hard. Then he looked me up and down slowly one more time that evening, making me feel sexy as hell. Yes, that was the last straw. At that moment, I definitely could wring my panties out. I fought hard to keep a poker face during this final gush of feminine juices–for Ben's sake. He caressed my leg with his hand, starting from my ankle up to my thigh. Then he pulled my neck closer for one last kiss.

"You look so beautiful, Rick," he whispered to me. "And yes, tonight was perfect." He kissed my lips so softly and sweetly, and then he rested his forehead against mine. He held his eyes shut tight for a couple seconds. Then he quickly got up from kneeling, put his shirt and blazer on, and headed toward the door. He looked back at me and said, "I can't wait to see you again." I wondered if he would have to take a cold shower. That sounded like a good idea for me as well.

Chapter 11: Iced.

I could hardly sleep that night. I was on a supernatural high after Ben told me that he loved me. My fairy wings carried me through the house as I got ready for bed.

Ben texted me the next morning, asking if he could come over. "Of course!" I texted him back. He said he'd be over around noon.

The morning seemed like an eternity as I eagerly awaited his arrival. It was easy for me to keep busy, but I tortured myself by constantly watching the clock. I had cleaned the entire house, including all of the laundry, and I still had two hours to kill.

I decided to take my dirt bike out for a spin to keep my mind distracted. I got all geared up with my padded coat and pants, gloves, boots, and helmet. I really tore it up in the woods, pushing it hard with tighter turns and higher jumps. I also tried a few easy tricks off of some small dirt ramps that I had recently fashioned. When I got back inside, I had so much adrenaline shooting through my veins that it felt like my *whole body* would expand and then return to normal size with every heartbeat. Lub-dub equals big-normal. If that makes any sense. I left myself little time to freshen up before Ben arrived, so I jogged around the house to save time.

When I noticed Ben pulling in, I twirled around like a little girl bursting with excitement. I opened the door before he could lift his hand to knock. I grabbed his shirt and pulled him through the door. I stood there smiling, silent, holding onto his clothing. He smiled back at me and was silent as well.

Finally, I said, "I missed you." He didn't lean forward to kiss my lips as I expected, so instead I wrapped my arms around him, rested my head on his chest, and held him tight. He caressed my hair and kissed my head. After we unlocked from our embrace, I ascertained that Ben was not himself.

"What's wrong?" I asked.

"I need to talk to you about something," Ben said seriously.

"What is it?" That dire look on his face caused a deep pit in my stomach. We sat down on the couch facing each other. He reached for my hands and held them.

"I love you so much and I know that you love me, but you need to know some things about me before we continue on in our relationship." This sounded bad. The deep pit in my stomach turned into a sharp pain, and my mouth became dry.

I took a deep breath and said, "I'm listening."

"Remember when we talked at Hocking Hills? I said that I was angry as a young man when my mother left, and that I acted out with reckless driving, alcohol, and in 'other ways.'" I nodded. "What I meant by that is that..." He paused and swallowed nervously. "I went through a period of time where I...I slept with a lot of women."

I can't explain how this happened, but I felt a fire burn a path from the back of my neck around to my temples. It surged into an instant headache. I unintentionally and unknowingly squeezed Ben's hands. We sat there quiet for several seconds. It felt like an eternity.

Finally, I said, "I, uh, assumed that you had been with three women because you told me that you had three long-term relationships."

"Yes, I thought that's what you'd assumed," he said. I breathed in deeply and exhaled slowly. Ben went on sincerely, "I felt like this was important to talk about now because of your religious beliefs, because you're a virgin, and because I don't want to hurt you."

I nodded and another silence came over us. He was either about to give me a number or he was going to wait until I asked. I was not able to make eye contact with him as I waited for the number. He adjusted his hands; that's when I realized how tightly I was gripping him. My mind screamed, "Just tell me the number before my head explodes!"

Ben went on, "Rick, I want you to know that I've been tested for STDs and AIDS, and I don't have anything like that." The fire in my neck and the pain in my head intensified. I winced as a result. I squeezed his hands even harder. I felt like I might puke. I took one hand away from his, only to place it on the back of my neck to try to cool it. My gaze was still fixed on his hands as he talked. "Before we continue in our relationship, I want you to know...that I've been with twelve women in my life."

My body instantly became hot everywhere. My ears started to ring. I pulled my other hand away from his in order to pull at my shirt collar and try to cool my body. I said nothing as I tried to focus on the coffee table. What he said next was kind of a blur to me. He explained that this occurred in his late teens and early twenties, and that he hadn't had a one-night stand in over twelve years. He also said he had done light drugs.

My mind darted in all directions: "Light drugs? What does that even mean? That doesn't even bother me. But all the women he'd been with; that's different. Is twelve a high number? It seems kind of high. He *is* thirty-five. Is that a high number for someone who is thirty-five and still single? One-night stands? Really!? I can hardly believe that! Twelve. That would make me...thirteen. Number thirteen! Number thirteen!! How could I compete with so many women!? I'd be number thirteen forever!!!"

My emotions torpedoed me off of the couch into standing. I breathed heavily and held my head to try to pacify the pain that overcame me. I looked frantic! Ben stood up quickly too. He didn't know what to say, or whether or not to touch me.

Finally, he said, "I'm so sorry, Rick. I'm so sorry. God, I'm so sorry." Now he was the one who looked frantic as he watched me react.

The intense pain in my head and shoulders was unyielding. My eyes welled up with tears. I winced again loudly in pain. Finally, I turned to him and grabbed his shirt, savagely pulling him closer to me. I held him at elbow's length with my forearm pressed against his chest. I was able to make eye contact with him again.

My words came out slow and choppy, but they were true. "I don't know how, and I don't know why, but I know that you're supposed to be *mine!*" I said in an angry tone with my teeth clenched. A single tear floated down his face, whereas mine was streaked with tears. I released him from my grip, turned my back to him and said, "I just need some time to sort this out." He held his breath when I had his shirt. Now that I had released him, he desperately tried to catch his breath. He definitely seemed relieved. I don't think he was expecting that type of reaction. Who could expect such erratic behavior accompanied by such loving words?

"Yes, take as much time as you need," he softly reassured me. He walked toward me and gently put his hands on my shoulders from behind and kissed the top of my head before he left.

I poured a bath after he left and soaked my head in really hot water. It helped a little. I then took ibuprofen pm and slept the rest of the day.

The next couple of days were so hard. It was my turn to play the piano for church, and it was hard for me to concentrate. Somehow, I managed to execute the notes properly. Everyone seemed to notice my change in demeanor. It was really annoying to frequently hear, "Are you all right, Ricky?" I got away with saying, "I'm just tired." No one ever seemed to question that reply. Our Sunday family lunch gathering fell apart, and I was grateful for that. Getting anything past Dad and Mom seemed impossible at times.

At work, my days would vary greatly. Some days I'd be completely engrossed the entire day. Other days, I would go through spurts of being occupied followed by slow spells. I wished that I would've thought to bring something to work to keep my mind busy during down time. I focused my heart to prayer. "God, please help me to get over this. He is supposed to be mine. I know this with all of my heart. I need to get over this. Help me get over this." My prayer was repetitious, but I felt like I had no other way of expressing my pain to God. My prayer was constant, as I thought it whenever I was not engaged at work. I *had* to pray constantly. I knew that I wouldn't be in control of my emotions if I didn't. Even though most of the time these prayers were silent and redundant, I knew that God cared how heavy my heart was, and that He appreciated how sincere my prayers were.

Each day of that week, my heart hurt a little less when I thought about being number thirteen. I rationalized that all of those failed relationships would make him appreciate me more, and that he'd be thankful to have me love him truly and completely the way that I do. I don't know if God put these things in my heart or if they were my own thoughts, but they were comforting nonetheless.

Ben and I had radio silence since Saturday. It was as if our relationship had been iced. I understood how sick he must've felt about this. I reflected on the one tear he shared with me. My heart ached as I reminisced. I texted him late Friday afternoon saying, "I need to see you. Do you have any plans Saturday?"

He replied, "My only plans are to see you. Come over anytime."

I just couldn't wait one more night to see Ben, so Friday night, I packed a few clothes and headed over to his house. I had no idea if he was even going to be there, but I went anyway. I don't know why, but I decided to not let him know that I was coming.

He answered the door with a surprised look on his face. "Rick, I thought you weren't coming until tomorrow. Please come in."

"I couldn't wait see you," I replied. He gave me a tired smile. Apparently, his week was rough too. He looked at the bag that I was holding and then back at me. "Do you mind if I stay the night tonight?" I asked.

"Of course not," he said. He put my bag on the couch for me. When he turned back to me, I hugged him.

"I missed you," I said as I rested my head against his chest.

He squeezed me tighter than he'd ever done before. "Not as much as I've missed you."

"Could we just hang out or something? I just want to hold you."

"That sounds wonderful."

We lay on the recliner section of the couch together. I had one arm around Ben's waist and the other on his chest next to where I rested my head. My leg was positioned on top of his. I listened to his heartbeat as he ran his fingers through my hair. We were silent as we listened to some music.

We continued to be in rare form the rest of the evening: just quietly snuggling. It was getting late, and I said to Ben, "Can I sleep with you tonight?" I thought, "No, that's not what I meant. Can I sleep in your room tonight? With you? Can I sleep *with you?*" Fortunately, I didn't ramble these thoughts out loud like I sometimes do. Instead, I tiredly awaited his reply.

He reached his hand out and softly touched my face. "Yes," he simply said. Then he leaned forward and kissed my cheek. I was taken with his gentleness. I was also surprised that he had kissed me, even if it were on the cheek. I imagined that we were going to be back to square one as far as romance goes, and that he would wait for me to make the first move.

We changed into our pajamas and crawled into bed. Ben was lying on his back, and I planned to lie on my side next to him. He was wearing long, loose pajama bottoms and no shirt. I remembered how wild it made me the previous week when he laid on top of me shirtless as he kissed and groped me. He noticed me looking at his bare chest as I lowered myself into a snuggling position.

"Do you want me to wear something else?" he asked.

"No," I replied. I lay there with my head on his shoulder, my lips touching his skin, and my top arm and leg wrapped around him. I let out a long sigh and went to sleep.

When I awoke the next morning, I was still on my side but Ben was facing me. I had my face buried in his chest with my arm around his waist. He had his arm around my back with his hand caressing my head. I started to stir, so Ben lightened his grip to allow me to stretch.

"Hey, baby. How'd you sleep?" he asked as he brushed my hair out of my face. He looked like he had been awake a bit longer than me.

"Good," I replied. Really good, actually. I smiled at how well I slept, but also because that was the first time he called me baby.

"Good," he said with a smile. I rolled back onto my side, reached my arm back around his waist and innocently kissed his chest. He continued to rub my back and play with my hair. After I stopped kissing him, he let me hold him several minutes longer before he said, "I'm going to shower, and then I'll make you some breakfast."

"Okay," I replied. He kissed me on the top of my head and then got out of bed.

Chapter 12: De-iced.

Conversation during breakfast was a little scarce and arduous. Our discussions about work and possible upcoming motorcycle trips seemed forced, so we were mostly silent. I wanted to spend the whole day with him, but I was starting to think that maybe this was a mistake. Neither one of us wanted to address the elephant in the room. He wasn't going to ask, "Are we good?" and I wasn't going to say, "We're completely cool." It seemed obvious to me that this was going to go unspoken for a while, and I decided that I was okay with that.

After breakfast, Ben changed out of his pajamas into a yellow, blue, and pink plaid shirt. He was also wearing his glasses. It was by far the nerdiest I'd ever seen him. My mouth hung open as I processed his new look when he exited the bedroom.

"If you don't mind, I'd like to do just a little wood work today," he said. I don't think that he would've wanted to work in the garage if breakfast hadn't been so heavy.

I looked him up and down very slowly. "I've never seen you wear your glasses before," I finally said.

"That's because I normally wear my contacts from the minute I get up to the minute I go to bed," he said as if I didn't already know that.

"I, I know," I said, still staring at him. It was unmistakable how attracted I was to him at that moment. It also felt a little odd.

He took it in stride. "I wear my glasses and this old shirt only when I do woodwork." He pushed his glasses up with his finger after he said that. I gasped a little at this dashing Clark Kent moment.

I looked down from him for a second and clenched my teeth as I fought to regain control. I looked back up at him and said, "No, I don't mind. I'll clean for a bit."

Ben gazed into my eyes for several long, empowering seconds. Then he said, "You don't have to do that," without breaking eye contact with me. Ben noticed the lustful look that I couldn't contain. I think he was expecting me to ask him not to go, or maybe he was starting to reconsider how he wanted to spend the morning.

"It's fine. Go," I said. Ben plugged in some music for me to clean to. We had been at it for just short of an hour when I heard Ben come in for refreshments. I continued to dust.

While I was dusting, the song "Just What I Needed" came on. I slowly stood up from a stooped position and remembered how much fun Ben and I had dancing to that song. I smiled to myself and tucked my hair behind my ear, mesmerized by my own thoughts. I came back to reality when I saw movement out of the corner of my eye. It was Ben watching me smile. He put his drink down and walked over to me. My heart rate escalated as he approached.

He advanced toward me with a villainous smile, which made me smile even wider. "What is he about to do!?" I wondered. He was full of mischief. Ben abruptly picked me up, holding me in the Marriage Carry position. I squeaked in surprise. He held me under my back and legs and spun me around backward. I giggled at his silliness. After several turns, he stopped and let go of my legs, and the momentum caused them to go sailing around behind his back. I squealed louder this time. He caught my thighs behind him just after they crash-landed onto his backside. Then he spun me around while he held me horizontally behind his back. I'm pretty sure I've seen a move like this on *Dancing with the Stars*, without the screaming and with more finesse. We both soon became incapacitated with laughter. Finally, he carefully lowered me to the floor. Then he turned around to watch me giggle uncontrollably as I lay there. He bent over with his hands on his knees and smiled as he watched me. He pushed his glasses up with his finger again.

When we were done laughing, I sat up. Ben extended his hand to help me up. He let me look deep into his beautiful brown eyes. It felt as if our situation was healed. After several treasured moments, he grabbed me, threw me over his shoulder and carried me around like a sack of potatoes.

"Ah! What are you doing!?" I yelled as I laughed. He hit me on the butt several times as he paraded me around the living room. "Nooo!" I said, laughing harder. I kicked my knees up and down in a defiant motion, so he restrained them and slapped my butt again. I stopped struggling because my hard, silent laugh debilitated me. He laughed too, knowing that he'd won. He carried me over to the couch and started to put me down. I stretched my foot toward the floor, but he stopped me by grabbing my thighs and pulling them around him.

"Oh, no you don't," he said. He flopped down on the couch with me sitting on him. He wiped the tears of laughter away from my face and caressed my cheek lovingly. Our spirits transformed from playful to affectionate once again. The way his hands felt on my skin made time stand still.

He gently lured me in for a sweet, soft kiss. I readily returned his soft kisses. Gradually, I increased the fervor by French kissing him and sucking on his lips, showing him what a good student I was. He wrapped his arms around my waist and pulled me as close to him as I could get. I loved it when he did that. The feeling of my legs wrapped around him and of his hands on my body just made me wild. I removed his glasses and we tigerishly kissed some more.

It soon became very clear to me that Ben had a rock-hard erection, which was easy to feel through his thin sweatpants and my yoga pants. I'm sure he'd had erections at other times when we kissed and touched, but those times he hid it well. I became breathless as he unmistakably held me tight against his erection. I pulled my lips away from his because these sensations were staggering. He replied by kissing my neck fiercely. I held onto his shoulders tight and randomly tried to push him away and pull him back to me. I didn't know *what* I was doing. It felt so good. I felt like a wild animal. In a moment of delirium, I grabbed his neck and pushed him back into the couch, freeing my neck from his lips. I squeezed his neck tight and held him there. I looked at him with unquenchable desire. Then I savagely started kissing his lips.

The control I just imposed on Ben sent him soaring. He grabbed my hips and started grinding me up and down on his penis. I stopped kissing him, for sounds of pleasure flowed out of me, making it impossible to keep my lips otherwise occupied.

My sounds quickly turned more distinct, then resounding. I held his hair in my fist and buried my mouth into his neck to muffle my sounds. This was escalating quickly, but to what end? I didn't know. I tried to speak. My mouth moved but no words came out.

Finally, I could hear myself speak. "Ben, I, uh." I don't think he heard me at first. "Ben. I, I, uh." He slowed down a little to listen. "I...I was going to try to wait until marriage to have sex." This seemed like a terrible time to say this. I should've said it before. Somehow, it didn't seem to disable the moment, partly because the look of desire in my eyes never left as I told him this, but also because I quickly added, "But we can do other things." I grabbed the front of his neck again, this time pulling him toward me. I bit his bottom lip and then sucked on it. We were covered in each other's saliva.

Ben pulled away from my lips to say, "Hell yeah, we can." He started grinding me at full force. After a few moments, I pulled at his shirt indicating that I wanted it off, and he swiftly removed it. I took off mine as well. We kissed and groped and grinded some more. Moments later, Ben removed my bra. I wasn't shocked or shy as I expected I might be. I was ready for this. He slowed down and touched my breasts tenderly. My body convulsed at the new pleasurable feeling. This was a new level for us. We had never even been partially naked together before this.

After I opened my eyes, Ben looked at my breasts as he held them and said to me, "They are perfect. You are so perfect." It sounds shallow, but I was moved to hear him say that. I tried to catch my breath. My head was spinning with emotions. He pulled up on my breast and began kissing the top of it as he held it close to his lips. I let out a loud gasp followed by heavy breathing. The room came in and out of focus as he held and kissed my breast.

His hands were so warm. I loved this feeling. I wished he would've just continued this, but he shocked me by putting my nipple in his mouth and sucking it. I let out a loud, "Ahh! What are you doing!?" I hadn't heard of anyone doing this before! Well, except for nursing babies. "No! I can't! Uhhhh!" I genuinely tried to push him away. "No, no, no!" I said.

He released me and said, "What's wrong?" My eyes felt so heavy. I grabbed my breast to protect it as soon as he let go.

"I don't know. I don't think I like that. I don't know! I, I don't feel so good. I'm kind of dizzy." I paused a couple seconds and said, "I, I don't feel so good."

"Actually, you feel *really* good," he said cunningly. Then he grabbed my other breast and started to suck on that nipple.

"Ahh!" I screamed. The room spun relentlessly. I became completely overwhelmed and was unable to fight him anymore. I thought I was going to pass out. When I told him that we could do other things, I really didn't know what I was saying. Despite the fact that I genuinely did not want him to continue this, I felt a gush of feminine juice flow out of me. "Aw fuck," I whispered in my delirium. My body became limp in his arms for several seconds and I was quiet. I think I actually passed out. When I came to, my body convulsed several times, but Ben just moved right along with me and didn't stop. Then I gasped several times as if I had just come up from being under water too long. I tried to push him away, but he fought me.

So he was grinding me *and* sucking on my nipple. Then he stepped it up notch by sliding one of his hands down my pants, grabbing my butt. He kept the other arm around my back to keep me from getting away from him. Another large stream of fluid discharged from my vagina as he continued to suck on my nipple. I squeezed him with my legs and let out an, "Uhhh." This wasn't soft and sexy like it was when he kissed my neck during our fancy date. No, it was deep and loud. I doubled over forcefully, and we carved down the couch together. I gasped for air three more times, but he wouldn't yield. "Please, stop," I begged, and he finally let go. I pulled back and held onto my breasts guardedly. Ben sat us back up on the couch and then gently floated his fingers down my neck and chest, inspecting the red blotchy areas as I breathed irregularly.

We were being so naughty and it wasn't even noon. Ben peered toward the living room window, noticing how the sun shined so brightly past the open drapes. "We need to take this to the bedroom," he said. He stood up, holding me in the same position I was in while sitting on him, and carried me to the bedroom. I felt defenseless in my overcome state. As soon as he put me down, I held onto my breasts again. He was terrible with surprising me, and I was scared about what he was going to do next.

He leaned forward and kissed me softly and sweetly on my lips. "Relax, baby. Relax." He lay his warm chest against mine, and I gradually relaxed my arms, allowing his full body weight on mine. It felt so amazing. A tear floated down my face. From anxiety, from pleasure? I didn't know. Ben seductively slid my pants off. I let him because of how gentle he was being right then. Then he removed his pants and gently started grinding with me. I had soaked through my panties and was just starting to get his wet as well. He kissed me everywhere: my lips, my ears, my neck, my shoulders, my collar bone, my breasts. He touched me everywhere too: my breasts, my torso, my pelvis, my face, my lips, my hair, my butt. I was completely overstimulated.

His grinding, touching, and kissing kept me in a state of constant lightheadedness. He was moving at a medium, rhythmic pace. My eyes rolled back in my head as he grinded himself up and down on my clit. I began stammering whispers. One for every grind, "No–I–uh–no."

He lifted his mouth from my neck and softly said, "You don't mean that." He didn't even break his grinding rhythm.

I never felt so crazy in my life. I wasn't sure if I wanted to pull him close to me or throw him off of me. My body was sending my brain so many mixed signals. By then, I was moving in perfect rhythm with him. He pumped more words out of me, "I–uh–I–I can't."

"You don't mean that either," he said with a sexy voice. "If you want me to stop, you have to say the word 'stop.' I don't believe that you want me to stop when you say no, but when you said 'stop' earlier, you meant it. That makes 'stop' your safeword. Got it?" He went on grinding, kissing, and touching me. It felt like we were in the bedroom for hours. And no, I didn't say "stop."

I continued to get wetter and wetter, to the point where Ben could finally feel this through his underwear. He turned his head to the side and made a pleasurable groan. He bit his bottom lip and turned back to face me. He untucked his bottom lip and got so close to my lips that I expected he was going to kiss me again, but instead he said, "You are like a perfectly ripe piece of fruit. When I sink my teeth into you, your sweet nectar gushes down my face and chin." I gasped. That was the sexiest thing I've ever heard in my life! He bit and kissed my bottom lip, and I quivered underneath him. Well, guess what happened next. Duh, another flood came. "Fuck yeah," Ben said as I convulsed twice beneath him.

His thrusts became longer and more forceful. I clenched my arms around his back and buried my head into his chest. My body still moved perfectly with his at times, and other times I still intermittently convulsed. Tears streamed down my face as I made indescribable noises. Finally, he let out a long moan and came in his underwear. It took me a few seconds to realize what just happened.

He lifted his weight off of me and pecked my lips. "Is that what you meant by 'other stuff?'" he asked daftly. I was speechless and breathless. I couldn't even smile at his cleverness. His demeanor changed as he noticed my face was wet with tears, and that my body was even redder and splotchier than before. After he looked me over for several seconds, he pressed his lips against mine one more time and passionately kissed me.

I was nearly out of it when Ben returned to the bedroom with some water. He made me drink, and then he tucked me in with warm blankets and a fan, just the way I like to sleep. I slept the afternoon away.

When I awoke, I did a quick hair fluff in the mirror, changed out of my drenched underwear, and put my clothes on. I smelled coffee, so I headed straight to the kitchen. I peeked in to make sure Ben didn't have any company over because I'm sure I looked atrocious.

"Look who's back from the dead." Ben smiled. "I thought the smell of coffee would resurrect you." I shuffled into the kitchen with my arms folded across my stomach. He walked over to me and snickered a little. "You look so messed up." As he got closer, he suddenly changed his tune. "You look so sexy. You look *so* damn sexy." He put his arms around me and pulled me close for a kiss.

I was set back by his paradoxical reaction to my disheveled appearance. "I just wanted a cup of coffee before I jump in the shower," I explained shyly.

He pulled out a chair for me and said, "Of course." He slapped me on the butt when I turned to sit down and said, "Good game."

I flinched and let out a tiny, high-pitched, "Ooo." I was too exhausted for any other type of reaction.

Ben presented me with a cup of coffee from behind. He wrapped his arms around me, kissed my neck, and then said, "I love you, Rick." It was only the second time I'd heard him say that. I felt so blessed to have found the right man at such a young age.

I turned my head toward his arm and kissed it. "I love you too, Ben."

Chapter 13: The Diagnosis.

Sunday was family day after church, which meant that we'd either have a potluck lunch together or go out to eat. I preferred the potluck because Dad and I would often end up watching football or movies. Sometimes we'd even play games as a family. Johnny would seldom come with Evie, and it was getting fewer and farther between times of seeing him. Mom and Grandma June would always ask Evie where Johnny was, and she'd come up with an excuse that I knew was bogus. He was probably hanging out with his loser friends, smoking weed or doing something worse.

Don't think me mean. I had good reason for despising him. He had a history of serving time for theft and drugs. Evie naïvely thought she could change him, despite our pleas for her not to marry him. I never bothered asking her where he was because I didn't want her to have to lie to me. I still hoped that one day she would wake up and divorce him.

Grandma June decided to eat out with some of her church friends, so that left just Mom to grill Evie on Johnny's whereabouts. I had pity on Evie, so while Mom was grilling her, I blurted out my secret about having new friends in order to save Evie from this weekly torture. Evie looked relieved. She was thankful for the quick diversion, and she waited on the edge of her seat to see if that was all I was going to say. After the confrontation with Scott, I decided to hold off on having Ben meet my family or even letting Dad and Mom know that I had a boyfriend.

I went on about how I met my new friends at the Mid-Ohio Swap Meet, that they live nearby, and that we ride together sometimes. This was just enough of a subject alteration to get the heat off of Evie. She sat back in her chair and said nothing to incriminate me. I looked at her and imagined that maybe she was merciful because she thought that I was withholding some of my story for the next time she needed saving. That could very well be. I smiled to myself.

I was relieved that Dad and Mom didn't pry anymore into this situation. But my relief quickly changed to hurt because I had just said I had *friends*–that I was *hanging out with*. Sure, Evie didn't pay any attention to how hard high school was for me. I guessed that was easy for her to do with her being three years older and much more popular than I was. However, Mom and Dad definitely knew how many *friends* had hurt me, and how I was a loner throughout high school as a result. I thought that maybe more than the "that's nice" that Dad had to offer was warranted, but I eventually dismissed my hurt because that's really what I wanted was for them not to ask too many questions. Mission accomplished. I sighed.

Other topics of conversation were how work was going for Evie and I, Dad's stories of what goofy things the dog and cat (Max and Fifi) had done that week, and Dad and Mom's upcoming topics for church and bible study.

During a quiet moment at the table with everyone having a mouth full, Evie grabbed her head and moaned a little. We all stopped eating and stared at her. She looked up at our concerned faces, but before we could swallow and ask her if she was okay, she said, "I just have a little headache, and I don't feel so good."

Mom blurts out, "Are you pregnant?"

"No, Mom," Evie said softly with an irritated tone. Now that Evie was married, Mom asked her that question often, not being able to hide her eagerness for grandchildren.

"Maybe you should lie down for a bit, honey," Dad said to Evie. She finished her meal and took his advice.

While Evie rested, we enjoyed our after-dinner coffee. I was sitting on the living room floor playing with Max and Fifi when Evie emerged from her nap. She walked down the hallway using the wall for balance. "That's weird," I thought. I got up and headed her way. "Are you okay?" I asked.

"I don't feel much better," she said. I helped her to the kitchen table and she sat down by Dad and Mom.

"You had a headache last week. Come to think about it, the week before that too," I said concerned. "How often do you get headaches?" I asked. Dad looked at me with an equal amount of concern in his face. Evie sounded exasperated at my questioning.

She exhaled quickly and said, "I don't know. Every few days. It eases up and then gets worse again. I thought I was getting used to them." Evie sat at the table with her hand on her head. I was upset at her response. A headache of unknown origin isn't something you should get used to! We were no doubt annoying her, which was probably not helping her headache. But we continued on.

"Maybe you should go to the doctor, Evie" Dad said earnestly.

"I'll go with you," I piped up quickly because I didn't think she'd follow through on this recommendation. "You know I can trade someone work days. It won't be a problem." Evie looked up and let out an exasperated sigh. Then she inhaled and let out a softer sigh. Her countenance changed.

"Okay," she said. I knew she had given in because she knew that I wasn't going to let this go. I had a slight lump in my stomach that started during this conversation. It didn't seem to ease up as the week passed.

The doctor ordered Evie a CAT scan, and she was scheduled quickly. I was thankful for that, but also I was a little worried. The doc had a very good poker face during her physical assessment. He said that the CAT scan was necessary in order to rule out any masses so that he would know how to proceed. Mom had always referred to him as a "Doom's Day Doctor" in that he always believed the worst and was never hardly right at that. We all prayed as a family and individually for Evie to be okay. When the doctor's office called, asking to schedule Evie for a follow-up appointment to go over her results, a wave of panic hit me.

"I'll go with you, Evie," I said intensely.

But Mom interrupted with, "No, Ericka, I'll go with her this time." I wondered if anyone else was feeling as uneasy as I was about her test results.

On the day that Evie had her follow-up appointment, I rushed over to her house after work to see how it went. Johnny,

Evie, Grandma June, Mom and Dad were all there. I saw their cars. I ran up the sidewalk and stairs, nearly barging in. At the last second, I stopped myself at the door, took a deep breath and calmly entered. It was difficult to hide my shortness of breath though.

I could see that it was bad news. Mom and Dad sat beside Evie on the couch. Mom held Evie's hand and Dad rubbed her back. Mom had tears in her eyes and tried to keep her lip from quivering. I'd never seen Dad's brow as deeply furrowed as it was before me then. Grandma June had her eyes closed and was muttering prayers that I could barely hear. She had her hands lifted and her elbows resting on the sides of the recliner chair as she rocked. Evie's pale face was long and tilted downward. Johnny was sitting in the loveseat with an expression that could only be described as distant. I stood there with my mouth hanging open, taking it all in.

Mom broke the silence by saying, "Ericka, Evelyn has a brain tumor." Those words punched me in the stomach so hard that I felt like I doubled over. "She's been referred to an oncologist at the Cleveland Clinic."

I gulped and quietly asked a series of questions in one breath, "How big is it? Where is it located? What's the course of action?" I clenched my teeth and pursed my lips together to try to keep other insensitive things from escaping my mouth at such a delicate moment. It was hard, but I held back the tears.

Mom answered my questions with a lot of pauses as she tried to control her emotions. "It's about six centimeters around. It's in the cerebellum near the brain stem." She paused a moment and blew her nose. I felt like I was going to throw up for a second. Near the brain stem, or the center for all basic life function, is a heart-wrenching thing to hear. Mom knew that I already knew the severity of the location, so she didn't bother to explain it further. "Um," Mom's voice continued to flutter, "The doctor said chemotherapy and radiation are common treatment options. That's all we know until Evelyn's appointment with the oncologist."

Something went off inside of me like a light, and the panic lifted. I walked closer to Evie and sat on the coffee table in front of her. "It's okay, Evie. God will heal you just like he did Grandma June's femur."

"Yes, He will!" Grandma June piped up. "He is the God of love, mercy, and grace."

I leaned forward and put my hands on her knees. "Remember the scripture that says, 'If two or more agree on anything, it shall be done.' And 'When you pray, ask and believe, you will receive it.'" I didn't know where those scriptures were in the Bible, but I knew they were true just the same.

Dad added softly without missing a beat, "And 'By His stripes we are healed.'" A few tears streamed down Evie's face, and she nodded silently.

Chapter 14: Niagara Falls.

My relationship with Ben slowed down almost to a halt after Evie got diagnosed with cancer. She was all I could think about, and I was spending much more time with her. I prayed as often as I thought about her, asking God to heal her and thanking Him for His mercy, grace, and healing power. Meditating on God's word, especially those already put into songs, helped me avoid having anxiety. I wouldn't have made it through my day otherwise, especially during the slow times. I switched from listening to Christian music partially, to exclusively listening to Christian music to help me keep the right frame of mind. I would also bring my music tracks over to Evie's house and play them while I visited with her.

Evie met with the specialist at the Cleveland Clinic and started radiation and chemotherapy. Since Evie had been diagnosed with cancer, Johnny made himself completely absent during my visits with her at the house. That was, in fact, a little unusual. Sure, Johnny would avoid family gatherings, but he was often around if I were visiting Evie alone, at least for a little while anyway. Typically, *I'd* try to avoid *him*, not the other way around. He liked me for some reason. He liked me a little too much and made me very uncomfortable at times, but that was our secret because I didn't want to upset my family.

I didn't notice Johnny's loud friends being around either. I would hear a car door suspiciously shut shortly after I arrived, and he'd vanish. On the few occasions that I did see him, he didn't look concerned at all, and that bothered me. He certainly wasn't being supportive to Evie, but I didn't bring to her attention the fact that I noticed this. I just reinforced to her time and time again that if she needed anything at all, call me and I'd be there. I figured that if Evie wanted to talk about Johnny, she would let me know. Or would she? We didn't have a history of being real close.

Evie had the full support of the church. They helped Mom and me with cleaning her home and preparing meals, but more importantly, they imparted kind words to inspire faith. Evie was so gracious in receiving so much sympathy from everyone. She'd reply with a simple "thank you." I imagined that I would be tired of hearing the same things over and over from different people: "Evie, I heard the bad news and I'm so sorry. We're praying for you," they would say. I preferred original words of inspiration such as those from seasoned Christian, Ms. Wanda, who stated with such vigor, "Jesus never fails! You might as well get thee behind me Satan! You cannot prevail because Jesus never fails!"

Evie and I grew closer after she was diagnosed with cancer. Not one visit would go by without me kissing her on the forehead, telling her that I loved her, and telling her that everything was gonna be all right. It was weird, kissing her at first, but it became more natural the more I did it. We were a loving family, but the affection surrounding me was limited to hugs and "I love you" from Dad and Mom. Dad occasionally kissed me on the forehead, but Mom always said that I didn't want to be kissed, like she kissed on Evie. I don't know if that were true or if I just wasn't kissed by Mom like Evie was. Certainly, Evie and I were never affectionate toward each other. Not only did that change, but Evie and I found ways to laugh together too. During our visits, I tried to keep the mood light, and Evie actually started laughing at my jokes. She especially took a liking to my sarcastic commentary during movies that she found so annoying in the past.

During one of my visits, Evie's mood grew serious. "You know, I've always wanted to travel," she paused, lost in her thoughts. After several moments, she went on by saying, "And I don't know if I'll get that chance."

"Where would you go?" I asked.

"Well, I guess I would go see Niagara Falls. Maybe see the Grand Canyon. Stuff like that." She smiled at the thought of it.

"That does sound nice," I said. My wheels were already turning about how I was going to get her there.

I immediately started an internet search when I got home. I found out that the best views for Niagara Falls were from the Canadian side. I looked up information on hotels and sites to see near the falls. I called Mom and Dad to tell them that I was going to take Evie to see Niagara Falls when she finished her second round of chemo and radiation.

"Do you want to come with us!?" I asked excitedly.

"Erika, are you serious? How can you afford this? What about Johnny?" Mom asked.

"I have enough saved. Johnny's not invited because I'm not paying his way. I'll just tell him it's a family trip or something. He's never around anyway. Come on, Mom. If I don't take her, I'll regret it, and I don't want any regrets."

Mom sighed and said in a lighter tone than I was expecting, "Okay. Let's do it."

We had to play it by ear, according to how Evie was feeling. Evie was feeling stronger a couple weeks after chemo, so I was grateful that work was understanding when I quickly scheduled the vacation.

The trip ended up being quite affordable. Dad and I split the bill including gas, a hotel stay, and the Niagara Falls Adventure Passes. We took Mom's van to give us optimal room, and we packed light so that Evie could lie down in the back. I bought a transport chair because Evie's activity tolerance still varied.

The trip there was pleasant. I particularly appreciated the time we spent reminiscing about our family vacations when we were younger. One of our family favorites was Sulfur Lake campground, a place we'd stay during Independence Day holiday. We talked about the canoe wars that we'd have, water volleyball, ice cream bars from the small store, and of course the fireworks. We also remembered our dog, Lightning, who would camp with us. He was quite the canoe lover. Life was so simple back then.

We really enjoyed the Maid of the Mist Cruise, the White Water Walk, watching the lights change on the falls at night as well as the fireworks. I cherished all the time we spent together, including the simple stuff like pushing Evie up and down the main strip in the transport chair, ordering whatever food we wanted despite the calories, and just being together as a family. Time really stood still on this vacation. I took some really awesome photos. One of those was of Evie standing in front of the rapids on the White Water Walk. Tears filled my eyes to see Evie happily lifting her head to the sky, closing her eyes, and letting the mist engulf her face while we were on the Maid of the Mist cruise. Life is so precious.

Chapter 15: Ben Meets the Family.

We'd seen the last of Johnny before we left for Niagara Falls. Evie was going into default on the house, so she moved in with Dad and Mom. It was easier on everybody. I was just a stone's throw away from my parents' house, so I was over most days a week. Evie never talked about Johnny at this point. I admired her bravery.

I urged Ben to meet my family as soon as possible because I wanted him to meet Evie before her third round of chemo and radiation. She was starting to gain weight and swell from the steroids she was on. I regretted waiting so long to introduce him to her and my parents. It's just that time had slipped away from me when Evie got diagnosed with cancer. Nothing seemed more important to me than spending time with her.

I was really nervous about how my parents would react, so I warned them ahead of time that Ben was much older than I. When I told my parents this, they stared at me in silence with concerned, shocked expressions. So I said to them, "Why does that surprise you so much? When have I ever hung around immature people, or people my age?" I implied that the two were synonymous. This seemed to make enough sense to them that they didn't verbally fuss about it.

The function went really well, actually. Ben was his usual charming self: full of life and laughter. He chatted with Evie without staring or making her feel uncomfortable about her hair loss or weight gain. My parents talked with him in length in the kitchen over a cup of coffee while Evie and I visited in the living room. It was as if my parents were enchanted by him. I marveled at this wonder. I was really pleased that this encounter went so much better than the one with his brother. Ben even sent me a glance with an ear-to-ear smile, indicating that he was pleased as well.

Of course, after Ben left, my parents started grueling me about whether or not he was a Christian. It didn't make them happy to know that he hadn't gone to church since his mom abandoned the family. Mom's eyes danced wildly at the thought of how broken he must be, and how far he must have pushed God away in his pain. I knew her well enough to see this. I painstakingly watched her think as I wondered what she concluded. Had she decided that Ben would be saved because of my faith and prayers for him, or did she think that he would bring me down? She remained silent for a few more moments.

Finally, Mom reminded me about how the Bible says that a man and woman should be "evenly yoked together," which basically means a married couple should have the same faith in God and Jesus. Even though I expected her to quote this scripture, I didn't really know how to respond because she was right. I thoughtfully answered her by saying, "I know women can't change men, Mom, but God can. So I'll just pray that God saves him because I'm absolutely head over heels for him."

Is this what Evie thought when she married Johnny!? Was I acting like my sister!? I dissected my brains and actions carefully and concluded that this was, indeed, different. Evie thought that *she* could change Johnny. I didn't want to change Ben. I just want him to be saved. Only God could facilitate that, and I put my faith in Him.

My heart ached as I waited for Mom's counterargument, but I was shocked to see that she had none! Dad remained silent as well! So I went on to tell them about how poorly the encounter with his brother went, and that this was the reason I waited so long to introduce him. It played on their sympathy, just like I hoped it would.

Chapter 16: The Grand Canyon.

I put a lot of thought on how to get Evie to the Grand Canyon. It came down to me needing to sell my dirt bike. It sold pretty fast after I put it in a trader magazine. I didn't want to tell Dad because I didn't want him to be upset, and I didn't want him to try to talk me out of it. He found out before I sold it, and to my surprise, he supported me. I could always tell what he was thinking though. He never did have a good poker face. He felt bad for me because he knew how much I loved my dirt bike. I told him that I could always get another one later on, and that nothing was more important than Evie at this time. That seemed to set him at ease.

I started vacation planning with Evie's help this time. Dad and Mom decided to sit this one out. Evie inquired about how I got enough money to do this, and I hesitantly answered her. She was upset at first, but her concern was dispelled after I explained that I still had my motorcycle and car, and that I could replace the dirt bike easily in the future. I even added, "I know you're going to be all right, but I don't want any regrets." She smiled because she had heard me say "No regrets!" numerous times just before I'd do something impulsive and crazy or before doing something really nice for someone despite the fact that it may have made me vulnerable somehow, like giving a ride to a stranger who had a disabled vehicle.

Come to think about it, Ben said something similar when we first met! "I regret nothing!" he yelled as he told his animated story. My heart thumped hard as I made this connection. "He is definitely the one," I pledged.

During this vacation, Evie and I found a lot of time for relaxing and kept the travel to a minimum. We stayed at a resort that had two outdoor pools, room service, and a bar near one of the pools. I developed a daily routine of having a piña colada or two. I wondered how I would manage when I got back home, not being able to drink piña coladas at will and having to return to work. The thought made me laugh. Of course I would manage because I would just have to.

The bartender seemed to take an interest in me and was flirtatious. He was tall, black, and very handsome. (I learned that he was actually from Detroit! Not too far from where I lived.) It could be that he was just trying to get a good tip. Regardless, I was polite and friendly as always. I wondered if he thought I was flirting back. I felt like *I* couldn't even tell if I was or not. I didn't have much experience with flirting. I concluded that I wasn't flirting because I didn't have butterflies in my stomach like I did when I'd flirt with Ben.

Speaking of Ben, he consumed my thoughts at every opportunity: in the shower, before bed, when I was driving while Evie rested in the car... It was peaceful for me to picture his big goofy grin with his fiery eyes illuminating. I fought to keep my mind pure. It felt so good the last time our bodies were entwined together.

The Grand Canyon South Rim was as amazing as everyone says it is. The weather was hot, but tolerable with a gentle, warm breeze. I gave Evie my parasol, covered in beautiful Chinese markings, to use as protection from the sun. She looked so cute with it. She generously let me take as many pictures of her as I wanted. I don't know how much I'd want my picture taken under the same circumstances, so I tried to take pictures conservatively. I only took ones that were fantastic, for her sake. Nothing stupid like her eating a sandwich.

We smiled and laughed a lot. I felt closer to Evie than ever. I imagined us being best friends in the near future. I pictured all of the things we would do together when she got better.

I planned a picnic one day. We took in the breathtaking views while we munched. Evie sat cross-legged and I sat in a Z position on our blankets. Our conversation started with me talking about random spiritual stuff, which was not uncommon.

"God is such a magnificent artist. Look at all of the wonders around us." I smiled. Evie replied with a much smaller smile. Maybe she was tired or maybe she just thought I was being weird. It was probably a little of both. Evie had never been shy about telling me how weird she thought I was in the past. Oh well. Since I was already being weird, I continued with my next thought out loud. "God must have kaleidoscope eyes, seeing the beauty in everything, being able to look at the same thing and enjoying the different gems that seem hidden to us. Brandon Heath said it so poetically, 'Give me Your eyes for just one second. Give me Your eyes so I can see everything that I keep missing. Give me your love for humanity.'" I was being serious, but Evie startled me when she busted up laughing.

"What are you, some kind of philosopher or something?" She tried to stifle her giggles when I gave her a look of surprise.

After I got over the initial jolt, I gave her an ornery glance to egg her on. "I always wanted to be a poet," I said. She laughed again. "No really. I'll recite a poem for you." She rolled her eyes and gave me a muffled laugh as she bit into her sandwich.

"This is called 'My Magical Mystical Pony,' by Ericka Janelle Marshall." Evie laughed so hard that she snorted, knowing that I hated using my given first name, let alone my entire name. I cleared my throat and put my hand on my chest. I raised my other arm and moved it about dramatically as I recited my poem.

"My magical mystical pony
Meets me at the forest every day.
I'm always so happy to see her.
I bring for her apples and hay.
In return, she gives me rides on her back,
And we go soaring through the blue sky.
I miss that sweet magical pony.
It makes me sad when we say good bye.
But that's okay, the sun will still shine
And I can always see her again.
I love that sweet pony with all of my heart
And we'll always be best-est of friends."

I enacted each line of my poem as I spoke it, using my arms, body, and expressions to liven it up. I ended the poem with both hands over my heart as I looked toward the sky. Quite honestly, I was being ridiculous. No new news there. I looked back at Evie to see that she had stopped eating and had listened intently. I eagerly awaited her snarky reply.

"Ha! Hahaha! That was pretty good!" she said as she clapped for me. I let out a surprised laugh at her reaction. "Maybe you *should* become a poet. How many poems do you have?"

"Oh, between ten and fifteen," I replied.

"Do it," she said. "You should put a book of poems together."

"Maybe I will." Her encouraging words made me smile. We hadn't often taken interest in each other's personal hobbies before she became ill. We continued to finish our lunch quietly.

After a long period of silence, Evie said to me, "Thank you, Ricky, for everything." I planned a cordial reply, but when I opened my mouth, I became tearful and speechless. Evie seemed to notice and forgave me for not responding. We finished our meal in silence as I fought to work the lump out of my throat. In due time, I was able to relax and dispel the lump. Then I thanked God for the beautiful day and for the time I was spending with my sister, but especially for Him watching over her and healing her. The warm breeze blew our way again. This moment felt divine.

Chapter 17: Motorcycle Accident.

Even though I had a lot of fun with Evie at the Grand Canyon, I was glad to be back in Ben's arms. I found it challenging to manage my time between seeing Evie and Ben, work, and keeping true to my obligations as part-time pianist at church. My visits with Ben upon returning were brief, so there wasn't time for groping, just innocent kisses and hand-holding. I was glad for that. I felt like, even though I had talked to Ben about abstinence, it was going to be hard to follow through with.

One afternoon while I was driving home from work, I received a text from Ben, so I took a quick peek. It read, "Hey it's Scott. Ben was in a serious motorcycle accident. We are at Blanchard Valley Hospital." I pulled off to the side of the road, quickly bringing my car to a screeching halt in order to re-read the text. My heart began to race. I texted Scott back, "Is he okay!? How serious is it!?" I didn't wait for a reply. I already performed a wicked U-turn, peeling out as I headed toward the hospital in the next city over. I glanced down at my phone several times, waiting for Scott to reply as I sped down the back roads, but he didn't. I was going so fast that I ramped the front end of my car up and down over the uneven terrain. I felt sick to my stomach as I wondered if Ben was hurt or worse. I prayed hard for Ben's safety. I also said a quick prayer asking that I wouldn't have to pull over to vomit, and that I wouldn't get caught by the cops because that would slow me down.

After I pulled into the parking lot, panic struck me. I began to imagine the worst. I burst into tears after I shut off the car, but I quickly sobered up and headed into the Emergency Room. As I walked through the parking lot, I began deep breathing to control my anxiety. I figured the ER secretary wouldn't let someone in who was crazed. I walked up to the secretary and said with no pauses in my sentences and several cracks in my throat, "Hi I'm Ben Blake's fiancée. He's here because of a motorcycle accident. I need to see him. I need to be with him." I took a deep breath after that quick run of sentences. I hoped the fiancée thing would get me in the door faster.

"Calm down, miss, I'll see what I can do." She picked up the phone to make a call. Just then my vision went a little blurry, and the background noises became jumbled as my ears started to ring. "Miss." I tried to collect my senses as I turned my attention back to her. "He's in room four. Go through the double doors and hang a right."

"Thank you," I think I said loud enough for her to hear.

I double-timed it to his room with my heart pounding out of control. I could just start to see him as I rounded the corner and approached the door. Thank God! He looked okay. He was sitting upright on the gurney, and he wore a sling on his left arm. He caught my eye in the hallway as I advanced. He was definitely surprised to see me. My senses were still jacked-up from high blood pressure due to stress. I saw only him as I proceeded his way, for my peripheral view was still hazy. I rushed up to him and gently pressed my face on his cheek, kissing him twice.

"I love you. I love you so much," I said as my tear dripped onto his neck. I pulled back a little and said, "Are you okay?"

"Yeah, I'm okay," he said softly with his eyebrow intensely furrowed. Judging by the look on his face, I gathered that he didn't know Scott had texted me.

"So, you're Ben's fiancée, eh?" I jumped around to see Ben's dad walk in. He smiled cunningly. I then noticed Scott's presence as well. He was sitting in the corner of the room. Notably, I just told Ben that I loved him unknowingly in front of his family: one of which I hadn't even met yet, and the other who (I'm pretty sure) didn't like me.

I quickly pulled myself together. I walked toward Ben's dad, Martin, extending my hand. "Hi, I'm Rick. It's nice to meet you." Martin shook my hand firmly, keeping his smile the whole while. I suddenly felt weird at having made a formal introduction while Ben lay there on the gurney. It didn't seem right somehow. "Yeah, I told a little white lie so that I wouldn't get sent away." I turned toward Ben to get a glimpse of his reaction. I was glad to see that he was amused with my fabrication.

Martin said to me, "I'm glad to see my boy hasn't turned gay like I thought he had when I heard he was dating a 'Rick.'"

"Oh!" I laughed a little uncomfortably. "That never crossed my mind."

"That my son could be gay or that your name makes it look like he's dating a man!?" Martin said a little too boisterously.

"Dad," Ben moaned.

"Neither. I mean, both," I said. I walked past Scott to get back to Ben's side. "Hi, Scott," I said as I smiled politely. He nodded at me.

"I didn't realize Scott had your number," Ben said investigatively.

"He used your phone," I said to Ben. I got the feeling that Ben already suspected that, and that he was just confirming it. He clenched his jaw and gave Scott a menacing look. I've only seen that look twice. Both times it was directed at Scott.

I interrupted his glare by taking his hand and saying, "Don't be mad, Ben. He did the right thing. I want to be here with you now." I assumed that Scott intentionally made the situation more dramatic than need be by leaving out major details, such as the fact that Ben was okay, just to upset me. I wasn't going to call him out on this. My job was to be there for Ben, and Scott had facilitated this for me. My hands and soothing words did calm Ben.

We found out that the X-rays were negative for a fracture, thank God, but other tests confirmed a mild partial rotator cuff tear. The doctor recommended that Ben take a week off of work. He gave him a script for medication to manage the inflammation and pain and a script for Physical Therapy. He told Ben to follow-up with his doctor in a week.

I told Ben that I would come over every day after work to make sure he got some supper because it would be hard for him to cook with one hand. Ben reassured me that this wouldn't be necessary, but I insisted. I drove him home and got him all comfy-cozy for the night.

I tucked him in bed and made sure that he had everything he needed right there on his night stand. He had water, a snack, his pain meds, his cell phone, tissues, a flashlight…he stopped me there. "Rick, I have everything I need. Thank you."

"Yeah, okay," I said. I took a deep breath and tried to calm myself. I have a Type A personality all the way, and things like this throw it into high gear. I closed my eyes tight for a second and said, "I'm just glad you're okay." I opened my eyes and gave him a tired smile.

"I'm okay, thanks to you," he said. "Come here," he beckoned me to kiss him. I moved in to give him a naughty kiss.

"Can I stay the night tomorrow?" I asked softly and somewhat passionately, with my face still close to his.

He answered just as softly and passionately as I, "You don't have to do that."

I caressed his bottom lip in between mine and then whispered, "But I want to." Then my eyes got bright. "I'll make you coffee and breakfast in the morning. Ya know, mornings are kind of our thing." I smiled as I thought about the time Ben and I jammed in the kitchen at Hocking Hills, how we wrestled in the kitchen before his brother came in, and how he kissed and groped me on the couch after Scott left. I also reminisced on how we snuggled in the morning after that night I slept with him in his bed. His return smile let me know that he was thinking of the same type of things too.

"Okay," he said. We kissed again, but this time he grabbed the back of my hair, keeping my lips pressed tight on his for a deep, sexy kiss. We were both breathless after this kiss. We rested our foreheads together as we caught our breath. I won't lie, it felt awesome that he wanted me just as much as I wanted him.

"I'd better go," I said, not wanting to pull away.

"Yeah," he said, still holding my hair in his fist. "Rick. I love you so much too," he said to me as a reply to the affection that I bestowed on him when he was in the ER. I smiled and let out a quick exhale. He caught me off guard with that one.

"Yeah?" I asked as I looked deep into his beautiful eyes.

"Yeah," he affirmed. We finally separated from each other. I walked backward out of his bedroom so that I could see him every step of the way. I kissed my index and middle fingers and gave him a two-fingered up and down wave good-bye, instead of blowing him a kiss. It was a little weird, but that's status quo for me. He flashed me his beautiful, big smile, which made me lose my concentration. I bumped into the door frame as I turned around to exit.

"Ooh, I'm okay," I said as I turned out the light.

"You are *so* much more than okay," he said to me with a smile. My heart fluttered.

"Good night, Ben," I whispered.

The next evening, I showed up to Ben's house after work with a rather large duffle bag. Ben looked at it with a puzzled expression. "What's this?" he asked. He was truly perplexed.

"I'm staying the week, actually," I said with an I-dare-you-to-challenge-me expression.

"Is that so?" he contended.

"Yuh-hunh," I replied. I set my duffle bag down on his couch and walked into the kitchen to set down the brown paper bag I had. I pulled out some homemade chicken noodle soup and a salad that I picked up from the local café. We sat at the kitchen table, where I insisted on spoon-feeding Ben just to entertain myself. He tried to act a little annoyed by this, but he still let me do it just a few times to please me. I giggled at his reaction.

"You know I'm right-handed, right?" he said sarcastically. He knew very well that I knew that. He was making a point that there was no need for me to feed him with his left arm being the one in a sling.

"You are?" I said melodically with a look of surprise on my face. He shook his head at my silliness and let me give him one more spoon full. I giggled some more as some of the soup ran down the side of his mouth. He started to lift his hand to wipe it away, but I blocked his good arm and said mischievously, "I got it." I leaned forward and licked the soup off of the side of his mouth and went straight into kissing his lips.

After I slowly backed away from his lips, Ben said to me earnestly, "It's going to be a good week." He penetrated me with his eyes. I was taken with the sincerity of his words and the sexy way he looked at me. I exhaled quickly and became a little breathless. My eyes drifted away from him as I became completely engrossed in my thoughts. I pulled at my shirt collar because I was feeling a little hot. I let go of my shirt and unconsciously ran my hand from my collarbone, down my chest, and to my stomach seductively. My attention came slowly back to Ben, and I fully realized what I had just done, including the fact that he had intently watched me do this. My face turned positively flushed. I quickly looked away from him and timidly tucked my hair behind my ear. I definitely didn't have a poker face when it came to Ben saying sexy things, so he knew that he really got my motor running. There was a sexy, tense silence.

I got up from the kitchen chair and said, "Let me refresh your drink," with a quiver in my voice. And I let him eat the rest of his meal in peace while I sat beside him.

When it was time for bed, I was sort of backpedaling by making sure not to kiss him too passionately, and I was careful not to do any seductive moves. It was kind of hard (wink), but I managed.

"Are you going to sleep with me?" Ben asked.

I replied shyly, "Do you think I should?" I sure did want to, but I didn't want to hurt his shoulder.

"Absolutely," he replied.

I had to stay on Ben's right side to avoid hurting his left shoulder. He was on his back, so I lay on my side and gently wrapped my arm and leg around him, like I did the last time. I listened to his heart beat as we drifted off to sleep.

In the morning, I snuck out of bed early and made some coffee. I had to go to work, and I wasn't sure if I should wake Ben up before I left. Ben ended up being lured into the kitchen from the smell of coffee, so I didn't have to worry about it any longer. It was so good to see his smiling face.

"This is nice," he said. "Waking up to my girl and the smell of coffee."

He kissed me sweetly before I sat him down for breakfast. We talked about our plans for the day. Ben had physical therapy, and his dad was going to give him a ride. I told him that it was going to be a pizza and movie night after work.

Later that evening, just before I was about to head out to pick up the pizza, Mike showed up at the door. He came in and boomed, "What the heck, man!? I hear you freakin' trashed your bike!"

"Yeah," Ben moaned. Mike was pleased to see that his good friend was okay. He smiled and shook his hand.

"Did you trash your shoulder too?" Mike asked, smiling at his own mischievousness being that he asked about Ben's bike first and his shoulder second.

I entered the living room. "Mike, long time no see. I was just starting to miss you," I said sarcastically.

He smiled at my snarkiness. Then he looked at Ben sharply and asked, "Is this a thing now?" as he pointed back and forth between us.

Ben smiled widely and answered, "Yeah, this is definitely a thing." I smiled too.

"No shit!" Mike said with a look of surprise.

I cleared my throat and said, "I'd love it if you'd join us for pizza, Mike. I'll be back in fifteen minutes."

"Yeah sure," Mike said as he plopped down on the couch next to Ben.

When I returned, I entered through the garage door into the kitchen. I heard the guys talking about me, but for some reason, I decided not to use my superpower. Instead, I shut the door loud enough for them to hear, in order to make myself known. I immediately regretted that. Why have a superpower if you're not going to use it? I could have easily listened in on their conversation.

"Hey guys," I said as I entered. "I picked up some pop too." I got them table trays and brought them their food.

Mike remarked jokingly, "You don't have to serve me, woman."

I snapped back in jest, "I don't mind serving you at all, provided you don't call me woman." Mike looked at me with a big grin on his face. I really, really wished I had ease-dropped.

Mike started in on me. "So, uh, what's the age difference here again?" His face beamed with how much he wanted to annoy me. Ben rolled his eyes.

"I don't know. Something like twenty years," I said seriously. Mike busted out laughing. Ben couldn't help but to join in with Mike.

"So, uh, you think this is really gonna work out?" Mike asked me. I looked into Ben's beautiful eyes. He looked so sexy. I'm not sure if he was giving me a sexy look, or it he just plain looked sexy. I do know that Ben wasn't afraid of what I was going to say next.

I looked back at Mike and said, "I have no doubt." Ben and I smiled dreamily at each other.

Mike laughed. "Damn," he said to Ben. "Straight from the horse's mouth." We all laughed. "You know when you're 30, he'll be 43; and when you're 50, he'll be–"

I interrupted swiftly with, "I can math, Mike!"

Ben doubled over as he sat on the recliner chair. "Uhh, huh, ha ha," he laughed as he rubbed his hand across his face.

Mike was the serious one this time when he said, "Yeah, but ya don't talk good, do ya?"

"That's obvious," I grumbled. "I combined 'I can add' with 'I know math.'"

"Yeah, we know," Mike said as he flashed Ben an ornery smile as if to say, "You sure about this, man?" But then he turned back to me and gave me a sincere smile.

I felt all warm inside and decided to share this feeling with Mike. "It feels kind of good that you're okay with this."

"How could I not be? My best bud is so happy right now." I blushed a little. "So, are you two living together?" he asked.

"No," I replied abruptly. "I'm just staying for the week to help Ben out. I kind of insisted."

"You insisted, huh?" he asked. "I bet Ben didn't put up too much of a fight though, did he?" He smiled at me. I smiled back. Mike was so charming and funny when he wasn't rolling his eyes at me. I wished for him to be as happy as Ben and I were some day. I prayed for the best for him in love and life.

I caught up on all of Mike's business such as work, his workouts, and his ever-changing dating life. He was single at the moment, but he was never available long. I talked with Mike about how Evie was doing, including how she was on her third round of chemo. He listened intently and politely.

Mike stayed pretty late, but I didn't mind the break from the intimate moments that Ben and I were having frequently. Every affectionate moment we shared made me feel like we were closer to having sex. I knew that Ben wasn't going to ask me to, but I feared that I was going to change my mind. I struggled with guilt from being as intimate as we already were. Ultimately, I rationalized our physical relationship by asserting that what we were doing was keeping us from having sex. But I knew the truth: that it was getting us closer to having it.

The third night at Ben's house was Friday night. We listened to music in the living room that streamed from my phone. My jam "Me Without You" by Toby Mac came on. I got really excited about the music, and I popped up on the couch to tell Ben how much I loved this song and how much I loved to dance. He smiled at me and replied, "I know." I went on to explain that my dancing was mostly like a narration of the song; therefore, each song consisted of totally different moves. Ben was amused with my excitement, so I decided to show him my moves, which were pretty impressive if I do say so myself. I sang along as I did my interpretive dance, but I also added a lot of popular moves for Ben's entertainment, such as The Sprinkler and The Car with my own little bouncy spin to it. Ben laughed and clapped his hands softly so that he wouldn't hurt his shoulder.

"Oh, you liked that, did you? Then I have one more for you," I said as I jogged over to my phone to put on "Earthquake" by Family Force Five. If you knew this song, you'd understand that there's a lot of room for crunking, housing, as well as butt and shoulder shaking. I grooved very well and intended for it to be humorous, as evidenced by the bizarre facial expressions that accompanied the rug-cutting. It definitely was not meant to be seductive, although I could've pulled that off perfectly too. There's even a few cheerleader lines in it that I acted out with my imaginary pom-poms. At the end of this song, Ben was holding his stomach doing a hard, silent laugh. Finally, I had gotten him to that pinnacle. The same one he had gotten me to so many times before. I laughed and skipped over to him. "Someday, you're going to take me dancing at a club."

"I'd love to," he said, still smiling wildly.

I carefully straddled him, making sure not to bump his arm as I moved in to kiss him. Ben reached around me and lifted my hair to the front of my shoulder, and he twirled it around his fingers, just like he did during our first kiss. I kissed his lips and face and brushed my lips across his course stubble. He hadn't shaved since his accident. One more day of not shaving and he'd have a full beard. I loved the rough feeling on my lips and the taste of salt from his skin. Ben took his arm out of the sling while I kissed him and started caressing my back.

I quickly removed my lips from his and asked with concern, "Are you allowed to have your arm out of the sling?"

"Yeah," he said without missing a beat. "My P.T. said that I could occasionally, as long as I don't overdo it."

We kissed gently for a long time. This was one of my favorite memories. We had to keep it easy to avoid hurting Ben's shoulder.

Later that night, I was acting just a little too perky before bedtime, so Ben asked me, "What's up with you?"

"Tomorrow is Saturday. We get to spend the *whole day* together." My eyes gleamed as I smiled at him. He approached me, and he kissed my lower lip.

"Do you have something special planned?" he asked curiously.

"No, not at all. Just to spend the *whole day* with you." I was smiling just a little too big. Yes, spending the whole day with Ben was that exciting to me. He pulled me close, kissed me again, and hugged me tight. I could feel that his shoulder was getting better.

At night, Ben had been sleeping on his back while I slept on my side with my appendages wrapped around him. That night, he decided to sleep on his right side.

He said to me, "Do you think you can sleep on your right side?"

"Sure," I said, not knowing why that would matter. I rolled to my side and looked back at him to see what he was doing.

"Lie down," he said, and I did. He scooted up close to me, put his chest against my back and his left arm around my side. Even though he did this so gently, it caught me off guard because it was a new position for us. I let out a light gasp and was tense at first, but the warmth of his body soothed me into a relaxed state within seconds.

He kissed the side of my neck and whispered, "Is this okay?"

"Yeah," I said breathlessly. "This feels," I paused and closed my eyes tight for a second, "so good." After lying there a couple seconds longer, I said, "Wait." He carefully moved his arm as I reached for a small pillow. I got back into position and placed the pillow between his arm and my body for better support to make him more comfortable. "There," I said. He kissed my neck one more time, and we fell into slumber land.

When I awoke, Ben had an erection pressed up against my backside, but he was still sleeping. I turned onto my other side to face him. I marveled at this situation for a moment. I brushed my fingers down his chest as he slept, and I gradually became turned on. I felt a small fire start to burn in my body. I kissed his chest very gently. He stirred a bit but was still mostly asleep. This fire started to burn much hotter.

Before I knew it, I had one of my hands down his pants and the other on his butt. I pulled his butt toward me and pushed him away as I stroked him. It only took a couple strokes to awaken him. He inhaled quickly in shock. I loved that. Every couple of strokes, I would hear him softly say, "Uh." The more he did that, the more vigorously I massaged him. As I did so, I noticed that I was becoming wet. "How is this possible?" I wondered. "He's not touching me; I'm touching him." I kissed his chest fervently, confounded by what I was feeling. That fire in me progressed to full-body consumption. I sat up and pulled on Ben's cock and butt, lifting him onto his back. He let out a louder, "Uh!" I leaned forward and sucked on his nipple hard, paying him back for the time he'd done that to me. He took it better than I imagined. He grabbed the back of my hair and was vocal, but he didn't try to push me away.

Ben and I, in fact, hadn't said anything to each other yet that morning. I straddled him, grabbed his jaw, turned his head sideways, and started kissing his neck while I continued massaging his penis. Ben continued to be vocal as he moved his body up and down with my hand. He was so sexy when he did this. So sexy.

I stopped for a second to remove my pajama shirt and bottoms. Then I quickly resumed everything I was doing except I had my bare chest up against his as I did so. After several minutes, I stopped again to remove Ben's pajamas. This was the first time I'd seen him totally naked. Then the whole mood changed. I studied and felt his beautiful body by gently sliding my hands down his chest, abdomen, and genitals. I had never seen a man naked before. Never. Not even in a magazine or on TV.

I touched his genitals gently as I beheld his body in front of me. I slowed down with touching him until I came to a complete stop. I stared at his dick.

Ben sat up quickly on his right shoulder and said, "What's wrong?"

I stammered, "I've just, have never seen…" I stopped, realizing how stupid this was going to sound, but I had already started. Judging by the look on his face, there was no way I could get away with saying "never mind." I finished my sentence after a long pause by saying, "…one before." I caressed his scrotum and penis in my hands. He watched me as I did so. I grazed my fingers up and down his shaft, and then a worried look overcame me. Ben was still watching me and no doubt wanted to understand the look.

"What is it? What's wrong?" he asked again.

"It's so…big. I don't…I don't think…that it's going to fit," I said sincerely. I swallowed hard and felt a little peakish.

Ben was taken at my naïveté. He moved from leaning back on his elbow to sitting upright. He grabbed the back of my hair, kissed me passionately, and reassured me in his sexy voice, "It'll fit." He pulled me down to the bed, kissing me along the way. We kissed a while longer before I started fondling him again. Ben stopped me for a moment and said, "Here, try this." He grabbed some lotion and put it in my hand. I gently kissed his chest as I stroked his penis softly. I tried different angles with my hand until I found a position that seemed to flow smoothly. The lotion helped me transition from awkward to proficient quickly. Ben started moving his body rhythmically with my hand. "Uh," he said softly with his eyes closed. His reaction to me pleasuring him really turned me on. I responded by *firmly* pressing and rubbing my lips against his chest and squeezing him tighter in my hand. "Uh, uh," he moaned some more. The louder he got, the harder I jacked him. Listening to him and watching his body made me insane. I breathed heavily, pressed my lips harder against him, and clenched him even tighter. "Ah, ah," he moaned a little louder. That hot and bothered feeling that I had when I first started touching Ben that morning escalated into significant wetness and a throbbing sensation below. Finally, I popped up, straddled his thighs, and started a downward trust followed by an upward glide using both of my hands. "Ah. That's it, Rick. That's it," Ben said.

"Hah," I squeaked lightly as my juices intensified in response to him saying my name. My panties were soaked. I jacked him for quite a while. I didn't mind because watching him was intoxicating. When my triceps fatigued, I had to find another way to continue, so I locked my arms in place and moved my body up and down so that my legs were doing most of the work. His penis glided perfectly in between my firm grip. I was surprised at how quickly I mastered this. His moans became more pronounced.

"Oh yeah. Oh yeah," he said with his teeth partly clenched. After a while, his body tensed up and he said, "I'm gonna cum."

"Do it," I replied daringly. I held him tight as he came in my hands. The noises he made as he did so were breathtaking. I held his cum in my hands in wonderment. It was like nothing I'd ever experienced. The consistency, the smell; it was very distinct.

"Wow," he said with a smile. "I wasn't expecting *that* this morning."

"Neither was I. It just kind of happened," I said. I paused, looking at the cum in my hands. I finally said with full sincerity, "I really, really liked that."

"Lucky me," he said, chuckling. He gazed at me vibrantly and quickly sat up. Then he started to caress my breasts and kiss me aggressively. I couldn't fight him off, even if I wanted to—with his cum in my hands, I mean. He got out of bed and said, "Let's get your hands clean so I can take care of you now."

I smiled and said, "That won't be necessary. That was plenty pleasurable." I wanted him to touch me, but I needed to slow this locomotive down before it derailed. He gave me the weirdest look and laughed in disbelief and amazement at my comment. He gave me another kiss and escorted me to the bathroom to help me get cleaned up.

After our pleasurable rendezvous, I had a moment of clarity. "I got this." I was somehow certain that I could wait to have sex until we got married. I knew that Ben loved me enough to wait. If anything, me wanting to wait would get Ben to propose to me sooner. That's all I really wanted: to be with him forever.

Chapter 18: Deterioration.

By the end of January, Evie had been hospitalized due to breathing difficulty. She stayed at the local hospital where I worked, so it was easy for me to visit her daily. I had a substantial amount of experience with hospitals, which made me an annoying family member. I had seen plenty of medical professionals lie, or "cover their butts," when they were in a tight situation. Because of this, I was adamant that all those caring for Evie must wash their hands upon entering the room, even if they said they just washed them. I figured that fifty percent of those who said that they already did that were lying or had faulty perception. As a matter of fact, it's hospital policy to wash your hands or use hand sanitizer upon entering a patient's room, but that doesn't mean that it gets done. I wasn't about to let her get MRSA or some other nasty stuff. She couldn't afford another medical complication.

Ben came over to visit Evie one evening with flowers in hand. I got up and met him at the doorway. "Ben, those are so beautiful, and this was a great gesture, but we can't have flowers or plants in the room because of Evie's weakened immune system from the chemo."

"Oh. These are for my beautiful girl," he said with a gorgeous smile as he handed them to me. I giggled, knowing that they were really meant for Evie. Ben was just really good at rolling with the punches.

"Why, thank you, sweetheart," I said, smiling at his little white lie.

Ben peered into the room. "How is she doing?"

"She's sleeping," I replied. "Are you staying or just stopping by?"

"I'll stay a bit." I ushered Ben to the recliner chair that the hospital had for me. It was big enough for our slender bodies to fit side-by-side in the chair. We snuggled there. I fell fast asleep with my head on Ben's chest. It was the best sleep I'd gotten since Evie was admitted to the hospital. Ben said that I only slept for twenty-five minutes, but it felt like hours of rest.

After a week, Evie was transferred to the Cleveland Clinic to be near her oncologist. This was the most stressful period of time for me when Evie was sick because I couldn't be near her. I was only able to visit on the weekends, which didn't seem like much. Dad and Mom stayed in Cleveland with her while I cared for their pets. The oncologist painted a bleak picture and recommended that Evie go home with hospice care. So that's what we did. That, and we prayed lots of prayers.

When Evie came home, she continued to sleep a lot during the day. During the brief times that she was awake, she was only strong enough to whisper. We had praise and worship music playing most of the day to keep her spirits up. I'd often talk to her and quote her scriptures, even when she was sleeping. I'd also sing to her until I'd fall asleep with my head on her hospital bed. Mom and Dad held her hands while praying silently or aloud. The stress was taking a toll on my parents in that Mom looked like she had aged five years, and Dad looked like he hadn't slept in a month. Grandma June looked as good as ever. She'd walk around the house saying things like, "Thank you, Jesus, for your mercy, grace, and healing power." There was always one of the four of us near her bed in case she woke up.

The church members had a steady flow of food coming into Dad's house. I was so grateful for this because that meant we could spend more time at Evie's bedside. Several members would even come to visit Evie. Some were hopeful, but others offered us condolences as if she were already dead! I'd silence their unbelieving mouths with daggers from my eyes.

One day when Evie was more awake than usual, she struck up a random conversation with me. "Are you in love with Ben?" she whispered.

"Yes," I replied with a great big smile.

"Are you two going to get married?" she asked, after a few long blinks.

"Yes, but he doesn't know that yet." I smirked and giggled a little.

"You sound so sure," she whispered. "I believe you," she went on tiredly. "You were always…better than me…" She took a deep breath before being able to finish her sentence. "...at making good decisions."

"Don't say that, Evie," I said solemnly.

She brushed me off and continued with, "I was never...really happy...with Johnny. I mean, I thought I was...at first, but now I realize...it was...just infatuation. It wasn't love." Our conversation was taking a toll on her breathing. She inhaled deeply through her nose, allowing the oxygen running through the tubing to help her recover.

"Well, when you get better, I'll be your wingman and help you find Mr. Right," I said confidently.

"Do you really believe that I'll get better?"

"Yes. The Bible says, 'If two or three agree on anything, it shall be done; Ask and you shall receive, seek and you shall find, knock and the door shall be open unto you; By His stripes we are healed; We were made more than conquerors by the blood of the lamb; He is for us not against us;' and 'He will work all things out for our good and His glory.'" I couldn't tell you the location of any of these scriptures in the Bible, but I knew they were there and that they were true, just the same. She gave me a tired smile.

"You've been so great." She blinked such a long blink that I thought she had fallen back to sleep, but she surprised me with, "I want to tell you something."

"Anything," I said.

"If I do die...I want you to know...that I know...I'll go to heaven." I had been doing so well up until then. Tears exploded from my eyes into a short sob. I gasped for air twice. Then I wiped my tears away and sternly pulled myself together.

I nodded. "That's good. That's good, Evie." I didn't know what else to say.

"You know...some people don't get...the chance that I got: knowing when the end is near." She paused and breathed deeply several times and then continued with, "I've had time...to prepare my heart. If I had died suddenly...in a car accident...or something, I don't know...if I would've...gone to heaven." Her words barraged me like jagged razors, stabbing me in my heart, stomach, spine and neck. I was overcome with anguish.

"That's good. That's good, Evie." I didn't have anything else to offer in reply to such a profound statement. I swallowed the large lump in my throat and forced myself not to cry any more. Our conversation made her extremely tired, so she quickly drifted off to sleep. I gently brushed my hand across her head and across the few strands of hair she had left. As I watched her sleep, tears again gushed forth from my eyes. It was a silent cry this time because I didn't want to wake her. I tried to lightly sing songs of inspiration to encourage myself, but my body refused. Instead, I recited them in my head while my tears soaked my neck and shirt. Finally, I laid my head on her hospital bed while I held her hand, and my mind and body collapsed into inactivity.

Chapter 19: Pain-soaked.

At work I continued to focus hard and be efficient daily so that I could leave on time to see Evie sooner. I took the back roads from work to Dad's house, which allowed me to speed in order to get there faster. I was thankful that the cops hadn't caught on to my bad habit. I started a routine of jogging to and from my car to save time no matter where I was at.

I pulled into Mom's yard so that I didn't block the nurse's car in. I jogged up to the house, gave a short knock, and then let myself in, as per usual. When I walked into the house, I saw Dad and Mom sitting on the sides of the hospital bed, holding Evie's hands and crying. Each and everyone's painful expression was forever burned into my memory. Mom's cry turned into a sob when she saw me, but still no one spoke. I slowly stepped closer to where Evie's pale, sleeping body lay, but I carefully avoided looking directly at her.

"What's going on?" I asked softly in denial.

Dad stood up as I hesitantly stepped closer. "Ricky," Dad said, "Evie," he paused again, "she's dead." His voice cracked. "She's dead," he said again, and then he broke down into tears. Only moments later, he reformulated, "I mean, she's gone to be with the Lord." He collected himself for my sake, but it didn't hold. He then lost all composure and began to sob with his head in his hand. His whole body shook, and he staggered back into his chair.

My body and environment betrayed me. At first, the room repeatedly gyrated clockwise and would quickly returned to its normal position, just like you'd see with certain types of vertigo. I instantly became hot and began to perspire. After several long, agonizing seconds, the shock of it derived these new sensations: when I turned my head, it was as if the room was two seconds behind me; my surroundings slowly tried to catch up with my focus while the room still gyrated. It was a sickening feeling. Then my peripheral vision constricted as a white aura slowly took over my site. I gradually lost the feeling in my legs, and my arms became heavy and immovable. My face, neck, and tongue started to tingle. Then all became numb. I was starting to pass out. I was to the point where I could barely see when my face came within inches of the footboard on the hospital bed. I felt my body get jerked back, and then I floated over to the couch as my head hung lifelessly over to the side. The last thing I saw was Dad's exasperated, tear-stained face. Then all went black.

I'm not sure how long I was out for, but I woke up with a wet washcloth over my head. Dad and Mom were talking to men from the funeral home in the kitchen. Only some of my senses were restored to normal, so I carefully got off the couch and inched my way over to where Evie lay. I half expected that this was a bad dream and that I'd wake up soon. I sat down hard on the chair beside her because my legs didn't want to hold me. I held her cold hand in mine. Despite all the signs of lifelessness, I felt for a pulse in her wrist. I was unsuccessful, so I palpated for the one in her neck. Nothing. I collapsed my head onto her arm and sobbed. It was the most awful, heart-wrenching sob you'd ever heard. I gasped for air in between each painful cry, which sounded like a wounded animal, screaming for help. I felt a hand on my back, but I could not be consoled. I continued to sob until I made myself sick. A few of my dry heaves gave Mom enough time to get a bucket for me before I started vomiting. I crumpled down from the chair to the floor in my weakened state with Dad by my side, making sure that I didn't hit my head on anything. I continued to whimper as I caressed my bucket. I whimpered, wailed, gasped, choked, coughed, vomited, and repeated. Every nerve in my body was violated deeper than any knife could ever pierce. After allowing me to pitifully whimper on the floor and occasionally vomit for a while, Dad intervened by carrying me to my old bedroom and lying me down. Hours had gone by since I had entered the house, but it felt like days. I drifted in and out of a stupor while the men from the funeral home removed Evie's body from the living room.

The next couple of days were all a blur. I couldn't function at all. Ben had to call work for me to notify them that I'd be using bereavement because no one could understand anything I said through my sobs. It was brutal having to see so many people during such a difficult time. The best thing anyone could say to me was nothing. The worst thing anyone could say was anything religious. I just waved those people off, trying to silence them. Most people got the drift and stopped talking to me, but I had to get up and walk away from the others who wouldn't shut up about God's plan for Evie. The only time that I paused from crying was when I was mad at someone who wouldn't stop trying to console me spiritually. Hugs seemed to make me cry hard to the point of trembling, so I just wanted to be left alone. I guess this wasn't the time to be left alone, according to everyone and their brother. My face and my eyes were never dry during this time. I hadn't eaten since Evie passed. Mom pleaded with Ben to intervene, so he picked up some protein shakes for me. That was the most I agreed to consume.

At the showing, I didn't talk much at all. If I tried to talk, then I'd start sobbing uncontrollably, and no one could understand me anyway. My skin felt thick and boggy. I shook like a Chihuahua on and off during the day, and my fidgeting sky-rocketed parallel to someone mentally insane. The tears never stopped, but I wasn't always actively sobbing so long as I was quiet. There were a few times when everyone left me alone just for a bit. I was able to flip a switch momentarily at those times and slide into a painfully numb stasis.

The breakdown didn't start until my gang showed up. Ben must've warned them ahead of time not to try to console me verbally because no one said anything to me at all. Instead, they showered me with one very long, emotional group hug. The more I cried in their arms, the heavier I felt. They held me tight as I bawled. I was by far the biggest disaster at the funeral home. They helped this 103-pound derailed train over to some chairs and sat around me as I cried, whimpered, bawled, and dry-heaved. Ben held my head against his chest. Michelle, Aaron, and Mike sat around me, taking turns holding my hand, rubbing my arm, or just resting their hand on my leg. Their support was the most comforting.

Everyone tried to make the funeral as positive as possible. In the paper it said, "Please join us to Celebration the Life of Evelyn Jean Marshall-Moretti..." Cheerful songs such as "Mansion Over the Hilltop" and "I'll Fly Away" were played. Friends and family shared positive memories of her.

I scanned the funeral parlor thoroughly, looking for Johnny, who was nowhere to be found. He didn't even come to his wife's funeral! I gnashed my teeth and thought hatefully about him. "If I ever see that motherfucker again, I'll bust him up!" I promised myself.

The pastor read a nice remembrance speech that Mom had put together at Evie's Celebration of Life. It was accompanied by a picture show. Everyone seemed comforted by the pictures and memories of our family camping; and of baptism, cheerleading, and prom. Mom even compiled some of Evie's funny texts and sayings, but this didn't comfort me. I sat and watched as angry tears kept my face continually wet. Ben's caring arm around my shoulders didn't sooth me at all that day. Next up were the slides displaying our trip to Niagara Falls, followed by the ones of the Grand Canyon. I became vexed. Evie and I had gotten so close at that point. I had made future plans for our renewed sisterhood. Her smiles in those photos were so big and beautiful.

As I stormed on internally, I noticed a gradual increase in pain in my temple and neck from grinding my teeth. This pain got so strong that I barely noticed the whole in my stomach that I had endured since Evie's death. I got up and walked out during the funeral service, discretely using the wall to steady my path. It was necessary for me to use the wall because of my impaired vision from the high blood pressure that I suffered from as a result of my flooding emotions. I cared not for anyone else's thoughts or feelings at that time, save Dad and Mom's. I hoped that my walking out during the funeral didn't anger them. They didn't deserve to have a daughter die of cancer. And they didn't deserve to be subject to the wrath of a daughter who hated God for taking her sister away, when clearly He could've healed her.

After standing in the outer room for several minutes while deep breathing, I decided that I had composed myself marginally. I debated as to whether or not it was enough to go back in. Pastor Dan just finished the slides, and I continued to listen from where I was standing.

"Please bow your heads and join me in prayer for peace for the family and friends of Evelyn...." His prayer faded as the ringing in my ears drowned him out. My visual impairment returned, leaving me with severe tunnel vision. My heart raced out of control, and I breathed heavily through my clenched teeth. I stormed out of the funeral home, and I laughed crazily to myself. Then I said angrily, "I don't want peace! I want my sister back!!" I stomped over to my car with seriously impaired motor control. I had just enough self-awareness to recognize that I was in no condition to drive. I could only imagine that I looked like a crazed drug addict.

I stumbled into my car as furious tears burned down my face. My teeth were still clenched. I pounded on my steering wheel and screamed until I was exhausted. I finally laid my head down on the steering wheel and irrationally pleaded my case to God. "We did everything right," I mumbled through my sobs. "Two or more agreed. By His stripes…" I stopped. He knew the scriptures because He *is* the scriptures. It was useless to continue. What was I thinking? It's not like He was going to change His mind now.

By this time, my steering wheel was covered in tears and snot. My heart still raced and my chest began to hurt. Was I having a heart attack? I put my hand over my chest and laughed at the possibility. I sat there several minutes and finally acknowledged that this tormented state that I was in wasn't going to pass, so I decided to drive to the ER. It was only half way across town. I decided that I probably could make it. I carefully pulled out of the parking space and then saw Ben jogging toward me in the rear-view mirror. He had come to check on me, no doubt. I stopped the car, put it in park, and opened the door.

"Take me – to the – hospital," I said between gasping breaths. Ben quickly helped me out of the driver's seat and around to the passenger's side. He asked me no questions. My hand on my chest and difficulty breathing seemed to say enough.

The ER doctor diagnosed me with having an anxiety attack. She gave me a sedative and a prescription that only lasted a few days. After the sedative began working, it quickly became difficult to move or stay awake at all. The doctor explained to Ben that this was likely a combined effect from the medication and from coming down from the high anxiety. My heart was in over-drive, my blood pressure soared, and I was exhausted and needed sleep. The staff pushed me in a wheelchair to my car, and Ben helped me get in. The last thing I remember was Ben talking to either Mom or Dad on the phone. Then I fell asleep in the car.

Chapter 20: The Day After the Funeral.

The next day, I woke up in my bed around noon. I could hear stirring in the other room. I creeped to the doorway, using my hand to guide my way down the hall. I felt so weak. Ben quickly put down what he was doing and jogged up to me. He grabbed me and intended to help me along, but it turned into a long, emotional hug. His shirt muffled my crying and absorbed my tears. His arms practically held my body up. His face was so empathetic and caring. After a long embrace, he assisted me to the sofa.

"Are you hungry? Do you want some coffee?" he asked gently. Ben apparently took the day off of work to stay with me. I answered him with shaking my head no and then nodding yes. He gave me some coffee and a protein shake. "Drink this," he said. I did so because I didn't feel like arguing.

Ben inquired about where all of my furniture went. It was a good question since the only furniture I had left was the love seat, the kitchen table and chairs, and my mattress. My big TV was gone with a very small, spare TV sitting on a turned over laundry basket where the entertainment center used to be. (The TV screen was smaller than a laptop. I don't know why I still had it. It was a dinosaur from our camping years, but it still worked a little.) My mattress sat on the bedroom floor because I sold my bed frame, and my clothes wear neatly stacked along the wall where the dresser used to be.

"I sold most of it to go to the Grand Canyon," I replied weakly. I actually sold it after I returned from the Grand Canyon to be able to keep up on my bills. (Well, honestly, I was a money hoarder. I wasn't behind on my bills. I just got below that certain number in my savings account that would cause me anxiety. When I'd get that low, I'd do whatever I could to build it back up.)

Later, Dad and Mom came over to check on me. I told myself I'd be strong for them, but instead I completely fell apart. I cried and blubbered to Mom the hateful things I had said to God, which left her devastated. You could barely understand what I was saying, but Mom and Dad knew. Dad tried to comfort us both, but I was inconsolable. Ben watched helplessly from the sidelines.

Dad started sadly with, "Evie is in a better place, Ricky. God is all-knowing and His ways are not our ways." Blah, blah, blah! Was he trying to convince me or convince himself!? I wasn't sure.

"I don't want to hear it, Dad! He could've healed her, but He didn't!" I stormed out of the living room into my bedroom and slammed the door. I wasn't planning on coming out until they left. After a while, I started to doze off in between bouts of whimpering.

I could hear them softly talking in the other room. "Where is all of Ricky's furniture," I heard Dad ask Ben at one point.

When I awoke, I realized that my parents had left, so I emerged to fetch some wine. Ben rhetorically asked me if that was a good idea to drink while I was on the anti-anxiety medication. I simply said, "Nope," and continued on drinking.

After I drank my wine, I took another nap for a couple hours. When I awoke, I was dismayed to see that the pain was still there, just as stabbing as it was before my nap. I lay there on my side and cried. "I hate You," I told God in my mind. "I hate You for not healing her. What reason could You possibly have for not healing her?" I wondered how I was going to make it through the day, it hurt so much. I whimpered and wallowed in my hatred.

Ben must have heard me crying, although I thought I was quiet enough. He came in the bedroom and lay down next to me and snuggled. His hands and body were so warm. This comforted me enough to allow me to rest somewhat.

My mind wondered in and out of dreams. Evie and I were smiling and laughing together. She looked so healthy and beautiful. We were sitting on a blanket at the Grand Canyon. I watched the warm breeze blow Evie's hair in her face, and I could hear the birds chirping. The sun grew so bright that it blinded me. I squinted and held my hand above my eyes so that I could see her better. Evie flickered in and out of my sight.

Gradually, she became much harder to see, so I reached out for her. I was startled by the sound of a loud shatter. I looked at the ground and saw a broken mirror where Evie's face had been. It was destroyed and she was gone! I knelt over the broken pieces and frantically tried to put them back together as I cried. "No. No! No!!" The shattered pieces cut my hands, and my blood dripped over the mirror fragments as I persisted with the impossible puzzle. I twitched several times in my sleep until I flailed awake into an upright sitting position. Ben sat up quickly after me and put his arms around me.

I started to sob. "It's okay. I'm here. I got you," he whispered kindly to me. He coaxed me into lying back down with him. We lay on our sides and he rubbed my shoulder, trying to comfort me. After recovering from my startled condition, I returned to my state of continual tears and whimpering. I rocked back and forth on my side as I cried. The pit in my stomach rang so severe.

After a while, I turned to Ben and whispered to him through my sniffles, "Will you, um, k-kiss my neck and touch me a little?" Tears continued down my face. "I can't bear the pain anymore and it felt s-so good when you did that." His slightly perplexed facial expression made me think that he believed it to be a strange, possibly inappropriate request. He wiped the tears away from my face with his hand.

"Anything for you," he whispered to me. He leaned over and started kissing my neck very gently. I wiped the rest of my tears on my long shirt sleeve and tried to stop crying. I figured crying would make him feel terribly awkward. This was, in fact, the first time I had wiped my tears away since Evie passed. Prior to this, I had found it to be pointless because my tears were never ceasing. So why bother wiping them away? I fought to collect myself. It took me a while to calm down. In time, I was pleased to see that my idea was working. I felt less and less pain, and the tears had finally stopped altogether for the first time.

I ran my hands underneath Ben's clothes, feeling his back, chest, hips, and butt. He replied by kissing me more vigorously and fondling my breasts. Our touching escalated very slowly until I writhed in pleasure underneath him. It felt so good to feel something other than pain.

I grabbed a handful of Ben's hair and rolled him onto his back. Then I quickly unfastened his pants. He looked surprised, but he let me continue. I leaned forward and raked my thumb across his bottom lip while I forced my other hand down his pants. I kissed his mouth and playfully sucked and bit his lips while I rubbed his cock up and down. It was thrilling to touch him like this. I enjoyed touching him, dare I say, more than he liked being touched, it seemed. He moaned ever so slightly and rocked his body along with my hand movements. We did this for quite a while. Gradually, I felt the craziness building inside of me. I started doing some weird stuff, like pinching and twisting his lips while I vigorously rubbed him harder. The intense look on his face, his body movements, and the sounds of pleasure he uttered made me drunk with delight. I paused for a second, sat straight up, and straddled him.

"Take off your shirt," I ordered as I took off mine. He reached for my breast, but I intercepted his hand and said, "Oh, no you don't." I leaned forward and pressed my bare chest against his and went back to kissing his lips. Ben readily kissed me back. His arms and hands on my back felt heavenly. I was pain-free. I started to peel Ben's pants off; he helped me finish the task. Then I took mine off as well.

I slowed the pace down a little when I went back for his lips, and I seductively kissed my way down to his chest, abdomen, and pelvis. I handled his genitals with dove-like gentleness as I rubbed my open mouth along his pelvis. He breathed heavily as if he knew what I was about to do. At last, I pulled his underwear down and put his dick in my mouth. I heard a loud, "Uh." I started off gently, but the more noise he made, the more I sucked and fondled him aggressively. I didn't understand why I felt this crazy while I pleasured him. I loved it. I yanked his underwear off because it was hindering the quality of my blow job.

I've never seen or heard of this before, but I instinctively jacked him off while I sucked him. It seemed so natural. The more I did this, the more things got weird and forceful. I ran my lips and tongue up and down his shaft while I fondled his cock fanatically, like a whore. Once, I accidentally let his penis go very far down my throat. I didn't gag but it was close to that point. I was shocked at how loud he got. It was on now. I grabbed his penis and pulled it up and as far down my throat as I could repeatedly and forcefully. I was amazed at how well he moved with my mouth. Saliva dripped down my face all over his body.

"Aw yeah," he said. I looked up to see that he had one arm draped across his eyes and the other one had a fist full of bedding. He couldn't stop being sexy, even if he tried.

After a while he said, "I'm gonna cum. I'm gonna cum!" He obviously didn't think I heard him the first time.

I removed him from my mouth and continued to pump him. He came in my hands. I watched intently at the force of his ejaculation. It was such a surreal moment.

As he caught his breath, I said to him most seriously, "That was fun. We need to do *that* again."

"I'm not really sure how this happened," he said. "I was supposed to be kissing and touching you."

"Apparently, you kissing and touching me makes me wild," I said as a matter of fact. He then got up and retrieved some paper towels for my hands. Obviously, we weren't prepared because, once again, this wasn't planned.

When I finished wiping off my hands, I noticed Ben hovering over me with a fiendish, sexy smile on his face. He started to crawl over top of me, lying me down on the bed.

"What are you doing?" I asked nervously.

"I'm going to make *you* feel good now, and you don't get to tell me no this time," he said.

"I, I don't like that look you have." He liked my hesitancy. He smiled even more devilishly than before.

He grabbed a handful of my hair, turned my head to the side and started kissing my neck. He slowly inched his hand down my panties. I gasped and grabbed his forearm.

"Relax," he whispered, "and trust me." I relaxed a little, but I did not let go of his wrist. He sucked on my ear for a moment, causing me to exhale and unintentionally lightened my grip. He started moving his hand around my vagina, and I tightened my grip on him again. "Relax," he whispered even more softly in my ear. "Trust me." He transitioned to kissing me deeply on my mouth, and I eventually let go of his arm. He was so good with his tongue. I started to feel lightheaded. After I relaxed completely, I really started enjoying this. He continued to rub his fingers around my vagina, barely inserting them into me, until I was nice and wet. I could tell that he liked the noises that I made, which weren't nearly as soft as the ones he made earlier. He also reveled in the way my body moved rhythmically with his hand. I could tell by how he watched me so.

"Oh, Ben," I said breathlessly in my intoxicated state. "Ah, ah, ah," I said with a higher pitch each time. Just then, he grabbed my panties and pulled the back of them into my butt crack. I squealed. He laughed at me, and I replied by slapping him hard on his shoulder. He tried to pacify me with his kisses while he still giggled.

"Just let me relieve you of these," he said in between his laugh-kisses. "They're in the way." I nodded. He transitioned back into a serious, passionate mood. He scooted down on the bed as he seductively removed my panties, clawing my legs intentionally in the process. I winced partly because of the surprise of it. Then he moved slowly up my inner thigh with his lips. My anxiety began to build. I pulled away from him quickly and sat up.

"What are you doing? I don't want you to do that," I said quickly.

"Oh, but you're going to like it," he said confidently.

"No, I said no!"

"Okay, okay," he replied. He didn't miss a beat as he wrapped his hands around my waist and pulled me back down on the bed toward him. That was the second time he'd done that. He did that when we were on the couch after our fancy date. I was starting to like that move. He could tell. He could tell everything. I felt so vulnerable lying there completely naked. I had seen him completely naked when his shoulder was healing, and now he was seeing me completely naked for the first time. My heart began to race.

He grabbed the back of my neck, pulling my head toward his. He looked deep into my eyes and said, "I love you, Rick." He kissed me passionately again. I melted. I couldn't get enough of that kiss. We were back where we left off, but without my panties hindering his performance. He quickly got me back to that overwhelmed state I was in just before he hiked my panties up. Well played, Ben. It sure did get me out of them. He kissed and sucked my lips. My eyes rolled back and I began to moan lightly as I gushed feminine juices. His fingers were saturated by now. I definitely had a lip fetish.

I was done trying to keep my wits about me as our passion escalated. I clawed his back, pulled at his hair, and clenched my teeth on his shoulder as I moved my body up and down underneath him. "I want you. I want you so bad. I want you to fuck me, Ben." He paused for a moment because, naturally, he was shocked by what I had said. After a moment's hesitation, he touched me more aggressively down below. This felt so good. I was a full-blown animal, writhing up and down and making crazy noises. I tipped my head backwards and grabbed onto the sheets to give his body a break from my death grip. I slid one leg up and started moving more vigorously in sync with his hand. "I want you to fuck me!" I said again. Now, I knew that it wasn't possible that day, since he had just came. I just wanted him to know that I had changed my mind about waiting, and that I was serious about it.

He moved close to my face and agreed, "Yes. Yes, but not right now. I want your first time to be special."

He caressed my breast with his free hand and then began kissing and sucking on my nipple. I let out a deep, low groan. It felt different this time. It felt good, but I still fought the urge to push him away. Instead, I grabbed his hair and pulled him closer. I just needed some control I guess.

Shortly after this, he slid his wet fingers up to my clit. I yelped, grabbed his shoulders tightly, and squeezed him hard. This was more of an intense feeling compared to when we grinded. His precision was perfect and there was no clothing separating us this time. There was no more relaxing either, and he didn't bother to ask me to again. The animalistic behavior I described moments ago, seemed like nothing compared to what I morphed into. I can't explain this moment, except to say that I sounded like a wild animal groaning as he pleasured me. I had no idea I was capable of such noises. I tensed up my legs and my ass so tightly that my butt began to cramp a little.

I was no longer moving with him. Instead, I was fighting him when I could, in between my involuntary body tremors. I groaned deep and long, and then I would gasp for air and groan again. I started to drool a little about the time that I noticed the burning sensation in my feet. I could only tolerate this barrage of sensations for a couple of minutes total. I couldn't unclench my teeth in order to tell him to stop. Finally, I mustered up enough strength to roll him off of me.

I held him down on the bed as I breathed heavily. I had red blotches all over my chest and neck. I released him from my grasp in order to wipe the drool from my cheek as discreetly as I could. I flopped on my side and continued to catch my breath. He rolled onto his side, facing me for a few moments as I lay there feeling weak and breathless. He looked so devilishly handsome and proud of himself. He watched me lie there for a while, and we said nothing. Finally, he leaned forward to kiss my forehead, and then he quickly got up. He returned with some water for me that he set down on the floor next to the mattress. Then he got back into bed and wiped away a small measure of drool that I had missed on my chin.

"I don't know what all just happened," I said, referring to my behavior. I wasn't sure if I should be embarrassed about it or not. I was feeling insecure about lying there naked in front of Ben, so I positioned myself to cover my naked body with my arm across my chest and my top leg turned down on the bed.

He replied with, "What happened is–that was sexy as fuck." He crinkled his nose a little when he said fuck. I could relate to that facial expression because I crinkle my nose when I laugh or smile real hard. I took that as a very genuine statement. I convulsed with a silent laugh as I lay on the bed, still facing him. I was so exhausted from all of the noise I made, from all the water I'd lost, and from all the endorphins just released into my body. I was convinced that I had a clit orgasm. I didn't even know that an orgasm was possible without having sex.

Ben got a gleam in his eyes and said to me with a spirited look, "That was fun. We need to do *that* again." He was mocking me, but it still took my breath away. I reveled in the affirmation that no one else got to see that devious look he just gave me.

"Definitely," I replied with a hoarse voice. He kissed me deeply and passionately.

Chapter 21: Day 2 After the Funeral.

I slept so good that evening. I spooned and caressed Ben the whole night, so naturally I awoke when he got up for work. He left early that morning. That's when hell started for me all over again. I couldn't go back to sleep. I went through all of the emotions I had just gone through the day before: sadness, anger, resentment, sorrow, more anger. I cried myself to the point of dry heaving and I hadn't even gotten out of bed yet. "What time is it?" I thought. "Only 7:30! Shit. I'm not going to make it through today." I had a few anti-anxiety pills left, but then what?

I got out of bed and shuffled through the hallway to the bathroom. I splashed my face with cold water and let it drip down my neck and onto my clothes. Then I made the mistake of looking up in the mirror. I saw Evie looking back at me! I didn't realize before just how much I looked like Evie with my head tilted down like that. I had the same long, flowing, black hair and oh, how our faces looked so similar in this light. I was *enraged* by the resemblance. I breathed heavily in my anger as I looked at our face, gnashing my teeth together with my incisors showing like a panther. I inhumanly groaned and savagely thrusted my forearm into the mirror, shattering it to pieces. My anger was then replaced by dizziness. I closed my eyes and held onto the sink for support as I told my heart to be still. Finally, I looked at the remainder of the broken mirror to see only a few pieces of my face, but definitely *my* face. Pain surged throughout my arm while blood dripped into the sink. Ah, the physical pain, a welcomed feeling. Anything other than the loss I felt was welcomed. I stood there for a minute and fully understood why some people cut themselves. I confess that I used to wonder if they did it just for attention. My new experience gave me better insight. I closed my eyes and concentrated on the throbbing sensation in my arm. As I did so, I became a little more lightheaded. I decided to assess the situation. Lacerations on my left forearm–not too terrible I supposed. I cleaned it off, held my wound together until I could carefully wrap it, and then iced it. I took some ibuprofen and an anti-anxiety pill and then drifted off to sleep for a while.

I awoke to an intense throbbing pain in my arm. I looked at my bandages and saw a substantial amount of blood soaking through, so I decided to call my doctor. I phoned the office manager and told her about my anxiety situation that resulted in a trip to the ER. I mentioned that I only had a few anti-anxiety pills left. I went on to say that I didn't think I'd be able to return to work after my bereavement was over, and that I was requesting FMLA. Lastly, I told her about my lacerations. She instructed me to go straight to the ER. I pleaded with her to talk to Dr. Hall and see if he could get me in. "I just can't see anyone else!" I blared. My anxiety became exposed and quickly floored. She asked me to hold so that she could talk to the doctor. Thankfully, he got me in right away.

I wore a hat and dark shades to the office, which made me look presentable upon first glance. I took off my mask only after Dr. Hall came into the treatment room. He beheld the train wreck before him and couldn't conceal his concern. My troubling appearance would certainly help my case for FMLA. There's no way I could return to work anytime soon. That was for sure.

Dr. Hall and his office had all known Evie. They'd known us both since we were kids. Firstly, Dr. Hall gave me his condolences and I thanked him for the flowers. Then his attention went immediately to my forearm, which was wrapped and still bleeding.

"What happened here?"

"I don't want to tell you, but I guess I have to if you're going to help me?" That was sort of a question and a statement.

"Yes," he replied.

"I broke a mirror." That was all I offered. Instead of replying, he inspected the area.

"This is pretty serious, Ericka. Why didn't you to go straight to the ER like you were told?" he asked.

I interrupted with, "I can't go back there! Can't you suture it here!?"

I was losing control at the thought of going there again. I began rubbing my face repetitively with my good hand. My lip quivered as I tried not to cry. I rocked back and forth as I envisioned the ER staff judging me, even though they didn't know me. It was one thing for Dr. Hall to judge me, a man who has known me practically my whole life, but a strange ER doctor? No! They'd write something down in my chart in a criticizing manner and then it'd be stuck with me the rest of my life. I've seen how irreversible medical charts can be first-hand.

Dr. Hall tried to halt this second barreling train before it derailed. One train wreck was enough. Two may have sent me to a mental institution. He held out his hand in a comforting 'calm down' manner and said, "Yes, we'll do it here."

The nurse prepped the area and Dr. Hall went straight to work. We talked about my condition at the ER and my request for FMLA. He said that he could approve FMLA for my "anxiety disorder." He continued talking, but I zoned out as I watched him stitch my forearm. Not only was I not hearing him, but my vision was blurred too. This time the impaired vision was just from fatigue and a lack of focus. Despite my diverted mind state, I could still recognize the severe look of concern in his eyes when I looked up at him. He asked me a question. I didn't hear it. I blinked hard several times and everything came back into focus. I sat forward in the chair to help with my attention.

"I'm sorry, what did you just ask me?"

He paused a minute, studying my face, which was stained red from tears. I had black circles under my eyes, and my skin was pale. "How long do you think you will need off of work, Ericka?"

"I have saved up enough money to have three months off, and I'd like to do that."

He didn't even bat an eye at that, rather he continued stitching. His assistant took notes while he stitched. He was an older doctor, and he never did switch to computerized documentation personally. I could hear his assistant clicking on the computer as he talked. I was used to this, but I just hated the lack of privacy about it. I really didn't want his assistant to know all of my business, but I knew that it wouldn't leave the room–

what with HIPAA and all. Well, it wouldn't leave the office at least. He talked to me about hydration, proper eating, rest, and the medication he prescribed. He even tried to refer me to my choice of a psychologist or a church counselor. I wasn't able to hide my facial grimace and scoff at the thought of going to see a church counselor. Yeah, that wouldn't go over real well. I didn't want to upset him, so I snapped out of it and said something I thought he'd like to hear.

"I'll just let time work on this, and if I can't pull it together by the end of two months, then I'll see a psychologist." He was satisfied with that answer. "Good job, Rick," I thought. "You've always had a knack for saying the right thing. It's just that this time, you didn't mean it."

On the way home, I filled my prescription and bought an excessive amount of booze at the store. I was a little nervous that the cashier would call me out on it, so I bought party snacks as well to make it look like it wasn't all for me. It worked; she said nothing about my order. I also purchased some hair dye.

I got home by 11:30 a.m. Yes, all of this chaos happened in the morning. I wondered if Ben was going to come over to see me in the evening. I just knew I'd be better off as soon as I could be with him. I was even willing to drive over to his house. I squirmed restlessly at the thought of having to wait so long to see him.

Mom called and left me a message. I listened to it right away and texted her. "I'm not doing okay. I don't want to talk about it. Let's just text for now. I don't want company."

This broke her heart, and I could hear her sobs through her texts. She said that she was worried about me and that we could get through this together as a family. After that heart-wrenching text, I decided that I wasn't going to be honest with her any more. I couldn't take how torn up I made her feel, nor could I take how terrible she made me feel because I wasn't grieving normally. I sat on my bean bag in silence and drank my wine while I cried, sobbed, cursed, whimpered, and cried again. "What time is it?" I thought. "Only 12:20! Shit. I'm not going to make it through today."

I took another Xanax with a couple glasses of wine to wash it down. I got up in my drunken, medicated state and walked over to the table. I sat down and grabbed a pen and paper. "Write my book of poems, you said," I muttered as I wrote out a title out on paper.

Behind the Mask
Behind the Mask.
It's scary you know.
When you first discover,
That you're your worst foe.
You've just found out
What's at the pit of your soul.
To gain sanity back
That'll be your goal.
The ringing in my ears.
I'm bound by tight chains.
Agony of defeat.
Pleasure in pain.
Behind the Mask,
I ask how to correct.
Is this insanity temporary?
Or has it a chronic effect?

The words flowed so angrily and easily. I put my head down on the table for a long, silent cry. My shoulders shook as I did so. "You could've saved her," I whimpered. "You could've healed her. Didn't we know your word? Didn't we confess healing? Didn't we have faith!?" My soft cry turned into fury. "We did nothing wrong!" I yelled as I stood up, knocking everything off the table in one forceful swipe. "I've seen You heal *worse* off people! I've seen You heal *better*! You said that I could move a mountain with faith the size of a *fucking mustard seed*!!"

In a fit of rage, I flipped over the table. I grabbed a chair and slammed it onto the overturned table. To my surprise, it didn't break. It merely chipped the wood. The chair rebounded off of the table, and I went sailing back into the counter as the chair bounced from my hands. I hit my head on the counter, and the handle on the cabinet gouged me in my back as I flung to the floor. After the shock of the impact passed, pain soared all throughout my body: my head, my back, my forearm. I was stuck there on the floor with my neck bent up against the cabinet. It was difficult, but I managed to squirm my way out of that terrible position. I noticed blood leaking through my bandage. I faintly smiled and let out a weak, one syllable laugh. Pleasure in pain indeed. The more my body ached, the less sorrow and anger I felt. I looked up at the counter to see my unopened Pendleton beckoning to me. How convenient. I tiredly smiled again and reached up for the bottle. I gladly consumed a third of it before I passed out.

"Evie?" I said as Ben jostled me. "Evie?"

"Rick! It's Ben. It's Ben! Oh my God," he said as he continued to shake me. "Rick." I heard a quiver in his voice that time. Then I heard a quick outburst that vanished the instant it occurred. I think he cried for a second.

I started to fade away again, but he tapped my face with his hand several times to keep me awake. I barely opened my eyes wide enough to see him kneeling over me. I closed my eyes again, only to feel him zealously slapping my face again. I gasped and weakly tried to push him away. He grabbed my good wrist and lifted me up, putting my arm around his shoulder. "Ow, ow," I said. My head hung low, and I barely put weight on my feet as we staggered over to my bed. He sat down on the mattress with his back against the wall. Then he lay me down with my head resting on his lap.

"What the hell happened today!?" he asked in dismay. He stroked my hair so hard that he was hurting me.

I tried to stop him. "My head. I hit my head." He stopped stroking my hair and got up to get me an ice pack. He returned and gently put my head back in his lap, holding the ice pack in place for me.

"Rick, what happened?" It took me several moments to realize what he was talking about.

I was barely coherent, but I choked out these words with a weak pitiful whimper, "G-God could've healed her." I sniffled as tears streamed down my face, but then my countenance changed, and I finished my sentence strong with anger, "But He didn't. I *hate* Him." I continued with a whisper, "I hate Him." My blinks were long, my vision was blurred, and I was dizzy; but despite this, I got a semi-focused look at Ben's face for a second. Oh, how much pain he was in. A tear floated down his face and landed on mine, and our tears traversed down my face together. I lifted my hand toward his face to try to wipe his tears, and that's the last thing I remembered.

Chapter 22: I'm Outta Here.

I never felt more terrible in my life as I did the next morning. My head pounded, my back hurt where I hit the cupboard, my forearm throbbed in pain, and I felt sick to my stomach. I tiptoed to the bathroom, looking down with my hand placed across my brow, wincing with every step. I found a note above the sink where the mirror used to be. Ben had taken down the remainder of the mirror that didn't fall when I broke it. His note said, "I wish I could've stayed home with you today, but I couldn't miss work because the Regional Manager will be in. I bought you some Sprite, pretzels, and bananas. That should help you feel better. Drink plenty of water today. Try coffee and some aspirin. I can't imagine what you're going through but please try to chill today. I'm worried about you. I'll call you at lunch. I love you, angel."

He'd never called me angel before. I liked that. I looked down at my forearm to see that my bandages had been replaced. Ben was very smart. I'm sure he figured out what happened, even though I didn't answer his question correctly the previous night.

I made my way to the living room and put my ball cap on as tight as possible. This provided only a little relief, but it was immediate relief. I was grateful for that. I saw that Ben had aspirin, water, bananas, and pretzels on the turned over laundry basket that I was using as a coffee table next to my bean bag. I sat in silence for a while as I munched. Oh, how I wished Fifi were there to comfort me like she did at Dad's house the day Evie passed. After I ate, I wrapped myself up in a blanket, curled up in my bean bag and cried myself back to sleep.

When I awoke, I felt terribly bad, which was improved from totally miserable. I had a few more bites of bananas and pretzels. As I nibbled, I decided that I had to change my hair. I knew that I couldn't handle the repeated heartbreak of seeing my sister looking back at me every time I looked in the mirror, and I couldn't afford to have another mirror breaking incident. What if something like this were to happen in public?

I started with cutting thick, straight bangs. I imagined that I looked as good as Zooey Deschanel with my long, wavy black hair and blue eyes. Next, I put several purple and turquoise streaks in my hair. It took me longer than normal to do this because I was trying to be careful not to reopen my wound. I used the hand mirror and looked at the finished product. Job well done. I looked fantastic. More importantly, I didn't see Evie anymore when I looked in the mirror. I was pleased, but I decided to tweak my bangs by cutting them in a zig-zag pattern. Now I looked like a punk rocker. By this time, I was exhausted. I cried myself back to sleep and took a nap.

Ben kept his promise and called me on his lunch break. "Rick, how are you?"

"I'm… Thank you for the advice. I feel better."

"What the hell happened yesterday? Start with your arm and the mirror."

I hesitated and let out a big sigh. I was very short with Ben when I said, "I looked into the mirror and saw Evie looking back at me. It upset me and I broke the mirror. Dr. Hall stitched me up with dissolvable sutures and steri-strips." He was silent on the other end. After several long moments of silence, I added sincerely, "Thank you for changing my bandage."

"You're welcome. What about the table?" he went on. I was a little irritated. He knew exactly what had happened. It was *obvious*. Why did I have to explain it to him!?

"I flipped the table over when I was mad! I picked up the chair and hit the table with it! Then I fell back and hit my head on the counter! And then I drank until I passed out!"

"Calm down," he gently urged me, but I interrupted him.

"Did you just tell me to *calm down!?* " My heart started to race. After all I was going through, I did not want *anyone* to tell me how to feel or what to do!

"Please, please," he interrupted me. "I just meant... Don't you have any pills left?"

"Yes," I said as I broke down and sobbed.

"Rick, please take it. Take *one*. Don't do this to yourself. Don't do this to," he gasped for air and finished with, "us." He was very emotional at this moment.

"You don't understand," I continued through my sobs. "It feels better to be in pain, *physical pain*, than, I don't know," I stopped there. I really didn't want to upset Ben more than he already was. "Don't leave me, Ben. I couldn't take it." I started to hyperventilate.

"Rick, no. No. No, I'm not going to leave you! I love you!" he sniffed. "I love you so much," he said softly.

I tried to control my breathing. I was able to reduce my hyperventilation to an occasional gasp of air. "I," gasp, "love you too." Gasp. "I'll do better. I promise." Gasp, gasp.

After we hung up, I took the Xanax as promised, and I took another nap. I awoke to Dad and Mom pounding on my door.

"Ericka!" Mom yelled. She pounded some more.

"Ricky! It's Dad and Mom! Let us in!"

"No," I muttered to myself. "I can't *do this* right now."

I hoped that they'd go away if I didn't answer right away, but they persisted. I dragged myself out of bed, grabbed my ball cap, and shuffled to the door. I stuffed my hair in my hat because I didn't want an argument about how stupid Mom thought it looked. I grabbed a long-sleeved jacket to hide my bandage. As I dredged on, it just occurred to me that Ben probably called them. I glanced toward the kitchen to see that Ben cleaned it all up for me. I hadn't even noticed when I was in the living room earlier. I expelled a sigh of relief and forgave him for siccing my folks on me.

"Hi, Mom, Dad. I don't feel up to having company," I said, peering through the mostly closed door.

"Nonsense!" Mom said as she forced her way in, glaring at me angrily with tears in her eyes. "Ben called us! He's worried sick about you! *We're* worried about you! You are not going through this alone you know! You are not the only one hurting!"

It was her last sentence that packed the hardest punch. I burst out into tears. My body shook uncontrollably. My legs felt as weak as kitten. Dad, who was also tearful, gave Mom a sharp look. He approached me and hugged me.

"What we mean to say, Ricky, is that we're here for you, and we need you to be here for us," he said to me gently as he held me. Mom joined in the hug too. I tried to reply, but nothing coherent came out. Instead, I babbled and cried to the point of dry heaving. Mom grabbed the trash can and Dad guided me to the kitchen table where we all sat down. He straightened my ball cap that was bumped a little sideways during our group hug. I gasped and gasped for air.

"Breath in slowly through your nose," Dad said. I fought and fought to do as he said. I really didn't want to pass out.

I finally said in between my gasping sobs, "I can't be...here for you now...because all I'm doing...is causing you *more* pain. I don't mean to, I don't mean to." I gasped for air some more.

"Come on. I'll make you some coffee," Dad said. That seemed to be my family's go-to drink. We sat in silence around the table for some time. Mom was on one side of me with her hand on my leg, and Dad was on the other side with his hand on my back. This was exactly how Dad and Mom comforted Evie when she was first diagnosed with cancer. I politely tried to sip on the coffee, but I was too sick to stomach it. So I faked it.

"You know, Ricky," Dad said, breaking the silence, "Evie is in heaven where there is no more suffering or pain. She's at peace and happy." His voiced cracked at the end of his statement.

"I don't doubt that, Dad," I replied quickly. "Evie told me that too." I paused for a moment and then replied, "It didn't have to be this way. We did everything according to His word."

"His ways are not our ways," he said, referring to a scripture in Isaiah in the Bible. "His ways are higher than ours. He knows all outcomes of all situations. It's possible that maybe she would not have been saved if she would've lived longer." I am not normally an eye-roller, but I blatantly rolled my eyes and gnashed my teeth. I listened to him with my arms folded because I was his captive audience. I was incontestably irritated. He continued with, "I brought you something that I want you to watch." He handed me a DVD titled "Heaven." I took it from his extended hand and placed it on top of my neatly organized pile of paperwork that Ben put back on the table for me. I noticed that the poem I just wrote was on the top of the piled paperwork. That led me to believe that Ben had read it. I positioned the DVD to cover up as much of the poem as it could.

Exhausted from my emotional outburst and the medication that I just took, I nodded off several times while Dad and Mom were over. It felt like they were there forever. Finally, they decided to leave me to sleep. Dad helped me to the bedroom and covered me up nicely. I asked him to get my phone for me. He plugged it in and put it on the floor by my mattress. After they let themselves out, I mustered up enough alertness to set my alarm for three hours.

"I can't take another episode like this. I'm out of here," I thought. I drifted off to sleep, thinking of places that my motorcycle could take me far away from there.

Chapter 23: On the Road, Part 1.

When my alarm went off, I got up with a sense of urgency. I staggered to the kitchen toward the coffee pot as fast as my body would allow me. Then I stumbled to the shower. I was pleased with how much better I felt after I showered and got a cup of coffee in me. I looked at the time, noting how long I had before Ben got off work. I hustled around the house to pick out some clothes from the stacks along the bedroom wall. Next, I headed to the shed to grab my sleeping bag and tent. I meticulously packed enough layers for warmth, and I carefully distributed the weight evenly on my motorcycle. I planned on being gone a while, so I took my checkbook and my tablet to pay bills online. Also, I packed my 9mm semiautomatic and a knife for safety. Because of my general organizational skills, I was able to get up, get packed and out the door in just over an hour.

I stood outside, all geared up next to my running motorcycle. I paused for the first time since I'd gotten up and took a deep breath. I looked at my phone and sipped on my coffee. My thoughts began to dart: "What was I going to tell Ben exactly? He definitely won't understand. Will he leave me because of my rash decision? No, he loves me. He won't leave me, but he won't understand either." A tear trickled down my face. Actually, that was the first tear I shed since I'd gotten up from my nap. That realization sparked a glimmer of hope in me and calmed my nerves. I now knew that I needed this trip, not just to get away, but to heal too. Ben would be upset, but he would forgive me. I believed in him. I believed in us. I began to text him.

"I'm going on a long motorcycle trip. I can't take another day like today. The guilt I felt when Dad and Mom came over was unbearable. I need this trip to get away from the pain and to start to heal. I hope you can understand. I don't want you to be hurt or angry. I love you immensely and I'll miss you every day. I'm leaving now and going to California for my dream trip. I'll keep in touch daily."

I felt some immediate relief as I wrapped my leg around my bike. It was about five in the afternoon, and I was off to I-80 westbound with no plan on where to stop for the night. The cool air dulled my pain. When I made my first stop for gas several hours into the trip, I decided that I needed to contact Ben to see what the damage was. I read a series of texts from him, pleading for me to reconsider. This made me anxious. My heart began to race as I dialed his number. I had my opening line ready.

"Rick! Where are you!? What are you doing!? Are you okay!?" My ears started to ring a little. He kept talking, but I no longer heard what he was saying. I finally interrupted.

"Ben, I'm okay. Listen to my voice. I'm okay. I'm *not* crying." What I said must've struck a nerve with him because he stopped talking. There was a moment of silence because I didn't know what to say next. I surely wasn't expecting to stop him dead in his tracks.

"Can't you come home and let me help you through this? Move in with me. You won't have your parents so close to you then." It did sound logical.

"I can't move in with you. That's not a thing in my family." Never mind what God thought. I just didn't want to hurt my parents anymore. Evie moved in with Johnny before they got married and the whole house was in turmoil. "I'm already on my way," I continued. "I need to do this, and then I'll be right back into your arms, right where we left off." I smiled at the idea of it.

"Rick, I just think–" Ben started, but I quickly interrupted again.

"Ben, I promised Evie that I'd write a book of poems, and that's what I'm going to do on this trip." That was an impulsive lie. I hadn't really *promised* her this, and this didn't even cross my mind until it came out of my mouth. But it seemed like a good argument, knowing that he read my poem on the table.

I could tell that he was flabbergasted by his erratic breathing. He had no more leverage to get me to come home. "Oh, shoot," I thought. "Now I have to write a book of poems. Oh well, it's not like I don't have the time for it."

His next series of questions had to do with where I was going to sleep for the night. This was a bullet I knew I needed to dodge, so I lied and told him I was planning on staying at a motel in the next town. I had fully planned on using the tent. I wasn't one to lie, but I didn't want to fight about it.

As we said our good byes, he made me say I'd keep good on my promise to pick up where we left off when I got back. I giggled a little.

"That was *so* nice to hear," he said. I giggled again.

After the phone call, I put on my chaps because it was getting cold out. I rode on, only to end up staying in a motel because I couldn't find a place to pitch a tent. (Funny how my impulsive lies would come true after I said them, so that I really hadn't lied at all.) After that night, I started to plan ahead a little better, knowing that I was living off the money I made selling a lot of my personal items.

After I checked in for the night, I walked to a nearby store and bought a couple pens and a pad of paper. I might as well be prepared anyhow. I took a very long, hot bath and savored every minute of it, not knowing when I would get another one. I broke out the Pendleton and drank myself to sleep.

What an eventful couple of days. I rehashed the events as I drifted off to sleep: the funeral, my anxiety attack, a trip to the ER, a passionate evening with Ben, my rage, the broken mirror, my appointment with Dr. Hall, my meltdown in the kitchen, Ben comforting me, my new hair, how much alcohol I'd been drinking lately, Ben's concerned call from work, how I hated that I was dependent on Xanax, the devastating visit from my parents, my rush to get out the door, and how this was all God's fault. As I lay there ready to pass out from exhaustion and drunkenness, I could see these recent memories spiral above my head like a cyclone. I lay there in the eye of the storm and stretched my hand out, feeling the wind and debris against my fingers.

That night I dreamt that I walked down a long corridor that opened up into a coliseum-like room. I peered through the archways, looking out at the gray sky. I turned around slowly to view the room. There was nothing in it. I noticed that the entrance was gone from whence I came. My attention turned to a woman who was floating around the outside of the coliseum. She wore an all-white flowing dress. Her hair was also white, long and flowing. Her face was gray–more so than the sky–and her eyes burned red. I watched her float, no, be pushed by the wind. Wait, she could've been flying. I don't know. I was mesmerized. I started to get dizzy as I turned to watch her go 'round and 'round. How long would I have watched her? I'm not sure. The spell was broken when she held out her hand for me. I walked toward one of the archways and waited for her to come around. I didn't know if she needed help or if she wanted to help me. She may have even wanted to pull me out and have me fall to my death. I waited by one of the pillars getting ready as she neared. Then I grabbed her!

Chapter 24: On the Road, Part 2.

Not much to speak of my first full day on the road. The cool air kept me reasonably numb. Chicago traffic kept me on my toes with not much mental downtime for wallowing in despair. I navigated to a free campsite. It was a little out of the way, but I was trying to save money.

I hadn't been eating well since Evie's departure. The pit in my stomach finally nagged me enough to get something to silence it. Nutrition had become quite the obstacle since most of the time I had no appetite, and everything tasted off when I did eat. I lost some weight in just a few days. Any amount of weight loss was alarming in my already thin condition.

I stopped at a grocery store, thinking that there's gotta be *something* in there that I could eat. Once I got my walking legs back under me, I sped up and down each aisle scanning right and left, hoping something would stop me in my tracks. Something that I could stomach and that would tackle that nagging pain. It felt good to be on my feet, yet I was so fatigued from being battered by the wind.

There it was. I stopped right at chocolate Boost. High calories and nutrients is what I badly needed. Also, it was a flavor I could tolerate. I grabbed a box of Clif Bars, too, just in case I'd be able to eat something more substantial later.

Normally, I'd just go grab some Pendleton Rye and be on my way, but this time I stood with the rye in my hand searching for other options. Medication plus exhaustion seemed to be the only way I could fall asleep, and it wasn't foolproof to say the least. So alcohol seemed like a necessary addition.

As I studied the shelf, a man of about thirty walked up and grabbed B&B Liqueur off of the shelf. He looked at the Rye in my hand and noticed me searching the shelf. "You like whiskey, huh?"

"Yeah," I replied.

"I bet you'd really like this stuff." He showed me what he had in his hand.

"Oh really?" I said, inspecting his bottle.

"It has a hint of a sweet taste to it. You can't have a lot of it though 'cuz it'll really knock your socks off. Five sips and I'm out like a light," he said as he motioned his hand in a horizontal manner.

"Really?" I said wide-eyed as I looked up at him. He smiled. I grabbed a bottle off of the shelf for myself and said, "Are you my guardian angel?" He laughed a little uncomfortably. "Because I have a terrible time sleeping and I'm at my wit's end." He laughed genuinely the second time since he knew where I was coming from. I put the Pendleton back on the shelf and grabbed a second bottle of B&B.

"I, uh, don't know if *that's* a good idea," he said to me with a smile.

"You *are* my guardian angel," I confirmed in jest. "Don't worry. I'll be all right." I winked at him and smiled as I walked away. He smiled back. His girlfriend, who caught up to her man after he and I exchanged smiles, looked me up and down with jealousy as I passed her by. I felt bad for him. I'm sure he had some explaining to do.

So the extent of my daily intake for the next several days due to my lack of appetite was chocolate Boost, several pieces of a Clif Bar throughout the day, water, and eight sips of B&B.

This was the day I had to call my parents to tell them what I had done–what I was doing. I called them from the campsite. I kept a positive tone for their benefit as I talked with them. I explained to them how the cool air dulled my pain a little. They were both very upset just like Ben was. Dad, being a motorcyclist himself, made it a little easier on me than Mom did after I worked hard to convince him, but he expected me to check in with him every evening. "Great," I thought. "Now I have to check in with Ben *and* Dad."

I sighed long and hard after that phone call and rubbed my hand over my throbbing head. That was stressful. I stopped riding a little early to be able to stay at the free campsite, so I had some daylight on my hands. I decided to go for a brisk walk. As I walked, my headache started to minimize, so I decided to jog some. Again, I felt a little better. When I got back to camp, I stretched and strengthened some too. I was good and tired by then. I decided to relax in my sleeping bag and write in my notebook, but instead I lay there and looked at the blank, college ruled pages.

Instead of writing, I daydreamed. At first, Ben and I danced across the notebook pages in stick figure forms. We laughed as he spun me around and dipped me. Then I was able to picture us as 2D cartoon characters, still dancing around and laughing. We danced right off of the page and disappeared. "Wait, don't go," I pleaded. Seconds later, Evie started dancing onto the page from the other side. Her dance was more slow and graceful. Musical notes floated above her on the paper as she spun. Her dress followed her twirls just seconds behind her. I smiled and wondered what song she was listening to. She jumped through the air twice in a row. I laughed a little. That was one of her old cheerleading moves I think. She danced over to the right side of the page and then paused to look at me with wide eyes and a large grin. She walked off of my page and into the sun that shined so brightly; her shadow lagged behind her. I cried when she left, and I ruined the first page of the notebook with my tears.

I tore off the page and crumpled it up as I tried to collect myself. I still sat there with a blank mind, and so I concluded, "Why not write about what I just experienced?" So that's what I did. That's how I broke my writer's block. I wrote about the dancing figures, the mirror and coliseum dream, and I re-recorded the "Behind the Mask" poem. That was four entries in my notebook, and that was success. I drank myself to sleep after that.

Chapter 25: Nebraska and Wyoming.

Nebraska, you harsh bitch, so flat and boring. You nearly killed me. It was unseasonably warm, so there was no comfort in the dulling sensation that the cool air had been providing. The wind was a warm and tiring. My mind was in control of me, not the other way around. I cried most of the day, so I had to keep my full-face visor cracked in order to keep my sunglasses from fogging up as much. It was quite the travel hazard, but I was too tired to let it concern me.

Nebraska
Never
Ending
Bitch
Ready to
Afflict
Suffering.
Kindly
Asphyxiate.

Ha! I was amused with how quickly that came to me. That wasn't one for my notebook though.

I drove pretty late that night, and I pitched a tent behind a rest stop. Not the safest thing I've done, but I slept with my 9mm under my pillow along with a knife strapped around my thigh. Honestly, I was more concerned about getting in trouble with the law for illegal camping than I was for my safety, so I set my alarm and left early in the morning.

I didn't think it'd be hard to sleep in a tent because the fatigue I experienced from the combination of grieving, driving, medication, and alcohol was supposed to knock me out; but I discovered as early on as my second night that it was, in fact, very difficult. Ewan and Charley made it look a lot easier than this. I supposed that the differences in our frame of mind may have accounted for some of the dissimilarities, among other things.

When I got to Wyoming early the next morning, I was completely exhausted. I looked for a local diner, for I was in dire need of coffee. I got quite a few looks from the locals. Maybe they don't see too many female motorcyclists. Oh yeah, my purple and blue-streaked hair and jagged-cut bangs may have had something to do with it. I nodded kindly to the locals as I walked by to seat myself. Apparently, I was famished. When I was served, I scarfed my ham, egg, and toast breakfast like I hadn't eaten in a week. I wasn't real hungry until the flavor of the food hit my tongue. I had three cups of coffee; most unusual for me.

While filling my third cup of coffee, the waitress kindly asked, "You okay, honey?"

"Oh, yeah," I piped up with an assertive voice. "I'm on a road trip and I just haven't had much of an appetite, except for today it seems." I smiled at her, and she smiled back as she finished filling my cup. She seemed genuinely concerned. What a nice gal. She was young, plump, spackled with heavy makeup, and had large teeth to match her wide smile.

I was enjoying my breakfast and trying to mind my own business, but it was impossible not to eavesdrop on this one lady because she talked so damn loud. She was at the register paying her bill.

"Well, I lost another hand the other day!" she said loudly to the cashier. She had a bit of an accent, but I couldn't place it. The loud lady had thin, long, gray hair that hung down straight underneath her hat. Her skin was dark from the sun.

"Oh no, honey. Not again," the cashier said as she shook her head sympathetically.

"They don't give no notice either! They just go!" The loud lady swiftly threw her hand up in the air as a gesture of frustration. The cashier was still giving her full attention and shaking her head.

"Well, you know the drill: free board, same pay, if you know anyone interested send 'em my way."

I was on my way up to pay when I spontaneously turned the woman to say, "If you need immediate help, I could work for you a couple days or a week until you find a replacement." She stared at me blankly. I went on, "I know you couldn't tell by my looks, but I grew up caring for horses. I don't know anything about cattle, but I learn fast." She still looked at me blankly. I thought maybe I should say something else, so I took in a small breath just before I was about to speak. But I exhaled only air, no words. I was done. Take me or leave me. I don't care. There was a treacherous silence as I paid my bill. She looked at my leather jacket and then turned her attention outside to my motorcycle that was carefully packed high.

"You on a road trip!?" she asked boisterously.

"Yeah, I'm on my way to California, but I don't have a deadline."

"Oh, oh," she said in a normal decibel as she looked me up and down, weighing her options. "You good with horses, you say!?"

"Yeah, I ride well. I clean hooves well. I clean stalls well." What else could there be? "I've never been thrown off one yet." I chuckled a little. I paused a moment, not sure what all she'd want from of me. "I don't break horses though."

"No, no. You wouldn't need to do that. Mainly feeding, cleaning, roundin' up cattle. That sort of thing," she said, mumbling.

"I think I could do that, just until you find someone permanent."

"Well!" She was back to her usual roar when she said, "Ain't ya gonna ask how much!?"

"I'm sure it's a fair wage," I replied.

"It's eleven dollars an hour, six hours a day, seven days a week. Three hours in the mornin' and three in the evenin'. Don't matter what cha do the rest of the day. Boarding ain't much but it's uh free room attached to the barn," she swiftly explained.

"That sounds just fine. The best part for you is, I'll be on my way and out of your hair as soon as you get a replacement."

She paused for a second. "Well! You ready now!?"

"Yeah!" I said loudly with a smile. Apparently, her clamor was contagious.

"Well, let's go!" She gave an exaggerated gesture for me to follow her.

I followed her to the barn, which was several miles down a stone road. I was thankful for my Adventure bike. It was tricky, but it could've been much worse with a cruiser. I got out my notebook and followed her around as she walked me through the morning chores. Oh, my Lord, she had chickens, geese, cats, twenty-plus horses, fifty-plus cattle, and a couple of bison. Thank God there were no pigs. Out of all the chores, I thought that rounding up the cattle on a four-wheeler might be the hardest part. I guess rounding up cattle via horses was kind of an old-fashioned thing. I was grateful that I wouldn't be operating any heavy machinery, such as the hay-mover thingy.

The room was just great; it was really old though. It had a small twin bed and a love seat in the living room. The kitchenette had a small fridge, a sink, and a microwave. The bathroom was divided by a curtain and was limited to a toilet and a pedestal tub.

"You can fluctuate your hours some if you need to, but generally I would try to stick to eight to eleven and four to seven!" she said just before she walked away.

Mad was her name, short for Madeline. I loved that nickname, of course, and she liked Rick just as much. My reply was "that's awesome" when she told me her name. It was a great icebreaker. She didn't seem to think much of me at first. I'm sure part of it was my 100-pound frame. The other part of it was my hair. However, she warmed up to me when she noticed my excellent organizational skills, especially with the horses that she boarded. I wrote down their names, their stall number, their markings, their diet, and any behaviors that they exhibited.

She left me to my own devices until four, so I quickly unpacked and called Dad straight away. He was excited to hear how excited I was. He was also relieved that I had a nice place to stay. He hoped that I'd be content enough to come right home after I was done in Wyoming. Needless to say, he was disappointed to hear that I was sticking to the plan of driving to California. I told him that I loved him very much, and I asked him to give my love to Mom. It was a choke-in-the-throat moment, but somehow, we both made it through without getting too emotional.

I was quite tired from not sleeping well, so I took a little catnap. When I awoke, the thought of staying sober until four and not having anything to occupy my mind made me mental. I did some push-ups, sit-ups, dips, and a few static core exercises, but that didn't take up a lot of time. I got online to look up some local places that I could visit the next few days during the five hours in between my shifts.

I still had some time on my hands, so I decided to go out a little early and brush the horses that didn't get to go out to pasture for various reasons, such as being too old, too young, or injured. I trucked out there with the brushes, hoping that Mad wouldn't mind. I didn't want to get in trouble my first day.

She didn't mind at all. Orientation went well. The bison stayed in their elaborate run, so I didn't have to round them up with the four-wheeler. Hallelujah. I'm not sure how that would've played out. The chickens were just nasty smelling, but I guess that's chickens for ya. I didn't know geese could be such bastards. They followed me around a lot and hissed at me. When they'd get too close, I'd turn around and kick at them. They'd back off and then retaliate almost immediately, giving life to the power struggle. All in all, the geese had it the best. They had the run of the farm and came in on their own when it was supper time.

I watched a video on the internet to see how to round up cattle using a four-wheeler before my second shift came, but those people were just idiots. I decided I would be fine as long as I didn't do what they did. There were two people "herding," and they had cattle darting everywhere. Actually, rounding up the cattle was much easier than I expected. They knew when it was time to eat, so they willingly trotted into their pens.

Believe it or not, the horses were the complicated ones. Bringing them in for supper was a super chaotic. Mad added to the confusion, in my opinion, by letting them all run in at once. They didn't go to the proper stalls once they were in, so it was challenging to figure out which horses were in the right pen. Mad did a lot of yelling and butt smacking during this process. I quickly learned which ones were the good horses that went right to their pen and which ones were trouble-makers. Next time, I decided that I'd take the good ones in first, and then deal with the trouble-makers after. I noticed that it was stressful for the well-behaved horses to get run around by the brats. I could see it in their eyes.

When chores were done, I practically ran to my room to start on my B&B. I savored a shot while I poured a hot bath. I took a Xanax to help me sleep. I was hoping for no dreams. In all the turmoil of this eventful day, I almost forgot to call Ben.

It was great to hear his voice. He felt the same about me. He was flabbergasted that I had changed my plans because this meant that I'd be gone longer. "It's only for a couple of days," I told him. "And I could use the rest and the money." He didn't argue any longer. I went on to say, "I'm not much of a selfie-girl, but I have something for you." I sent Ben a picture of me lying on my back on the bed in just a tank top, doing a come-hither pose.

"Oh my God! Your hair! I love it!" he said. He was silent on the other end of the phone for a few moments. "Uhh," he growled. "You shouldn't have sent me this." I knew what he was saying. He thought that I looked sexy in that picture.

I laughed. "I had to, so that you don't forget about me while I'm gone."

"No chance of that," he said.

During this phone call, it occurred to me that I had some upcoming massage appointments that needed canceled. I asked Ben to do me the biggest favor by calling all twelve of my clients and canceling them…indefinitely. I had no idea when or if I was going be able to return to those close relationships. How could I tolerate their caring faces or heartfelt words regarding my loss? Ben agreed so promptly to my request that I became overwhelmed by his devotion to me. This emotional trigger caused me to remember all those times that he carried me around while I was in my drunken, destructive element. That thought produced a flood of more emotions. I was a snowball rolling downhill. I couldn't stop thanking him.

"You know how you can thank me?" he interrupted. "By being safe and coming home as soon as you can." It was a fair statement. He didn't ask me to come home immediately, and yes, I promised I'd be safe.

After our phone call, I thought about Evie. Specifically, about how close we were getting before she passed. My heart grew larger as we grew closer together just in time for God to blast a hole in it. I drank and cried myself to sleep.

Chapter 26: The Ranch.

Working on the ranch was the most peaceful time for me during the grieving process. I kept busy feeding and tending to the animals. Most days, I made a full day out of it. I'd brush the horses, clean their hooves, and keep the barn in impeccable shape. These were all things that were not required of me. Mad would even let me ride ole Marge during my break time. Other days, I'd plan quick road trips–just local stuff.

Vedawoo was a delight. I went there a couple times and hiked around, enjoying the unique boulders of Medicine Bow National Forest, but Curt Gowdy stole my heart. It was only a forty-five-minute drive from Mad's place, so I could spend a good couple of hours there before I had to return. The hike to the waterfall was my favorite, naturally. It was a popular place–not too busy– but I was never alone at the waterfall. It was just as well. It was easier to observe others than to be captive by my own thoughts when I was alone.

The water there was ice cold–much more contrary than that of Hocking Hills. I made a goal to submerge myself in the water before I left Wyoming. It would be a mental toughness challenge. I bought a cheap bikini for the job. Normally, I wouldn't be caught dead in something so revealing, but I was on a budget. Four dollars for the top and four for the bottom.

The water felt even more frigid the day I planned to master my challenge. I jumped into the water and thrashed closer to the waterfall. It was painfully cold. It was now or never. I turned around and did a Nestea plunge. I came up wide-eyed and sort of regretful.

"Wow, you're an adventurous little lass."

I looked over to see a young woman standing with her dog on the stone's edge. Her words didn't seem to match her age. She couldn't have been more than twenty-five. I hustled toward my towel. My feet were burning from the cold.

"It seemed like a good idea at the time," I said with a forced laugh.

"Did it? Did it *really*?" She was snarky. I liked her immediately.

"No." I laughed even louder. "But I did it anyway."

"Well, one can't argue the wild ways of young women," she said with the slightest smile. I was still smiling at the way she chose her words. I wrapped myself up in my towel to try to head off the shiver I had acquired.

"Yeah? What are your wild ways, pray tell?" I said to her.

She turned her head sideways, still looking at me, and raised her eyebrows playfully as if to say, "Do you really want to open up this van of worms?"

Finally, she said, "Well, I rock climb, travel quite a bit, and dabble a bit with scuba diving." That sounded nice. I was glad I asked. "What about you, pray tell?"

"I ride motorcycles, and I'm on a road trip from Ohio to California. During my quest, I put the wanderlust button on pause to become a farmhand in Cheyenne for a while."

"Frankly, that sounds a bit made-up, if you don't mind me saying."

I laughed really, really hard. "But it's not!"

"What qualifications do you have for being this farmhand?"

"I can ride horses, clean hooves and stalls, and drive a four-wheeler–which is how you round up cattle in this day and age, I guess. But what really qualified me to take care of bison, chickens, geese, cattle, and horses was the lack of the previous farmhand giving his notice and the immediateness of my availability." I thought I was clever, but she just casually smiled.

"I'm pretty sure you mean you're a *ranchhand*," she said slowly and deliberately as if I were a child.

"Quite possibly," I replied. I bent over to pet her pit bull.

"This is Bowser, and he's a big, fat baby."

"Hi, Bowser," I said in that annoying voice that all women have when talking to animals. "You're so cute, Bow Wow. So cute, so cute, so cute."

"Yes, and he knows it," she said in a flat tone.

Elane was her name. She was quite a delight. She lived in Cheyenne at the time, and so we decided to meet up a few times before I was on my way. We met in town for lunch a couple times, and I even talked her into meeting me for lunch at the ranch once, just for the experience. She was charmed by my living quarters. We became good company for each other. I wished I had someone like her back in Ohio. Michelle was great, but it was different with her being a mom. Also, she was essentially a friend of a friend. Or better said: we would never hang out just the two of us. Making and keeping friends wasn't my strong suit, but Elane and I planned on keeping in touch after I moved on.

Mad had given me two days' notice; she'd found a replacement. I rode ole Marge for the last time. We traveled out quite a ways, so I kept the oil field in reference to keep from getting lost. I saw a lone coyote while we were out. I couldn't believe how small it was: just bigger than a fox. I had my 9mm holstered to me, but I knew that I wouldn't need it. Later, I asked Mad if that was a full-size coyote, and she said yes! I laughed.

"They are much smaller out here than the ones in Ohio. Now those coyotes would strike some fear into you!" I told Mad. They get as big as German Shepherds in Ohio.

"Bet they don't have no mou-in lions in Ohiuh neither!" Well, she was right about that!

The next two days, I realized how accustomed that I had become to the cozy room attached to the barn at Mad's ranch. I feared that I had softened up too much for camping, so I bought a camping mat with some of the money I made working for Mad. I had never done this rustic of camping prior to this road trip, and I quickly learned that it was hard on my back. I was hoping to prevent backaches in the future.

After researching various areas for my next camp spot, I came up with Argonite, Utah–less than eight hours away. That should be do-able.

Chapter 27: Thoughts Unspoken.

I left Cheyenne early in the morning so that I could get to my next destination while it was still daylight. The drive through Wyoming was beautiful with partly cloudy skies all day. I was able to savor all of the breathtaking landscape around me since I was on I-80 the entire way and traffic was light. This drive was a mental struggle for sure in that I was so high in altitude that I felt like I could touch the heavens. Normally such things would lead me to praise God for his marvelous works and tell Him how awesome He is, instead I gulped down any thoughts of Him and buried them in the pit of my stomach. Despite this emotional challenge, I was in fair spirits. I saw a good number of antelope on my drive. They were a nice distraction.

I turned on Exit 56 as planned, but I never made it to Argonite, Utah. The area was eerie and desolate. This eerie feeling worsened the farther I drove, so I decided to stop and find a spot off the road to hide my tent and motorcycle out of sight. The area was secluded enough. I was mindful of the threat of animals, but at that time I believed that a bad encounter with people was a more likely scenario. Just to be safe, I carefully inspected my tent, clothes, and sleeping bag, making sure no bugs or snakes would plague me, and I had my gun and knife in a handy location. (Hindsight: my mindset just wasn't accurate considering how desolate of a location I was in. I should have been deathly afraid of the animals out there. I was just lucky.)

It was still early but getting cold, so I decided to wrap up in my sleeping bag and try to write. Nothing came to me initially. There was no cell service there, so that meant that I didn't have to bother with checking in with Ben and Dad. I started to write about my trip because I had nothing else to say. I was a bit cautious with the whiskey because of the sketchy sleeping arrangement, but I drank enough to get nice and warm and lethargic. Despite my worries, I slept well and left early the next day.

I was off to Reno and decided to stay at a hotel because they were just so darn cheap there. I suspect that cheap hotels lure gamblers there and cause them spend more money on gambling.

The hotel was exquisite. I enjoyed walking around the casino, but I spent most of the evening in my room. I took a hot bath, drank B&B, and watched Tosh on TV for a while. His dark sense of humor was just what I needed. This was the first time I really laughed since Evie died.

Since Evie died... I was using that reference a lot. Life had changed so much since Evie died. I wished I could stop thinking that. Damn commercials. They were too long, and they gave me too much time to think. That's when I consumed the most whiskey. Oh well, Tosh. Nighty-night from Rick. Maybe some other time.

The drive through California made me so excited about how close I was getting to my destination that the hairs stood up on my neck. The first stop of my planned dream trip was Muir Beach. It was amazing. It was beautiful. It was all that I wanted it to be and more. But as I walked toward the beach, I felt my heart drop into the pit of my stomach. My excitement vanquished and was replaced by pain and grief. My eyes began to tear up. No. No! My anger pacified my sorrow temporarily. The closer I got to the beach, the heavier my heart became. Every step became more difficult than the previous one, as if I were walking in quicksand.

A transformation started taking me over, like vines of anguish and hate piercing from my skin as it built an armor around me. The armor: to keep God out, to keep in my hate? It certainly didn't protect me from pain. My blood flowed like acid freely to the ground due to the cuts from the jagged vines. I could feel the blades of grass suffocating beneath my feet as I walked on.

I headed for the nearest large rock by the ocean in search of a little seclusion, knowing that I was about to have a colossal explosion. I held in the eruption as I dredged by quite a few strangers. I didn't want their pity, their condolences, or even their attention. I pulled at my collar to try to relieve the sensation that the vines were choking me. My vision was blurred, and I could feel my neck deviate to the side with each mammoth ejection of blood from my heart to my head.

Just as I made it around the large rock, I collapsed to my hands and knees and wailed long, hard, and loud. I could feel the earth crack deep beneath my body. The power of my cry pushed the waves back to sea. The waves rolled in, saturating my hands and knees, only because I sucked them toward me as I gasped for air. Everything in my body ached. I imaged dying would be less painful than what I was experiencing.

"Didn't You create the *entire world* in only six days!? Didn't You cause Lazarus' dead bones to come forth just by telling them to!? Didn't You say a mountain could be moved with faith the size of a mustard seed!!?" That damn mustard seed. Why did that scripture vex me the most? Certainly, my faith was mustard seed sized, I imagined. I sobbed some more with piercing moans from the deepest part of my soul. "But you wouldn't save Evie's life?" I choked out. I was fully exhausted from my emotional outburst, and I collapsed further onto the sand face-first. The last thing I remembered was the feeling of the waves crashing over the side of my face and the taste of salt.

I lay there for I don't know how long. The ocean had covered my head enough times to drench my entire upper body and thighs. As I lay there, I dreamt of Evie. The sun gleamed on her beautiful face. Her long black hair blew in the breeze. Her bright blue eyes twinkled in the sunlight. She breathed in deeply, enjoying the fresh air that the cool breeze had brought her. She looked so happy. She turned to look at me, and her smile slowly faded from her face.

"Ricky, wake up," she said in a serious tone. I must not have been listening to her. "Ricky, wake up!" she said more intensely. By now she looked quite distressed. "Rick! Wake up!" She never called me that.

My head shot up from the wet, heavy sand. I choked and spat up the salt water in between my gasps for air. I crawled away from the water closer to the rock and flopped down with my back against it, still coughing from all of the water I had swallowed. A shiver befell my whole body. Too cold to cry now. I sat with my jaw clenched, my head down on my knees, and my arms wrapped around my legs. I was sick and lightheaded with misery.

In my mind, I started to put words to my torment. I was so angry with God. I wanted to tell him how badly He ruined me. Despite all of my sorrow and anger, I still believed in the power of the tongue. The Bible says that your tongue is a two-edged sword. I really wanted to tell God off, but I was afraid to. I felt helpless–not being able to say what I was thinking for fear of unleashing worse spiritual calamities in my life. I had already said too much. "I hate you, God." Yes, that was one of them. "Thoughts Unspoken." That's what I'd call it.

Thoughts Unspoken

The things I think but cannot say–dare not say.
They light me like a fire within.
The glow illuminates from my eyes, my mouth, my fingertips.
Brighter with fury until I'm motionless,
Powerless to move.

My head tipped back with my mouth open slightly,
Looking to the sky.
My arms extended at my sides
As if chained to the floor.
I burn brighter with fury.
My body trembles.
I fall to my knees.

The angels that camp about me
Are standing at attention–first in wonderment.

An eruption of sound occurs and a horrible cry is birthed,
Heard throughout the heavens.
The animals join in this sad song of agony
Because truly it is a beastly resonance
Unrecognized by man.

The angels, now alarmed by these beastly sounds,

Stand with their backs to me.
They are ready to fight on my behalf,
But there is no foe in sight.
They look around sharply, perplexed,
As the wail continues
With no signs of wavering,
Still exhaling.

The light now radiates through my entire body
With nearly no visible signs of me left.
The earth now shakes beneath my feet
Until the light explodes from me.
Too bright to see.

Silence.

There, now on my hands and knees,
I breathe heavily,
Dripping sweat, naked,
Arms and legs trembling.

I collapse further to my chest and face, still breathing heavily.
Too weak to move, to numb to care.
Sleep comes, warranted.
My face covered in tears.
Each tear named...
Anger, Hate, Despise, Sorrow, Vengeance, Malice,
Injustice, injustice, injustice!!!

No man heard this inaudible cry
That discharged from all of my pores
And stained all that it touched.
No man; just beasts, angels, and God.

Alarm clock sounds, another day.
A better day?
Absurd.
Still these thoughts remain...

Unspoken.

I looked completely disheveled with my hair and shirt soaked, but the worst of it was how much sand was caught in my hair. How was I supposed to get off of this beach without people asking me if I was okay? Or maybe they'd report me to the cops because I looked like I was strung out on drugs thanks to my eyes being blood shot from the salt water.

I was exhausted and, at last, hungry again. After what felt like several hours of sitting by the rock shivering, I decided to find the closest hotel and just crash for the day. I took a couple Xanax, had a Boost, and called it a day. I went to bed hungry, but I was too tired to care.

Chapter 28: Dream Flop.

My dream trip to California, driving on Highway 101 along the majestic Pacific Ocean, was a sad and incredibly painful experience. Every day was the same. It was so beautiful. The awareness of how omniscient, omnipresent, and omnipotent God is was on my mind. This would quickly cause me to become stricken with anger and sorrow to the point that I'd have to pull over and vomit. I wasn't able to keep anything down for days.

I stopped checking in with Dad and Ben for a couple days. They both left me numerous voice and text messages about how concerned they were. Mom called several times as well. One night, I finally gave everyone a quick text message, saying that I hadn't been feeling well and that I had been resting. That wasn't true, of course. I was powering through the days, going eight to nine hours, pulling over frequently to vomit, and then collapsing at a motel.

After I sent out this message to all, the return texts fired back. Dad and Ben both wanted me to call them immediately, but I refused. It wouldn't have been good for them to hear me in this state of complete despair when I was supposed to be healing. After several text messages, they both began calling me. I got firm with them by informing them that I was *not* going to pick up the phone, that I was going to rest, and that they needed to stop calling. I ended by expressing to them how sorry I was for upsetting them (and I meant that sincerely). Dad's last text said that he loved me very much and that he was praying for me. Ben ended with, "I love you. Feel better. Please please call me tomorrow. I need to hear your voice." I was too sick to drink alcohol that night, and that made me mad. More tears filled my pillow. Each one named: injustice, injustice, injustice.

When I reached the Red Wood forest, my debilitating despair elevated to heavy sorrow. I had exhausted myself from being at rock bottom for so many days that I honestly couldn't have gotten any lower. There was something about the forest, something almost peaceful that took ahold of me. My first day there, I walked through the forest and found a secluded spot, so I decided to rest. I nestled myself in the thick brush, using my coat for a pillow. This was fairly comfortable. I set my alarm so that I wouldn't sleep long and get stuck in the forest at dusk. I listened to the lullaby of the forest: the melodic sounds of the birds and the wind making the trees sing. My eyes grew heavy, heavier. Sleep. Warranted. No dreams.

To my surprise, I awoke feeling pretty good. I was hungry too. I sought out some food at a local restaurant and greedily filled my belly, not caring that the locals stared at my disheveled appearance and my lack of manners while I ate. I was then ready to call my family and relieve them of any worries they had.

I called Ben first. We talked a bit while he was on break. I convinced Ben that I was doing okay, but I wasn't able to mask my anguish from Dad. Like I said before, Dad has the Holy Spirit, which means that often he just knows stuff sometimes. Evie couldn't hide many things from him, and I never had anything to hide from him until recently.

When Dad asked me how I was doing, I told him that I was doing okay in a semi-perky manner. I was an artist. I was painting a solid picture through my words and by controlling any variations in my vocal chords. But he replied, "You're not even *close* to being okay." Then the paint washed down the canvas as tears exploded from my face. Even though I was feeling better, rehashing the past few days was emotionally exhausting. Dad was ready to get on a plane and come get me. He said that we'd have the motorcycle shipped back; it was no problem at all. I told him no. I explained that I was doing better since I got to Oregon, and that I planned to stay another day. By then, I felt like I'd be ready to travel. I promised him that I would come straight home after that. Dad hesitated but finally agreed to this, partly because I insisted.

Later that evening, after I had quite a lot to drink, I called Ben again. "Hi, I miss you. I shouldn't have left you. I don't know what I was thinking. I'm coming straight home tomorrow." There was a quiver in my voice when I said, "God I miss you so much."

Ben took a second to take this all in. I'm sure he was confused because my previous call went so differently. "I, ah, miss you too," he said. I pictured him running his fingers through his hair as he said that. He looked so damn sexy when he did that. "Yes, come back to me. I'll take care of you. I'll never let you go, Rick."

I wept softly and rocked back and forth as I lay on the bed with only a few sniffles to give me away. "I m-miss... I n-need...your touch," I sniffled. He was starting to get the idea of how drunk I was. "My shoulders, my back, my face..." I said as my voice trailed off. He was still quiet on the other end. "Your lips are, *so* fuckin' sexy," I breathed in deeply. There was another long pause. "Are, are you there?"

"Yeah." He exhaled heavily.

"Could you, just tell me about your day, or talk about something? Anything at all, so I can hear your voice? I just need...to hear your voice." I was talking with long pauses in between my words and in a softer voice than usual in my drunken state.

"I have a better idea," he started.

"Yeah?" I said, waiting for him to finish.

"I want you to slide your hand down your pants and touch yourself," he said in a sexy voice, "like I did the day before you left."

"What?" I said in tired disbelief. I was pretty sure I didn't hear him right.

"You remember how I touched you?"

My breathing and heart rate increased. I did hear him right, and how could I possibly forget that? "Yes," I whispered.

"I want you to do that while I talk to you." He was such a bad boy. I loved it.

"Um, um, I d-don't know," I said breathlessly.

"I'll walk you through it." He paused to listen to me breathing heavily on the line. "First, slide out of all of your clothes," he instructed.

"This is crazy," is what I thought, but I hesitantly followed his directions. Anything, just as long as he'd keep talking to me. "Um, okay," I said as I put my phone on speaker.

"Now bend your legs up and let them rest out to the side. Put your fingers in your mouth and get them nice and wet."

"You've got to be kidding me," I said with my hormones in full throttle.

He laughed a little sexy laugh. "Make sure you leave your fingers in there a while. Rub some of that wetness on your lips." He remembered my lip fetish of course. "Now slide your hand down there and stroke up and down until you're nice and wet." I was several steps behind him, still in disbelief that I was doing this.

"You'd be surprised how wet I am already, just listening your voice." He liked that, I could tell by his light gasp. "Uh," I let out my first moan. "Please tell me you're being a little naughty too right now."

"Hell yeah I am! This is phone sex, baby," he said unashamed. I'd heard of the term before, but I never really stopped to think about it. He stepped it up a notch by talking dirty to me, as if things weren't feeling crazy enough. "Keep your body relaxed. Now move up and down on the bed as if I'm moving inside you, making your body glide with my every thrust." My hairs stood up on the back of my neck when he said that. I had a lump in my throat. I did what he asked, vividly imagining that he was moving inside of me. I broke out into a light sweat.

"Ah, ah," I moaned softly.

"Are you doing it, Rick? Just like I asked you to?" Um, he knew the answer to that. Every time he spoke, I got a shiver throughout my body.

"Yes, yes," I replied in between moans.

"I'm going to press my lips against yours and slip my tongue in your mouth as I continue to *thrust* my dick inside you." I instinctively rubbed my fingers across my lips when he said this while I continued to stimulate my clit. My moans got louder as I visualized this. Finally, I could hear him moaning on the other end occasionally. I gasped and smiled for a second. The noises I made, caused him to grow louder. I respond by laughing a little. "Uh!" he went on. "Here I go! I'm going deep and hard! I can't help myself! You're so beautiful! I shove your breast into my mouth and caress it with my tongue!"

I grabbed my breast hard and squealed. "No, slow down! It's too much!" I said, as if I wasn't in control of my own hands.

I was completely saturated, on the verge of a clit orgasm, when he said to me, "I can't! I can't control myself! I grab your ass and pull you toward me as I continue to ravage you hard, for a deep, deep fuck!" My pussy started throbbing, so I rolled to my side and grabbed it to subdue the pain while I continued to massage my clit.

"Holy shit! Ah, ahh!" I said in ecstasy. How was he so damn good at this? He painted a really explicit picture for me, one I couldn't form on my own. "I can't, I can't!" I said.

"Wait, wait, one more thing. You gotta do one more thing for me, baby. Roll onto your stomach and keep going, but keep your legs apart, far apart." I tried but my body was starting to convulse, so I stayed on my side. My moaning was out of control and not sexy sounding at all. "Grab your breast with your other hand and squeeze tight. Now go harder, faster, just a little bit longer." I was in a full clit orgasm and was so loud that I had to bury my face in the bed to muffle my sounds.

I could only go hard about ten more seconds then I yelled, "No more! No more! I'm done!"

I heard him let out a light, "Uhh." He breathed heavily for a couple of moments and gave me a sexy laugh. Then he said, "That's my girl."

"You're so bad," I said as I tried to catch my breath and keep the room from spinning in my drunken state.

"You're gonna see just how bad I can be." He laughed.

I giggled a little. "How did this happen? How did I end up lucky enough to have you?" I said breathlessly. It did perplex me.

"It's like you said, 'I was meant to be yours and you were meant to be mine.'" That was a modified version of what I told him when I had a fist full of his shirt after he confessed that he'd been with several women, but it was correct nonetheless. "I love you, angel," he said. Funny that he calls me that when clearly he's my angel.

"I love *you*, Ben."

Chapter 29: Trip Home.

I woke up with an urgency to get home to Ben as fast as I could. My body was bombarded with pain at the disappointment my dream trip had been. The cycle of flooding emotions never ceased. Despair, sorrow, anger, hate...the whole ride home. I tried to concentrate on Ben, the one good thing I had going for me.

Montana was an exceptional interruption on the ride home. I was amazed at how her beauty engulfed me. During this part of the ride, I was able to dissect the Creator away from His Creations. It was a self-preservation technique. I couldn't afford to think about Him because of the pain it brought. I just couldn't survive another day of internal cyclones tearing up my insides.

I pondered other reasons as to why Montana was going much better than California. California was my destination. My quest didn't provide me the relief I was expecting. Now I was on my way home, which was tied to a good feeling. This pep helped me soar on eagles' wings through Montana. She was so majestic. It's no wonder that the folks in Cheyenne say that their loved ones go to "Montana" instead of heaven when they pass.

It was so cold in the mountains, especially in the morning. It monsooned past the normal satisfaction I'd get from the numbing sensation. I had to stop to buy liner gloves and a leather neck cover just to make it through. I got a hotel that evening because I was chilled to the bone and was in dire need of a hot bath.

It took me less than a week of travel to get home because I pushed it on my motorcycle longer than I should have each day. This was completely exhausting, and I slept well each night as a result. I decided I was going to head straight to Ben's house and forgo the trip to my own house. That would come soon enough.

Chapter 30: Motorcycle Lessons.

I learned a good deal about motorcycling on this trip. I made a fair number of mistakes. Some of which weren't repeated but others took a smidge more time to work out. I parked downhill in the stones once at a gas station parking lot because I was hurrying to get out of the way of fellow traveler. It was time consuming to get gas because my tank was on the seat behind me and my bag was on the back of the motorcycle seat, so I had to take my bag off every time I wanted to fill up. I was trying to be kind to the person waiting behind me by moving out of the way as soon as I finished gassing up. In my haste, I made a poor choice by parking downhill on the stones. I didn't fall in the stones, but I sure did have a near miss. Park in the stones downhill? Never again.

The wild wind in the western states taught me a quick lesson as well. I learned to rely on my rear-view mirrors more. I like to use my mirrors *and* turn my head to check my blind spot. Well, not in windy Wyoming. The wind nearly took my head off! My neck was jolted back quickly and my visor flew up a couple of times. It scared me half to death! Turning my head during high wind? Never again.

I learned that your motorcycle swag is not only good for protection from the sun, wind, and in case of a crash, but it also protects your pants against nasty bugs. Being that I traveled light and didn't have the luxury of a washer and dryer too often, the first day that my jeans were covered in bug juice was the last day. I made a habit of wearing my chaps more. Bug juice on my pants? Never again.

Other lessons not learned so quickly included how difficult it was for me to go from first to second gear when I was traveling in town. On several occasions, I'd shift from first to neutral instead of second gear. This only happened in town. I think that it was a motor planning problem—my brain just couldn't work out the right signal to my foot—which is why it took longer for me to learn my lesson. This never happened when I accelerated quickly on the highway.

The throttle lock was a life-saver, but it was very difficult to turn on. I'd drop ten miles per hour just trying to get the thing in the right position! The motorcycle would lurch back and forth as my speed fluctuated until I could get it right. I got a little better at this, but I'm still not great. Now I hold my thumb on my cramp buster and use all of my other fingers to lock it in place. This works a heck of a lot better than trying to lock it into place with my middle or ring finger, which is the way you have to do it if you leave the palm of your hand on the cramp buster like it's intended for. Still a work in progress.

I discovered that thick socks and gel inserts in my boots were a must have. Without them, I would get tingling sensations in my feet from the vibration of my machine. Something I've never had before because I'd never gone long distance before.

Most importantly, I was reassured that I have the perfect bike for me. I loved how I could stand up on the pegs and straighten my legs as I was going through city limits at a slower speed. I also liked how my back felt sitting in a more upright position, instead of sitting back like you'd do on a cruiser. I appreciated that I could lean forward completely on the tank when my butt needed a little unweighting or when my neck needed a break from the wind.

Speaking of wind issues, I opted for the tallest wind shield available for my bike, but my head still towered over it. This left me vulnerable to the wind. I hated how my head would bobble on really windy days. I'd have a headache within twenty minutes of this. So my solution was to lean forward and rest my chest on my bike. This worked well for a while, but then I started to get neck pain from looking up at such a harsh angle. I came up with a simple solution: I taped a sweat shirt into an oblong pillow shape, secured it under my jacket, and then leaned forward onto my tank. It was a perfect solution that I only used when I had to. You can imagine how silly I looked, being so thin with a huge sweatshirt hiding under my jacket. I looked like Santa!

I love my bike, but it has one more flaw. The seat isn't comfortable for long distance riding and there aren't many upgrade options. I tried an inflatable cushion on top of the seat. It was comfortable, but it brought me up so high that my feet didn't touch the ground well. Obviously, it also would raise my head even higher above the windshield, and you know how that story ends. Having a cushion on the seat also caused me to lean down onto my handle bars more, which resulted in neck and shoulder pain. Simple solution: I wore bicycle shorts with the gel inserts at my sit bones under my clothes.

Other motorcyclists revealed to me that we are all part of a family. They'd make friendly chit chat at every stop. I also learned that some men are driven wild by female motorcyclists. I was followed on several occasions and gawked at, and strange men would often flirt with me. Some guys were nice; others were creepy. I didn't think much of it either way. I just needed to get back to Ben.

Chapter 31: Arrival at Ben's House.

I parked along the side of the road near the back entrance to Ben's house and sat there for a couple minutes until I could muster up enough strength to dismount. My stiff legs were unable to comply with my desire to run into Ben's arms. I stood tall and straight for several seconds, enjoying the stretch. I started walking toward the back door with my helmet in hand, trying not to limp. I saw Ben look out the window momentarily just before he tore through the door. I couldn't match his free movements, but my "I missed you" smile perfectly matched his. He picked me up with a hug and swung me around. It was painful, but I didn't want him to stop. He put me down, looked longingly into my eyes, brushed my hair back from my face and kissed me. The warmth from his lips gave some life back into my cold body. Ben then put my arm around his shoulder and assisted me up the stairs. I thought it was a little dramatic at first, but I was so tired that I wasn't about to fuss. (Hindsight: I did look pretty rough, and it wasn't dramatic. It was dead-on because of my fatigue.)

We entered the house, yet we still hadn't spoken a word to each other since my arrival. I was too tired to talk. We said all that we needed to say to each other over the phone the past few days: "I love you, I need you, come back to me, don't ever leave me again," and "I love you, I need you, I won't ever leave you again."

Ben unzipped and removed my leather jacket. After he hung it up, he guided me over to the kitchen chair where he sat down. Then he gently pulled me down on top of him–just like we were for our first kiss. Even though I was so tired, a thrill rushed over me. I had goosebumps because of his clever choice of positioning. He caressed and kissed me several times, but then he suddenly stopped and abruptly jerked me back by my shoulders to look at me. He manipulated my arms and body as he visually inspected me, making me feel like an object.

"Oh my God, Rick!" he said, noticing my weight loss. Yeah, I dropped under 100 pounds. "Oh, no. Oh, no," he said as he ran his hand across my pronounced collar bones. After he was done scrutinizing me, he noticed my angry-hurt expression and the fact that I wasn't making eye contact with him anymore. He back peddled heavily. "It's okay. It's okay," he reassured me. "You're back in my arms now. I'm sure you'll get your appetite back." He tried to guide my face back toward him, but I refused. Yes, I was that upset.

He gently pulled me forward onto his body, and I rested my head on his shoulder. I was as weak as a kitten and couldn't have fought his hug, even if I wanted to. He caressed my back as my body lay against his chest. I began to feel sedated. His touch was so therapeutic that I soon forgot why I was mad at him. He could feel my body relax completely over the next couple of minutes. I still hadn't said anything to him yet.

After a long embrace, Ben sat me back up off of his chest. He gently lifted my chin and started to kiss my lips. I oafishly received his kisses in my tired state. He didn't seem to mind my lack of coordination. My lips accidentally brushed against his coarse stubble, and I flinched. It hurt so much that I instinctively put my fingers on my lips, checking for blood. But then I smiled at him as I slowly realized that this was all on purpose: his unshaven face, me sitting on his lap, his intentional brush of his stubble across my lips. It was *exactly* like our first kiss after our Hocking Hills trip. It was perfect. Everything was perfect. He was perfect. I loved how much thought he put into our reunion.

My exhaustion and lack of food combined with the pleasure of Ben's lips and touch started to have an LSD-like effect on me. The colors in the room seemed off. I felt dizzy. It seemed like time had slowed down to a crawl. I kissed his neck as he slid his hands up my shirt. He soon unfastened my pants to be able to grab my butt more easily. He wasn't messing around. The room spun as he groped and kissed me. I might have let him do anything to me, but I felt filthy.

After he unfastened my bra, I said to him, "I love what you're doing, but I need a shower in the worst way."

"Of course," he replied understandingly. He smiled cunningly and continued with, "Would you like some company?" My heart raced. I didn't know what to say. I stared at him blankly with my lips slightly open. I hadn't even thought of the possibility of getting sensual in the shower. He reveled in the fact that he stunned me. "No, I think a shower can wait," he said, making my decision for me.

He smiled and went back to making me touch heaven. After several more minutes of intense groping, he grabbed me and carried me to the bedroom. I was so weak and tired. He was definitely running this show, with me not being able to reciprocate well like I had done in the past. This didn't seem to bother him a bit. He started to undress me. It felt like my heart was going to explode through my chest.

"Are, are we going to have sex now?" I asked apprehensively.

He smiled and took his good ole time answering that question. He loved to toy with me. "Not today, but I *am* going to make you feel good."

He was just about finished removing my clothes when I said, "Wait. I need to freshen up a little."

"You have two minutes," he said as he removed his shirt.

"I need five," I said as I headed to the bathroom.

"Two!" I heard him yell at me as I walked away.

I returned to the bedroom within two minutes and said, "Ben, I'm so tired. I don't know if I can," I paused briefly and then finished with, "do whatever it is you're thinking."

"Don't worry, baby. You just need to lie there while I pleasure you. And then you're gonna return the favor, but' you don't have to do anything but just lie there."

I blushed hard, my heart raced again, and my hairs stood up on the back of my neck. He just said we weren't having sex, but I was going to return the favor by just lying there? I was so confused.

"I-I have no idea what you're talking about," I said as my mind wondered. He grabbed my arm and pulled me toward the bed and removed my panties.

"I know," he said, fully pleased with himself that he was torturing me with secrets. My head spun like a vortex because this was the first time we were completely naked together. He started off with a deep French kiss while his body lay heavily on mine. I was overwhelmed with his naked body pressed against mine because we hadn't touched in so long. He then progressed to biting and sucking my lower lip *hard*. I grabbed his shoulders and squeezed them as I winced in pain. I was getting a little scared, and my body tensed up. I feared that I wasn't going to be able to handle whatever it was that he had planned. He must not have realized what state I was in.

Ben noticed my conspicuous distress and backed off some. He moved on to kissing my neck and running his hands down my sides more gently. His transition to gentleness caused me to melt like butter in his hands. He started grinding with me gently. His gentle grinding, kissing, and touching felt so good that I eventually involuntarily started moving with his body. I had forgotten the concerns I had moments before about him being too rough. I became breathless beneath him. Ben grabbed my leg and bent it up a little as he continued to grind with me. I gasped from the surprise of this new position.

He whispered into my ear, "Are you nice and wet yet?" The answer was yes, but him asking me that doubled my flow.

I gasped for air again before I could answer him. "Um, y-yeah."

"Good." He fondled me, guiding some of the moisture from my vagina up to clit.

"Uh!" I yelped as I clenched his shoulders. Ben did this motion repeatedly. "Uh! Ah! Ah!" I exclaimed with each stroke. He looked at me so voluptuously. Somehow, I knew that this was only a warm up. The suspense and the look he gave me had my stomach in knots.

"I'm gonna put my dick right here and rub you up and down," he said as he placed his shaft directly on my clit. "Bend your leg up." He grabbed my other leg and slid it up with his hand, causing my breathlessness to turn into a squeal of apprehension. His first grind in this new calculated position sent a sensation through me as if the room had picked me up and thrown me back onto the bed. As he continued to precisely move on me, I felt the ceiling and the walls bounce in and out at me, making me nauseous. I couldn't breathe. He had one hand under my low back and the other on my butt while he moved forcefully up and down. I'm sure I was loud, but for the life of me, I couldn't remember what I sounded like. That LSD-like effect came back hard with a vengeance. I was so exhausted that I couldn't begin to push him away, and believe me, I wanted to. The best I could do was hold onto him tight. Every touch from him was perfectly designed to push me just short of dizzying every time we embraced. After a bit, I could barely hear him moaning over the deafening sensations that bombarded my nervous system. My eyes began to water. I squeezed my legs together around his hips.

Ben's volume escalated, and I could finally hear him over the trumpets in my head. I collected my mind and concentrated on his sounds of pleasure that pleased me so. "You can do whatever you want to me, just don't stop making that sound," I said breathlessly in between my crazy, random noises. I was completely caught up in the moment. Of course I didn't mean that. That was like telling a thief to take whatever he wanted, which would be *everything*. My words made him hornier. He grabbed my breast and put my nipple in his mouth, not missing a beat with his thrusting down below.

"Oh shit! Oh no!" I yelled. My body stopped flowing with him. Instead, I convulsed as he sucked on me. After he released my breast from his mouth, he arched his back, changing the angle at which he was grinding me and split my clit wide open. I screamed loudly. He thrusted harder, making me regret what I had just said. "Ah, ah, ah, haaa!" I wailed.

He kept his end of the deal by saying, "I love you, Rick. I love you so much. You're so sexy. You're absolutely perfect." He stopped talking so he could kiss my mouth deeply, all while he kept grinding his body on mine. The force of our bodies caused the bed to bump against the wall. All I could do was to hold onto him tight.

He put my nipple back in his mouth, and I screamed in pleasure and pain. "You've gotta be fucking kidding me!" I shrieked. I punched him in the shoulder twice like a crazed maniac. He removed his mouth from my breast, grabbed my hands and held them over my head. He smiled and laughed while he continued to grind on me. "No," I whimpered in dismay at my newly restrained position. Then Ben pressed his lips against mine again and continued to savagely manhandle me. His lips on mine allowed me to handle the restraint. All of these staggering sensations were nothing like I'd ever felt before. How was feeling this beastly possible when we hadn't even had sex yet? What kind of sorcery was this!?

I got to the point where I couldn't continue on with this, so I broke contact with his lips to try to wiggle out from his grasp. But he didn't budge. I went off the deep end and started screaming, "Oh fuck! Oh shit! Fuck! Shit!" as he continued grinding his dick on my clit. My body convulsed as I had a yet another clit orgasm. My feet were completely on fire. He still wouldn't let up. "No, no, no! No more!" I yelled, but still he held my arms tight above my head and moved forcefully on me. I couldn't stop him; he was a freight train. I couldn't tolerate any more! "No! No! Stop, stop, stop!" I screamed. And he did stop. It was then that I remembered Ben telling me in the past that he wasn't going to stop until I said the word "stop."

"Are you sure?" he asked sarcastically.

"Yes, ya jerk! Now let go of my arms!" I yelled breathlessly. He laughed at me and he didn't let go. Instead he kissed my lips.

"You're amazing." He laughed as he lay on my chest with his body rising and falling with each of my deep breaths. "You're so fucking amazing," he said more seriously. He let go of one of my wrists, grabbed me behind my neck, and gave me that deep kiss known for causing wet pussy 100% of the time. I think my eyes rolled back in my head. "You lasted a lot longer than I thought you were going to," he said. "Now are you ready to keep up your end of the deal and just lie there?"

"What!? I don't know!?"

He smiled deviously, amused at how genuinely upset I was. He grabbed a bottle of lotion nearby and rubbed a generous amount on his dick. Then he straddled me and grabbed my breasts, shoving them together hard. I gasped. He thrusted his dick up and down between my tits vigorously as he held them tight together. I was in complete shock! After I realized what was happening, I decided that I kind of liked this, but obviously not quite as much as he did. I insolently scratched his thighs as he went on. He winced in pain and slowed down just for a second. Then he tipped his head back and laughed wildly, and then he resumed moving at a crazy-fast pace. I was amazed at his strength, endurance, and flawless movements. After a bit, his thrusts became slower and more intense. Finally, he came between my breasts.

"That was so sexy," I said. Ben laughed a little and smiled as he worked to catch his breath.

"Don't move. I'll be right back." He returned with some paper towels and cleaned me up.

"Do you have a secret life you are hiding from me? Are you a porn star?" I asked jokingly.

He smiled and laughed so hard that his nose crinkled. "No," he simply replied. There was a brief silence.

"Did you have this much fun with the other girls?" I asked him after my smile faded. I immediately suffered a huge pain in my stomach. I squeezed my eyes closed tight and swallowed hard. My head started to hurt. I did a mental head jolt, trying to change the channel, but it doesn't work like that. I couldn't change the channel because now a reply was inevitable. Even saying nothing would have been a reply. Why did I ask such a stupid question!? Of course I didn't want to know the answer to that! It was too late. My heavy regret hung out there on a frail limb. I didn't think about being number thirteen much anymore, but the number would sometimes flash in my face, leaving me blind for a few minutes. My tone was light enough during my question, but Ben easily read the regret on my face. A satellite could've done so as well.

I felt his breath on my face as I held my eyes closed. He had bent over and was nose to nose with me. I slowly looked up and gazed into his beautiful brown eyes. Then he said in the most serious tone, "No, not even close." He kissed me sweetly, caressing my bottom lip with his. I believed him, and I never asked him a question like that again.

Chapter 32: Forever.

Ben took the next day off to be with me. I couldn't have been more thankful to be able to spend the entire day with him. I slept so well wrapped in his arms my first night back, better than I had in a long time. I smiled at the thought that I didn't even need alcohol to accomplish that. I'll also thank fatigue and the endorphin rush that Ben gave me for my good night's sleep.

I woke up kind of late, 8:30 a.m., and Ben had breakfast ready for me. My heart danced to see him smiling in the kitchen first thing in the morning. I was tired, but you couldn't slap the smile off my face. I stood at the edge of the kitchen, watching him.

"Good morning, sunshine," he said, smiling back at me. He continued to shovel breakfast onto my plate. He grabbed a cup of coffee, and placed it on the table with waiter-like finesse. As he was setting things down, he looked up at me and did a double-take. He seemed surprised to see me still standing there, smiling at him. He walked over closer to me and put his arms around my waist. He tipped his head to the side a little and squinted as if to evaluate me. "You got something on your mind?"

I smiled even bigger. "I love you."

He rocked me side to side as if we were doing some sort of uncoordinated dance. I giggled at his goofiness. "No ma'am, I love you." He bent over and kissed my neck, intentionally tickling me.

"Ahh!" That's about as high pitched of a shriek as I've done. My laughing and trying to push him away only made him fight me worse. "Stop, stop, stop," I said as I laughed uncontrollably. He picked me up and carried me to the table while I still giggled. He put me down and pulled my chair out for me like a gentleman.

"Thank you, Ben," I said, gleaming at him.

"My pleasure, my fair lady." He couldn't have been more charming. "How many weeks do you have until you return to work?" he asked nonchalantly as we started to chow.

"I think a whole month." I frowned a little. "I wonder if I can get that shortened up a little. I don't know. I don't know what to do."

"Well, take a couple days and you'll figure it out."

"I'll probably go home tomorrow and unpack, and then visit my folks while you're at work."

He looked up at me sharply. "Then you are moving in with me? Cuz it sounded like that's how you were going to finish your sentence."

I smiled widely at his stubborn persistence. "I would like that very much, but that's not what I was going to say. And that's not what–" I stopped and was startled by his abrupt interruption. He had literally jumped out of his chair and was on one knee in front of me in two seconds. He grabbed my hand and put it on his chest.

"Rick, move in with me." I could feel his heart beat underneath my hand.

"I, I, uh, I can't," I said. It broke my heart to tell him no this time because I truly wanted to move in with him. I just knew I'd be happier, but you know the story. I began to tear up.

"No, no. Not acceptable. Tell me that you'll seriously think about it. I'll accept nothing less than that."

My heart ached, and one tear escaped my eye. "I'll think about it," I promised. He squeezed my hand against his chest and closed his eyes as he let out a sigh of relief. He got up and wiped my one tear away, and then he kissed my cheek where that tear had been. I was taken with his sweetness, hence another tear escaped when he returned to his chair. I quickly wiped it away before he could notice.

The morning went by so slowly, but in a good way. No, in a great way. We were just hanging out, being stupid. Ben convinced me to dance with him in the living room as we listened to music. "I promised to take you club dancing a while back. This is one step toward keeping that promise," he said to me as he ushered me to the dancefloor.

We danced close together around the living room with our bodies constantly touching in one fashion or another. Ben was not a great dancer, but I didn't care. It was the spirit of it that

I loved. At one point, Ben was doing an intentionally goofy dance. He said to me while he was shakin' it, "Are you sure you want to be seen in public with this?" He had his arms over his head as he moved his pelvis around in discontinuous circles. I placed my hands on his chest while we danced and giggled.

"I'm ready to go public with this," I said in jest. He dipped me and kissed me.

This day was amazing. Why did I leave him to go on that road trip? It seemed like a stupid decision in hindsight. Oh yeah, I really didn't leave *him*. I left because I needed space from my parents. Moving in with Ben would give me more space from my parents, but that would make all future encounters with my folks terribly coarse.

The mood changed when the song "Sweater Weather" by Neighborhood came on. This song always got my motor running; I don't know why. I started dancing seductively around Ben, touching him in naughty places. He gradually stopped dancing with me and intently looked me up and down as I bewitched him. After I slithered my way back around to face him, I did a sultry twist. As I twisted down, I glided my fingers down the outsides of his thighs. As I twisted up, I glided my fingers up the insides of his thighs. Then I unfastened his pants and put my hands down his backside. He let me touch him in any way I wanted. He looked at me with the devil in his eyes, yet he remained frozen. This was uncharacteristic of him. I found his motionless state to be enthralling.

As I danced, I listened to the lyrics of the song and realized that I was doing a seductive dance while Neighborhood sang about two lovers living together. When this realization hit me, I quickly averted my eyes from Ben and became almost paralyzed. I felt like I was conveying the wrong message to Ben. I, of course, knew the words to this song, but I didn't think about how this looked to Ben after he had just asked me to move in with him. "She knows what I think about. And what I think about: One love, two mouths, one love, one house..." This was a coincidence and was unintentional. Ben ascertained what had just happened. He graciously saved me from myself by lifting me up and carrying me to the couch.

We kissed on the couch, but there was no heavy petting this time. This kind of surprised me, what with the way Ben was looking at me and all. Ben stopped kissing me for a second to explain. "I just want to keep it easy for now." No, he really didn't, but that was fine with me.

"Whatever you want," I replied. It felt like an amazing high school make-out session. I certainly wasn't disappointed.

After our make-out session ended, we caressed lovingly on the couch while one of the original Godzilla movies played in the background. Ben was watching it, but I had my head on his chest, listening to his heart beat. I lightly caressed his torso while he stroked my hair. It was so therapeutic. When the movie was over, Ben told me to get ready for lunch because he wanted to take me to the local café.

We walked up to the café entrance with newlywed-like bliss, evidenced by our big goofy grins and me hanging on Ben's arm. Ben ran into quite a few locals that he knew, and he readily introduced me to them. Each of them stared at me just a little too long. He got several different reactions from each person. My favorite was, "You're kidding, right!?" This man wore a flannel shirt and a ball cap. He looked to be about ten years older than Ben. He was unshaven and dark from the sun. I wondered if he were a farmer. He sat down beside me a little too close and whispered to me, "Tell me his secret so I can get a hot, young babe like you."

I glanced over at Ben, who looked amused. I laughed and said to his acquaintance, "There's no secret. He's just being himself, and that's all I want from him." I looked back over at Ben to see him looking at me with a small smile and with those big sexy eyes. My, his eyes did luster, and they told the story much better than his smile: that he was taken with my words.

"Damn!" his acquaintance said. "Don't you let this one go!"

I laughed again. "He couldn't shake me if he tried." I got a laugh out of Ben that time. The man got up, hit Ben on the shoulder and then departed from us.

Ben's smile was so incredibly beautiful. I was staring and smiling at him again, much like I had done in the kitchen earlier.

Ben leaned forward, put his elbows on the table, tilted his head to the side, and analyzed me with a squint. "You got something on your mind?" he asked in a quiet voice. My smile grew at how clever he was, asking me the same question he had done earlier. He gave me an ornery smirk.

I leaned forward, put my elbows on the table and gently cupped my fingers round his. Then I said with the utmost confidence, "I'm gonna marry you, Benjamin Warren Blake."

He laughed at my boldness. We had never talked about getting married before. "When exactly did you decide that?" he asked, egging me on.

"Hocking Hills, actually. After you put your foot in my stomach and sent me soaring over your head." I had a big, stupid smile on my face with that big, stupid crinkle in my nose.

His smile slowly faded, and a stunned look replaced it. He exhaled quickly and breathed in deeply. It wasn't often that I caught him off-guard. It felt nice. "We weren't even dating. How, how could you possibly know then?" he asked.

"I just know things sometimes," I replied. "When you wrapped me in two towels, and as I stood there shivering in front of you, I knew right then." He smiled and his lighthearted mood returned. His eyes gleamed at me.

"You never cease to amaze me, Rick. Do you know when I fell in love with you?" he asked.

"No," I said a little excited. I didn't expect for him to indulge me any further with this conversation.

"It's complicated," he paused for a minute, thinking about what to say. "I wanted to kiss you so bad at Hocking Hills, but I couldn't because I thought I was too old for you. I could tell that you were falling for me hard and fast, but I struggled with my feelings because I thought maybe you just had puppy love. I thought that I knew I loved you when you let me recklessly drive you around in my STI," he said. He smiled as he reminisced about that day. Then he grew serious again. "But I fought those feelings because I just knew that I was going to ruin this relationship somehow. And that would have ruined me." I was on the edge of my chair listening. "Remember the day you first told me you loved me?" he reminisced.

"Of course," I whispered. I was so caught up in his story.

"And you were so sure," he reminded me.

"Yes, I am," I quickly replied, changing his past tense to present.

"Your certainty took my breath away." We were somewhere else for the moment, with the diner sounds and background conversations fading away. He paused for a moment and then continued, "I thought I was going to lose you for sure when I confessed my past to you." He squeezed my fingers and looked emotional for a moment. My mouth hung open, for I was awe-struck that he would open up so much to me. "So I prepared myself to be crushed," he paused and continued in a much softer voice, "like I have been so many times before." He shook his head and swallowed hard. He could barely choke out this next sentence. "You *blew* me away when you grabbed my shirt and told me, 'I don't know how, and I don't know why, but I know that you're supposed to be mine.'"

I remembered vividly how I felt when I said those words, and it was hard for me to control my emotions as I listened.

Ben sat back into the chair and ran both of his hands through his hair. He tried to recapture his cool as he looked off into the distance. "Fuckin' blew me away," he whispered as if he were talking to himself. After a few moments, he leaned forward again, and this time he clasped his fingers around mine. "That was the day I knew you'd be mine forever." I swooned at his use of the word forever. He went on to say, "Who could love a monster like me, except my sweet angel?" My heart stopped, like someone clenched it tightly in their hand, and I winced in pain. Is that what he really thought!? That he was a monster!? I became queasy as I felt his internal discord as strongly as if we had the same heart.

"No. No." It was all I could do to control my tears, but I managed. I had to because we were in public, and I didn't want to embarrass him. "You were just lost, but now I've found you. And I'm never letting you go." He was moved deeply by my words.

The rest of the day was just as magical. I was high from being in love. We sat on the couch and let the afternoon float on by as we cuddled, caressed, and innocently kissed.

At one point, Ben got up to use the restroom. Just after he returned and sat down, he said to me, "Oh shoot. I think I left my phone in my room. Could you go get it for me?"

"Of course, babe." I popped up without hesitation.

When I entered his bedroom, I saw rose petals leading from the doorway to the bed. Candles were lit in the room and "Sweater Weather" was quietly playing. I stopped dead in my tracks and reached for the door frame for support as the room spun around me like a vortex. I hadn't breathed since I entered the room. Did this mean what I thought it meant? Ben came up behind me and caressed my waist and stomach while he kissed my neck. I turned around to face him and let him kiss my mouth. My body trembled in his arms.

"I think it's time," he said to me in his sexy voice. I blacked out just for a second. Ben held me up until I got my feet back under me. My respiration increased as I came back to earth. He backed me up to the bed and started to undress me. I felt shy even though he'd seen me naked several times before. I acted like it was the first time he'd removed my clothes.

After he seductively undressed me, he gave me face to face unwavering eye contact as he lowered me to the bed. I was getting wet with anticipation. Once my head touched the pillow, Ben kissed my lips gently for quite a while as he lay on top of me. He slowly progressed from kissing me gently to kissing me passionately. It was a smooth transition. He was such an artist. He slid his hand down my stomach to my vagina and gently started to stimulate me. He quickly realized that I wasn't going to be high-maintenance. I was full-on wet. He gasped into my neck, very pleased with what he felt. His breath on my neck caused me to quiver.

"Uh." I flinched slightly. This was the first thing I said since we entered the bed room.

He moved down to kissing one of my breasts while he fondled the other one. Then he advanced to moving his body up and down, rubbing his genitals externally against mine. Judging by the escalation in passion that he indulged me with, I knew that he wasn't going to be able to wait much longer. Right about the time I thought that, he reached for a condom.

"You won't need that," I said.

"What?" he asked.

"I've been on the Depo shot since we started dating."

"Are, are you sure?" he asked me, and then he held his breath as he waited for my answer.

"I'm sure."

He put the condom down, exhaled deeply and went back to kissing my lips. I watched his face as he kissed me. So much passion in his expression. He looked like he was barely in control. He stopped kissing me and whispered to me, "Are you ready?"

I instinctively grabbed his shoulders and whispered, "Yeah."

He inserted himself into me, and I gasped harder than I had in my entire life. I went from grabbing his shoulders hard to wrapping my arms around him tightly like a bear hug. Every muscle in my body was tense. He let me hold onto him tight as he gently moved inside me. I wondered how he could move at all with me holding him as tight as I did. He moaned so softly and moved his body in slow rhythm with the music.

He continued to move gently for quite some time. My legs were straight, my body was rigid, and I clung him so tight. I tried so hard to relax. It was a mind battle. I was able to relax only a little when I focused on my breathing. After a while, he whispered to me, "Are you okay?"

"I think so," I replied. "I can't relax. I just can't relax." He pressed his lips against mine and continued to move inside of me. After several moments of this, my body relaxed a whole level. I was still really tense, but it was a quick, noticeable change. Then Ben started using his tongue in my mouth. I relaxed another level, and then one more right after that. He continued French-kissing me, and I inadvertently squeezed him with my vagina. "Ah!" I yelped from the pain of it.

"Uhh!" Ben let out a deep moan and stopped moving. He buried his head into the pillow, just next to mine, and tried to control his breathing. I lay there afraid that he wasn't going to be able to control himself. Finally, he started moving slowly again.

He resumed kissing my lips. I was just getting used to this when he said to me, "I'm gonna go a little deeper."

"Deeper!?" I asked in dismay.

"Yeah. I haven't been giving you my full length."

"Oh fuck!" I said with full apprehension. Ben smirked at my reaction. I tensed up again.

"No, no, angel. That's not going to help anything," he said as he continued to give me half of his length.

"I like when you call me that," I confessed.

"It's so true. You were sent from heaven to save me." He kissed me deeply for several moments, and then he gave me his full length.

"Ahh! Oh my God!" I clutched to his shoulders and back for dear life.

"You got this, angel," he said confidently. Despite the full penetration, he was still being gentle, although it didn't feel like it at the time. He moaned in pleasure as I occasionally let out painful and exasperated noises.

Soon Ben's movements changed from fluid to a little choppy, with sporadic changes in speed and depth. He was clearly about to lose control. My body tensed up 100% and I squeezed him inside of me again. I yelled in pain simultaneously with Ben's moan of pleasure. I hoped he was almost done. Just like I called it, he lost control and was giving me his full length with a pelvic thrust at the end.

I shrieked in pain and quickly moved my hands down to his hips to try to keep him from going deeper, but it was futile. He buried his face in the pillow to muffle his moans, which were not so soft now. No! Those sexy sounds were the only thing helping me to tolerate this. I was sweating and still wincing in pain, but I refused to tell him to stop or even slow down.

In between painful outbursts, I finally said, "Ben, move the pillow! Just get rid of it!" He quickly did so without asking questions, and he continued on, with my hands still on his pelvis as I fought for some control on his depth. Good. Moving the pillow worked. I could hear him again. I concentrated on his sounds and I let out my first sound of a little pleasure–pleasure from hearing him moan. He caught the difference and immediately remembered how I love to hear his voice.

He instinctively slowed down and whispered in my ear, "I love you, Rick. I love you so much." I let out more small sounds of pleasure in between the ones of pain. "You're mine forever." I quivered beneath him and loosened up a little. He again moaned with this pleasurable feeling. "It gets better in time, baby. Just hang in there. You got this, angel," he whispered to me. After that, he slid his hands under my back and grabbed my shoulders, pulling down on my body for better leverage. It was all I could do to not scream in pain or yell at him to stop.

Instead, I yelled in between my painful moans, "Keep talking to me, please!" I was then grimacing with every painful thrust. Tears ran down my face, but it was okay because I knew he was almost done.

"You're so amazing. I'm never going to leave you. I'll take care of you. I'm yours, forever. Ah, ah, uh! My angel!" Finally, he came. I was so relieved that it was over. He laid there on top of me and kissed me for quite some time before he got up. "You're my lifeline, Rick," he said sincerely. "I was drowning in a sea of loneliness, but you rescued me."

The idea of me rescuing him was powerfully ironic. More tears fell from my eyes onto the bed beneath me. I put my hand on his cheek and gently rubbed my thumb over his lips, trying to comprehend what he had just said. He kissed me passionately again and then removed himself from me. There was so much blood on the towel, more than I was expecting, but what did I know!? Practically nothing. He helped me up to the bathroom because I couldn't walk well or even stand up straight. He started the bathtub for me and left me to my own devices.

I should've felt ashamed for fornicating, but I didn't. I was planning on waiting until we were married, but in my anger and disregard for God, I changed my mind. Ben may have actually waited for me. That's probably why he got so creative with me physically, knowing that I originally wanted to wait. As I sat in the bath, I talked to God in my head for a brief second, "Go ahead and tell Dad. I don't give a fuck." I was certain that God was going to tell on me and that there'd be family drama as a result.

I had trouble getting to sleep, knowing that Ben had to go back to work and I'd be alone the next day. The thought punched me in the stomach, but regardless, I slept well. It felt so good to have his arms wrapped around me. His body warmth compelled me to sleep.

I awoke when Ben got up to shower. I got up to get him coffee and breakfast. I walked around the kitchen bent over a little, still unable to stand up straight and still bleeding from the night before. Because Ben got ready quickly and I was moving slowly, I was only just finishing up in the kitchen when he walked in. He looked touched that I had gotten up early for him. I forced myself to stand up straight when he walked in.

He walked up to me, hugged me, and kissed my forehead. "How do you feel?"

I'm sure the answer was obvious, but I down-played how sore I was to save his feelings. "I'm okay," I said. He grabbed the back of my neck and pulled me close to him for a deep, passionate kiss on the lips.

After we disengaged from our kiss, he said, "It gets better, baby. A lot better." He held me against his chest for a bit.

"I love you, Ben," I said with my head resting on his chest and my arms around his waist.

"No ma'am. I love you," he said as he rocked me back and forth in an ornery fashion. I let out a one-syllable laugh that was muffled from my cheek being pressed against his chest.

Chapter 33: Moving In.

The previous day with Ben was one of the longest good days of my life. I had so many long bad days. My thoughts ranged dynamically from being so happy and in love, to being so sad and in deep despair at the loss of Evie and at knowing my God failed me. And let's don't forget about my anger and fits of rage. The good news–I hadn't broken anything since the mirror incident. My forearm healed nicely despite all of the riding I had done.

I knew that I couldn't see Dad and Mom my second day back with the way I was moving around. I knew they'd question me, and I wasn't in the mood to lie, so I decided to lay low for a while. I did talk to them on the phone for a bit, however. I told them I was a little under the weather from all of the riding, which didn't seem like a lie to me. Surprisingly, our chat went over well. So God hadn't told on me. I wondered why. I suspected that He was waiting for the right time. I didn't dwell on it because I had too many other things on my mind.

It was an extremely uncomfortable motorcycle ride back to my place. If anyone saw the way I was moving, I could certainly pass it off as my legs being sore from my cross-country trip. I unpacked my things and became really emotional when I got to my notebook. I reviewed some of the pages and wondered if Evie would be disappointed with what I had written so far. I missed her so. I thought about how much in love I was with Ben, and I became angry that Evie only knew the affections of assholes and never found true love. Once again, I thought about how close we were getting, and how our relationship would have blossomed into a great one. A *deep* sorrow swept over me. I dislodged a long, loud, body-fatiguing sob as I knelt down on the floor next to my bean bag. I cradled my arms and rubbed them as I rocked back and forth on my knees. I choked several times on the mucous that built up in my sinuses from my wailing. I don't know how long I broke down for, but the severity of my mourning caused a complete depletion of my energy.

After becoming exhausted from my emotional discharge, I collapsed further into the bean bag. I lay there in a fetal position for what felt like hours. My head hurt so bad that I didn't want to move. I became weary and vexed that the pain didn't seem to lighten up with rest, so I crawled over to my purse and looked for my nearly empty bottle of Xanax. I momentarily weighed the benefits and consequences of taking one mid-day because of how dizzy they made me. Then I hastily took one. I crawled over to the kitchen and stood up with the help of the countertop. I fumbled for my nearly empty bottles of wine, whiskey, and vodka (pretty much everything I had in my house), and I drank one bottle after another. I put on Porcupine Tree and let the melodies sweep me away to a place with less pain and heartache. I listened to the sad lyrics of the artist and felt bad for him momentarily, instead of feeling bad for myself.

Just before I passed out, I wondered if Ben was thinking about me. Then my thoughts transitioned to my parents. I wondered if they were doing okay. Did they wallow in pain, seeking comfort in ways they shouldn't like I had been doing, or did their faith and commitment to each other keep them from crumbling to pieces? I knew Dad and Mom better than that. Did I really need to wonder?

The last thing I remembered before things grew dark was Evie's conversation with me right before she died. The one where she said that she knew that she would go to heaven if Jesus didn't heal her. This was the first time I held onto something positive regarding her passing. Where would I be right then if I didn't have that? I was in so much pain. I couldn't imagine hurting more, but that's exactly where I'd be if I believed that she went to hell. This was the first time in a good while that I had been thankful for anything other than having Ben in my life.

I dreamt of Ben. I heard him call my name. He was trying to wake me up, but I was so tired. Why wouldn't he just let me sleep? I gave him a leave-me-alone look and drifted back to sleep. I kept feeling and hearing disturbances around me such as tremors on the floor from abrupt walking, things zipping and unzipping, and the car door slamming. I'd flinch at the noise and then immediately fall back to sleep. Finally, Ben starting tapping my face aggressively with his hand. I angrily defended myself. He looked upset or hurt; I couldn't tell which.

"Rick, wake up!" I just realized that I wasn't dreaming, but there was no way I was about to wake up and stay awake. He scooped me up and carried me to the car. I looked disheveled. I opened my eyes one last time and glanced at his blurry countenance as he put my seat belt on me. "You're moving in with me," he said firmly. He put my pillow on my lap just before he shut the car door. I was unable to reply. That was the last thing I remembered for the night.

The next morning, Ben woke me up early. "Rick, get up. I need to talk to you." He was dressed for work. I fought to sit up against the headboard with my hangover battling my every movement. Ben sat down by my legs and held my hand. "What happened last night?"

I was so tired of this question and he'd only asked it twice now. His irritated tone with asking me this hurt me more than his stupid question did. What did he think happened!? Did he think that I was completely over everything!?

My heart raced and my face turned several shades of red. My voice trembled in anger when I said, "What are you talking about? It hasn't even been three months!"

"Do you want me to stay home from work today?" he asked with a slightly improved tone.

I pulled my hand away from his and scoffed. "I don't need you to babysit me."

He sat on the bed a few more seconds. He rubbed his hand on the back of his neck, fully exasperated, but he remained quiet. Then he got up slowly and started to walk to the door. "No," I thought, "I can't have you mad at me. My whole life would be destroyed!"

"Ben, wait!" I begged, and then I burst into tears. "I, I'm sorry." He turned around, walked back to the bed, and sat down beside me. "Please don't be mad. You're, the only thing, keeping, me going." I tried to control my breaths. I put my hand over my chest, trying to coax it to stop hurting.

He sat down beside me and held me. "Just breathe," he said kindly. "Just breathe." He put my head against his chest and stroked my hair. His warm hands on my body slowly pacified me. After a few minutes, my breathing normalized and my heart rate came back in control.

"I can stay home today. Just say the word."

"No. I'll be okay."

"I don't know that you will. You never used to drink this much."

"It's just temporary. Just to help me get through this—pain." I put my hand in between my face and his shirt to make sure my tears didn't moisten his work clothes.

"Maybe you should go back to work early to keep your mind off of things."

We were silent for several moments. "I would have to go back to the doctor and get my FMLA shortened."

"Yeah," he agreed.

"I could start with calling my clients and seeing if they want me back," I added.

"That sounds like a great place to start," he assured me.

"I'll, I'll make those phone calls today, including a call to the doctor."

"Good. I'm going to call you at lunch. You better answer the phone or I'm coming right home." I nodded to acknowledge his threat.

The morning eked by. The doctor couldn't get me in until early next week. I lay on the couch and watched movie after movie with tired tears streaming down my eyes. I had some wine after breakfast, but I made sure to keep it minimal so that I could get the phone when Ben called.

It was so great to hear his voice. He told me that we were meeting my parents for supper after he got off from work. I felt like he was also telling me to be sober without saying those words directly. I was eager to see my folks. It'd be the first time I'd see them after I got back from my trip. I asked Ben some questions just to keep him talking. How was work going? What time would he be home? That's all I had but, fortunately, he kept talking. He asked me if I called the doctor. He was disappointed to hear that I had to wait about a week to get in, but he lightened the mood a little toward the end of the call by asking me what I was wearing.

I giggled and replied, "Cookie Monster PJs."

"Mmmm, those are my favorite. I can't wait to chomp those off of you." I giggled again. "I should probably get going," he said. "Oh, could you do me a favor today?"

"Sure."

"Could you do the dishes and maybe vacuum?" He was asking me this to keep me busy so that I wouldn't wallow in despair and drink. I wasn't that naïve.

"Of course, love."

"See ya soon, babe."

It was good to see Dad and Mom at the restaurant. They couldn't disguise their concern regarding my apparent weight loss as I approached them, but they both gulped it down as I grew closer for a hug. I hugged them both tight. They each held me a long time. I heard a very slight wince in pain as Dad's hands caressed the ribs on my back. It physically hurt him to hold my anorexic body. After we said our hellos and sat down to order, Ben nonchalantly smoothed over my parent's concerns regarding my weight loss by mentioning what a good cook he was and by promising them that he'd make sure I started eating better.

All in all, dinner seemed to be going well. It had been over two months since I had seen my folks, and I missed them so. Somehow I pulled off normal ambulation, hiding that fact I had lost my virginity. Dad seemed to be in good spirits, so I knew that God still hadn't ratted me out.

After we finished our meal, our conversation took a serious turn. Ben said to Dad and Mom, "I wanted to let you know that I love your daughter very much. I believe that we are soulmates, and we plan to marry in the future." My heart danced. He had never actually told me that he was going to marry me, although I assumed that's what he meant when he told me at the café that he knew I'd be his "forever." He continued on with, "I invited you to dinner to let you know that I made Rick move in with me." My jaw dropped wide open. You could hear a pin drop. I was in complete shock. I angrily stared at Ben while carefully avoiding eye contact with Dad and Mom. I thought that somehow we were going to keep that a secret. I even planned to keep paying rent on my empty house to maintain a little harmony. Ben went on, "She has turned me down several times before due to her religious beliefs, but I don't think she should be by herself right now. She's been drinking more than she should." He had genuine concern and love in his voice. I knew that he was doing this so that Mom and Dad wouldn't give me grief about moving in with him, and so that we didn't have to keep it a secret. But he should have told me what he was going to do! I had been through so much emotionally that I didn't need any added shock to my nerves!

My eyes filled with tears. I hesitantly looked at Dad for a second and then at Mom. They both remained shocked and silent. I could see sadness or pain, I'm not sure which, and concern in their faces. They really didn't know that we were moving in together either. Maybe God didn't care enough about me anymore to tell on me. I stood up abruptly and accidentally knocked over my chair. I bent over to reach into Ben's pocket to grab the keys. I hastily made my way to the car, not having said a word. Somehow, I made it to the car before I broke down in tears. I sat there on the passenger's seat sobbing while I waited for Ben to leave the restaurant.

After several minutes, I saw Ben walking toward the car in the rear-view mirror. I wiped away my tears and forced myself to stop crying. I leaned my head on the car window and sat with my arms folded across my body to comfort myself. Ben sat down in the driver's seat and looked at me not looking at him. He put his hand on my knee for several seconds. We sat there silently for another minute. Good choice. Anything he would've said at this point would have only angered me more. We drove home in silence.

When we got home, I marched inside and grabbed my wine bottle–forget the glass. I locked myself in the bathroom and ran the bath water. I took a very hot, long bubble bath. I was a third of the way through the bottle when I imagined how worried Ben must be. Maybe he was thinking, "What if she passes out in the water? I can't help her if the door is locked." I sighed a long, heavy sigh and had mercy on him by getting out of the tub and cracking the door. I thought maybe that would ease his mind. I returned to my bath and wine.

I was so angry, but I felt somewhat relieved at the same time. I felt bad for my parents, but I was too emotionally drained to perseverate on it any more. I finished my bath and bottle of wine with a free mind. When I finally came out of the bathroom, Ben was already in bed. I stumbled across the room to the other side of the bed and flopped down next to him. I moved into a spoon position behind him and put my arm across his stomach with my hand resting on his chest. I buried my forehead in his back. He grabbed my hand and held it tight on his chest and he let out a choppy sigh. I felt like he received my silent communication: "Even though I'm mad at you, I can't make it one day without you." And I received his as well: "Thank you for not holding a grudge, even though you're mad at me. I did what I thought was best."

The next day, I awoke to the sun rays piercing through the curtains. Ben was awake and holding me. I jumped up in bed and said, "You're late for work!"

"I have today off." That was code for, "I took the day off to be with you."

"You do, huh?" I said with a hint of sarcasm.

"Yeah, I do." He smiled.

I changed my tone to a pleasant one. "Good," I whispered just before I kissed him. He wrestled me back onto the bed and kissed my neck playfully as I squealed. I jostled him off of my neck and said, "What are we going to do today!?"

"I can think of a few good things," he said as he friskily grabbed my breasts. I laughed and shoved him off of me. Then I ran to the living room and returned with my purse. I pulled out my breath spray and squirted some in my mouth and some in Ben's. Then I quickly removed my clothes. Ben followed suit. His eyes glowed with anticipation. I lunged on him and started kissing and groping him. He hungrily returned my affection.

After several minutes of intense kissing and groping, I sat up on him and began rubbing myself back and forth on his dick, just like he did to me several nights ago. He ran his hands down my sides and began moving with me. This feeling quickly went from feeling good to feeling great. I went from being moist to being quite wet. Ben did something to my libido that no one else could ever do. I took his breath away when I carefully mounted him. I'm sure he was surprised by this, knowing that I was still very sore from two days ago. I winced and quickly leaned forward onto my hands, which landed by Ben's shoulders. Sitting upright was just too painful.

"I can roll you over if this is too much for you," he said.

"I think I can figure this out. Give me a second." I kept my weight forward on my hands, and I began moving up and down very cautiously. I quickly learned at what depth to stop.

There was something very intimidating about being on top. Ben studied me intently. He watched my body, my face, everything. There was just enough distance between us that I felt like I was under a spotlight. It felt like he even looked into my soul. He had the sexiest look of desire on his face. This turned me on even more, and I tried to go deeper to please him–and boy did it. So did my erratic breathing that accompanied my movements. At one point, I went a little too deep. Ben let out his first moan and I lurched forward in pain, crashing my chest against his. I rested there for a moment to recover. I slowly sat back up and rested my hands by Ben's shoulders again. He ran his hands up both sides of my torso and to my breasts. He looked at me lustfully as he did so. I turned my head sideways and let my hair fall forward to cover my face.

"No, Rick. Don't hide from me." He reached for my chin and turned my head forward. Then he seductively ran his thumb across my bottom lip. An increase in moisture streamed out of me, and I inadvertently squeezed him tight.

"Uhh!" It was the most pleasurable sound that I got out of him that morning so far. I smiled at this. He ran his hand down from my lips to around my neck as I continued slowly up and down. I tried to go just a little deeper, but I just couldn't. I winced in pain again and stopped for a second, and then resumed my cautious movements. My face and neck started to flush, and I began to sweat from the combination of pleasure and pain.

"Rick, do whatever you want. Just have fun. You don't have to go hard."

"I want to make you feel good," I said as my forehead continued to bead up.

"There's no way you could fail at that. Trust me," he said with a smile. I laughed and inadvertently squeezed him tight again in the process. He let out another loud, pleasurable sound as I flinched a little from the pain, which wasn't nearly as bad as when I went too deep. He grabbed me by my shoulders and pulled me down face to face with him, and he said, "If you do that too many more times, I don't know if I can control myself. I don't know what I might do to you." He was dead serious and had so much passion in his face and voice. Was that a dare or a threat? I kissed his lips most passionately, and then I gave him another intense rebellious squeeze.

He was right. It was like a switch flipped inside of him, and he went crazy on me. He grabbed my ass and began thrusting up and down, pulling me down on him with each upward thrust. I started screaming in pain, and my body tensed up. The tension only caused my pain to intensify unbearably. I was in a position where I couldn't possibly resist him or even slow him down. If I had pushed him away and sat upright, it would've surely be devastating for me, but also he was just too strong for me to do that. Instead, I lay there on top of him with my legs bent up and my chest pressed up against his, focusing on trying to relax my body. I thought to myself, "I should've listened to him. I won't make that mistake again." Relaxing did help with the pain some, but I had to focus intently on my breathing to make it through this. Ben made animalistic groans that sounded much like myself when I had a clit orgasm. Despite the pain, I gushed with feminine juices only when I focused on his sounds of pleasure. I imagined that his balls were dripping wet and that thought pleased me so much that I became even more saturated. He held me tight for two final thrusts as he came inside me. We were both short of breath, and I was dripping sweat.

I watched Ben gradually came back to himself as he tried to catch his breath. I could see that his return was not immediate, rather it was a process. I was amazed at my discovery. He turns from Dr. Jekyll to Mr. Hyde in an instant with the right sexual trigger, but he returns to Dr. Jekyll from Mr. Hyde via a slower transformation. Finally his eyes met mine. He grabbed my face with his hands and wiped away some of my sweat. The he said with genuine concern, "Are you okay?"

"Yeah, yeah. I think so," I said with a hoarse voice. I lied. That was unbelievably painful. "I might need some water though," I added. Once I awkwardly dismounted him, we noticed quite a bit of blood. "Is that normal?" I asked.

"I-I don't know. I imagine so. It was only your second time and we went pretty hard."

"Yes, of course." I walked toward the bathroom bent over with my hand on my lower abdomen, looking even worse than I did the first time we had sex.

"Do you need any help?" Ben asked. He walked up to me and supported my arm with his hand. He looked upset at my posturing, because I just couldn't stand up straight.

"No, I'm good." I'm not really sure what he could've done for me. I paused in the bedroom doorway and said, "That was amazing, right? I mean really, really amazing?" I seemed to need some confirmation. He laughed so loud and ran his hands through his hair.

"It was nuclear!" The fact that he reacted that way made it easier for me to tolerate the pain.

Ben beat me to the kitchen and had coffee and French toast waiting for me. I slowly made my way over to the table. Ben had pulled my chair out for me when I got closer. I sat down so slowly. I wasn't being dramatic. I was really a mess. He kissed my cheek after he helped push me in. As we started on our breakfast, Ben said to me, "Scott is dropping by this morning to let me borrow his truck. I figured we could pick up the rest of your stuff today. I'll do all the lifting, of course." I nodded unsure whether Ben saw me or not. It was a nice gesture, but a necessary one, considering I couldn't even walk well.

Seconds after he had said that, Scott pulled in. He knocked at the door and Ben answered it. "Hey, man. Come on in. Would you like some coffee and French toast?"

"I'll have a quick cup of coffee, thanks." Scott sat across from me at the table as Ben served him a cup.

"Rick, I'm very sorry to hear about your sister," Scott said sincerely.

"Me too," I said just before taking a sip of my coffee.

"So, you're moving in, huh?" he asked.

"Yeah. That was Ben's decision," I said as a matter of fact. Ben peered over at me while he poured his blueberry syrup.

"Well, I'm sure it's for the best," Scott said. I tensed my jaw and squeezed my cup, realizing that Ben had told his brother of the circumstances that led to me moving in. "Nice do, Ricky," Scott said teasingly to lighten the mood. Scott hadn't seen my punk rocker bangs and wild colors yet. "Jesus! It makes you look like a minor!" He laughed heartily and was pretty amused with himself. Ben sent him daggers, but Scott didn't notice. Scott did, however, notice my smirk. Consequently, he went on, "Thirteen is my final answer!" He laughed even harder. I couldn't help but smile bigger.

"That's the plan. I'm trying to get Ben sent to jail." I smiled as Scott laughed on. Ben smiled at the notion that Scott and I were getting along.

"Will you be at it all day?" Scott asked, making polite chit chat.

I scoffed. "No, I just have a table with chairs, a bean bag, a sofa, kitchenware and some clothes left. That and a mattress."

"You don't have any other furniture?" Scott inquired with a hint of confusion.

I sighed a little before I continued. "I sold it to take Evie to the Grand Canyon. It was worth it."

"Wow," he marveled. "That's pretty great," he said after some thought. "I'm sure she really appreciated that."

"She did," I replied. I gulped hard, trying not to tear up.

Scott tried to elevate the mood again. "Well, Dad is excited that you are moving in," he said cheerfully. "He's already counting how many grandchildren he's going to have." I produced a small courteous smile. Ben nervously rubbed his hand on the back of his neck–his telltale sign of stress.

Scott finished the last of his coffee and said, "Well, bro, I gotta jet off to work. You know I'm gonna bring her back dirty, right?" he grinned.

"I wouldn't expect anything less. No dents please." Scott got up and took his cup to the sink. "Thanks again for the truck, man," Ben said as Scott headed toward the door.

"No problem, bro." Scott turned to me just before leaving and said, "Again, Ricky, I'm very sorry. I can't imagine the pain you're feeling." He turned from me and looked at Ben affectionately, trying not to imagine life without his little brother. I nodded acknowledging his kind words. "Later, bro," Scott said as he walked out the door with Ben's car keys in his hands.

Ben and I ate mostly in silence. As we were finishing our second cup of coffee, he said to me, "So, do you want to talk about last night?"

"Nope," I said, giving him a sharp glance. I returned to sipping my coffee. I stewed for several moments and then blurted out, "You should've told me ahead of time."

"If I had told you ahead of time, you would've tried to talk me out of it."

I was angry at his truthful words, but I said nothing at first. He was right, of course. At last, I said, "My nerves…I-I just can't take…" I couldn't finish either of those statements without losing control. Instead I looked down at the table, clenched my jaw and hands, and successfully fought back the tears. There was another brief silence between us.

Finally, Ben said, "I'm sorry, Rick. I didn't mean to hurt you." That was enough for me. I nodded, accepting his apology.

Despite my obvious abrupt changes in mood that morning, I was so glad it was Friday and that Ben had the day off. This meant that we had a three-day weekend together.

On our way to my place, Ben turned the radio on for me. He tuned in to K-Love, a previous favorite of mine. A very good song was on that I used to like called "It is Well with My Soul." It was at the beginning where it says, "When peace like a river attendeth my soul..." I quickly turned off the radio.

"We don't have to listen to the radio right now if you don't want to," I said. I felt like he was testing me, trying to see how bad off I was with my religion.

"Naw, it's all right. Whatever you want," he said.

We sat in silence for a short spell, but then something came to me. "Ben, I need to pay part of rent if I'm going to live with you."

"I don't think that'll be necessary," he quickly replied.

"All the same, it won't feel right to me if I don't share the expenses. I don't want to feel like a free-loader."

"I don't think *I* would feel right if you did pay me."

"We have to think of something." I sighed. Maybe he didn't think my offer was sincere, or maybe his words were true. "What if I paid for utilities, water, and other things like that directly? Then I wouldn't be paying you." He paused to consider my offer.

"I think we could work something out like that," he answered. I was relieved.

During our time packing together, I grew sad about having to move from the country into a small town. I shared my feelings with Ben. "You know, I'm really going to miss living in the country. I loved going over to Dad's and riding Diamond and Priscilla with him. I rode my dirt bike in the woods back there often. It's just that is was an amazing lifestyle."

Ben stopped packing for a moment and came over and kissed me. "Yes, but look what you are getting in return. Not *too* shabby of a deal." He smiled at me, and I smiled back.

"No, not *too* shabby at all," I admitted.

Later that day, I called Dad. It was the first time we talked since the incident at the restaurant. I was nervous.

"Hey, Dad. How are you doing?"

"I'm good. How are you?" he asked cordially.

"I'm good. I'm good. Um, I haven't gotten to see you and Mom much, with me just getting back and all, and I was wondering if, if you wanted Ben and me to come over sometime to, uh, visit." I gulped on the other end of the phone, waiting for his reply. I wasn't sure if he would hold a grudge against me for moving in with Ben. I didn't think I could handle that; I was so fragile right then. I held my breath until he answered.

"That sounds good. Why don't you both come over Sunday afternoon for lunch? I'll have Mother fix us up a good meal." I breathed again, and my anxiety diminished.

"I'll bring something of course," I paused for a moment. "Dad, I don't think I could handle..." I paused again. "C-could we not talk about me moving in with Ben while we are there? I-I mean I already know, w-what you think about it," I said, chopping up my sentences.

I hated how I came into stuttering since Evie had passed, during anxious and angry moments, I mean. I squeezed my eyes closed tight, waiting for his reply.

"I think we can do that, since you *already* know what we think about that." He said "already" almost like he was making fun of me. He had compassion on me and was trying to lighten the mood. I appreciated that so much that I teared up.

We talked a bit longer on the phone. I told him how I was looking forward to going horseback riding with him in the near future. I confided in him about how disappointing my trip was and how it didn't seem to help me heal any. There was no hiding the tears then. He told me how Jesus could bring me peace, if I let Him. I rolled my eyes at the irony. I was mad at Jesus for not healing Evie–for letting her die. So why would I ask *Him* for peace, or anything else for that matter? Funny, at the time I didn't think of it this way, but my question should have been, "Why would He give me peace when I was acting the way that I was?" To which Dad would've replied, "Because He is full of mercy and grace."

Ben and I watched movies together the rest of the day. It was relaxing. There was no sexual tension. He could obviously tell that we wouldn't be having sex for a while with the way that I was moving around. Oh, and the blood was partly from me starting my period. I was irregular with being on Depo, so I just never knew when it was going to hit. I was never so thankful for my period in all my life. We needed to take it down a notch for my body to recover, and now I had at least a couple of days.

Chapter 34: Basketball Bet.

Saturday was day two of our three-day weekend. My spirits were high knowing this. "What are we going to do today?" I asked Ben bright-eyed, as if he were supposed to entertain me.

"Well, we could go to the park and shoot some hoops," he replied. I thought about that for a few seconds and then smiled.

"Okay, let's do it."

It was overcast that day in Ohio. Imagine that. I didn't mind the frequently droll Ohio weather because my eyes were always exceptionally light sensitive. I wore my ball cap and shades despite the mostly cloudy weather.

Ben surprised me at how good of a shot he was because he didn't play basketball in high school and he didn't have great coordination in general. I was a good shot as well, but I had lots of training. Our leisurely activity quickly became a competition. I was in no condition to play one-on-one, so we resorted to playing Twenty-One and Horse. Now that was a tight competition. On our last game, Ben proposed a wager.

"Do you want to make this one interesting?" he said with a smile.

"What do you mean?" I asked, narrowing my eyes at him.

He walked up close to me and said, "If I win, I get to choose the next sexual position, and no matter what it is, you have to agree to it." How twisted of him, especially since I was not that experienced and because I was still hurting from yesterday.

"Okay. When *I* win, I get to pick something sexual too. And I have no idea what that would be right now. It could be to refuse something that you want, or to pick something that *I* want. And I have a whole year to decide what and when this thing occurs. This thing that I can't be specific about right now." Ben laughed at my string of awkward sentences and the weird facial expressions I made that accompanied them, which openly declared that I knew how ridiculous I sounded.

He got right in my face and said to me with a determined look, "You're on."

"On top? Well, we'll see about that. You can't be making demands right now. It's too early to say." I thought I was being funny.

He gave me a look, advising me that I wasn't as clever as I thought I was. I smiled at how gorgeous he looked with whatever expression he was giving me.

We decided on another game of Twenty-One. It was tight; we had our game-faces on. There was a lot of smack-talk during this game. Ben was in the lead and feeling cocky, so he said to me, "When I win, I think I'm gonna do you from behind and use your piggy-tails as reins." My heart skipped a beat as I envisioned this. How was he so perverted and creative? Despite the fact that I was still sore from yesterday morning, I became unsettled from his description. I was silent for a spell. He had caught me off guard again, and he savored those moments. He walked around behind me and wrapped his hand around my pony-tail and gave it a firm tug. I turned around quickly and shoved him back. He snickered a little.

"When *I* win, I may or may not let you do that," I retorted. I made my next foul shot and was back in the lead. Then Ben made his next foul shot. We went back and forth, changing leads constantly.

"Why are you trying so hard? You don't want to win," he said.

"I don't ever back down from a challenge, and I *do* want to win, actually. Maybe I have something better in mind." Ben raised his eyebrows at the notion of that.

Despite my best efforts, Ben squeaked a win by me. He jogged after the ball and then back to me. I was lost in thought for a moment, noted by the distant look on my face and the way I held my shirt collar closed a little. I quickly tried to re-group as Ben approached me. I swallowed hard and nonchalantly changed my hand position, hoping he didn't notice how fragile I just looked. My heart pounded hard as he smirked at me.

He leaned in and kissed me on the cheek. Then he said in a soft, sexy voice, "Don't worry, angel. I'll give you one more day to recuperate." His breath on my neck and his assertive words caused me to quiver. I swallowed hard again and remained silent. He took my hand, and we walked back to the house, fingers intertwined.

Chapter 35: Visit With Parents.

I was eager to see my folks Sunday afternoon, but I also had a fair amount of anxiety about it. Would Dad stay true to his promise? Of course. Could he get Mom to do the same? I wasn't so sure. Obviously, they knew that I hadn't been to church since Evie passed. (We did go to the same church.) I bet that they didn't know I had no intention of going back. I hoped that conversation wouldn't come up during our visit.

I was quiet all morning except when Ben spoke to me. On the ride over to my parent's house, Ben said, "Just relax. Everything's gonna be all right."

I raised my eyebrows and lowered them quickly as if to say, "How can you be so sure?" Then I turned my head away to look out the window. He wasn't there at the cataclysmic event that consumed our house when Dad and Mom found out that Evie moved in with Johnny. I didn't tell him the details, just that it was bad. I didn't feel like talking about it, so I continued to silently look out the window. How could I have broken my own vow to not put our entire family, including myself, through that again? I didn't care what God thought. I just didn't want Dad and Mom to hurt any more.

When we entered the house, we were sweetly greeted by Mom and Dad; however, Grandma June didn't greet us well. She intentionally ignored us. I was angry that Dad didn't mention she was coming. I wouldn't have come at all if I knew she was going to be there. She had a history of having harsh words, all in the name of Jesus. Regardless, I guess I expected her to receive me a little better than she did. She hadn't, in fact, seen me since the funeral. She was probably holding that against me too. I'm sure my folks told her that I hadn't been around because of my motorcycle trip. Maybe they told her that I just moved in with Ben. Maybe she was rude and ignored us because she didn't know what all I was going through emotionally. Maybe she knew and didn't care.

Mom had coffee ready, and we sipped on our drinks while she made the finishing touches on lunch. It felt good being in their home again. I missed my parents so. I was starting to feel emotional, and I struggled with containment. Dad turned the football game on, and it felt nice. Football season spared me from having to listen to Christian music, like we'd done so many Sunday lunches before. I firmly told myself that I'd handle the music without a fuss if need be, but I didn't really know if I could follow through with that.

Dad, Ben, and I chatted casually while we watched the game. Dad decided to head back into the kitchen to check on Mom to see if she needed help. Ben was sitting on the love seat watching the game, I stood next to Ben with my coffee in hand, and Grandma sat in the recliner chair on the other side of the room. That's the moment that Grandma decided to blindside me.

"Well, Ericka, I didn't figure *you* to make as poor of decisions as Evelyn did. God rest her soul." These were, in fact, her first words to me since the funeral!

I winced in pain at her comment as if I had been punched in the chest. My eyes went a little blurry as the rage inside of me quickly ensued. I felt a pressure around my head, like a vice was being tightened. I looked around the room, waiting for it to come back into focus. I felt unsteady. Finally, I was able to make eye contact with Ben, who was sitting on the edge of his seat with a very concerned expression. I tilted my head to the side toward the door, indicating to Ben that we were leaving. Ben kept on my heels while I slowly walked toward the door. On my way out, I haphazardly put my cup down on the desk by the door, nearly missing it entirely. Ben steadied the cup and kept it from falling to the floor. My thoughts were not about myself, only about Evie. How could she talk so jaggedly about my dearly departed sister!? And how could she do this so close to her passing!? Her statement may be true, but it was in poor taste and poor timing!

Dad came around the corner, fully hearing what June had said but not fully aware of my reaction to her boorish utterings. Dad saw Ben catch my coffee cup and noticed his distress. He rushed over to try to appease us. Ben stopped to talk with him in the doorway, but I continued on, not hearing their words. My ears began to ring as I descended the steps. I felt like I was moving in super slow motion. I touched my face, which felt like it was going numb. This sensation thrived.

On the last step, I blacked out and crumpled to the sidewalk, hitting my head and nose hard enough to leave an abrasion on each. I didn't pass out entirely, so I could just barely hear the alarms coming from Ben and Dad over the ringing in my ears. Ben rushed to me, buckled to the ground, and turned me over on his lap. My vision slowly returned. My eyes darted around, unable to focus on anything. I looked up at the sky. The ringing in my ears lightened up enough for me to hear Dad's siren.

"Oh my God! Oh, God, have mercy!" He burst into tears for a few seconds.

"Rick, are you okay!? Rick?" Ben said as he gently squeezed and shook me in his arms.

I gradually became more responsive. The more I did, the more I felt like my head was on fire. Ben helped me up off of the ground. My footing came to me slowly, like a newborn calf. By the time I was fully standing, my breathing was rapid like a rabid dog. After I was fairly steady on my feet, I pushed Ben away angrily. I had gone off into the extreme deep end.

"What the fuck!? Who the *fuck* does she think she is!? How can she talk about her like that!?" My body trembled. Ben reached for me, trying to pacify me. I pulled my arm away from him and almost fell. I staggered back and then said, "I don't feel...I can't...my head...my head's gonna explode!" I put my hands on my head and grabbed my hair. "My head's gonna explode!!" I was completely frantic. I looked to Ben for help, despite the fact that I just pushed him away and then pulled away from him. I didn't know what I expected him to do. I didn't know what to do myself. Maybe I was going to have a heart attack or a stroke. As this feeling escalated, I felt like I could drop dead at any second–from a ruptured artery or something like that. I started behaving erratically, like pulling my shirt away from neck, hyperventilating, and aggressively rubbing my face. I made strange moans of anger and pain as I did so. Dad and Mom were horrified. They never imagined that their perfect daughter could act in such a way. They've never even heard me say a curse word before. Dad started praying. Mom watched from the doorway as she held her hand over her mouth crying.

I whipped my shirt off and flung it to the ground in an attempt to alleviate the choking sensation. I stood there outside in my bra, still breathing erratically and grabbing at my hair. Ben grabbed my shoulders and shook me. "Get it out! Get it out! Punch me and get it out!" He held his hands up as if I were to box with him.

"What!?" I exclaimed, still acting erratic.

"Punch me and get it out, so your head doesn't explode!"

It sounded ludicrous, but I didn't hesitate. I punched his hand once, then twice. Hard, then harder. Fast, then faster. Then continuously. I punched and I screamed. I put everything I had into him. I continued punching and screaming until I was exhausted. I collapsed onto my knees and sobbed. Ben and Dad got on their knees beside me. I breathed in and in; I couldn't exhale. Ben lifted my head with his hands. My face was quite red. I was plagued with dizziness once again.

"Rick, watch me. Breathe like me," Ben said calmly. He looked into my eyes and breathed in through his nose slowly and out through his mouth even slower. His hands became full of the tears that burned down my face. I tried to mimic his breathing, but it was so difficult. The pain in my stomach was too much. I pulled away from him and vomited as I balanced in quadruped. Gravity assisted my tears to the ground that bathed the grass before I threw up again. I was surprised that the pain in my stomach didn't let up any. I dry heaved three more times. By then my arms were trembling. Ben caught me just as my arms gave out, saving me from landing face-first into my own emesis. He pulled me near and turned me over. I was back to looking at the sky. My breathing slowly started to normalize.

"This is how–I am." I continued to take small gasps of air in between my words. "This is how–I feel. *Crazy inside,*" I confessed to Ben and Dad in a soft hoarse voice. "I'm ready to react, or overreact. How can I go back to work?" I gnashed my teeth at the thought of it. "I could *hurt* someone. I could get fired from, from throwing a table if, if someone says something that upsets me." I felt so drained from my meltdown. I looked up at Ben and said, "I'm ready to go. Help me to the car."

"Only God can heal your heart," Dad said to me as he walked with us to the car. "Only God can give you peace. I'll keep praying for you, Ricky. I'll pray that God heals your heart and that you let Him." One could say that the last part of his sentence was little harsh, but I wasn't offended. I was too crippled by my outburst, and also there was truth in that.

Ben helped me get my shirt back on, buckled me up, and then drove me home. I slept the rest of the day. It was the last day of our three-day weekend. Before he went to bed, I tried to wake up and talk to him. I could barely open my eyes. My head felt concreted to the pillow. I mumbled to him, "Ben, I'll be all right tomorrow. Don't take off work again. I'll probably just sleep most of tomorrow."

I don't think he was comforted by my words. He lay silently with me on the bed and held me tight. I was unable to assess the situation in my debilitated state. Was he mad at me? I tried to stay awake, waiting for his reply, but I couldn't. I quickly fell back to sleep without the help of medication, and without the help of alcohol. Meltdowns are exhausting.

Chapter 36: Off to the Counselor.

Ben touched my face and said my name softly twice. I scarcely awoke with heavy eye lids. He brushed my face again with his hand. I put my hand on his and tried to focus.

"Rick. Rick. I-I'm heading to work," he said hesitantly.

"Yes, yes. I'll be okay. I promise," I mumbled. I blinked long blinks. He leaned forward and kissed my cheek. Then he exhaled heavily, for the weight of my suffering was on his shoulders. He held my hand tight for a few moments. I fought harder to keep my eyes open. "I'll be okay. Call me at lunch and I'll answer. I promise."

"Okay." He kissed my hand and then left for work.

I awoke at 9 a.m., which meant that I slept for about nineteen hours! I got up with a pounding headache. I poured myself a very hot bath and took some ibuprofen. I grieved heavily for Ben because of all that I put him through. This pain was in addition to the pain I felt from hurting my parents, and in addition to the pain that vexed me from June's hurtful words. And, of course, in addition to the pain I felt from losing Evie.

I got on the scale. I gained back two pounds of the twelve that I lost from not eating well on the road trip, which meant that I was still under 100 pounds. The sickness I was currently experiencing had me worried that I'd lose more weight. After I finished a cup of coffee, I forced myself to eat some pretzels. The phone rang as I ate. I slapped my face a couple of times and smiled widely before answering the phone. I was trying to psych myself up so that I wouldn't blow this conversation.

"Hi, Ben," I said with a forced smile.

"How are you feeling, baby?"

"I feel okay." I didn't know what else to say. There was a lull. I'm not sure that he believed me. He was smart like that.

"I'm glad to hear that," he finally said. There was another silence.

"I'm g-going to clean today. And I'll make you supper!" It was obvious that I was trying a little too hard.

"I made you lunch today. Check the fridge." He paused a minute. I felt bad that he took time to do that before work.

"Thank you," I replied softly.

"Why don't you just relax today?" he said. I sighed heavily. More silence.

"I'll just play it by ear, depending on how I'm feeling," I conceded.

"That sounds good." Silence again.

"I don't know what else to say," I said with a sigh as I adjusted my ball cap lower on my head.

"I know. We'll talk when I get home."

"Okay. I love you, Ben," I said to my angel.

"I love you too. See you tonight."

"Bye."

I hung up the phone and began to worry that Ben might start an intervention for me or something like that. How likely was that to happen? I had no idea, and my imagination ran wild.

I watched a movie and then did a bit of cleaning. Then I drank and watched another movie. My heart was heavy all day. "I can't pretend I'm okay for everyone else's sake," I thought. I was fooling myself when I theorized that maybe I could pull that off when I returned from my road trip. I irrationally worried that I might lose Ben if I didn't pretend.

I moseyed along to the refrigerator, even though I wasn't hungry. I decided that I had to make an effort for Ben's sake. Since I had moved in with Ben, I quickly realized that he was a pretty clean eater, aside from when we'd occasionally go out to eat. That had to be at least part of the reason he stayed so thin. I'm sure some of it could've been genetics. He certainly didn't take after his dad, like Scott did, and I hadn't seen any pictures of his mother, so I wasn't sure.

I kept good on my word and had the house clean with supper waiting on the table when he got home. He looked so tired, as did I.

"How was work?" I asked him while I assisted with his coat.

"Work was work," he replied.

I sat down across the table from him. We stared at each other for several long seconds. Finally, we both started talking at the same time. We both stopped at the same time too. I gave him a tired smile.

"You go first," he said.

I paused. "I-I can't pretend that I'm okay. I want to pretend that I'm okay so that I stop hurting you and everyone around me. I'm sorry. I don't want to hurt you, and I don't want to lose you." We talked with little emotion. Fatigue will do that to you.

"You're not going to lose me because that would mean I'd lose you." That felt like a profound statement to me. I finally got it: he needed me just as much as I needed him.

I reached for his hand and squeezed it in mine. Then I said, "That makes sense." After that, I never senselessly worried that I would lose Ben.

He looked at me as if he saw the revelation in my eyes. He put his other hand mine and reassured me, "We'll get through this together." After a moment of silence, he added, "We've got to do something though." I didn't know what he meant exactly. My anxiety rose.

"What then?" I asked nervously.

"Maybe you should see a counselor like Dr. Hall suggested."

I sat back in my chair rebelliously and folded my arms across my chest. I didn't think that was the answer. "Let's try to think of something else," I said. I realized my attitude immediately and assumed that Ben wouldn't appreciate it, so I changed my posture and quickly added, "But if we can't, I'll do it." That seemed to appease him. We had a lazy evening because we were both fatigued from my abnormal grieving. Ben just held me as we sat on the couch together. He watched an old western movie as I rested my head on his chest, listening to his heart beat rhythmically.

Chapter 37: Here's Johnny.

It was the day before my appointment with Dr. Hall. I was just starting to dread it. It was originally supposed to be about getting approval to return to work early, but I wasn't sure what it was about now. Was I going to see a counselor? If so, would I be going back to work or not?

I resorted to starting an exercise program to keep my mind off of it. I found an intense program online that combined cardio and core exercises. I worked up a good sweat and I felt good when I was done. I also did all of the laundry and quite a lot of cleaning. Ben's house was spotless.

Ben and I had planned on going out to eat after work, so I made myself look real good. I went all out with heavy eye makeup, lipstick, curls in my hair, and a nice casual outfit. I met Ben at the door with a big smile on my face when he arrived home from work.

"Hi, I'm ready," I said as I continued to smile.

He looked a little stunned. "Wow, okay. I'm ready too."

"Let's go. I'll drive," I said as I grabbed his keys from him. We usually traveled in Ben's car since mine was a clunker.

Things felt normal in the car. I talked about my exercise program and how that I thought this was going to help me if I stuck with it. I told him about how I planned to buy a punching bag and add boxing to my new regimen. I joked about how this purchase was essentially his fault because it was his idea to use punching as an outlet for me at Dad's house. It seemed to work well too. Ben was encouraged by my excitement, my motivation, and the fact that I was able to joke about my meltdown so soon. We listened to Chill on the way over; one of my top music choices. We headed to our fine dining destination: Bob Evans, my favorite restaurant. (I'm kind of a cheap date.) We were in such good spirits.

When I pulled in, I saw Johnny walking out of Bob Evans with a pretty girl hanging on his arm. I parked the car, got out immediately, and stomped over toward him. He didn't even see me coming. How could he not see the trail of fire behind me?

How could he not feel the ground crush beneath my feet? How could he not perceive the cataclysmic force spewing from my mouth with every exhale. Surely, the explosion in my chest could've incinerated him from thirty feet away! He didn't react in time to my warning fireball, "You stupid son of a bitch!" I already had my hand in a fist when I finished that sentence. I directly gave him a right uppercut to the abdomen that doubled him over in pain. His girlfriend shrieked. I continued with a forceful downward punch with my left fist to his face that launched him onto his hands and knees. My form was flawless– with my core tight during each punch and complete follow through of motion. "You didn't even come to her funeral! You fucking piece of shit!!" I was bent over so he could hear me loud and clear.

His girlfriend was in complete dismay and was petrified against the wall, as if I were going to hit her too. Ben caught up to me, but he didn't restrain me. Two men stopped at the door and watched carefully, trying to decide whether or not to intervene.

"What did he tell you?" I asked his girl. "That he's a widow? Yeah, he is. My sister married him. Then she got cancer, and he left her as soon as he found out!" Johnny started to move around on the ground. I bent over again and yelled, "I swear to God, if you get up while I'm still standing here, I will send you to the hospital!" He stopped moving. I turned back to his girl. "He didn't even go to her funeral." My words were lighter, as I could barely get that sentence out. "Evie didn't deserve that," I said softly to myself. I spaced out for several seconds. "Nobody deserves that!" I blared down at Johnny with my hands still clenched.

I wanted him to get up. I wanted to knock him on his ass again, but he remained still. He wouldn't even look up at me. "Good call, Johnny," I thought. "Probably the only smart thing you've done all day."

I looked up at his girl and said, "Run. Run while you can." A single tear coursed down my cheek. I turned back to Johnny for one last fireball to hurl: "If I ever see you again, you're gonna need plastic surgery! I swear it!"

I looked at the girl; she was still horrified. Then I looked at the two strangers, who nonverbally bestowed compassion on me. Ben lightly touched my shoulders from behind, trying to comfort me. Johnny was still on the ground silent. We turned around and walked back to the car. I gave Ben the keys and got in the passenger's side. I figured he didn't want me to drive in that condition. I took a deep breath. My heart still raced. I marveled at how someone under 100 pounds could drop someone Johnny's size. The element of surprise? The fury in my fists? I think it was a combination of both.

Ben got in the car and started the engine. Then he looked over at me as I still breathed heavily from all of the adrenaline pumping through my body. Finally I said, "That felt *so* good." I pressed my lips together, trying not to smile. Ben remained silent and expressionless. "Say it!" I finally said to him in an annoyed tone.

"Say what?" he asked calmly.

I put my hands up in the air and said, "Whatever it is you're thinking!" I was ready to be reprimanded.

He put his shades on, tipped his head back on the headrest, and then turned his head to look at me again. "I think he had that coming," he said sincerely.

I exhaled quickly, shocked at his words. I was swept up in a whirlwind of emotions. Ben had never looked as sexy as he did just then. I grabbed his shirt and pulled him closer to me, and then I kissed him passionately. "Let's go home and get our freak on," I demanded. In this moment, I felt a *Natural Born Killers* kind of vibe. My heart started racing again.

After Ben pulled onto the main drag, I unzipped his pants. "Whoa, whoa. What are you doing?" he asked.

"I was just going to warm you up a little."

"I, uh, don't know if that's a good idea."

"Well, let's just find out," I said. "You know the safeword." I was amused at my cleverness. I inched my hand down his pants and gently stroked him. It quickly had the desired effect. I was a little surprised that he let me do this. When we were safely out of city limits, I carefully went down on him. He gasped lightly. I thought for sure he was going to ask me to stop, but he didn't. I pleasured him gently for the remainder of the drive home. He was stone-cold silent.

It was a different story as soon as we got home. We were barely through the door when we mutually started tearing each other's clothes off. In the process, I said to Ben, "I'm calling the shots, got it?" I was making myself clear because of the bet I had lost shooting hoops with him a few days ago. He raised his eyebrows as if to say, "Oh really?" I finished by saying, "You're on top, *facing me*, because I need to see your beautiful face today. That's after some really exhilarating foreplay."

He laughed. "Sounds like you've got it all figured out."

I backed up to the bedroom wall, pulling him along. "Put your arm here," I said as I placed his forearm against the wall. "Put your hand here," I said as I placed his other hand in my hair, indicating that he was to have fist full of it. He looked intrigued. I kissed his lips and vivaciously sucked on them. Then I whispered to him, "Now I want you to fuck my mouth." He had a look of confusion or disbelief just for a second, but his disbelief vanished as I slid down the wall. I put him inside my mouth and grabbed his hips, moving him back and forth until he started moving them for me. His erratic breathing and the noises he made declared how off guard he was, but he quickly pulled himself together and transitioned to his usual soft sounds of pleasure. He was careful at first until I proved that I could handle myself. Then he started moving more aggressively. Perfect. He was doing exactly what I wanted.

I didn't account for how difficult it would be for me to breathe during pleasuring him. In order to breathe comfortably and give a great blowjob, I had to forfeit control over my saliva. It ran freely down my face and neck. I decided to come up for air occasionally, masking this break by jacking him off. He was really into this. I could tell by the intermittent crazy sounds he made and by how he'd pull my hair too tight on occasion. I refused to succumb to the pain.

I was very generous with my time. Finally, he stopped me and pulled me into standing by my hair. I was thrilled to see his face had turned a couple shades of red. He helped me wipe the saliva away from my mouth before he kissed me. "I'm gonna make that *very* worth your while." He kissed me again and then carried me over to the bed. He carelessly tossed me down, and I landed with my butt on top of a couple of pillows. He lunged on top of me and began kissing my neck and groping my breast. I tried to move the pillows because they were in an awkward place, but I was unsuccessful because Ben wouldn't let up on me. I decided to let it be. He put his other hand under my butt and slid it up to my low back and side. His hands were so warm. He then grinded his genitals up and down on mine externally. Pleasurable sounds escaped my lips as a tingling sensation down below progressed into a hard throb. He did this for a good while before he inserted himself inside of me.

Up until this time in my life, this was by far the most pleasure I had ever had. I enjoyed watching Ben's body move as fluently and powerfully as a mighty, crashing wave. I closed my eyes and could taste the salt on my tongue and feel the sand in my hair, similar to the day I collapsed at Muir Beach. I bent one leg up and moved my body perfectly with his. We ended up doing a deep grind together. It was complete ecstasy. Our moans were uninhibited. He still had his hand on my side just at the top of my pelvis. This felt so amazing, so I moved his other hand from my breast to the other side of my pelvis just to see how it felt. *Indescribable.* I found this to be something comparable to my lip fetish. Ben leaned his body back so far away from mine that he was out of arm's reach. My eyes rolled back as Ben pulled my hips toward him with each forceful grind. Something was happening or about to happen, and I didn't know what it was. I felt a little anxious.

"I-I-I don't know," I kept saying as I became more and more wet. My pussy was on fire. Was I going to lose control of my bladder? "I don't know what's happening, what's happening," I finally said. My body would alternate between tensing up and relaxing. "I don't know. I don't know!"

Ben said, "Just relax, baby. Let it happen, whatever it is." I kept trying to relax, but I would involuntarily tense up again. Ben could see the struggle in my face, so he said, "Just relax, let go, and let me love you."

"Let go and let me love you." Those were the words that caused my body to melt completely. Several moments later, fluid started gushing from my vagina. "Oh no. Oh no! Oh no, no, no!!" I cried. Soon after, my cries turned into very loud moaning. I put my hands over my face to soften my sonic booms.

"You're cumming," Ben said. "Oh yeah! You're cumming!" He grabbed my sides tighter and grinded me deeper. "Uh! Uh! Ah!" he went on. I stretched my arm out to try to push him away, but his torso was too far away for me to reach. I bent my legs up, trying to get away from him because, even though this felt so good, it also felt so wrong. This backfired, however, because he grabbed my legs and wedged them between his arms and his body. He then leaned his body back some more. I was so saturated at this point that we made a disgusting squish sound as he pounded me. I went back to holding my hands over my face, because there was no use in trying to reach him to slow him down. He continued thrusting while pulling my hips toward him. I became hoarse from all of the noise I made. It didn't seem like he was anywhere close to being done.

"You can cum! You can cum now!" I said exasperated. "I can't take this anymore." He wasn't slowing down at all. "Please, Ben, please cum already!" I said after a short while longer. My pleas only seemed to make him wilder. I felt an unusual zinging sensation up and down my neck, and my feet were on fire, just like when I had a clit orgasm.

"Aw yeah! Fuck yeah!" he said as my feminine juices completely saturated his genitals and the pillows below my hips. I may have had three different orgasms, or maybe it was one long one with three increases in intensity. I'm not sure which, but it was exhausting.

That feeling in my neck was unyielding. I thought I might pass out. I was no longer able to speak or even moan for that matter. Instead, I gasped for air intermittently. It sounded like I was gasping for my life. Finally, he came.

As we tried to catch our breath, Ben said to me, "I love you. I love you, Rick." He kissed me.

That zinging sensation in my neck very slowly started to dissipate. I felt all kinds of butterflies in my chest and stomach from him professing his love. He pressed his lips against mine one last time. I was barely able to utter, "No, sir, I love you." He smiled at me and kissed me again.

Ben left the room and returned with some water. "Here, drink this. You lost a lot of water," he said. I consumed it as Ben headed to the bathroom. I was exhausted and fell asleep before he returned. I was out for a couple of hours.

When I awoke, I could hear Ben rustling in the kitchen. I was surprised to see that it was 9:30 p.m. I got up and took a hot shower and then headed to the kitchen. When Ben saw me, he jogged up to me and he hugged and kissed me. He looked so happy. I loved to see that lightning in his eyes. I smiled at him as he escorted me to the table. He'd had a pizza delivered when I was sleeping, and he piled it high on a plate for me. He had great intuition. I was famished. He sat the plate in front of me and then sat down beside me.

"That was epic," he said, smiling at me as I took my first big mouthful. I giggled and nodded with him in agreement as I chewed and swallowed my food. "No one compares to you, Rick." I was taken with this compliment. He could tell by the silent, long look I gave him. After all, I was number thirteen.

After I recovered from his being lost in his eyes, I said, "It felt so wrong." I pressed my lips together, wondering if I should continue with what I was thinking. "I thought, I thought was going to pee myself." I laughed a little. "I didn't know what was about to happen." He smiled widely and laughed at my honesty.

Chapter 38: Return to Dr. Hall.

A lot had happened since Evie passed: the anxiety attack at the funeral, the laceration on my forearm from braking the mirror, various outbursts such as flipping the table over, my dramatic hair change, my recent dependence on alcohol, the solo dream trip that was supposed to help me heal–but it didn't, Ben and I becoming intimate, the blackout I experienced at Dad's house from uncontrolled anger; and most recently, my attack on Johnny. Now I was on my way to see the doctor to request to return to work early.

I knew that I couldn't flat out lie to Dr. Hall. It wasn't my nature, so I contemplated ways I could answer his questions vaguely enough to avoid lying.

"So how are things going?" he asked me. All the preparation was for naught because I was like a deer in headlights. How on earth could I answer that without looking like a maniac? I didn't anticipate such an open-ended question.

After quite the hesitation, I said, "I think it'd be better for me to go back to work, to keep my mind off of things." He wasn't as happy as I was with that reply.

He looked at me for a few seconds and said, "You didn't answer my question."

I gnashed my teeth for a second but quickly collected myself. "I'm not sure what you want me to say."

"I want you to answer honestly," he said with compassion and understanding. He cornered me very well, and in such a short amount of time. I was upset, and my heart started to pound.

"I can't *do* this! I'm going to cry for sure and ruin my chance to return to work!" I thought. Then I said more calmly than I thought I'd be able to, "It's only been two months. How good am I supposed to be by now?"

"Everyone experiences grief differently, Ericka. You're here because you want to go back to work earlier than we had talked about last time. We discussed your anxiety level and I wrote you a prescription for Xanax. Did you use the prescription?"

"Yes, up until I ran out."

"When you ran out, did you still have problems with anxiety?" I felt like the vein that started to protrude from my neck answered that question for me, but I had hoped that I wasn't as transparent as I felt.

"Yes."

He paused waiting for me to elaborate, but I didn't. "Why didn't you call for a refill?"

"I wanted to try something else." Well, I knew I couldn't just leave it at that, so I went on to say, "I went on a motorcycle trip to California–something I've wanted to do for a long time."

"Did it help?"

"No."

"Describe what you feel or what happens to you when you get anxiety and you don't have medication to help you."

I felt numb for the next minute as I gave him examples. "I cried until I collapsed in the sand, and I almost drowned in the ocean. I blacked out from anger and fell down a step when someone said something disrespectful about Evie. I punched Johnny in the stomach and the face and told him what a shit he was for leaving Evie right when she got cancer and for not coming to her funeral."

Yep, that about summed it up. I figured I was never going to be allowed to work again. Dr. Hall didn't know that Johnny had left Evie. I gathered that by the look on his face. I knew there was a chance that Dr. Hall could report me for attacking Johnny, but I guess I really didn't care at that point.

He was silent as he absorbed all I had told him. "Let's back up to the blackout. Tell me about that."

"I didn't pass out because I was awake the whole time. My vision went black when I was angry. I became weak and I fell to the ground. My vision returned in about a minute."

"Anxiety and anger can be a very dangerous thing. They affect heart rate and blood pressure. If this goes unchecked, you could have serious medical complications," he explained. I was already fully aware of this.

"The medication did help, but I felt like a zombie when I took it. So I would just sleep a lot."

"Are you still financially stable enough to have the three months off?"

Oh, no! I didn't want to answer this! "Yes," I said after several seconds of silence and a hard gulp.

"I think you should see the grief counselor a few times a week before you return to work."

I'm not sure if he was done talking or if I interrupted him at this point. "You know not everyone likes to talk about their problems!" I wasn't really yelling at him. I was just talking very intensely. "When I talk about my problems, I get upset again and it feels like I'm reliving the experience! It's like having a cut on your finger. If you keep bending the finger, how is it ever supposed to heal!?"

"A grief counselor doesn't have you just talk about your problems. You'd learn ways to manage your anger and anxiety without needing medication. This might include things like controlling your breathing to keep your blood pressure and heart rate in check so that you don't blackout again."

I had nothing left to argue save this, "What am I supposed to do the other twenty-three hours of the day when I'm stuck at home and not with the counselor?" I thought it was a valid point but, damn it, he had an answer to everything.

"You would start implementing what you learned from the counselor."

I clenched my teeth again and shook my head in disgust.

"Ericka, you assaulted a man and you almost drowned. You need to take my advice. You know that I care about you and your family, and I just want you to be safe. I think the best way for you to do that is to see the counselor for two weeks and get your anxiety and anger under control. Then you should be well enough to return to work."

I felt a pressure behind my nose as I tried to control my nervous ticks and facial expressions in front of the man with decision-making power over me. I was definitely only doing a fair job at that. I was unable to cork several obvious clenches of my jaw in between bouts of me pressing my lips together firmly, and God only knows how pronounced the tension was in my forehead. But I *did not* jolt my head, damn it. I *did not* jolt my head.

Finally, I said, "I know what you are saying, but you don't know what you're asking of me." A single tear trickled down my face despite my best efforts. "I just can't talk about it." I paused for a moment. He was actually silent for a spell. I quickly wiped my tear away and added, "You know, I just started exercising and I have a boyfriend who makes me happy. I guess I thought that would be enough for now."

"That's good, both of those things, but you can't use your boyfriend to distract you from the healing process. That's not fair to him or you. Besides, being distracted might only prolong your healing." I hated that he was right. He gave me a script for a different medication, and his office called to make me an appointment with the counselor. I was mad the rest of the day.

I couldn't wait for Ben to get home. I coerced him to the bedroom as soon as he walked in. We had another round of amazing sex, which relieved some of my stress. When we exited the bedroom, Ben was surprised to see supper was ready for him in kitchen. He was pleased with his evening so far. I told him what Dr. Hall had said and how disappointed I was.

"He sounds like a smart guy," Ben said, not looking up as he chowed down on his supper.

I scoffed and replied, "He is," under my breath. It didn't make me happy that Ben was on his side. I guess I was hoping for a little sympathy because I wouldn't be returning to work as early as I had hoped. I worried about what I would do to bide my time: exercise a little, drink probably.

I called Dad and Mom later that evening to update them. Dad had taken my side and was disappointed that I wouldn't be returning to work earlier. He also thought that work would help keep me focused on something other than my pain. Dad had a suggestion for me.

"Why don't you try playing your piano?"

I hated to burst his bubble, but that's exactly what I did. "I only know how to play church songs, and I don't want to play church songs right now." The words "right now" were added so that I didn't hurt Dad. I didn't plan on playing that damn piano ever again. Surprisingly, he left it at that.

"Why don't you come over tomorrow and we can ride the heifers." Ah, Priscilla and Diamond, my sweet nags.

"That's a great idea! Let's do that." I was grateful that he had the time. He was a very busy man.

Oh, how I missed my pets. Well, I claimed them as mine anyway. I was their babysitter when Mom and Dad would go away, and I often chipped in for the more expensive vet bills. Before Evie passed, I was over there three times a week, whether my parents were home or not. I'd clean the stalls, give the heifers apples, and brush them until my heart was content. Of course, I'd spend time with Fifi and Max as well. That was another good thing with regards to living so close to Mom and Dad. I love animals. The only reason I didn't have one of my own was because I traveled a lot, but I sure did get my pet fix whenever I needed it. Unfortunately, Ben didn't have any pets.

Later that evening, I had two glasses of wine. Ben didn't seem to mind, but I did notice him monitoring me. What he didn't know was that I had some before he had gotten home. I was hiding some alcohol in the spare bedroom, the one that I occasionally slept in before I moved in with Ben. I still had a lot of stuff in that room and in essence, it was my room, but I chose to sleep with Ben in his room. "I must be careful," I thought. "If he finds out how much I'm still drinking, it would put a terrible strain on our relationship."

The next day, I was more lighthearted than I'd been in while. Normally, I felt overburdened when Ben wasn't around, but this day was different. Ben was my saving grace, but Dr. Hall was right about it not being fair for me to rely on Ben so heavily for my happiness. I needed to get to the point where I felt okay when he wasn't around. That was my goal.

Priscilla and Diamond were being precious angels. It was apparent that they missed us and our rides together. I enjoyed their mood wholeheartedly. For a moment, I felt as though nothing could dampen my mood, but I was wrong. It was as simple as Dad saying, "What a beautiful day. 'This is the day that the Lord has made. I will rejoice and be glad in it.'"

Yes, I used to concentrate on the scriptures like that too, but now stuff like that upset me. My mood transitioned from lighthearted to disheartened. Isn't He wonderful, all-powerful, able to make the planets orbit around the sun? But He didn't think it worthwhile to let Evie live? How many miracles had I personally seen? Several. These thoughts repeated in my mind, almost to the point of insanity.

We rode the rest of the way in silence. I struggled to keep my thoughts under control. I focused on how happy the nags were. This in turn made me happy.

Mom had lunch ready for us when we returned. It was nice that they made a day out of it. I bet that I would've had three drinks by then if I were at home by myself. Maple Crown Royale in my coffee had become one of my favorites.

Fifi was a darling, letting me hold her like a baby and rock her in my arms. Her purrs were so soothing. I decided that Ben and I needed a cat. I wondered what he'd say to that.

When I was getting ready to leave, Dad asked me if I watched the video he gave me. "No, not yet," I replied. "But I will. I love you," I said to them, and then I hugged them tight before leaving. I could hear the choke in their throats as they returned the sentiment.

I was tearful as I walked to my car. This made me angry because I was *so damn tired* of crying, so I decided to try an experiment. I grabbed my wrist and twisted my skin around to see if the pain would stop the tears. This was similar to what was known as an Indian-burn when I was a kid. It was something mean that kids would do to each other by grabbing your lower arm with both of their hands and then twisting your skin in opposite directions, all while saying "Indian-burn" as they did it. (I never noticed that this phrase was a bit racist until recently. Not something you think about as a kid. I put it out of my mind because my problems seemed much deeper than that of the world's.) This maneuver worked to decrease my pain to a degree. I felt the tears pause for a moment, but this technique just wasn't as effective doing it one-handed to yourself. In addition to twisting my arm, I also razored the inside of my lower lip with my incisors hard enough to draw blood. Ah, between the two of them, it was enough pain to keep me from tearing up any further.

Chapter 39: Psychotherapy.

It had come. The day of the psych eval, as I called it. It was just as painful as I said it was going to be, but I had to cooperate in order to get back to work sooner than I originally planned. We rehashed my feelings together and determined that me being angry with God was holding me back. The counselor said that if I continue to blame God, then I may be stuck in the anger phase of grief for a longer time than what is usual for most people.

Well la-dee-fucking-duh! I'll just stop being angry then! Give me just a second to stop. There! I've stopped! Are you kidding me!? My stomach was twisted in knots when I left. Although I had cooperated with her, I made a point to tell her how much worse I felt when I left. "This is not for me," I thought. "Why can't anyone just *believe* me!?" I went home and drank the rest of the day. Then I passed out on the couch.

Ben was so upset to see me like that when he came home, but I didn't care. I made that clear to him. When he confronted me, I told him how therapy wasn't working and that nobody listens to me! He paced around the house as I lay there in a drunken stupor. I heard him on the phone moments later. I guessed maybe he was talking to Scott, but I didn't know for sure. After the call, Ben sat down in the recliner near the couch. He put his head in his hands and let out a long, troubled sigh.

"I want a cat," I mumbled. "It felt good to have Fifi purr in my lap, and I want a cat."

He looked up at me and said, "Okay, we'll talk about it later." He sighed deeply again.

The next couple days, I tried very hard to keep occupied and minimize drinking. It was such a long day. I exercised a lot. In fact, I did three different thirty-minute workouts and a twenty-minute ab workout each day. I cleaned the entire house, made supper for Ben each night, and watched numerous movies. I even watched *Heaven*. I justified having a few shots of whiskey while watching this because I knew that it was going to be tough to watch. I was down from seven drinks a day to about four or five, but I never let Ben see me drink more than two a day. Ben never did find where I was hiding all of my alcohol.

The next psych session was more of the same. I had to use the anti-stress techniques that I learned from the counselor while I was in counseling because I was mad at having to be there. I told her how ironic that was. She wasn't happy with me. Whatever. Dr. Hall will no doubt let me go back to work at the end of three months as previously agreed. He's not going to let me go broke and lose…well, what did I have left to lose? I had sold so much of my stuff to get Evie to Niagara Falls and the Grand Canyon. I smiled at the thought. I didn't regret that for a second. All I had left in my name was my motorcycle, my clunkmobile, my table and chairs that don't break, my mattress that I didn't need anymore, my bean bag, my clothes, and my keyboard. I owned my beater car. I didn't have an apartment anymore because I was living with Ben, and I recently sold my sofa. If Dr. Hall made me wait longer to go back to work, the only thing I had to lose was my motorcycle, which wasn't quite paid off yet.

After I muddled through two weeks of therapy, Dr. Hall agreed to let me go back to work a whole week early. Gee, thanks. I pondered how I would do with drinking less as a result of working the same shift as Ben. I wouldn't be able to have whiskey in my coffee in the mornings anymore, and then I'd only be allowed two drinks at night with Ben monitoring me. This thought soon became futile because I learned that I had been rotated to second shift. What a nightmare. Spending more time away from Ben was going to be treacherous for me. At the same time, it'd be easier to drink without him knowing. I cried when I found out my schedule change. It seemed like I was always crying though, at least when Ben wasn't around. Sad tears, angry tears, hateful tears... I sat in my chair with my arms folded as I rocked my body back and forth. I looked crazy. I decided to try the lower-dose anti-anxiety med that Dr. Hall gave me, hoping it wouldn't make me feel like a zombie. It worked better than the prior dosage, but I still felt tired. Better that than feeling crazy, I supposed.

As soon as I found out I was going to be on second shift, I dragged Ben off to the pet store to pick out a cat. I was grateful that he let me choose. "What kind of cat should I get? Hmm." I decided to get a cat that might not be picked by others, like an older cat. So that's what we got: an older indoor cat that was surrendered because his owner passed away of old age. The cat's name was Boomerang. He was a fifteen-pound tiger cat, and he was perfect.

I had just a couple days left until I returned to work, and I was completely wrapped up in orienting Boom to his new surroundings. He acclimated kind of quickly. Well, I guess anything is better than a kennel. "I'll be good to you, Boom," I told him. "As good as, if not better than, your previous partner."

As my return-to-work date neared, I decided that I needed to come up with a game plan for how I was going to manage myself at work during brutal down-time. I dug up my Netter flashcards and decided that I would review anatomy during those times. I felt hopeful, like I had enough foresight to prevent a crisis at work. Between my medication and flash cards, I thought that I could pull off quasi-normal at work.

The worst thing about the first day at work was all of the condolences that I received from my coworkers who hadn't seen me since Evie passed. I appreciated the sentiment on one hand, but on the other, it felt like another fracture formed in my non-healing heart with each voice of sympathy. After the first day, I found it necessary to hide during breaks, and that proved to be less painful for me. I avoided the break room and went out of the way to use the more secluded bathroom. This worked well in conjunction with using the flashcards.

I was down to four drinks a day. Two, early morning before my shift, usually whiskey and coffee, and two more in the evening. It was a tough first week. It was actually quite exhausting to keep my mind focused on other things. Every minute was a battle.

I didn't see Ben until late Friday. He stayed up late so that he could see me when I got home. He actually met me at the door with a glass of wine. I gave him a surprised, grateful look. He took my coat and purse in exchange for the glass.

"Thank you," I said in a defeated tone, just before taking several swallows. We took a seat on the couch.

"What's the verdict? How did your first week go?"

"I survived," I replied with low energy. He rubbed my back.

"I'm proud of you," he said. Then he kissed my cheek.

I finished my glass quickly with no regard as to what Ben thought of that. Surprisingly, he immediately filled my glass again. I gratefully accepted and was moved by how compassionate he was toward me, so much so that a few tears floated down my face. I had no strength to hide them from him like I had done countless times before. He put his hand in mine, and we sat in silence as I slowly drank my second glass of wine. After I finished, I said to Ben, "Do you think we could…"

He quickly interrupted with, "I'm one step ahead of you, babe." He grabbed my hand and led me to the bedroom. My heart smiled at how well he knew me, but that's all I had the energy for. No typical giggle this time. After we undressed, he kissed me for a while. Finally, he asked, "What did you have in mind?"

"Something simple I guess." I wouldn't dare say to him, "Whatever you want," knowing his history of lavish love-making.

He spent a good deal of time with foreplay by kissing my lips and touching my body. Simple, but it got me going really fast. He transitioned from kissing my mouth to my neck. Then he slid his hand from my bent leg to under my butt. Our bodies rocked together as he mastered foreplay. I thought about the first time he kissed my neck, and how that it was the first time I had thought about anyone sexually before. This memory, along with the foreplay, quickly pushed me to the point of feeling hot and ready. I felt an intense throbbing sensation down below. I imagined that this had to be similar to how guys feel with an intense hard on.

It was clear that he was gonna let me call it, so after a few more minutes, I said breathlessly, "Okay, let's go."

The hornier I got, the more I could do anything in the bedroom. I was a complete ragdoll, letting his body move mine however he wanted. He went for deep, hard thrusts. Good, good choice. There was no shame in my moans of pleasure. I was hoping that this wouldn't be a short session, and I got my wish somehow. I loved running my lips and tongue up and down his shoulder and neck while he pleasured me.

Once we were done, I felt a lot better. I had one more glass of wine, to which Ben said nothing about, and we cuddled ourselves to sleep. It was a good way to end a very rough week.

As the weeks went on, work continued to be a struggle; Ben continued to be his amazing self and tolerated my drinking so long as I wasn't passing out; Boom was a comfort to me when Ben wasn't around; and I tried to visit Mom and Dad every week.

Chapter 40: Rick's Thanksgiving Fiasco.

I battled a heavy depression as Thanksgiving grew near. On several occasions, I silently stewed to the point of having mini-attacks of anxiety. Being that I weaned myself off of medication, I relied more on alcohol, Ben, Boom, and my breathing techniques to keep myself checked. I hadn't seen June since her insulting words toward Evie. She hadn't even tried to contact me to see if I was all right. I didn't get that. I blacked out and hit my face on the concrete for Pete's sake! I certainly wasn't expecting an apology, but I was surprised that I didn't get a simple concerned phone call about how I was doing.

Ben was excited about the opportunity to introduce his "One True Love" to his entire family. I'll admit, his excitement was a little contagious. I couldn't really tell if his excitement was strictly about having me meet his family, or if it was a combination of that plus him trying to cheer me up. No matter. I thought no more of it. I just enjoyed his energy when he would talk about it. He joked about how his family gatherings get harder each year, with more pressure to start a family. He was thrilled to be able to shove me in his uncle's face in particular.

One morning, I surprised Ben by bursting into tears when he was simply talking about what we were going to bring to Thanksgiving dinner. He hugged me firmly and rubbed my back. "I'm so sorry, Rick," he said as we embraced. "I know how hard this is for you. I'm doing everything I can to help you through this."

"I know. I know you are," I said as I tried to control myself. My face was firmly pressed against his chest. His shirt grew damp from my tears. "You're so amazing. I'd *die* without you," I said clinging to him. I really meant that. Without his love, my destructive behavior surely could've been the death of me. He squeezed me even tighter. It felt like nobody in the world loved each other as much as we did.

We were off to see my side of the family first when Thanksgiving finally came. June and I didn't make eye contact, much less talk. I stayed close to Ben most of the time, hanging onto his arm, like he was my life jacket and I was on the Titanic. Even though it was nice to see my aunts, uncles, and cousins–a rare treat–it was a very difficult day. People were still giving me their condolences and saying how much they missed Evie. I had a constant lump in my throat.

Dad and Mom looked tired but well. They were comforted by the Holy Spirit. Dad told me so several times. He also told me that I could be, too, but that I had to focus my heart to God and let him give me peace. I still reacted with a strong jaw clench at the simple thought of God.

My parents seemed to be watching how much alcohol I drank, but they didn't say anything. And I didn't care. By that I mean I *couldn't* care. I had to focus all of my energy on mastering my feelings in order to continue this fake-normal that I struggled with.

Dad made some friendly chit chat with me. "How you doing, kid?" he asked just before he kissed my forehead. I really didn't know. Good? No. Okay? I'm not sure. Better? I guess.

"Better," I said, hoping to appease him.

He gave me that one-handed side hug, or squeeze, that he's known for. "That's good," he said. "If you need anything, let us know."

"I will. Thanks." I really wasn't sure what he meant. What could he have for me? Prayer I guessed. He was no doubt already praying for me.

"Did you watch that video yet?" he asked.

"Yes," I replied. He seemed pleased with that.

I introduced Ben to my family as we mingled over hors d'oeuvres. Everyone was so nice and pleasant to him. My cousin, Lisa, stopped me as we were headed back toward the kitchen for more drinks. She was intrigued with my man.

"So, Ben's cute," she said, smiling at me with her eyes lit up.

"Yes." I smiled back.

"He's a little thin though," she said as she observed him from a distance. She didn't notice that I had rolled my eyes at this. I hated that Ben's size was one of the first things that everyone went to. It's so annoying how people are blinded by outward characteristics. It's shallow. He's funny, charming, and smart, but also very attractive. That's what I fell in love with–his inner traits. "How old is he?" she asked. I snapped out of my internal rant.

"Thirty-five," I replied.

She dropped her jaw and exclaimed, "Huh!" Then she gave me a look that indicated how naughty she thought I was for pursuing an older man. It was quite funny; we laughed together. "How serious are you guys?" she questioned.

"Very," I said as I let my smile shine. "He's the real deal." Lisa mirrored my smile, hung on my arm, and escorted me further into the kitchen.

"That's awesome, Ricky." She walked me up to the two bottles of wine that I brought, and she poured us both a drink.

"Um, you're gonna get in truh...bowl," I said melodically to her. "I'm already in trouble." I tilted my head and raised my eyebrows, and then I said in one of my funny voices, "Are you sure you want to follow me down that road?"

"This is a good exception," she said undeterred. "To love," she celebrated with a toast. Lisa did a great job of elevating my spirits. We talked softly, but I'm sure Ben heard us because when I glanced over at him, he was smiling widely at me with his eyes just gleaming. I reflected his smile. It was a magical moment. Those beautiful brown eyes; I could get permanently lost in those.

My night turned from arduous to delightful, thanks to the help of Lisa and Ben. I was successful in avoiding June, and I hoped that pleasantry would continue throughout the evening. Dad seemed encouraged by my elevated mood.

It turned out that my luck would change. I ran into June while getting desert. It was inevitable, I expected. Unfortunately, we made eye contact. I was satisfied with this moment being silent and awkward, and so I started to walk away from her. Ben graciously stayed close to my side all evening like he promised.

Before I could get past her, she said to me with a heavy dose of disgust, "So you're living in sin now, and a drunk too, I suppose. What's next, Erika? Are you going to get pregnant?" Her words cut me like a knife. Dad happened to just walk in during this encounter and heard the end of her crushing words.

He was shocked, and had a horrified look on his face. What was the probability of something like this happening twice!?

Pain instantly seared behind my right eye, the top of my head, and down into my jaw. I was nauseated. A lump formed in my throat that was so severe that it felt like someone was choking me. I tried to clear my throat several times in a row. Dad and Ben walked up to me, not knowing what to do or what to expect. I tried hard to keep it together for Dad's sake.

"I, uh, sh-should, um..." I cleared my throat again, but my words came out so softly. I scarcely uttered, "...gu-go." I squeezed Dad's arm in place of a hug and whispered, "Love you." Ben shot June a look of fury and started to escort me to the car.

On my way out, I could hear Dad's angry words, "June! Why would you say that!?"

"Well, I'm not just going to stand by like you and my daughter and watch her go to hell!" she retorted.

We just made it out the door when I heard Mom come into the equation. "Mom! Rod! What is going on in here!?" And that was the last thing I had heard.

The tunnel vision that inflicted me was spectacular, so much so that it was necessary for Ben to escort me down the stairs very slowly arm in arm. I lost my footing once, but Ben kept me from falling. "How are you doing?" he asked.

"Na-not so good," I replied with a quiver in my voice. I cleared my throat several more times, pulling my collar away from my neck and holding it down.

As we inched toward the car, the commotion I once heard like symbols in my head was now fading. I was left with the pain in my forehead that continued to blaze behind my right eye and down my jaw. The pain intensified until I was bent over with my hand against my head, wincing with each step. I dredged on. Ben changed his position from arm in arm to putting my arm around his shoulder while he supported my waist. He was ready just in case I collapsed. By the time we got to the car, my surroundings seemed to repeatedly pound close to me then pulsate away, which was a very troubling feeling. I would've fallen to the ground for sure if Ben wasn't there. My winces changed to a combination of whimpering and nearly crying from the nauseating, overwhelming, and depleting atmosphere that trapped me. The pounding-pulsating sensation tossed me to and fro, like I was on a ship during a storm.

"Back seat," I voiced dubiously. I also pointed just in case Ben didn't understand my words. He assisted me into the back seat where I toppled over onto my side. During the ride home, I transformed from a girl who was helpless and in pain (and out of control) to one who was raging and in pain (and out of control). I punched the seat several times in between bouts of holding my head and groaning as my body melded to the seat. In between moans, I growled and laughed with my teeth clenched like a maniac. I pulled at my hair to compete with feeling that my head was splitting.

Ben said to me, "Hang in there, baby. We're almost home." In retrospect, I'm not sure how he put up with this, but I don't know what I would've done without him.

He helped me out of the car and up the stairs. By this time, I was exhausted but ready to fight. I looked to Ben to see if he was going to let me punch him like he did before. I put up my fists, not knowing if I could really put any force into it this time.

Ben had an intense look on his face. He looked into my eyes for several long seconds. "I have a different idea this time," he finally said, but then he hesitated.

I pushed him back with both of my hands forcefully and thundered, "Well, do it!" I was surprised at the power I had in my conflicted state.

He staggered back a few steps. Then he lunged forward at me and grabbed my wrist, pulling me toward him. He spun me around, similar to the way he did in the hot tub at Hocking Hills, but this time he did it so aggressively, and he ended up holding me with my arm *behind* my back. He then grabbed a hand full of my hair and pulled my head back. I yelped in pain and surprise.

"I would never have considered something like this before you told me that story," he whispered in my ear.

Which story was he talking about? I could think of several stories that I shared with him where I had self-inflicted physical pain to dull my mental anguish. He walked me as his captive to the bedroom. I became more breathless with anticipation the closer we got to the bed. "Don't forget your safeword is 'stop,' right?" he said with his breath heavy on my ear. "Not 'no,' 'no more,' or 'I can't.'" Those were some of the things I commonly said when I felt overwhelmed during intimacy. "Got it?" he asked.

I felt the word "yes" escape my lips, but I could barely hear myself speak. He began to disrobe me aggressively while I had my back to him. Once we were naked, he folded me over the bed, forcing me down face-first by my hair. He allowed me to turn my head to the side so that I could breathe better. With his free hand, he grabbed my arm and pulled it behind my back again. He held me in that position as he alternated between kissing and caressing me gently to viciously grabbing and biting me.

Finally, he stood back up and forced himself into me. He unpredictably transitioned between gently moving inside of me to violently ravaging me. He'd pull my hair, claw my sides, and reach around to grab my breast. Then he'd press his forearm into my back to keep me folded over the bed, all while he held my arm behind my back. It was so random. My neurological system was in a constant state of shock. There was no predicting what he was going to do next.

The screams coming from the bedroom sounded like someone was being raped or tortured. After several minutes of this, Ben stopped and turned the music on loud. We lived in town with the neighbors only a stone's throw away. He didn't want anyone to hear me scream and call the police. He also used this opportunity to tie my arms behind my back with the long-sleeve shirt that he seized from me.

This freaked me out and I yelled, "No! No!! I need one arm! I need one arm!!" I didn't use the word stop, but he listened to me anyway because of the urgency and panic in my voice. Instead of binding both hands, he tied my left arm behind my back and anchored it to my opposite thigh. Now both of his hands were free to violate me, and my right arm was free to brace myself on the bed. The bed was a tall one, so my feet were useless to help stake myself down because my toes barely touched the floor.

After he turned the music up, he sailed past being unpredictable and morphed into pure sadism. He went from grabbing my breast, to pinching and twisting my nipple hard. I made a noise equivalent to someone coming up for air who had been under water too long. I tried to regain my senses enough to grab his hand to pull it away from my nipple. As soon as I did this, he grabbed my hair again and pulled my head back off of the bed while he continued to fuck me hard. This caused me to put my free hand back of the bed to support myself to ease off of the pain I felt from him lifting me by my hair. Not only did I not say "no," "no more," "I can't" or even "stop," but I couldn't form any words at all, just beastly noises and screams.

Ben was surprisingly very loud too. At one point he said, "I'm gonna fuck you into next year!" to which I replied with a gush of feminine juices. This made him mad with delight. I thought he was giving me all of his force, but somehow, after I saturated his genitals, he was able to fuck me even harder. "Uhh! Can you feel me in your throat, Rick!?" It sounds corny now, but he was dead-on in the moment. Each time he said something, my body involuntarily responded, and that made him more and more crazy.

Ben decided to pull out for a second and flip me over. We were facing each other for the first time since we entered the bedroom. He paused for a second to inspect my chest and neck, which were completely blotched pink. I was grateful for a break, even if it were only a couple of seconds. After Ben realized I was okay, he pulled me closer to the edge of the bed where he was standing, and he mounted me again. He wrapped his arms around my thighs and had my legs bent up as far as they could go. It was deeper and harder than anything we'd ever done. I stopped all other noises except screaming. Somehow, I was able to free my arm from behind my back. Eventually, he let go of one of my legs so that he could grab and squeeze my neck. I instinctively grabbed his wrist and futilely tried to lighten the pressure on my neck. My other hand changed positions several times in desperation. I'd try to push his chest away unsuccessfully, and then I'd move it to join my other hand with trying to lighten his grip on my neck. He was totally gone at this point and didn't seem to be monitoring my well-being. He was like an unstoppable freight train. Fortunately, he only lasted about thirty seconds more after he put his hand on my neck before he came. Oh, I'll never forget his loud sounds of ecstasy. His orgasms weren't usually that loud. Finally, he let go of my neck, and I immediately gasped for air and started a deep, hoarse cough. He seemed to come-to more quickly because of my reaction.

He dismounted me and said, "Oh my God! Rick, are you okay!?" I rolled over to my side, still coughing. He brushed the hair out of my face and then ran off to the kitchen to get me some water. When he returned, my coughs and gasps had lessened considerably. He lifted me into sitting. "Here, baby, drink this." He helped me with the water and studied me as I drank. I noticed the horrified look on his face.

I composed myself, then I looked into his eyes and said in a hoarse voice, "Well, I didn't hate that." I smiled at him. He gasped deeply three times in a row. He almost looked faint for a couple of hot seconds. He rested his forehead against mine and caressed my face.

"I went too far. I went too far," he said quickly and softly.

"Maybe so, but I didn't hate it," I said with a smirk. My hoarse voice persisted. "Mission accomplished, right?" I said, reminding him of why he did this in the first place. He gave me a small, exasperated laugh and kissed my cheek.

I was totally exhausted and would've been happy to call it a night and just sleep in my filthy, sweaty state, but Ben insisted on drawing me a bubble bath. He handed me a glass of Pendleton as I passed by him on the way to the bathroom. After he got a clear look at my naked body, he exclaimed, "Oh my God!" He forced me into the bathroom where the lighting was better. He did this so abruptly that I spilled much of my drink, but he didn't even notice. Ben grabbed my shoulders and spun me around as he inspected my body. I was covered in red marks, scratches, and bruises. "Oh my God. Oh no. Oh no!" he said as he assessed the severity of each mark. I looked in the mirror at myself and giggled a little. The most upsetting part of this for Ben must've been the clearly defined fingerprints on my neck.

"It's fine, babe. I'll wear a scarf tomorrow. It's winter. It'll be fine." My smile reassured him little if any. He looked over my body again with a heavy frown. I set my drink down, grabbed his face with my hands to make him look me in the eyes, and said, "Hey, I'm in better shape now than I was before we started. Or have you forgotten?" There was a little sarcasm in my tone. "My headache is completely gone." It was no joke of a headache either, if you even can fit it into that category. Near death experience–now that sounds a bit more like it. He kissed me softly on the lips and helped me get into the bubble bath. It was very, very hot. Just the way I like it. Once I had settled in, he handed me my whiskey.

We slept like cherubs that night. Our bodies were entwined the entire night in one fashion or another. When we awoke, we were very refreshed and in good spirits, ready for another family gathering.

Chapter 41: Ben's Thanksgiving.

Ben and I both had Black Friday off in order to attend his family gathering that afternoon. I was able to make myself look spectacular with makeup, a scarf, and spirals in my hair to hide all of the bruising. Ben did a double-take when I walked into the room, and he approached me with a smile. However, his expression turned grave as he came closer. He walked around me, inspecting me closely from all angles.

"Not only did you pull this off, but you look amazing," he said, converting back to a smile. Then he leaned over to give me a quick passionate peck. "How are you feeling?" he asked as he held me gently in his arms.

"Sore, *everywhere*," I said with a big smile. That must've upset him because his smile dampened. "I think I'll be okay as long as I don't stand up and sit down a lot," I said as I rubbed his shoulders, trying to appease him. "I'll try not to give us away, but that might be a little difficult because of my hoarse voice and slow movements," I said teasingly with bright eyes. He leaned over to kiss me again, but this time he did it ever so gently.

When it was time to leave, Ben escorted me to the car like a true gentleman. He held the car door for me and watched me try to sit down as normal as I could. When we arrived at the party, he hustled around to the passenger's side to escort me out of the car and up to the house. Ben's contribution was a cherry dessert, and mine was Bushmills Black. I asked Ben if my choice of beverage was going to be a problem; he assured me that it would not. I was glad to hear that because I needed something strong to medicate me, especially after my Thanksgiving catastrophe.

We certainly did turn every head in the house as a couple. I hadn't forgotten our age difference, but sometimes I'd forget that the turquoise and purple streaks in my hair made me look much younger than I was. I blushed as everyone in the house took turns staring at us. Ben did a nice job of introducing me to his family and making me feel comfortable. Everyone seemed so nice. We weren't there long before Ben's uncle, Chuck, approached us. He walked up to Ben and shook his hand.

"Hey, Uncle Chuck. How ya doing, man?" Ben inquired.

"I'm good, Ben, but not as good as you, I expect," he said as he smiled at me. I politely smiled back.

"This is my girlfriend, Rick," Ben said, introducing me.

"Pleasure to meet you," I started to say as I reached for Chuck's hand.

Chuck took my hand and promptly cut me off with, "Rick, is it?" He narrowed his eyes.

"It's short for Erika," I replied, "but I go by Rick." He looked uncomfortable at the thought of calling me that, so after a long awkward pause, I added, "You can call me Ricky if you like."

"All right, Ricky," he piped. Of course. It was all I could do to not roll my eyes. I was amazed at how many people preferred to call me Ricky when I clearly preferred Rick. There was no ambiguity about it. Oh well, at least Ben and the gang called me Rick. I guess it made it more special that way.

Chuck brazenly added, "It looks like there's a bit of an age difference here." Ben bowed-out of a reply and looked to me to respond.

"Love is not bound by age," I replied in a silly super-feminine voice as I reached for Ben's hand. I glanced up at Ben while holding his hand to see *fireworks* in his eyes. He granted me a small smile as well. The fireworks were hypnotizing. I was completely captive to his gaze, forgetting that we had company in our presence.

"I guess not!" Chuck trumpeted, reminding me that Ben and I were not alone. I was so gone that I almost jumped at this boisterous reorientation. "What *is* the age difference here?" Chuck pressed.

"Thirteen years," I replied.

"Is that all!?" piped Chuck.

"Yeah, I look a bit younger than I am," I added.

"Which is?"

"Twenty-two."

"My God!" He slapped Ben hard on the back. "How did you pull that off!?" Ben gave him a small, polite smile.

"Well, I can be quite persistent when I want something bad enough," I said, rescuing Ben from having to answer. I smiled at Chuck, leaned my head up against Ben's chest, and lovingly wrapped my arms around him.

"Something tells me that you probably didn't have to twist his arm *too* hard," Chuck said, smiling back. I laughed. Chuck laughed too, and then he was off to mingle with other family members.

"You are quite the ham today," Ben said just before he kissed me softly.

"I'm kind of enjoying it too." I giggled.

"Whatever you want," he said with his soft, sexy voice just before he kissed me again.

We were definitely the center of attention at the party. I think our age difference utterly intrigued people. Also, Ben and I were the most affectionate couple there. We were either holding hands, smiling at each other, or just being close to each other. I loved how he wasn't afraid to give me the occasional peck on the lips or behold me a little longer than he should've in his family's presence.

Ben's dad stopped me in the kitchen to feel things out. "Hey, girl. How you doing?" It hadn't stopped being a hard question. The hole in my heart that plagued me when Evie died seemed to have jagged edges. I wondered when that simple question was going to get easier to answer. I loved Ben so, but sometimes it wasn't enough to fill in the hollowness in my soul or chisel away the anger.

"I'm good, Marv." I was getting better at convincing people at least. "How are you?"

He smiled sadly and said, "Lillian used to call me that." It was the first time I called him Marv.

"I'm sorry," I said empathetically. "Do you want me to call you Marvin instead?"

"No, Marv is fine." I hadn't noticed until then that no one else seemed to call him that.

"Are you seeing anyone, Marv?" I asked him, not minding my own forwardness.

"No," he said. "I've, I've stopped looking," he said with a nod as if to finalize his statement.

I smiled widely. "That's good!" He looked at me with a shocked expression. "Sometimes the best things happen to you when you're not looking." I smiled over at Ben who was talking to Scott. He smiled back.

"Speaking of which, how are you guys doing?" Marv asked.

"Great!" I continued smiling.

"Any marriage plans in the future?" he asked.

"Absolutely!" I said without hesitation.

"Oh? Ben hasn't said anything to me yet."

I laughed. "He hasn't said anything to me either! But I told him that I was going to marry him and he hasn't run yet!" We laughed together. This was a true statement, actually. He had told my parents that we planned to marry in the future, but he really never told me that.

"Well, that *is* something," Marv said. As our laughter died down, Marv glanced over at Ben with a serious expression, and then he looked back at me. He was probably hoping in his heart that Ben wouldn't mess this up. Ben was talking with Scott and fortunately didn't notice his dad's grave expression.

"Don't worry, Marv. He's not getting away from me," I said reassuringly.

Marv smiled and nodded. He seemed comforted by my confidence. "That's great. That's really great, hon." He looked over at Ben again and said, "I've never seen him so happy." He turned back to me and gave me a light hug. Then he surprised me by kissing my cheek before he walked away.

I turned to see Ben and Scott talking and laughing together. They didn't seem to notice the heart-felt conversation I had with their dad. I watched them closely for a few seconds, envying the way they were enjoying each other's company. My mood morphed into a heavy one from missing Evie. Never again would I have the joy of her conversation or laughter. The smile I had on my face only moments ago, vanished straightaway. I turned my back to them both and leaned against the counter. I finished my first cup of whiskey in one big gulp. I closed my eyes, enjoying the burning sensation down my throat. Bushmills Black is so smooth.

I was startled by the clink of the Bushmills bottle on the rim of my glass as Scott filled my cup. I opened my eyes and breathed in deeply in place of a jump. My eyes had been closed just a little too long, I imagined. After he filled my cup, he said, "The first holidays are always the worst. Your cup should never be empty." I gave him a tired smile as I continued to lean on the counter. I was really impressed with his intuition. It seemed that Ben and Scott both had that in common. "When Mom left," he paused as if it were still hard to talk about, "I was *so* angry, for *so* many years." He shook his head and paused a few more seconds, "But it got better slowly, very slowly."

I turned to him, looked him in the eyes and nodded as if to say "I'm sorry for your loss and thank you for your kind words," but I was unable to verbalize any of that for fear of an emotional surge. I touched my hand to his forearm and squeezed him lightly to express my gratitude instead of using my words. I removed my hand after a few moments and took another sip. I was glad to be feeling the full effects of the alcohol.

"Ya know, Rick, I never told you that I was sorry for being a jerk when we first met." Scott went on to say, "I'm sorry. I thought that Ben was going through some sort of, I don't know, crisis. And that you were just some kind of playtoy." His face turned beet-red from being embarrassed by his own words. "Uh, I," he stammered.

I rescued him by saying, "It's okay, I understand. I actually forgave you already."

"Really?" he said with puzzled expression.

"Yes. The day you came over to let us borrow your truck, you were trying to be so nice. But you can't go wrong with an apology, even if everything comes out *entirely* wrong." I rolled my eyes when I said "entirely," and then I smirked at him as I took another sip.

"Uh, yeah," he said as he rubbed the back of his neck with his head bent forward a little. It made me smile to see how

Scott and Ben had the same nervous tick in common. This was Ben's signature move when he gets uncomfortable. "What's so funny?" he asked.

"I didn't realize how much alike you and Ben are until now."

"Really? How so?"

"I can't tell you because, in my experience, once you tell someone that something they say or do is cute, then they stop saying or doing it altogether. It's quite annoying, actually."

He laughed and said, "Fair enough, I guess." My heart skipped a little during our conversation. It was the first time that Scott called me Rick.

Ben came up behind me and put his arms around me and rested his cheek next to mine. He rocked me side to side and said, "See, I told you everything was going to be all right." He gave me a light peck on the cheek.

"Whhhy wouldn't everything be all right?" Scott asked.

It was a fair question, so I gave him a fair answer. "My family gathering didn't go so well."

"Really? What happened?" Scott seemed confused and concerned.

"I can't talk about it. Ben can tell you later if he wants." Scott nodded and we left it at that.

All in all, it was a great day. Ben was quite the gentleman, even up until the end when he held the car door for me one last time.

When we got into the house, Ben surprised me by cradling my head with his hands and kissing me. I mean, I barely got my coat off. He continued to kiss me as he walked me backwards toward the bedroom. It was a very steamy kiss. I stopped him in the bedroom by pulling his hands away from my face so that I could talk. He listened, but kept his lips close to mine. I explained to him, "I don't know if I can today. I'm so sore."

Ben brushed his hand across my cheek and placed his thumb over my lips. "Shhhh," he whispered as he rubbed his thumb across my bottom lip seductively. "I got this." He moved his other arm around my waist and pulled me tight against his body. He rocked with me side to side and whispered, "You're gonna like this." I was definitely intrigued. He was usually right. Ben kissed and touched me gently in all the right places as we undressed. He kept at least one hand cradling my head and his lips either on my lips, face, or neck. He mastered kissing my lips as if he had invented it himself. Finally, he swooped me up and snugged my legs around his waist, and then he slowly lowered me onto the bed. He caressed my bottom lip in between his–one of my favorite moves. I squeezed him tight with my legs as he did so. I couldn't believe he was making me hot. I didn't think that'd be possible for at least a week after the extravaganza from the previous day. He firmly ran his hand down my side, another one of my favorite, although simple, moves. I was completely lost in the moment.

Ben pulled away from my lips and said, "I'm completely in love with you, Rick." He kissed my lips again several times, and then he went on to say, "And I *will* marry you."

My breathing became shallow and quick as if he was putting all his weight on my chest. I didn't reply. I was unable to. My eyes misted over. He continued to kiss me and touch me gently until I was fully ready. He made love to me so softly and tenderly. He was actually gentler with me than he was during our first time. I was amazed at his restraint and glad for it because I still felt all of the bruises, bite marks, and scratches from the day before. It was like every nerve in my body was exposed and hypersensitive. I could see, hear, taste, and feel everything far better than ever before. That day couldn't have been more perfect.

Chapter 42: Plan to Return to Hocking Hills.

A few days later, Ben waited up for me to get home from work. He approached me, gleaming with excitement as I walked in the door. "I need you to get the second week of January off. I'm taking you back to Hocking Hills." He helped me out of my coat and took my bag as he talked. I was so tired because I found second shift to be quite draining, but I smiled genuinely, for his enthusiasm was infectious.

"Cool. I've never been to Hocking Hills in the winter." We got online, and he showed me the cabin that he was going to rent. It wasn't as nice as the cabin we had last time, but it was still great. Boom jumped on my lap, and I scratched his back as Ben explained all of the activities that we could do there in the winter. "I'll put in my request tomorrow," I said. I didn't think I'd have any problem getting this off because Ben had given me a month's notice.

Ben had been incredibly attentive to me after the Thanksgiving drama, more so than usual. Not only was the love-making phenomenal, but he was very considerate and polite in every way imaginable. I assumed that he was doing this because he knew Christmas would likely be just as hard for me. I made it clear that I had no intention of going to my family gathering. Instead, we planned a small dinner with just Dad and Mom. My parents were grateful for this because they didn't expect to see me at all over Christmas because of the Thanksgiving fiasco.

I had plenty of time to contemplate June's words that cut me so deeply during Thanksgiving dinner. I came up with, "Yes, she's right. I am doing wrong, but her reaction was just as wrong." I wondered how her actions may have affected Ben, who hadn't been to church since his Mom took off. Unfortunately, I had seen so many instances of Christians acting out in one way or another, which turned off non-Christians from Christianity altogether. "If that's what being a Christian is, I don't want anything to do with it," I've heard several times. And June's coarse words towards my sister–unforgivable.

Not only did I think about the accuracy and hatefulness of June's words about me, but I also thought about how I didn't care. Her words didn't stir me to change the way I was living. Now I was just going to avoid my family gatherings. I focused on how Mom and Dad must still be hurting from losing Evie, and now also from the drama June and I had caused. That made my heart heavy. I wondered how long it would be until Ben and I got married. Quite a while, I supposed, since we had only been seeing each other six months, and he just recently told me that he planned to marry me. My head starting spinning with all of these thoughts, so I tried to cling onto the fact that Ben reciprocated my feelings about marriage. But I had difficulty dismissing the thought, "If we could just marry now, this whole family chaos would be contained." I couldn't tell Ben that because it'd be too much pressure on him, and it wouldn't be fair.

Chapter 43: Christmas.

Ben's excitement about our upcoming trip lasted the whole month; it was catching. He was also being a little secretive. This had me intrigued. I didn't know what he was up to, but I didn't let on that I was onto him. He received some boxes in the mail that he quickly hid, and he tried to act nonchalant after abruptly ending a phone call or two when I walked into the room. Christmas was just around the corner, so I assumed that he was getting me something special. I decided I'd better get on the ball with getting him a present.

I struggled with what I was going to get him. He had a great job and had been single for so long that he'd just get whatever he wanted without hesitation. After long consideration, I bought him communicators for our motorcycle helmets. Ben hadn't been on his motorcycle since his accident, but I was still pleased with this decision. I was sure that he would be ready to ride next season. I foolishly hoped that he hadn't gotten me the same thing, even though the probability of that was minute.

It was getting a little easier at work during downtime. I wasn't entirely dependent on my flashcards to keep from getting depressed about Evie's death, and I didn't obsess much about how I was not going to be able to attend any family functions as long as I was unmarried and living with Ben. I completely weaned myself off of the anti-anxiety meds. I was able to control my emotions by meditating more on Ben: how much I loved him, how he returned my love, how happy I was to be with him, and how that we'd eventually be married.

Our Christmas dinner with Dad and Mom was quite delightful. They treated us very well despite the tension June and I had caused the family. Christmas without Evie was hard, very hard, but it seemed like we all rescued one another several times throughout the evening. As soon as someone looked down, even for a second, someone was there to cheer them up with a hug, a kiss, a joke, or just some Christmas cheer.

Dad and Mom really seemed to take to Ben more this holiday, in that they were paying him quite a bit of attention. I realize that sounds silly given that there were only the four of us, whereas there were so many of us at Thanksgiving. Nevertheless, it just seemed different somehow. They were treating him like he was already part of the family. Not that they ever treated him with anything less than respect and courtesy. This occurrence was nothing like when Evie moved in with Johnny. Maybe they were cutting me some slack because of all I had been through. Maybe they recognized that being with Ben was helping me. Whatever the case, it was nice and I appreciated it.

Ben's Christmas gathering was also smaller than the Thanksgiving one. Marv confided in me that he started seeing someone, and that he hasn't dated in about ten years. "Marv, that's *marv*elous," I said accenting the *marv* in marvelous because I'm that corny. "I told you that good things happen when you're not expecting them!"

Scott and I were getting along as if there had never been any conflict between us. In fact, I think we were actually closer than we would've been if there had been no conflict at all. Scott seemed really happy. He told me that he and his girlfriend were starting to get serious. He said that they had been taking it really slow because she has two children.

Ben grew a beard for me that winter. He was normally a clean-shaven guy, but for some reason he offered to grow one for me if I wanted him to. I jumped at the opportunity. He looked so incredible with his neatly trimmed beard. I couldn't believe that he didn't think so himself. I could hardly keep my eyes off of him at his Christmas party. He seemed to notice and revel in it. He'd flash me his gorgeous smile when he'd catch me staring at him. He was handsome for sure, but I really loved how distinguished he looked. As I mentioned before, his dark eyebrows, beard, and eyelashes highlighted his light brown hair and eyes. I also loved the fact that he had several gray hairs and smile lines. He was dreamy.

Later that evening, Ben and I exchanged gifts at home. We sat on the floor near our small, charming Christmas tree. It was synthetic, snow-frosted, heavily decorated with pine cones, and had minimal white lights. I helped Boomerang open his present first. He happily kicked and scratched at his cap-nip toys. I monitored him, making sure the old chap didn't overdo it.

I insisted that Ben go next. He was very pleased with the helmet communicators. He admitted that he had also thought of getting me a similar gift, so I guess I *wasn't* being ridiculous when I worried that he might get me the same thing. I also presented Ben a coupon for a full body massage with a "happy ending." He was more amused with that than I thought he'd be, and he laughed heartily.

"One!? Really!? Only *one* coupon for this?" He laughed again. "I'll be looking forward to that." He leaned forward to kiss me.

"Well, birthdays are a freebee," I spontaneously added. "So I suggest you don't use it then."

"My dear, you *are* a vixen," he said. Then he grabbed me and kissed me again.

I opened my present next. I was surprised to see a turquoise dress with spaghetti straps and a straight-cut top, just like the classy black and silver one that I wore on our fancy date. I held it up and marveled at the gift. It wasn't what I expected at all.

"It's beautiful! Thank you, Ben!" I said.

"There's more," he said. I looked down to see a white shawl with turquoise embroidery in it. I gasped at how well they went together. Before I could say anything else, he said, "I have plans for you in this outfit." He smiled at me. "I loved the way you looked in that black dress on that glorious day when we proclaimed our love to each other. And you're going to look amazing in this color. It'll accent your beautiful eyes."

I couldn't have smiled any bigger. I was moved by all the thought he put into this gift and by his touching words. I put the dress carefully back in the box so that Boom couldn't mess with it. Then I lunged at Ben with a kiss that knocked him from a sitting position to lying on his back on the floor.

"What kind of plans?" I interrogated him as I lay on top of him.

"I'll let you know when it's time," he said coyly. So that's what all the secrecy was about! He was planning on taking me some place fancy again in the future.

I continued kissing him while we lay on the floor, with my eyes open of course. I loved the feel of his prickly beard on my lips. I was awestruck to see how the Christmas tree magnificently illuminated Ben's face. I paused from kissing him and marveled at his beauty. I brushed the back of my fingers against his face and said, "You are so beautiful, truly, inside and out." He furrowed his brow and had so much emotion in his face. I imagined that he was in limbo between feeling perplexed or in disbelief. Judging by his reaction, I figured that no one had ever told him that before.

After several moments of gazing into each other's eyes, Ben responded by turning his head toward my hand and kissing it. He closed his eyes as he did so. I leaned forward to kiss his cheek. Then without warning, he turned his head toward me and started barking like a dog loudly at me. I screamed in surprise, and then he whisked me onto my back and bit my neck as he growled. I punched him on the shoulder and yelled, "You tool!" Now *he* was lying on top of *me*. He smiled at me; he loved to catch me off guard.

It was just like him to disable a serious moment with his playfulness. I figured that he wasn't too comfortable with my sincerity being forced upon him. And I was okay with his avoidance. He leaned forward and graced me with one of his lengthy, infamous, amazing kisses. He then said to me most sincerely, "Rick, I love you. You've unlocked parts of my heart that," he paused for a moment searching for the right words, "that I didn't know even existed. Being with you has made me a better person." I was stunned that he transitioned back to being serious. He continued with, "And no one is more beautiful than you, inside and out." His words were so touching. I can't even begin to express the emotions that flooded over me. I just wanted him to understand how much he meant to me, but he turned it around completely, making *me* feel amazing. The hairs on the back of my neck blossomed. His words were so stunning that I couldn't seem to breathe. It was as if someone had punched me in the stomach. I wondered if he saw the panic growing in me from my breathlessness.

He leaned forward and kissed me again. I felt my breath come back to me tempestuously. Ben, knowing how emotional I can get, took this in stride. He continued to kiss me and my breathing finally regulated. I caressed the back of his neck as we kissed. The more he kissed me, the more my blood started to sizzle. He carelessly thrashed his beard across my lips, causing me to flinch. I went from caressing the back of his neck to grabbing a fist full of his hair. He replied by kissing me deeper. I was mad with passion. I let go of his hair so that I could untuck his shirt. I rubbed my hands up and down his back as I bent my leg up. Then I unzipped his pants, grabbed his butt, and pulled him up and down on me, indicating that I wanted more. With his lips still pressed against mine, he unfastened my bra and jeans and groped me perfectly. My sounds of pleasure were muffled by his lips. We stopped kissing only long enough to remove our clothes, and then his mouth was back to mine. A chill rushed over my body as we lay uncovered on the carpeted living room floor. Ben rubbed his hands up and down my body, warming me. He made love to me with his mouth rarely off of mine. The more he kissed me, the more I involuntarily squeezed him inside of me. The more I squeezed him, the deeper he would crash into me. The intensity of his thrusts seemed to be ever growing to the point where my lips were unresponsive, for my entire body was overcome with ecstasy. My paralyzed lips didn't deter him. He continued to pound me as he sucked my lips into his mouth. My body became a complete rag doll. It was clear that I was broken-in. As much as Ben loved that everything he did was new to me, I could tell that he loved this feeling just as much. The chemistry between us was off the charts.

Chapter 44: Return to Hocking Hills.

It had finally come! It was time to go back to Hocking Hills! I beamed with excitement as I packed the night before our departure. Ben was elated to see me like this. He said that he had every detail planned.

"We're going ice-skating, winter hiking, and we're going on a horse-drawn sleigh ride."

"Oh my gosh!" I exclaimed. "What's the occasion!?"

He moved close to me, caressed my face with his hand, and said in his fake, sexy voice, "Love...doesn't need an occasion, baby." He smiled devilishly at me. What a dork. I loved it. I grabbed his shirt and pulled him toward me. I could barely stop smiling long enough to kiss his lips.

"Gee, Ben, I don't know what to say," I said in my very smitten, damsel-been-rescued voice, "'Cept I, I love you." He smiled at my silliness. I kissed him again and then I said in my most sincere voice, "I love you, Ben, with all my heart. You're so amazing." I moved in for yet another kiss.

The next morning, I noticed that Ben had packed more than I expected. I paid attention to see if he was going to pack the dress he got me, but he didn't. I do know that he was in charge of packing our ice-skates, so I figured that was part of the bulk. I decided not to pester him about it.

I was surprised to see that Ben rented the same cabin that we had the last time we were there! He tricked me when he showed me a different cabin on the internet. I bounced around the place in jubilee after we set our luggage down. I jumped at Ben and wrapped my legs around him after he caught me. He swung me around in a circle and then we kissed.

"I hear that vacation sex is something to be reckoned with," I said with a mischievous smile.

"And I'm gonna give you all you can handle." He smiled back at me. "But not tonight."

"What?" I asked in surprise. He had never refused me before. I let myself down off of him. "Why not tonight?" I asked with my arms still around his neck.

"I want you to want it *so bad* tomorrow."

"I always want it bad," I said confused.

"I know, but I want you to want it *more*. I promise it'll be epic."

"All right." I sighed lightly, trying to hide my disappointment. I walked over to retrieve my luggage and said, "I am kind of tired tonight anyway." As I unpacked, it occurred to me that Ben and I hadn't had sex since Christmas. He just seemed too busy lately. We had never gone so long without it. I furrowed my brow as I pondered why. No matter, I'd surely get some tomorrow like he promised.

The next morning, we went hiking. I'd never hiked in the winter before, and I found it to be quite enjoyable. Ben and I came across a small meadow with fresh snow. I scooped up some snow and whipped a snowball at the back of his head. Before he could turn around, I hit him twice more.

He wiped the snow off the back of his neck and said, "You dirty dog. You have no idea what you've unleashed!" He darted toward me at full speed. I hesitated for a moment as I decided whether to counterattack or evade. I chose to evade him, but it was no use. He tackled me into the snow and pinned me down with his legs straddling my body. The snow was so soft and deep that I sunk several inches in the powder. He took fists of snow smearing it across my face, like he was the school bully and I was his prime victim.

"No! Nooo!" I let out blood-curdling shrieks. I bridged up and down, trying to throw him off of me, but instead my feet sank deep into the snow. Then I grabbed his legs at his inner thighs, pulled myself down lower so that my head was near his crotch, and I kicked my legs up together. I was trying to latch my heels around his shoulders and pull him off of me. I've seen similar things like this done in kung-fu movies. It would've worked, too, if he wasn't so tall. I hit his shoulders with my feet twice. He turned to look behind him and immediately knew what I was trying to do. He leaned forward to dodge my kicks.

"You sneaky little brat! *Now* what are you going to do?" He laughed, as I was in quite the predicament. My head was still stuck in his groin area, and I had done this to myself. He wasn't going to win this time! I was determined. I forcefully spun around onto my stomach. I grabbed his thighs, got my footing, and then pushed him off of me using my shoulders for leverage. He landed forward into the snow on his hands and knees. (This maneuver would not have been possible without the deep snow that allowed me to turn over.) I wasn't satisfied. I lunged at him from behind and grabbed his one arm, causing him to land cheek-first into the snow. I held one arm behind his back and leaned my body weight on him as I stuffed snow down his pants with my free hand.

"Ya like that, baby? Do ya? Huh? Do ya!?" After I stuffed him a few times, he somehow rolled me onto my back and freed his arm. Then he turned over and pinned me down again. I squealed in dismay. Ben smiled just before he grabbed my coat and pulled me forward. To my surprise, he kissed me.

"You have stooped to a new low, Ericka Janelle Marshall," he said. "I love it. You win this time." He leaned forward and kissed me again. "Don't press your luck though," he warned me as he got up. He pulled me into standing by my coat. No, I wasn't going to press my luck. I smugly took the win.

We ate a late lunch at a local eatery, went back to the cabin to chill, and then got ready for our sleigh ride. Ben told me to bring my camera because he wanted to show me something spectacular along the way.

I took some photos during the sleigh ride, but, for the most part, I wanted to be more in the moment. I smiled and squeezed Ben tight as we passed the beautiful snow-covered pines, enjoying their fresh scent. Ben and I commented on how lovely this winter wonderland was, but we sat silently most of the ride, holding each other close.

At one point, I felt overwhelmed by the beauty of it all. I almost said to Ben, "Isn't He wonderful. He's in every ray of sunshine, every infinitely unique snowflake..." But that thought quickly caused my throat to choke. In a matter of ten seconds, I went through a whirlwind of emotions. First, I thought I was going to cry, but instead I suppressed that with anger. I restrained that angry monster only to let panic take its place. I didn't want to ruin this treasured moment, so I tried to redirect my mind. My heart raced as my thoughts darted. I abruptly jolted my head to the left once to change the channel. "You look crazy when you do that, Rick," I thought as I flicked my tears away with my glove before they could even hit my face.

Ben noticed my short nonverbal outburst, and he squeezed me tight to comfort me. "It's so beautiful. It's quite beautiful. Thank you for this," I said nervously, trying to cover my tracts.

"I'm so glad you're enjoying this," he said just before he pecked me on my cheek. I desperately clung to him until the wave of emotions settled. "We are almost there," he said with a spark in his eyes. I smiled at him and got my camera ready.

The driver brought the sleigh to a stop. Ben hopped out first and lifted me down. I giggled because, obviously, he didn't have to do that. He took my hand, and we leaped through the snow. I laughed at his sprightliness as he dragged me behind him. The closer we got to our destination, the deeper the snow got. We staggered through the deep snow, leaving trenches behind us. Finally, we stopped. We were both short of breath. Ben pointed to the sun starting to set over the cavern. The cavern was covered in snow. Stalactite-like waterfalls were frozen in place. I dredged closer to get a better look. There was a light blue hue deep in the frozen falls. It was indeed beautiful. I lifted my camera and took a few shots. Then I put my camera down and I fell into a trance, as I was captivated by this splendor. I was so far away that, just for a couple of moments, I forgot that I wasn't alone. I turned around to find Ben. There he was kneeling in front of me, holding a ring. I felt a wave of numbness and tingling flood through my body. My legs felt weak.

"Rick, I can't imagine my life without you. I want to be part of your life forever. I can't wait another day to ask you: will you marry me?"

I collapsed to my knees in the powder. Honestly, I don't know how I stood there long enough to let him finish his proposal. I knelt there silent and in complete shock. I had no idea that this was what this trip was about! I was motionless and in complete awe at how romantic his proposal was. I tried to speak. My mouth was moving but nothing came out. Finally, after several attempts, a barely audible "yes" came out. Ben smiled, grabbed my hand, and pulled off my glove. He put the ring on my finger and smiled even bigger. I sat there expressionless because it still felt like a dream. He leaned forward and kissed me. At that moment, everything felt real. My senses came back to me. I let out several gasps or laughs, I'm not sure which, as I looked at my ring.

"I love you, angel," Ben said to me. He grabbed me by my coat and pulled me forward to kiss me again.

"I love you, too, Ben," I replied. He wiped a tear of joy from my face.

We frolicked back to the sleigh where the horses and driver awaited us. We held each other so tight and kissed often on the ride back. When we got back to the cabin, I tackled Ben down to the couch and started kissing him.

"When should we get married?" I asked him joyfully.

"I'm so glad you asked," he smiled coyly. "Tomorrow."

"Whaaat?" I asked with a laugh.

"I've hired a minister. I rented a gazebo. I got you an outfit; your mom helped with that. And I've secured a handful of guests: your parents, my dad and grandma, and Scott."

"You're serious?" I asked. It sure did sound real.

"Yes." He tucked the lock of my hair that fell into his face behind my ear lovingly. "I can't stand to see you and your family at odds over us living together," he said compassionately. "We were going to get married sooner or later. Why not tomorrow!?" He beamed.

Tears filled my eyes. I was speechless for several moments. Gravity took one of my tears down to his face. I brushed it off of his skin and said, "I love you so, so much." I smiled and kissed his lips. "Tomorrow sounds perfect." I kissed him again and then laughed. Another tear fell down my face. I was overjoyed. After several moments, I pulled away from him and said, "So that's what all your sneaking around was about!" He laughed a little.

"So you noticed!?" He laughed even louder.

"Of course I *noticed!* That's what I do! I notice things!" We laughed together. I tried to kiss him again, but it was hard because we were both still laughing.

He patted my waist and said, "Let's go try on your outfit and make sure it fits."

"Well, it's too late now if it doesn't!"

"It'll fit! Go!" He guided me to the bedroom from behind with his hands on my hips. He opened up the mystery luggage and pulled out a beautiful cream colored, thigh-length Snow Princess Cape Style coat with large buttons down the front.

"Wow! It's beautiful!" I snatched it from him and held it up in front of me.

"I'm *so* glad you like it," he said, beaming. By the time I put it down, he had the rest of my outfit in front of me. There was a cream-colored hat that matched the coat perfectly, a red fleece long-sleeve shirt that I was to wear under the coat, warm-looking black pants, and fleece-lined black boots. The pants and boots were cute but practical. I liked that. I wondered if Mom or Ben knew me better. In general, I desire practical more than stylish clothing.

"Who picked out the outfit?" I asked.

"I did," Ben replied. I smiled to myself. Of course he did. "I went through your closet and found your clothing and shoe size," he boasted. He had every right to boast. "I talked to your mom as well, because sometimes you wear bigger clothes than your size." I put the clothes on the bed and grabbed his shirt to pull him closer to me so that I could kiss him. He embraced me as I did so.

"I love the idea of an outdoor wedding in the winter," I said excitedly.

"Yeah, that was a gamble. I'm glad to hear that," he said as he gently rocked me side to side.

"What are *you* going to wear?" I asked.

"A black trench coat, black pants and boots, and a red tie."

"Wow. That sounds great. You picked out the colors yourself, or did you have help?"

"All me," he said. "Oh, there is just one more thing," he said with a cheeky grin.

"What is it?" I asked hesitantly, only because of his smile.

"Could you wear these in your hair?" He reached in the luggage and pulled out two red ribbons.

"Oh my gosh! That's so specific!" I laughed. By the look on his face, I gathered that he was a little embarrassed to ask. "Of course! Anything for you, Ben." I took the ribbons from his hand and put them in my pocket. I kissed his hand and then spun myself around, landing my back into his chest and holding his arm across my stomach. I leaned my head back on his shoulder and raised my other arm in order to put my hand behind his neck. I stood there in the renowned *Dirty Dancing* pose. He put his free hand on my side and laughed heartily.

"Whaaa..." He couldn't stop laughing. "What the heck was that?" He laughed some more.

"That was my sexy move," I said, taking full credit. Then I puckered up very large and obnoxious-like.

He laughed some more. "You, ha ha," he started. "You need some work on your sexy moves."

"Kiss me," I instructed him. I leaned my head back toward him and pulled his neck forward. He kissed me from behind. Our silliness and laughing quickly changed to something else. It was invigorating to do anything new together, even something as simple as kissing in a different position. I sucked on his bottom lip and he slid his hand up my side and to my breast. Seconds after he did that, he defused the situation by pulling his lips away from mine and turning me around to face him.

"Rick, I, uh, hope you don't mind that I did all of the planning. I just wanted to surprise you. I want you to be happy with the wedding." He sounded a little concerned.

I looked up at him and said wholeheartedly, "Ben, the only thing I need is you." I shook my head side to side and declared, "Nothing else matters." I pulled him closer to me and raised up on my toes so that I could kiss him again. Then I flashed him an ear-to-ear grin and said, "Everything's perfect." I grabbed his shirt and jerked him back and forth as I said boisterously, "I can't believe that everything's going to be perfect!" He couldn't have smiled any bigger himself. "*You're perfect*," I said earnestly. I kissed him long and passionately. I caressed my hand around his neck and the other around his back. Our kiss quickly became hot and heavy.

He pulled away from my lips and said, "We have to wait one more night. We can do that, can't we?"

"Yes, we can," I assured him.

"I hear just-married sex is something to be reckoned with," he said. I smiled at his wit and then realized that's why we hadn't had sex in a while. He wanted our wedding night to be special. When I looked into his eyes, I knew that I was the luckiest girl in the world. That knowledge was unbreakable.

It was a ten o'clock wedding, and I was grateful for that. I couldn't imagine waiting until the afternoon to get married. We were going to meet our families for breakfast and then drive to the gazebo together.

We pulled into the restaurant parking lot and waited for the gang to arrive. Dad and Mom arrived first. I jumped out of the car and darted toward them.

"Mom! Dad! I'm getting married!" I yelled as I ran toward them, but I knew they already knew that. I hugged them both individually.

"Yeah, we heard," Mom said in a playful, sarcastic tone.

"We're so happy for you," Dad jumped in. Then we group hugged together. Dad kissed me on my cheek.

"You look so darling," Mom said as she touched my low ponytails that I had in front of my shoulders. She looked at the red ribbons and added, "Nice touch." Her mood turned a little stern when Ben walked over. "I thought it was bad luck for the groom to see the bride before the wedding," she said.

"Pish-posh," I said jovially. "There'll be no talk of bad luck today."

Scott, Marv, and Ben's grandma pulled in right after we greeted my folks. "Grandma isn't coming?" I asked Mom as I watched them park. It was the first time I called her Grandma, instead of June, since her insults toward Evie.

"No, honey, she couldn't make it." I was quite sure that meant that she didn't want to come. I swallowed down my tears, and I welcomed the new arrivals.

"Marv! Scott! Lindsay! We're getting married!" I waived and jogged over to them. I hugged Marv and Grandma Lindsay first.

"You look remarkable, hon!" Marv said as I hugged him.

"Oh, hon, just call me Grandma," Lindsay said after she pecked my cheek. Ha! So Marv takes after his mom with regards to using the word hon.

I hugged Scott last. "Wow, just wow," he said to me after we hugged. He looked me up and down.

"Ben picked this out," I said as I smiled widely.

"I know," he said as he smiled back.

I grabbed his hands and skipped around in a circle, forcing him to turn with me. "I'm gettin' married. I'm gettin' married," I said in a childish sing-song way. He laughed hard at me. Ben rescued Scott by snatching me from behind with a bear hug.

Ben smiled lavishly and said, "Here, let me take this trouble off your hands."

Mike, Aaron, and Michelle pulled in last. I had no idea that they were coming! Another one of Ben's surprises. I turned around to face Ben and gave him a shocked, but pleased, expression. I couldn't say anything to him because I knew that I'd cry. I walked up to my best friends and hugged them all. I was quiet for several moments. I finally felt composed enough to speak, so I said, "This is a surprise. I didn't know you were coming. I didn't even know we were getting married!"

"Yeah, we found out before you did," Michelle said.

"I'm so glad you're all here," I said to the gang.

"We wouldn't miss this circus for the world," Mike said. We were all in great spirits during breakfast.

When we arrived at the gazebo, I was speechless. Ben and I walked hand-in-hand toward the frozen pond. The powder generously covered the ground, the bark on the trees, and the ice-covered pond. The morning sun peeked over the tall trees, glistening off of the snow. It was surreal. I grabbed Ben's bicep with my other hand. So I had a double grip on him: holding his hand *and* hanging on his arm. I continued to walk beside him, wrestling with my emotions. I unconsciously squeezed his hand and arm tight as we walked together. He stopped dead in his tracks and turned toward me. He put his hand on my cheek and smiled.

"No," Ben said and then pecked me on my lips. "No," he said and kissed me again. "Not yet. You have to wait until the ceremony." He let out a little laugh. I looked down and pressed my lips together. I took a deep breath and regained control. He lifted my head up to look into my eyes. "It's breathtaking, isn't it?"

"Yeah," I replied softly.

"But it's nothing compared to how radiant you look." He gave me a longer, sultry kiss.

"Whoa, whoa!" Scott protested as he caught up to us. "No one said 'Man and Wife' yet." I smiled at Scott and then leaned my head onto Ben's chest and hugged him. He wrapped his arms around me. I closed my eyes for a few seconds and let his love surround me.

Mom and Dad were right behind Scott. Mom walked up to Ben and fastened a red rose to his trench coat collar. "I'm so happy to have you as my son-in-law," she said before she kissed his cheek. Then Mom fastened one to my coat as well. "There," she said triumphantly. Shortly after that, the pastor pulled in. Mom turned to Dad and motioned for him to accompany her to go greet the pastor.

I looked Ben up and down. He looked amazing in his black pants, black boots, black gloves, black trench coat, black knitted hat, red tie, red rose, and his full, neatly trimmed beard. The red rose took him to a new level of dashing. He noticed my pining gaze. He put his arms around me and rocked me side to side. "You got something on your mind?" he asked coyly.

"You look *dashing,"* I said breathlessly.

"*Do* I?" he said with a smirk. He liked to make fun of the words I chose sometimes. This was one of those times.

"You have *no* idea," I said with a serious tone. We gazed longingly at each other.

Mom motioned for us to come over to the gazebo, and we had a quick conference with the minister. He asked us if we needed help with our vows, but we declined. I was just as stirred about the vows as I was about getting married. Mom presented me with my bouquet of red and white roses that Ben chose. They were perfect.

I looked at him and said, "You…are a Jedi master." He gave me his crinkle-nose smile and unrestrained laugh that revealed the vein in his forehead.

The time had come, and the ceremony commenced. It was better than anything I'd ever imagined. The sun shined brightly through the clouds with the rays scattered across the frozen, snow-covered pond. The minister spoke about the roles of a man and wife from a Biblical sense. I appreciated that Ben asked for a religious ceremony. I had a warm feeling blanket me, as if God himself showed up to our wedding. Of course He did, in that he is Omnipresent, but it felt more personal than that.

Ben had asked me if I didn't mind going first with my vow, and I had no problem with that. It was important for me to be concise and short, because I didn't want to bawl at my wedding. We held hands as we exchanged vows. Mine went like this:

"Ben, I have always kept people at arms-length because I've been hurt so many times. But when we met, I was completely immersed in your world. I knew even before our first kiss that you were going to be mine. I know without a doubt that we were meant to be together. I promise to be your everything, forever."

Ben was pleased with my vow. Mom started to sniffle. Ben said his vow next. His vow to me was raw and seemed unrehearsed, but smooth. It went like this:

"Rick, I have screwed up so many times in my life and made so many mistakes that I thought I was destined to be alone, or at best, I'd have to settle and not be truly happy. But then you came *crashing* into my life and turned everything upside down. You make me want to be the best I can possibly be. I have never been so happy in my life as I have been since I've met you. I will be your one-and-only, forever."

The honesty in his words wrenched my heart to the point of tears. Mom was on stand-by with a hand full of tissues. Michelle was tearful too.

We exchanged rings and were pronounced "Man and Wife." The warmth of our kiss could've melted all the snow around us. Our loved ones cheered as we walked down the gazebo steps.

Scott planned a surprise for us just after we descended from the gazebo: Ben and I repeatedly got pelted with snowballs as we walked past our family. Even Grandma Lindsay got off a few good shots. It caught us both off guard. I could tell by Ben's face that he had no idea this was coming. He picked me up and swung me around to block the snowballs from hitting me. Meanwhile, Ben continued to get pelted in the back.

"Well don't just stand there! Get 'em!" I bossed. We picked up the snow and packed it tight and whipped it back at the intruders. We were nice and cautious about it with the elders, but we were out for blood with Scott, Mike, Aaron, and Michelle. Scott got hit full-on in the face numerous times. He was no saint either. Ben and I both took a couple shots to the noggins.

Eventually, Mom busted up the ruckus saying, "No more! They still have pictures!" I looked around for the photographer, who was documenting the whole snowball fight. I was elated about that and couldn't wait to see how those pictures turned out.

Mom pulled me aside to help me fix my makeup. Then the formal pictures began. I insisted on having formal pictures taken *after* the wedding when our smiles would be maximal. It took some convincing because it wasn't the norm. It was cold enough to see our breath, so we all dressed for the occasion. It was charming that everyone kept their hats and gloves on during the pictures. We had a forty-five-minute session, so we let the photographer start us off with the usual poses. After he finished, he asked us if we had any other poses in mind.

My brain sprang into action. "I got this," I told Ben. The photographer nailed all of the serious poses, such as me leaning my head on Ben's chest with our arms wrapped around each other, so I opted for nontraditional poses. Some of those included me riding piggy back on Ben, Ben holding me with my legs wrapped around his waist (a static pose and then one with Ben spinning me around), and Scott and Ben posing with snowballs ready to be tossed. I quickly grabbed Dad and Mom and got us into a three-man pose, simulating how the Monkees walked during the theme song of their TV series. We stood side-by-side with our arms wrapped around each other, and we all had our right foot forward and around front of the person to our right.

Our photography time was coming to an end when I thought of something funny that I wished to have a picture of. I was kind of bummed about not having thought of it sooner. "Ooh," I moped. "I would've loved a picture of Ben looking like Hawkeye Pierce."

The photographer looked intrigued. He tilted his head to the side and said, "What were you thinking exactly?"

"Well, remember the episode where Hawkeye did a movie for the army, and he had the fake nose and eyeglasses prop, along with the cigar?"

"I have a pair of those glasses in my car," he announced.

"Are you serious!?" I cheered.

"Give me a sec and I'll get them." He started toward his car. I shot Ben an excited glance. Ben rolled his eyes at me, but he couldn't hide his smile.

"I actually have a cigar in my car," Scott said. I shrieked in joy, clapped, and bounced up and down. Ben laughed at my excitement. Scott took off toward his car, knowing time was of the essence.

"Unbelievable!" I said to Ben just before I grabbed him and kissed him.

"*You're* unbelievable," he retorted insolently.

My eyes got real big. "Dad! Do you still have that stethoscope in your car!?" Dad often had one handy so that he could check for gut sounds on the horses in case of colic.

"Yes I do!" he said. Then he headed straight for the car to grab it.

Mike rolled his eyes and then smiled at me. "I have the perfect hat in my car." He took off for it.

It was a dream come true. I had Ben, my Hawkeye Pierce, dressed up in prop glasses with a fake nose while holding a cigar. I had Mike stand in the back ground with bad posture, Dad's stethoscope in his ears, his hat on, and his eyes crossed. I couldn't believe that between all of us, we had enough props to make it look like we planned this ahead of time. We all had a big laugh about it after we were done. It was a great picture to end on. I kissed Mike on the cheek for being such a good sport. It was a perfect wedding.

After the wedding, our family and friends headed back home, and Ben and I headed back to the cabin. Ben had reserved the cabin for five days for our honeymoon. He startled me when he swooped me up to carry me over the threshold.

"You didn't think you were just going to walk in, did you?" he said as he carried me into the cabin. He smiled at the fact that he startled me.

"I didn't think..." I stopped. "It didn't occur to me..." I stopped again. "Yes, I thought I was just going to walk in." He smiled at my awkwardness. I smiled back. He put me down and I started to take my coat off, but Ben stopped me.

"Allow me," he said. It took him a while to take off my coat because of the numerous buttons. Finally, he removed my coat and hung it up beside his. He led me over to the kitchenette where he poured us a glass of wine. He had two bottles, his and my favorite. He poured himself Cabernet Sauvignon and Riesling for me. We stood at the kitchenette island and drank our wine together.

"Ya know, everything's gonna be okay," I said to him most sincerely. He knew what I was talking about. I wasn't talking about our love; that was solid. He leaned forward and rested his elbows on the counter to get closer to me. "I didn't think I was going to be able to pull it together," I continued. "I mean, I'm still mad, and I still don't understand," I paused a moment as I fought to control my emotions, "but I'm gonna be okay, thanks to you." He reached for my hand and held it in his warm hands. I placed my other hand on top of his and gently stroked his fingers. "Is it selfish or silly for me to talk about this on our wedding day?" I asked remorsefully as I gazed down at our hands.

"No," he simply replied. We finished our wine in good time. He poured us another glass. This time red wine for me and white wine for him. He gave me a spirited look. I giggled as he handed me the red wine. Drinking each other's favorite wine was hopelessly romantic.

After we finished our second glass of wine, Ben walked up to me and took the ribbons out of my hair. As he did so, I thought about the song "Just What I Needed" by The Cars. I reflected on the lyrics, "It's not the ribbons in your hair." I wondered if he had wanted me to wear my hair like this because this was his song of choice the night that we first said "I love you" to each other. And this was the song that reconnected us after we had been iced. I was convinced that this was all done on purpose. My heart began to race. I was surprised at how clairvoyant I was feeling despite the intense buzz.

He combed through my wavy hair with his fingers and then pulled me close for a kiss. His kiss was so soft but intense. It felt like a first kiss in a way–like a first kiss between new lovers. His kiss elevated me to the point where I felt like I was floating. We kissed a long time. I refused to be the one to escalate this sweet kiss into the inevitable love-making, but only because it felt so right.

Ben finally picked me up and carried me to the bedroom. He sat me on the bed and began to disrobe. I sat there and watched him intently, so much so that it seemed like I had forgotten that I, too, needed to undress. Every movement he made was supernaturally sexy. He walked closer to me as I sat on the bed. I pulled his naked body close to me and kissed his stomach, and he caressed my hair. I suddenly became aware that I was fully clothed, so I began to undress. Ben eagerly helped me along the way. As I removed my shirt, he was unfastening my pants. By the time I dropped my shirt on the floor, he had unfastened my bra.

We have had sex so many times before, but this felt really special. Aside from our sounds of pleasure, the only thing we had said to each other in this matrimonial intimacy was "I love you." Another facet of our love-making that was different than usual was that we spent so much time watching each other's faces–watching each other revel in our celebration of marriage. I was amazed at how comfortable he felt–we felt–with this. In contrast to the love-making extravaganza near the Christmas tree just a couple weeks ago, we rarely kissed. Rather, we touched each other continually with our hands. He gently touched my lips, my face, my hair, and my legs. I touched his lips, his neck, his torso, and his chest. Every so often, I'd slide my foot up the back of his leg as he moved inside me. He'd occasionally get a little crazy and grab my butt for several hard, intense thrusts. I enjoyed watching his face as he came inside me. It was epic love-making, never to be forgotten.

Ben was tired from all of the planning. After we made love, we lay in bed, and I caressed his body as he tried to fight the impending slumber. I told him not to fight it. I gently ran my fingers through his hair, across his face, and through his beard, coaxing him to sleep. I periodically kissed his cheek and brushed my lips across his beard.

"I'm never shaving again," he mumbled in a stupor just before he fell asleep. The fact that he liked what I was doing so much to make him say that made me smile.

The remainder of the honeymoon was just as remarkable as the beginning of it. We ate well at the local restaurants, and we played hard via ice-skating, snowmobiling, and snow shoeing. Upon returning to the cabin, we drank readily from the assorted wines and whiskeys that Ben brought. And, of course, we brought the curtain down every evening with extravagant love-making.

One particular bedroom episode that was quite exceptional, was when I decided to be on top. I hadn't been on top since the second time we had sex! Ben was right, trying that position on the second time was way too soon, but I wouldn't listen. It was so incredibly painful because it was too soon and due to Ben's volcanic passion that I avoided that position altogether. My fault though because, again, I wouldn't listen. I never admitted to Ben just how badly it hurt, but he knew because of my avoidance.

Ben was thrilled when I insisted on being on top. I started off tentatively but quickly realized that wasn't necessary. Ben loved watching me morph through phases of realizing what I could do while sitting on top of him. At one point I laughed a little in between my sounds of pleasure, because I couldn't believe how good it felt.

After I did that, Ben said, "Aw yeah, baby." His words and sounds of pleasure *always* made me come unglued. I hammered him a little harder. "That's it. That's it," he said. I bent one of my legs up and put my foot near his shoulder and pounded him even harder. "Uh. Unreal! Ah! Fuck!"

"Say one more thing. I fuckin' dare you," I said breathlessly while I recklessly thrashed him.

"Fuck me, Rick! Fuck me hard!" I bent my other leg and fucked him as hard as I could. I had to use my hands on his thighs for balance as I did so. It took me a couple of tries to get the perfect position to where I could keep fucking him hard with the least amount of exertion. It was like playing a game of Twister. The game-winning position was with my left foot near his right armpit and my leg completely bent up, my right thigh resting along his chest with my knee pinning down his left shoulder, my left hand on his right thigh, pushing off for leverage, and my right hand behind his left shoulder to assist with pulling my body up so that I could come crashing down on him again. I've never heard him as loud as he was right then. We both were. It was absolutely a thunderous event.

After he came, he said to me breathlessly, "What were we both saying about vacation-sex and married-sex?" His neck and chest were blotched pink. His body had never reacted this way to sex before.

I laughed as I tried to catch my breath. Finally, I said, "That we heard it was something to be reckoned with?"

He smiled sheepishly at me. "Hell yeah it is!" We laughed some more.

So we made love, had sex, and fucked two to four times a day while on our honeymoon. At least one of those was always with me on top, facing different directions or trying different angles. Before our honeymoon ended, I found *thee position:* the position that caused me to cum 100% of the time. It was with me on top facing him, sitting as upright as I could while doing a slow, deep grind. The feeling before I was about to cum was just like before. It felt wrong. It felt like I might pee, but I didn't. It was a mental challenge to get past that wrong feeling in order to sail into ecstasy. I couldn't stop saying "no" or "I can't" to save my life. Ben had to coach me a little. "Don't stop. Keep going," he said while my cerebral warfare persisted. At first, I was satisfied with cumming for several seconds. But the next time I pushed it to see if I would keep cumming or if it just automatically stopped, like a male orgasm. As long as I sustained the position, I kept cumming! When I came, I seemed to do the same thing every time. I'd tip my head back, grab my breast with one hand, and slide my other hand down my torso. I don't know why. It seemed involuntary. My longest run was about three minutes. While this was happening, I said to Ben, "I'm just gonna keep cumming until you cum! Please cum!" Our bodies made that disgusting squish sound, and I saturated him and the linens beneath us. He was ecstatic that we both came at the same time on several occasions. Our physical relationship was electrifying.

When we returned home, Ben had one more surprise for me. We had the weekend left before we had to return to work. Ben told me that we were going out Saturday night, but he wouldn't say where. I had mentioned to him twice that I'd rather stay home because I was tired from our honeymoon. As a matter of fact, I'd rather spend the night alone with him just about any time. He decided that he had to pull drastic measures to get me excited and agree to go.

"You're going to wear your turquoise outfit tonight," he revealed.

"What!?" He totally had my attention. He smiled bigger knowing this.

"Yeah, so you can't say no," he gleamed.

"Where are we, where are we, where are we going?" I asked him excitedly while I pulled at his shirt in a child-like manner.

He laughed as he tried to fend me off. "No! I'm not telling you! Get off me!"

"Where, where, where are we going? Where we going?" I persisted annoyingly as I bounced up and down in his way at every turn.

"Ugh!" Ben grabbed me, picked me up, threw me over his shoulder, and carried me out to the living room. He tossed me down on the couch hard and held my hands down. "Ask me where we're going again? I dare you."

"Where are we going?" I asked without hesitation. Ben playfully chomped on my boob through my clothes. "Ahhhh!! No! No!!" I shrieked. I squirmed and fought him without success. He just laughed at me.

"Ask me where we're going again," he said with a puzzled look on his face, knowing full well that I wouldn't dare ask again.

"No! No! No! Unhand me, you oaf!" He laughed some more as I struggled hard to get away. Then he held his mouth open near my breast taunting me. I shrieked and thrashed some more, "Ahhhhh!" I screamed. He laughed so hard, but he wouldn't let go. I was laughing, too, in between my shrieks. I bridged my hips up and down fast, trying to throw him off of me and off of the couch. After I failed at this wild attempt, we were both almost paralyzed from laughing so hard. I couldn't fight him anymore and he was losing his grip a little. Finally, I mustered up enough strength to roll him off onto the floor. We both hit the floor pretty hard, which only prolonged our laughter.

As our laughter died down, I started tearing Ben's clothes off. "What are you doing?" he asked, only because I was intentionally being really rough with him.

"Whatever I want to," I said. I performed really aggressive fellatio on him as he squirmed on the living room floor. I'm not sure if he liked it, didn't like it, or was just afraid that I might hurt him. I figured that it was definitely a combination of all of the three at different points in time, depending on what I was doing. I made sure to mix it up a lot and be unpredictable. Something I learned from him. I do know one thing. I know *I* liked it.

During this floor session, I decided that I was going to push the limits. I started licking Ben's balls while I jacked him off. He gasped and was startled by this. He tensed his whole body up and held his breath. I smiled at his reaction. I gave him a few moments to adjust to this sensation just before I put one of his balls in my mouth. I sucked on it ever so gently. His reaction was priceless. "Uh! Ah! I don't know, if uh, that's a good idea!" he said with abounding alarm.

I removed him from my mouth and said, "Trust me. It's a good idea." Then I put his other side in my mouth and gently sucked on it.

"Uh! Ah!" he went on. "Please be careful," he whispered to me in full apprehension. I was very careful. And I was thoroughly pleased that I had steamrolled over his comfort level. I wondered if he liked the taste of his own medicine.

I finished him by jacking him off deep and hard. His reaction after he came in my hands was, "Uh, wow."

"You can expect more crazy shit like this now that we're married," I boasted.

"Uhh ha ha ha," he laughed deeply. I loved that crazy laugh. I'd only heard it about three times now. Each time was rapturous.

Later that evening, I exited the bathroom looking smashing. I left my hair down this time, accenting my waves with styling gel. I wore my bangs low with a straight across cut. Fortunately, I had cut the jagged edges out of my bangs before we got married. I walked up to Ben to see him wearing a black suit and a turquoise tie that matched my dress.

"Oh my God! You look gorgeous!" I said to him. I ran my hands down his suit and smiled.

"I had to try, in order to be seen with this pretty young thing, hanging on my arm." He twirled my turquoise and purple locks around his fingers.

"I would've taken these streaks out of my hair if I had known we were getting married." They had faded quite a bit by then though.

"Well, I'm glad I didn't tell you then." He leaned forward and kissed me. After he kissed me, he looked into my eyes and said, "I was right." I looked at him with a puzzled expression. "This outfit makes your eyes look even more beautiful." I smiled, and then he kissed me again.

"Where are we going?" I whispered to him just after he withdrew his lips from mine.

"You'll see," he answered patiently. I smiled at him.

We headed off to Findlay, but he still wouldn't tell me where we were going exactly. It was hard, but I tried to be patient and occupy my mind with random chit chat. We arrived at a large building that I've never seen before, even though I had been to Findlay dozens of times. There were quite a few cars. Maybe it was a dance club. No, we were dressed too nice for that. I was completely stumped.

When we walked in, I was startled by a large group yelling, "Surprise!" Loud noises accompanied the shouting, including kazoos and pops from confetti cans. I jumped into Ben, knocking him off balance a little. Then I wrapped my arm around Ben's after we recovered our balance, and I tried to regain my composure. Ben laughed at my reaction.

"What is this?" I asked Ben, because I was still completely baffled from the shock of it.

"This is our wedding reception," he said, amused that I had to ask.

"Oh wow!" I looked around to see our families and friends gathered and smiling at us. Ben had many more attendees than I did, which made sense in that he had more family and friends than I did. Actually, the only friends of mine that were there were Mike, Michelle, and Aaron, and they were Ben's friends first. No matter, they were all there for us and that felt wonderful.

I looked at Ben in complete amazement. I was stunned at all he had done for me. I was overwhelmed with his expressions of love and romance that he showered me with that week. I hung on his arm as he guided me around the room to greet people.

As we walked, I noticed the crazy display of food, and that the decorations were exquisite. The DJ just started to jam. "Did you do all of this?" I asked Ben.

"No. Your parents did most of this. My dad helped a little too. All of the other stuff before tonight–that was all me."

"Oh my goodness," I said, still stunned. I had to force myself to smile as we greeted people in order to get the emotional and dumbfounded look completely off of my face.

My cousin, Lisa, was there. I marveled at how much she supported Ben and me, even early on, because Lisa and I weren't really that close. She roped me into answering all of her questions. How long had Ben and I been dating before we got married, was one of them. Not long. We had only known each other for about eight months. We had only dated for about six months. After I answered that question, I immediately reflected on how that meant that Evie's cancer had progressed so rapidly. It made me sick to think about how our wedding anniversary would always make me think about how long Evie had been gone since the dates were so close together.

I thought about how nice it would've been to have had my sister there for my wedding and reception. I wondered if I should've been grateful that the cancer took her quickly. She didn't suffer long. The pain that accompanied these thoughts differed from the pain I felt right after Evie passed. I had pain along my upper jaw bilaterally, which was totally symmetrical. I had an ache deep behind my nose, eyes, and throat. I probably had been clenching my jaw as I tried to bury this pain.

I spent a lot of time talking to Dad and Mom. I told them how thankful I was that they helped out so much with the reception. Dad told me how happy he was for me because he felt that Ben really was the one for me. I wondered if God had told him that. I always had trouble deciphering whether Dad was giving me his personal opinion, or if God had showed him something. I'm not sure why it mattered, but I seemed to wonder nonetheless. Regardless of the reason for Dad's approval, I appreciated that he supported us. Well, why wouldn't he? I was no longer "living in sin." You see? That's what I do. Every thought inside of me has a pong for every ping. Why couldn't I just take things at face value? I should've just been thankful for their approval and thought no more of it. Instead, I had to wonder about all sorts of stuff. Mom told me numerous times that I was the kind of kid who always asked questions and always wanted to understand things on a molecular level.

"Grandma couldn't make it?" I asked Mom during a short lull in our conversation.

"I guess not," Mom replied in a slightly irritated tone. I didn't understand why she wasn't there. I thought that she'd surely support us now that we were married. Our family wasn't really known to hold grudges.

"I'm gonna get some air. I'll be back in five," I told Mom. I walked outside, unlocked the car, and grabbed my cell phone. I was on the verge of tears. I looked at the time. It was still early. I thought if I called her, maybe she would come. I didn't want any more animosity between us. My call went straight to voicemail.

"Hi, Grandma. It's Rick. I just wanted to let you know that Ben and I got married last week–it was kind of a surprise for me–and that we are having a reception at the Circle P in Findlay. We'd really love it if you could make it. Bye." I stood in the cold a while longer, enjoying how my sadness and disappointment slowly transitioned into a feeling of full-body numbness. Nothing felt better on my mental anguish than cold did. Physical pain was a close second. I closed my eyes and took a few deep breaths. I watched the cloud of condensation leave my mouth as I exhaled. Ben walked up behind me, startling me.

"What's up?" he asked me.

"I'm just getting some fresh air." I sighed. "I also called Grandma to let her know where the reception is," I said as a matter of fact.

"Oh," he said.

I took his hand and said, "I'm ready to go back in now." We walked back inside.

I ran into Michelle straight away and started with a little chit-chat. "I think they over-did the gifts, don't you?"

"No," she replied. "That's pretty common for a wedding reception."

"Well, that's so nice," I said.

Michelle talked about how excited she was that Ben and I were married. She reminisced about the part she played in our getting together. I down-played that fact initially but decided to give her props. She basked in that. She asked me if Ben and I had talked about when we planned to start a family. She was a little upset to hear that we hadn't even come close to having that conversation. I told her not to worry about it. Nothing could tear us apart.

We did a lot of dancing that night. I loved that Ben wasn't shy on the dancefloor. His dancing didn't improve since the last time we danced, but he loved to have fun. And that's all I needed.

All of our closest friends and family members brought their "plus one," and that pleased me. Marv, Scott, and Mike all brought their girlfriends. They all seemed to have a great time. I was also glad that Aaron and Michelle brought the kiddos along. They had a good time as well.

Several hours into the reception, Grandma June showed up! I really didn't think she'd come, being that she missed my wedding and all. When I saw her walk in and take her coat off, I immediately got tunnel vision. I walked toward her as if no one else was in the room. It felt like a slow-motion parkour moment.

"Grandma! Hi!" I said as I hugged her. "I'm so glad you came," I told her. She held me tight, and for a long time too. This type of embrace would've been awkward under any other circumstances, aside from condolences. It was a mutual "I'm sorry" hug. I was sure of it.

"Me too, Ricky. Me too," she finally said. And that was it. Grandma and I were back to normal. She didn't verbally apologize to me and I didn't apologize to her. Neither one of us seemed to need an apology. The conflict was over.

My outfit was a big hit. It was simply too cute and classy. The fact that Ben's tie matched my outfit perfectly was also a big hit. The turquoise locks in my hair were quite the talk, as they matched my dress as well. Ben gloated from a distance as I told everyone about my surprise Christmas present, the surprise engagement, and the surprise wedding.

Scott put together a slide show of our wedding pictures. It was fantastic. I appreciated the thought that went into it. The pictures of the snowball fight and of Hawkeye and McIntyre were quite the crowd-pleaser.

At the end of the day, I was so tired. I was thankful to get to sleep in on Sunday. On the ride home, I told Ben that he was "amazing beyond description."

"I wasn't before I met you," was his reply. After I thought about his response, I told him that I was sorry that I couldn't be there for him during the hardest time of his life when his mom left. I realized that it was an impractical statement because of our age difference, but it was heart-felt just the same. I told him that I didn't know where I'd be if he hadn't been there for me at the hardest time of my life: losing my only sibling.

He understood the sentiment. Then he replied, "We wouldn't have worked out back then." I was surprised by his response.

"Why do you say that?" I asked.

"Because I wasn't ready for you then. Our timing was perfect because I was ready for you now." I marveled at his insight.

"Of course," I replied. "And I wasn't looking for the person you were then. I need you the way you are now."

Chapter 45: Newlywed Life.

Newlywed life was amazing. We never fought, and we were inseparable. We spent plenty of time with family and friends as well as reserving enough time for us to be alone. We drank and partied a lot, and our love-making was still supernatural.

One day, on a drive back from a weekend trip, I saw a sex store. We were far enough away from home that I knew no one there would know us, and so I impulsively got off on that exit. Ben looked at me, nonverbally questioning where I was going. "I just need to make a pit stop," I explained.

When I pulled into the parking lot, Ben said, "What are we doing here?"

I replied excitedly, "*We* are going to have some fun shopping."

He gave me a chuckle and an eye roll. Then he said with a serious tone, "I don't really think we need to be here. Our love life is amazing just the way it is."

"That's true," I confessed, "but it'll be fun to look around anyway." I gazed at him devilishly.

He laughed again and said, "Well this oughta be interesting." I giggled at his spirit as we got out of the car. Instead of being embarrassed that I was dragging him into a sex store, he decided to roll with it. I loved that about him!

Ben let me guide him around the store by his hand. "Well, we won't be needing any of these," I said flirtatiously to Ben as we walked past the dildos. He gave me a closed-mouth smile with a full gleam in his eyes. Even if we left with nothing, I was thrilled at the opportunity to flirt with my new husband. After I said that, I think he was on the same line I was. We walked by the bondage section, and I stopped dead in my tracks with my mouth hanging wide open. I'd never heard or seen of such things in my life! I looked back at Ben to see an amused look on his face. I pulled at his hand and said, "Let's keep moving."

"Now wait a minute," he said playfully. "Maybe *I* want to look at this section." He smiled at my ever-growing upset expression. "Hmm. What do we have here? Nipple clamps? That might be fun. Ooh. Do you want a whip or a paddle?"

"Neither!" I whispered harshly to him. "Now let's move on."

Ben laughed boisterously and held his stomach. "You're the one who wanted to come here."

Next, we moseyed into the anal stimulation section. "How about this?" I asked enthusiastically, referring Ben to the anal beads. "For you," I clarified. "For me to use on you," I illustrated clearly.

"I *like* this idea...for me to use on you," he smiled as he nodded. "Or I could just," he said before he put his finger in his mouth, seductively saturating it. I gasped.

I grabbed his shirt and pulled him toward me. "They have video cameras in here!" I whispered harshly.

"Well, I'm sure we just made someone's day," he chided.

"You're impossible!"

"Yep. And you married me, knowing that." That's true. I pressed my lips together, trying not to smile. "Do you want to keep looking? Because, I can do this to you all day," he said daringly. We picked up the pace and ended up leaving with just a Kama Sutra book.

The flirting worked. We were wild with passion when we entered the bedroom. We tore each other's clothes off, and then Ben tackled me onto the bed. We playfully kissed and groped as we rolled around.

Ben rolled me to my back and gave me a long, sultry kiss. Then he said, "I'm cashing in on my bet today." I glowed with anticipation. I remembered him saying that he might do me from behind while using my piggytails as reigns. I thought that he didn't have anything that I couldn't handle.

"Really?" I asked as I prepared myself mentally.

He paused and silently gazed into my eyes for added dramatic effect. "I'm gonna suck on your pussy," he finally said.

"What?" I asked. I hoped he just said that he was going to *fuck* my pussy. He kissed my lips again and sucked on my bottom lip.

When he removed his lips from mine, he said just as determined as before, "I'm gonna suck on your pussy." I did hear him right. I gasped and subconsciously tensed my arms and tried to push him away.

"No," I said. He looked at me passionately and just shook his head yes several times before he kissed me again. I stopped his kiss with another, "No."

"Why not?" he asked.

"Because I don't want you to."

"Why don't you want me to?"

"Because it's gross."

"Why do you think it's gross?" I thought that was self-explanatory, hence the hesitation to reply. "Do you mean that you think it'll taste bad?" he asked.

"Yes," I simply said. There was more to it than that, but I kept that to myself because I could barely function through this conversation with all the anxiety I was feeling. I knew that it wouldn't feel good partly because I wouldn't be able to relax enough for it to feel good and partly because I couldn't imagine a tongue or mouth down there feeling pleasurable at all. It'd just *feel gross*.

"So just use a feminine cloth first then." He got up and grabbed one from the bathroom and tossed it onto my stomach. I remained still, silent, and shocked because I realized that there was no way he was going to let me out of this. He recognized my incapacitated state, so he took this matter into his own hands. He took out the cloth from the wrapper and started to cleanse me with it.

"No," I said in dismay as he finished the task.

He was undeterred. "Look what we have here," he said with a surprised expression as he reached for the strawberry flavored lubricant from the nightstand. "Mmm. I love strawberries," he said with wide eyes. He put some on his hand and massaged my vaginal area with it. I was speechless for several moments. Ben seized that opportunity to kiss my lips seductively. He held the back of my neck with his hand as he kissed me while using his other hand to stimulate me down below. I was really into this and would've been completely happy with this instead of oral sex. I didn't bother telling Ben that because, honestly, I knew that he already knew that. Immediately after removing his lips from mine, he lightly pressed his fingertips on my lips for a dual purpose: to feed into my lip fetish to buy himself time to kiss his way down to my pussy and to keep me from telling him no. It was working on both accounts.

So he had his fingertips electrifying my lips, his other fingers provoking my clit and vagina, and his lips grazing down my abdomen. My body rolled up and down in pleasure with the rhythm of his hand as he did all of this. As he advanced lower with his lips, I began to tense up. "Uh," I said nervously as I tried to close my legs. Ben responded by going more hardcore on my lips by pinching and twisting them, just like I did to him before I left on my motorcycle trip. "Uhh," I said in a deeper voice. My eyes rolled back in my head and my legs collapsed out of their tense state. Then he put his full hand over my mouth firmly. The control he took over me caused me to convulse a couple of times while natural lubrication flowed from my vagina, drenching my genitals and Ben's hand. I body was so jacked-up from all of the conflicting emotions I was feeling. I experienced shock from his persistence despite my attempts at refusing, combined with pleasure and total apprehension.

His first touch with his mouth was to my clit. He moved his mouth as if he were giving me an open-mouth kiss. His hand no longer could reach my mouth, so I was able to verbalize my first uttering, "Huh." It was a sound one would hear if someone were punched in the stomach. I squeezed my legs together and tried to pull my pelvis away from him. Ben adapted quickly, capturing the right side of my pelvis by positioning his left arm over the top of and around my hip. This effectively kept me from squeezing my right leg in or moving that side altogether. Ben's next touch was exactly the same. I gasped and flailed my left side up and down, trying to free myself from him. This time he reached his right arm under the left side of my butt and clamped his hand down on my hip. I marveled at his troubleshooting skills during intimacy. He effectively had my pelvis locked in place using his arms in a figure eight pattern, which also kept my legs apart so that I couldn't resist him. He gave me another slow and deliberate kiss to my clit. "Ahh!" I exclaimed, exasperated that he had me completely contained. He kissed me again and again with just a little more pressure. "Uh, uh," I said as my body swelled up and down. Ben flowed right along with me as if he were a boat being lifted and lowered by the ocean. Then Ben transitioned to using his tongue on my clit. I screamed, "No, Ben! No!"

He stopped for a moment and said, "No tongue?" Before I could answer, he licked me again.

I screamed and dug my elbows into the bed, trying to pull my body up and away from him. I ended up pulling Ben up in bed with me. I rested on my elbows and bellowed, "No tongue!" as I breathed heavily.

He looked up at me analytically for a moment and then said, "Remember the first time I put your nipple in my mouth?" he asked rhetorically. "You didn't like it," he reminded me. "But now you love it." He had a point, and that pissed me off. Ben didn't give me a chance to respond. Instead, he aggressively pulled me back down on the bed. To my surprise, he started kissing my clit again. He did this several more times. Now that I had a comparison, the way he pressed his lips on my clit was much more tolerable than when he used his tongue. I made mildly contained exasperated noises as he continued.

All too soon, Ben transitioned from kissing to constantly sucking on my clit. "Oh, shit!" I yelled as I clenched every muscle in my body. This didn't deter him at all. He had my movements in check. I pierced his ears with my screams. "Motherfucker!" I added, to which he replied with more sucking. My movements transformed from predictable and fluent with his kisses, to unmanageable and riotous with his sucking. Finally, I shrieked, "Stop! That's enough!" Ben stopped and unlatched my pelvis. I pulled my legs together, put my hands across my chest defensively, and tried to roll to the side. Ben caught me mid-roll and pushed me back onto my back. Then he began to kiss his way back up my abdomen and chest.

When he got to my neck, he stopped and chuckled a little. "You lasted longer than I thought you were going to." He laughed again. "So you didn't hate that?" he asked. We both remembered how Ben tore me up after the Thanksgiving fiasco, and how I said that I didn't hate it.

"I didn't *hate* it," I said expressionless as I tried to catch my breath. Clearly, I was indicating that I didn't *like* it either. "Kiss me," I instructed Ben. He started to move his hand towards his mouth to wipe my essence off of his lips, but I intercepted his hand. "No. Kiss me like you are." Ben had a full-blown deer-in-headlights gaze. He thought that I didn't realize what I was asking him to do. I used my hand to guide his face toward mine. I put his disbelieving, paralyzed lips into my mouth. Ben breathed out quickly and gasped for air twice as I sucked on his bottom lip. He tasted like strawberries mixed with my essence. I didn't mind the taste at all. After Ben realized that I wasn't going to abort mission, he started kissing me back. My experimentation really turned him on. He went from paralyzed to floored in six seconds flat. He inserted himself inside of me without missing a kiss. He was wild, ravenous and unpredictable, keeping my body in a constant state of shock. This whole experience was sensational and mind-blowing. I felt like I was keeping my promise to Ben to keep it crazy since we got married.

Chapter 46: Sleep-Deprived.

Even though my relationship with Ben was perfect, my relationship with God was agonizing. I struggled to keep Him far from my mind. I didn't hate Him anymore, but I didn't want anything to do with Him either. Yes, I was *still* mad. It was hard to keep Him away because He had been my right hand for all of my life, up until Evie died. That's how I was raised. I was with Him daily because He was around me everywhere! If there was something wonderful or beautiful, He created it! I couldn't see a beautiful sunset or revel in a fragrant light rain without Him being there. In short, every time I had a good thought, I thought of God. Every time I thought of God, I was angry again. It was maddening! I concealed this from everyone around me, including my husband. It was *my* burden that I locked deep inside my heart.

Along the same lines, I was so thankful in my heart to have Ben who loved me so. But who was I thanking? Not fate, not the stars, nor any other sort of nonsense. I was thanking God, of course. I believed that God brought us together. It was hard not to think of God when I thought of how wonderful Ben was. God gave Ben to me. So when I thought of Ben, I often thought of God. When I thought of God, I'd get angry. So I bitterly buried my thankfulness over and over, as it would tend to resurface often and cause me pain. I was able to maintain the appearance of normal for the sake of my loved ones, but when I was alone, the agony of being pulled in opposite directions resonated into the deepest part of my soul. It was maddening!

After several months of newlywed bliss, I was overcome with internal conflict, and I went back to crying a lot when I was alone. That same painful sob that I was so familiar with when Evie first passed. The one that spewed from the wound rooted deep in my chest, expelling as quick as lightning. The one that felt like I had exposed nerves wrapped around the hole in my stomach. The one that would cause me to cough or dry-heave in between each agonizing gasp for air. Because we lived in town so close to neighbors, I would hide these house-shaking sobs with the noise from the bath tub filling and my music. I'd lock myself in the bathroom, turn my music on, sit in the tub naked while it filled, and sob. I'd have a bottle of whiskey or wine with me as I did so. "Just leave me alone!" I'd say to God. It was his fault that I felt this way. He was pulling on my heart, and I wanted Him to JUST LET GO!

Several months had passed since we had gotten married, and it was getting harder to maintain the presentation of normal. I looked sleep-deprived, and Ben became growingly worried about my deteriorated appearance. He decided that another Rock Band party was in order to elevate my mood. That didn't go so well. I told the gang that I'd rather just watch and enjoy the evening that way. Everyone's face was paralyzed with concern. Yeah, I wasn't the same girl who used to dance around the room anymore.

"I just haven't been sleeping well is all," I explained. I thought that'd be the end of it. That strategy worked so nicely with my church family when everyone kept asking me if I was okay the time that Ben and I were iced. When I went to the kitchen to refresh my beverage, I heard them whisper their concerns to Ben as loud as if I were standing right beside them.

Michelle started intensely with, "What's going on with Rick? Something's wrong."

Mike added, "Yeah, man. I thought she was getting better."

"I don't know," Ben said exasperated.

"Well, you need to figure this out," Aaron chimed in.

It's true that the last time we were together as a group, I was energized from being a newlywed. Ben and I were so affectionate in front of them, almost to the point of fault, right after we were married. I remember squeezing my fanny in between Ben's lap and the couch arm rest while I draped my legs across his lap. I had my arm around his neck, playing with his hair and ear. I thought it to be harmless enough to sit like this in front of the gang, but we pecked a lot and looked into each other's eyes with desire often. At one point after we smooched, I brushed my thumb across Ben's bottom lip, pulling it down and letting it bounce back into place as we penetrated each other with our eyes.

Mike, who was sitting closest to us, interrupted with, "All right, you two lovebirds. You only have to wait another two hours or so before you rip each other's clothes off again." Ben chuckled at this and got up to get us both a beverage. I sat there in my renowned Z-position, fully flushed in the face. Mike turned and noticed my demeanor. He laughed a deep, hard belly-laugh at my disposition. I'd only heard him laugh like that a handful of times. Yes, newlywed life originally had me completely distracted from my internal discord.

When the gang left for the evening, Ben said to me, "You've been kind of down lately. I thought having the gang over would cheer you up. What's going on?"

"I don't know, Ben," I said wearily. I was completely intoxicated at that point and wasn't in the mood to talk about it, not that I would've wanted to talk about it anyway. "But I know what will cheer me up," I added with an I-dare-you-to-come-get-me look.

"Yes, ma'am," Ben said as he stood up and reached for my hand to assist me to the bedroom.

I made a quick stop in the bathroom and emerged with two ponytails in my hair. Ben was already in bed waiting for me. I crawled from the foot of the bed toward him and said seductively, "Do you know what I have in mind?"

"I think I do," he said with fire in his eyes. I smiled at him. Yes, he was right. I wanted him to do me from behind and use my ponytails like reins, just like he had threatened to do during our basketball competition.

Sex with Ben was always exhilarating, but this was the drunkest I'd ever been during sex. Every touch from him was like a surprise to me. My erratic breathing, moaning, and gasping went unchecked. Ben didn't seem to mind.

After a generous amount of foreplay, Ben flipped me over onto my hands and knees and mounted me. As he went on thrusting inside of me, my legs started to slide apart farther and farther, almost to their max capacity. I quickly grabbed a pillow and put it under my chest and rested down onto my forearms. I explained to Ben that I did this to keep my legs from sliding any farther apart. I also added, "Please be careful," because of how wide open I was in this position. If he went crazy on me, it could've been devastating.

I should've learned that lesson already. Remember when Ben said that I shouldn't tell him what not to do because that only makes him want to do it more when we were on our fancy date? He stopped for a minute and pulled me to the edge of the bed so that he could stand. He pushed down on my back to slide me open just a bit farther.

"Ah, ahhh, ahhhh!" I wailed as he continued to flow quickly and forcefully in and out of me.

"Oh, Rick," Ben replied in ecstasy. He'd lighten up on me for a bit, and then go back to fucking me hard. During one of the calmer moments of him pounding me, I closed my eyes and thought about how frictionless his movements were in my completely saturated pussy, on how my breasts were tossed to and fro with each powerful thrust, and on how his balls knocked against me with each impact.

I slept well that night, but it was more of the same right after that. Ben would ask me why I couldn't sleep, and I'd just chuck it up to "I don't know." As my sleeplessness progressed, he'd occasionally press me harder about it. At one point, I let it slip that I didn't do so well when he wasn't with me. As soon as I said that, it was immediately twenty-questions. Ben asked me if I was unhappy with him. Absolutely not! He asked if I thought my sleeplessness was related to Evie's death. No, not really. Maybe. I wasn't sure. He also asked me if I had gone back to drinking a lot. "Not like before," was my answer. This was true in that I hadn't totally passed out from alcohol since my first psychotherapy session. I had built up a tolerance to alcohol, so I was, in fact, drinking more. But I didn't lie because it was *not like before*. Ben said that I should go back to the doctor.

I told Ben that I'd try some over-the-counter natural sleep aids before going to see Dr. Hall. He thought that sounded fair. Melatonin worked for about a month. When it stopped working, I doubled the dosage with no results. I changed to a tryptophan supplement. That worked for about two weeks. Then I went back to melatonin, which stopped working after only a few days. Then someone told me to try a calming powder in my drinks. That had no effect, so I doubled the dose with some results, but it caused stomach pain. I tried a magnesium supplement and sampled *every* different variation of tea that advertised to help promote sleep. No dice. I finally went to ibuprofen pm with good enough results. Ben didn't like the idea of me using that to help me sleep, but he couldn't buck the results. I looked more rested and started taking care of my appearance better. Thankfully, that meant that Ben wasn't going to make me go back to the doctor.

I had two more months until I rotated to night shift. I feared that second shift was just going to kill me because it kept me away from Ben. I imagined that I would manage nights better because I could sleep while he was at work and then spend the evening with him before going to work myself. It's true that Boom was a comfort to me when I was on second shift, but he couldn't keep me from crying. I'd cry and soak his fur with my tears.

Chapter 47: The Promise.

I ran into Don at the grocery store. He was part of a group trip from the nursing home that was headed by the Activities Department. He saw me at the far end of the isle and darted quickly in my direction. Even though he had impaired coordination in one leg and fixed rotation of his neck, he could move fast. And he always moved fast.

"Hey! Hey you! I know you! You're Rod's daughter! I'm coming! Wait for me!" I wasn't walking away from him, but I guess he wanted to make sure that I didn't. The Activity Director, Brenda, jogged to catch up to him. The other activities gal stayed back with the group.

"Hi Don. How are you?" I asked cordially.

"Fine! Fine! I'm fine!" he said. By this time Brenda had caught up to him. "You play the piano with Rod! I haven't *seen* you! Where have you been!?" he said with wild eyes. He always had that same expression on his face. Like everything was urgent. Brenda reminded him to lower his voice. "I'm sorry," he replied. "I'm sorry," he whispered.

"Her name is Ricky," Brenda reminded him.

"Yeah! Ricky! Come play the piano for us, Ricky!" Don rocked side to side rhythmically.

I was completely flabbergasted. I hadn't played the piano since Evie died. I had no desire to touch those keys ever again. As a matter of fact, I wasn't sure why I hadn't sold my keyboard. I didn't know what to say to Don in my astounded state. I hesitated before I said, "I don't play the piano anymore."

"What!? But you play good! You play good for us! Come play for us! Come play 'Amazing Grace'!"

"I haven't played the piano in almost a year, Don," I said to him.

"Please come play for us! Please come!" he begged.

"I don't play anymore," I started to say before Don interrupted.

"Please! Please! Please come! Please come play! Please! Please!" he said relentlessly.

Brenda noticed the distressed look on my face and said to Don, "Don, she said she doesn't play anymore."

"But you remember how! It's easy!! Come play for us!" It was all I could do to keep from having a full-blown anxiety attack.

Brenda said, "Don, don't make her feel uncomfortable. She said no."

"She didn't say no," he said to Brenda with a confused expression. That's true, I didn't say no, but I'm sure he would've said "please" repeatedly even if I had said no.

"It's okay," I said to Brenda. "I could try," I said to Don.

"GoOOod! GoOOod! I love to hear you play!" He clapped as he laughed, "Ha ha ha!"

"I'll play for *you*, Don. Just you," I added.

He started galloping back to the group at the other end of the isle. "Hey! Rod's daughter is gonna play the piano for us! She said she'd play the piano!" he said with his hands in the air.

"I'm sorry," Brenda said sympathetically, as if she knew my reason for quitting the piano. I'm sure she figured it out by the timing of it all.

"I guess it seems selfish of me to stop playing if you look at it from Don's point of view," I said, trying to convince myself that it was going to be okay.

"Are you sure about this?" she asked, as if she could somehow give me an out.

"A promise is a promise. I'll see you soon," I said. I managed to give her a half believable smile as I departed. I left the store hastily without making a purchase. I set my basket of goods down next to the bagger and said, "I'm sorry. I gotta go." A storm brewed inside of me as I stomped to the car. I was so angry; it felt like I might burst into tears. I was tattered to and fro from these turbulent feelings of sadness and anger the entire drive home.

Fortunately, Ben was home when I got there and we didn't have any company. I marched into the garage where he was doing some woodwork and had a complete outburst.

"I ran into Don at the grocery store today!" Angry tears streamed down my face.

"Don who?" he asked. I had Ben's full attention.

"Don with the head injury from the nursing home!" I never really even talked to Ben about him. I had just said in the past that it felt good to play for the nursing home residents. "He made me promise to come and play the piano for him! He was *relentless!* He just wouldn't stop asking, like a little kid! Like he has a...head injury!!" I said, completely flabbergasted. "I don't want to play the piano!" By this time, I was outraged.

Ben walked up to me and lovingly caressed my shoulders. "You don't have to play the piano if you don't want to," he said calmly.

"It doesn't work that way! You don't make promises and then break them! And you sure as hell don't make a promise to someone with a head injury and break it!" I started to hyperventilate. He pulled me closer to him and held me. He comforted me as if what I was saying was rational. He rocked me side to side. I held onto his shirt, ready to either pull him close or push him away. I was balancing on the edge of a complete meltdown composed of sobbing or being physically destructive. Maybe even both. My vital signs were out of control. I could feel it.

"It'll be okay. You just go and play, and maybe it'll be okay." He was great. He was still talking to me so calmly. And he didn't tell me once to "calm down."

I inconsiderately pushed Ben away from me. I felt like a volcano ready to erupt. "I'm so angry! I'm so angry! Why am I so angry!!?" I grabbed my head and winced in pain. I gnashed my teeth and began to whimper a little. Ben walked over to my boxing gloves and then handed them to me. With my jaw still clenched, I put on the gloves and started on my punching bag. I was fierce. I felt like I could surely knock the bag clear across the room. Ben watched me as I punched myself into significant fatigue. It didn't take too long, actually. Punching a bag full force is quite exhausting, especially because it wasn't a regular exercise for me. It was more of an outlet. Usually a pretty effective one at that.

Ben walked up to me when I was done and took off my gloves. I was completely out of breath. He watched me rapidly transform from being on the verge of suppressing my tears with anger, to nearly having a colossal sobbing explosion. With each breath, I alternated from one torturous emotion to the other. I felt like I was in enough control that I could tip the scale one way or the other, but I didn't know which way to go! Which way would be better? I was trapped in this tormented state. I felt like I was going to puke or pass out if I didn't decide.

"No, no, no," I said as I tried to catch my breath. The punching didn't help like it had in the past. I shook my head side to side as this feeling of impending doom escalated. Ben couldn't help me. He had no idea about the mental oppression I'd been going through. This looked like certifiable madness to him, I'm sure. I started on my deep breathing techniques, but I had waited too long. It wasn't working. I fell to my knees. "No! No! Nooooooo!!" I screamed. Ben darted over to the radio and turned the music on loudly, trying to mask my meltdown. "Ahhh! Ahhhhh! Ahhhhhhhhhh!!" I screamed with my hands on my head and my body curled forward as I rocked back and forth on my knees. Ben stood in front of me completely helpless. I screamed some more.

"He did this on purpose!" I yelled. "You did this on purpose!" I wasn't talking to Ben, and Ben had no idea what I was talking about. Finally, I shouted, "I TOLD YOU TO LEAVE ME ALONE!" I fell limp onto my side in the fetal position and weeped.

I had just given Ben the last piece of the puzzle, and now it all made sense. I wasn't lucid enough to see for myself, but I imagined that Ben's face went from one of being confounded and horrified to being enlightened. He got my lack of sleep and my often disheveled appearance because the veil that concealed my depression and anguish was now torn. Just in case you're not following, I believed that God made sure Don and I were in the store at the same time, so that he would get me to play the piano again. God was tugging at my heart strings and I just wanted him to let go!

I cried and cried and cried, as if I had just lost Evie all over again. I gasped for air and dry-heaved, and well, you've heard all of this before.

Ben sat beside me while I lay on the garage floor. After my meltdown deflated to soft cries and whimpering, he said, "Let me help you inside." I didn't respond. He picked me up like a wet noodle and carried me to the bedroom. I rested my head on his shoulder so that I wouldn't have to exert my neck. My tears quickly moistened his shirt sleeve. He placed me gently onto the bed.

"Do you want anything from me?" he asked. I assumed that he meant sex. I shook my head no. He stayed with me a while longer.

Finally, I said softly, "Whiskey. The fan. A scarf, please." The scarf was to tie around my head to help with the headache. I often used a ball cap for this, but a scarf was a better option for sleeping.

Ben returned with my requested items along with a bottle of whiskey and two shot glasses, which surprised me. I thought he was just going to bring me one or two shots and leave the bottle in the kitchen, considering that he voiced to me several times how concerned he was about my drinking. He sat on the edge of the bed next to me, where I was lying with my back up against the headboard. He tied the scarf tight around my head, just like I like it, and he even made sure that it didn't pinch my ears. I was so weak from my outburst that I was only able to hold my head up just long enough for him to assist me with the scarf. Then I went back to resting my head back on the headboard. He wrapped me up in my favorite heavy blankets and turned on the fan for me. And then he poured us our first shot.

I marveled at his love and sympathy for me. He didn't fully understand this type of pain that I was experiencing. How could he? He was never close to God. That was his mom's thing. Yet, he treated me as if he knew. Pain is pain, and he definitely knew the pain of being abandoned. He lifted his shot glass and clinked it to mine. I had enough energy to give him a small smile. How could I not smile? I had the best man in the world.

He poured us another shot and we drank. Man, I loved that burn. I closed my eyes for a second and enjoyed the sensation. Ben put his hand on my face and kissed my cheek. "Do you want another?" he asked.

"Fuck yeah," I said softly, followed by a sniff. Ben smirked a little at my choice of words. Normally, I reserved that word for passionate moments and an occasional outburst, but that day I made an exception. He poured me another shot and handed it to me. I drank alone this time as he caressed my leg. After I finished, I said, "Just one more." He didn't even hesitate to pour. I sipped on the last one and my eyes grew heavy. In a moment of alertness, I wiped my last tear away and consumed the rest of my drink in a big gulp.

Ben took my glass from me and said, "You should get some rest." He stood up and picked up the whiskey bottle. I stopped him.

"Ben, I'll need something from you later, if that's okay." He knew what I meant.

"Of course." He leaned forward and kissed my forehead.

Later on in the day, I heard Ben poke his head in to check on me. He couldn't be real sneaky because the door was a tad squeaky. He had been in a couple of times before, but I was lethargic and in and out of sleep.

"Hey," I said. "I'm awake."

"Are you feeling better?" he asked as he entered.

"Yeah," I said. "Do you want to stay?"

"Yeah." He crawled into bed with me and we began to cuddle and kiss. It started off so sweet and innocent. But, as usual, it quickly transformed into passion. It was because of the way he kissed and touched me. He was a master. We groped each other as we undressed. It still amazed me that something so simple as having his naked body pressed against mine could get me into such a frenzy so quickly.

"What do you have in mind?" he asked me during this escalation. It was the perfect question, but I didn't know the answer. I didn't want something similar to the extravagant night we had after the Thanksgiving fiasco.

I paused a moment. "Something rough, but not too rough," I said.

He was so amazing. He didn't even hesitate. The way he kissed me shook me to my very core. It was sexy, deep, and a little rough. It was perfect. I was no angel myself. After indulging me with his mouth on mine, he turned me over onto my stomach and began kissing my back. I was so sensitive. I trembled and moaned lightly as he did so. He slid his hands down my sides while he kissed my back. You would've thought we were already having sex with the way I responded. I clenched the bedding in my hands and drowned my noises into the pillow.

Finally, he positioned his legs on top of and around mine as I lay flat on my stomach, and he drilled himself inside of me. We had experimented with several sexual positions with him behind me, but this was new. It felt so good, but it also felt like he was going to slide out of me with every stroke. I stopped him for a second and put a pillow under my pelvis. This effectively kept us intact. He was pleased with my modification and said, "Nice." I was surprised that he was able to go balls-deep in this position, but that's exactly what he did. It felt amazing. I started telling him what to do as if the sex were only for my pleasure. He didn't seem to mind.

"Keep your hands on my hips," I said. "Uhh! That's it." I grabbed onto the sheets again and held on for dear life. It was definitely rough, but not too rough. I buried my face in the pillow to keep my noises in check. I came up for air to tell him, "This is good. This is *so* good."

"Yeah it is," he agreed. He grabbed my ass and squeezed it together.

"Uh, uh, uh," I said just before returning my face to the pillow.

Even though we were married now, I occasionally still thought about being number thirteen, but my response to that was different than before. I'd change the channel if I didn't want to think about it, or I'd meditate on how Ben's life experiences made him appreciate me more. I never again got upset about it. That type of reaction didn't fit anymore. The pain of finding out how many women Ben had been with was insignificant compared to all that I had been through since we were temporarily iced. He was made for me. I needed him. End of discussion.

Chapter 48: Preparation.

I debated on whether or not to practice the piano in preparation for playing for Don. I stewed about it for a while, and then decided that I'd better practice. I had no idea what kind of emotional response I would have, and I couldn't chance having a meltdown at the nursing home.

I uncovered the keyboard in the garage and sat in front it for a really long time. I just looked at it emotionless and with a blank mind. I was chill. According to how I felt just sitting in front of it, I gathered that it was going to be easier than I anticipated. So maybe Ben was right after all. As I stared at the keys, I envisioned a plan for the dreaded upcoming event. This included me playing for Don only, and then rushing out the door before he could tie me down with another promise. I had only promised to play for Don, so I was going to show up unannounced and do just that. He was the one who blabbed to everyone else, but I had made them no promise.

I grabbed the first song available to me and started to play. It was "Sanctuary," or "Lord, Prepare Me to Be a Sanctuary." My fingers were a little rusty. No surprise there. I was only four measures in when I started to feel a burning sensation in my chest. I was getting angry: angry that Don had forced a promise on me…angry that I was playing a Christian song giving thanks to my Lord, who I didn't want anything to do with…angry that God had put me in this position in front of my keyboard, and that I was essentially playing into His hand. My body started to tremble. I stopped and stood up quickly. My chair rolled back across the garage. I started using my breathing techniques. It seemed to work well enough to get me to sit back down after a few minutes.

"This is stupid. What am I doing?" I thought. "He likes hymns. I just need to practice hymns and be done with it. 'Amazing Grace' and 'What a Friend We Have in Jesus' one time through and then I'm out." That's all I could do was one time through, and I had to breathe deep and slow the whole time to manage my anger. There was no way I could even think about singing. When I was done, I kicked my chair over in anger and stormed back into the house.

I decided to start on supper to keep my mind off of the piano situation. Consequently, I had time to think about other situations that fed into my anger, including how many times I tried to contact Elane. She was always too busy to keep in touch like we had intended. *She* was the one who originally made the plan to keep in touch! Maybe she would've given me her time if she knew what all I was going through. I didn't tell her. I didn't want to tell her. I didn't want friends because they felt sorry for me. I started to feel that sense of worthlessness resurface. I felt like that discarded piece of trash, like I did back in high school, except now my sorrow amplified the feeling tenfold. I paused from making supper to splash some cold water over my face. I held my stomach and head for a few moments while I cried. After several moments of feeling sorry for myself, I grabbed some whiskey to help me get through making supper.

Ben came home from work shortly after this. He accurately perceived the seriousness of the atmosphere as he entered the kitchen. I didn't greet him or even look at him for that matter. He didn't say anything to me for a while either. This was not like us. He took his coat off and hung it up. Then he approached me and watched me cut up the vegetables for a few moments. Finally, he said, "I see you took the cover off the keyboard. Did you end up playing?" I nodded and continued making supper without making eye contact with him. "It didn't go well, did it?" I shook my head no and continued chopping. "I figured when I saw the chair half way across the room," he said calmly.

I just finished chopping and said, "Supper will be ready in a couple minutes." I dumped the veggies in the salad. Ben came up behind me and gently hugged me. Tears started down my face. It was a soft, quiet cry, unlike my frequent outbursts. I turned around and hugged him for what I thought was going to be a few healing seconds, but it turned into at least a minute. And yes, it was so healing. My body noticeably relaxed in choppy, distinct intervals as he held me. The final wave of relaxation occurred when he put his hand on my head, pulling me tighter into his chest. I exhaled fully and expelled all of the anger out of my body.

We sat at the table quietly for a spell as we ate. Ben broke the silence with, "How was work?"

"I don't want to talk about it." I sulked. "But I would love to hear about your day," I added sincerely. I needed a distraction. Ben got that. He also knew how much I loved attention to detail, so he elaborated and possibly embellished on his stories for me. He saw my mood gradually improve the more he talked.

We cleaned the dishes together as we sipped on our second glass of wine. When we were done, he grabbed our wine glasses and said, "Follow me." We headed to the living room. Ben plugged his phone into the stereo and starting playing the song "You Don't Know Me" by Elvis. I was touched by his thoughtfulness. This was one of the songs we danced to in Toledo the night we proclaimed our love for each other.

"You-have this song on your phone?" I asked him.

"I put it on there after that night we danced to it," he said. I smiled at him. I couldn't believe he remembered that little detail. Neither one of us had pointed out that we had noticed what songs were playing when we danced. He finished his wine and then walked up to me and grabbed my hand to guide me closer to him. He held my hand tight against his chest. He put his other arm around my waist. "While this song was playing, you said to me, 'I love you, Ben. I know it sounds crazy but it's not. I know it seems too soon to know but I know.'"

I thought my heart stopped. That was word-for-word! I gasped for air. I was moved at that moment as much as I was the first time he told me that he loved me. My mouth hung open a little as I processed this.

He continued to quote me. "You also said, 'I feel like your previous relationship fall-outs were destined to happen, so that *I* could have you. You're mine. You're all mine. I need you.'"

I was overwhelmed with emotions. I squeezed his hand and shoulder tight. "I can't believe... I can't believe that you remembered all of that...word-for-word."

"I couldn't get it out of my head," he replied. "I thought nonstop about it for weeks. It helped me get through the week that we were apart." He kissed my lips and then smiled at me. "No one's come after me that hard before." I returned his smile. "And I've never wanted anyone so bad in my entire life."

I fought to control my emotions when I said, "You took my wrecked day, and made it unforgettable." He pulled my hand up to his lips and kissed it.

"You took my wrecked life and made it worth living," he replied.

Now I was bursting with emotion. No, I couldn't compete with him. He was the master of words and the master of love-making. All I could do was love him back, appreciate and respect him, and never let him go. I fought the tears, even though they were happy ones. Instead, I trembled in his arms. Frankly, I was just so damn tired of crying. Ben noticed my struggle to rebuke my emotions.

"You see, that's your problem," he said. "You try to hold everything in. Then you completely explode. It's not healthy. If you want to cry, then cry. It's better than having a meltdown."

"It's so easy to say, isn't it?" I said sarcastically. I looked away from him and fought to control my trembling.

Ben guided my face upward with his hand to make sure that his eyes penetrated mine. He still held my hand in his against his chest as he said, "You're all I ever wanted. You're all I need. I love you more than *any man* has *ever* loved a woman. My heart was consumed by flames and you revived it. Now I burn with desire for you." He said this with intense devotion and profound sincerity. It was too much to handle. He was too much. If I didn't cry, I just knew that I was going to pass out or something. And so I let go and cried tears of joy from being loved so completely. It was overwhelming to be loved so intensely and to be treated so respectfully. Naturally, I was speechless. He kissed me and caressed me as I cried. I didn't doubt anything he said, but I know that he said those things partly because he wanted me to cry. He thought it would help me heal.

My crying eventually dwindled. We kissed and groped each other scandalously. We headed toward the bedroom and made exquisite love with the ambiance of candles. Our evening ended up being perfect. We drank wine, danced to beautiful music, and made sensational love, all under our own roof. It was epic, just like our honeymoon. I was the luckiest girl in the world.

Chapter 49: Fulfilling a Promise.

I chose a day to play the piano at the nursing home when Dad wouldn't be there. I even picked a time just prior to an event that was planned in the activity room where the piano was. This would ensure that I would leave in a timely manner. I left no stone unturned.

I arrived forty minutes prior to the planned activity. This would give me ten minutes to find Don, five minutes to explain to him that I was there to play for him only, fifteen minutes to play the piano, and then leave ten minutes early to be polite and give the Activity Team enough time to put on the finishing touches for the two o'clock entertainment.

When I arrived, I found Don almost immediately. That was good. I had a feeling that it was going to take me longer than five minutes to explain to him that I was just going to play for him. I tried to convince Don of this, but he wouldn't hear of it.

"But *everyone* wants to hear you play!" he said.

"Don, we don't have a lot of time because the accordion player is coming in at two, and I only promised to play for you," I pleaded with him.

"He canceled!" Don threw his hand in the air. "He canceled!" he repeated louder. Then he leaned forward and put his hands on his knees. "Hahahaha!! That's goOOod!" He slapped his hand on his knee. "Now you can play longer! I'll go get everybody! Don't go! Don't go away!" He was off like partly uncoordinated lightning.

"You've got to be kidding me!" I thought. "This can't be happening!" I put my hand over my head and tried to keep the room from spinning out of control. I took a deep breath and walked over to the nurse at the nurse's station and asked if the accordion player had canceled his two o'clock appointment.

"One moment, I'll check for you." I heard her on the phone with the activities department. "Yes, he did."

"Okay, thanks," I mumbled quietly. My plan had fallen apart. I was going to be there forever! I could've lied and said that I only could stay fifteen minutes because I had an appointment, but I was never one for a pre-conceived lie. Or I could've just left! The room started to gyrate harder as I weighed my options. I had to just suck it up. I clenched my fists and dug my nails into my hands and concentrated on the pain it caused.

It took ten minutes for the usual gang to get rounded up. They came in droves: in wheelchairs, with walkers, with assistance from staff, or independently. Don was the only one who could walk without a walker independently.

It soon became apparent that the crowd was going to consist of many more people than the regular gang. They were expecting to be entertained at two, and there I was. Realizing that the crowd was going to be massive, fueled my anxiety. I held my music notebook across my chest and tried not to cry as I watched them all come in with hopeful hearts, looking to be entertained or spiritually guided. It felt wrong. I was in no condition to provide them either of those things. I closed my eyes and reminded myself that I made a promise to Don, and even though it wasn't supposed to happen this way, a promise is a promise.

My thoughts quickly shifted to the accordion player who canceled. These people had their hearts set on being entertained by him. They have limited opportunities for real enjoyment, stimulation, or entertainment–call it what you will. How *dare* he cancel! Didn't he realize how disappointed they would've been if I hadn't swooped in! It was outrageous to leave them high and dry like that! I stewed as I wondered what his excuse was for canceling. I closed my eyes and furrowed my brow at the knowledge that God had his hand in this. This was part of his plan–to get me there–to keep me there. This understanding did not change my emotions one bit. I was still mad as hell.

"We are so fortunate that you came today, Ms. Ricky," Brenda said to me. "Your timing is impeccable. One might even say it was divine intervention because of how sad everyone was that Jim canceled." I smiled at her best I could.

None of the residents could see my anxiety, but I felt like the staff saw right through me, especially Brenda. She saw me clutching my music notebook against my chest earlier. She saw my anxiety and my attempt to avoid coming at all while we were at the grocery store. She knew I had lost Evie just under a year ago, and that coincidentally, I haven't played the piano in that long. She was trying to be so nice to make this a little easier on me. Why else would she have said such a thing like "divine intervention" to me like that?

"Hi everyone, I'm Rick," I started. "I know most of you here, but I see some new faces. I had planned to play just a few hymns for you today."

I wasn't planning on singing while I played, like I had been known to do. I knew that there was no way I could sing even if I wanted to. I'd end up crying–no sobbing–and looking like a complete buffoon. I planned on telling Don that I couldn't sing because "I hurt my voice." It wasn't a lie really because I knew that it would hurt to sing. I also knew I could get away with this because of his head injury. He wouldn't question that logic, but I wasn't so sure the whole group would receive this information well. I imagined that Don wouldn't even ask me how I hurt my voice. I pictured him saying, "OoOOoh, you hurt your voice. I'll pray for you! Jesus will help you!" And that'd be it.

I intended to give Don a copy of the words, even though I knew he wasn't capable of reading well, with the hopes to pacify him so that he would sing instead of me. He had most of the words memorized anyway, and he'd just add humming or nonsensical words in place of the ones that he didn't remember. When he sang in a group, he would blurt out the words that he didn't know a little after everyone else had started to sing them.

I happened to have several copies of the words for the songs on the lineup. I handed out these copies and asked people to share. I told them, "I need you all to sing real loud for me and make a joyful noise because my throat hurts." I was surprised at how easily the Biblical words "joyful noise" came out of my mouth, considering the pain and anxiety I was feeling at the time.

I sat down at the keys and stared at them a little too long. I'm sure some were starting to wonder if I was going to play at all. In the past, I've heard one particular resident have several outbursts during our family's performance like, "That's enough! Go home!" The Activities Team would quickly and kindly remove her from the room so that the others could continue to enjoy. I pictured her yelling, "Play something already!" But she remained silent.

I closed my eyes and took another deep breath. I was tearful already, and I hadn't even started. I felt an unusual quiver in my chest–a heart palpitation possibly. I started my deep breathing techniques. It was fortunate that my back was turned to the group because of the way the piano was positioned. This discreetly hid my discomposure.

Instead of politely announcing which song I was going to play, as I'd done in the past, I just played an introduction to each song. This clearly and nonverbally let the audience know what song I was playing before their cue to start singing. It was easier on me this way. Less talking meant more concentration on trying to be calm. I also played the songs in the order that they were on the list to make it easier for all to follow. "What A Friend We Have in Jesus" was first on the lineup. I had to sing the first few words of every song to get the participants going on the same beat. I choked out each and every word, so I had no doubt that everyone believed my story about my throat hurting.

The group sounded terrible, really. No one had a good voice, many people were off key, and a lot of their timing was off. But their hearts were really into it.

Overall, the whole thing was just as painful as I originally anticipated. I tried to make my mind blank to minimize the pain, but it was so wearisome. It made me physically sick to hear "Jesus" and "peace" so many times in such a short interval. Because of this, I had to maximally concentrate to keep from having a breakdown. I played well despite my body trembling. I followed through on my deep breathing the whole time and somehow made it through a half an hour set. That was all I could do. I was mentally and emotionally exhausted!

When I finished, I said, "Thank you everybody. It was nice to see you all again. I have another appointment to get to." Just to be clear, that wasn't a lie. I had to work third shift that evening. I added, "Have a great day and God bless you." I had already grabbed my notebook as I spoke those words and was headed out the door. My ears had been ringing for ten minutes by then, surely because of high blood pressure from anxiety, so I didn't hear much of the group's reply as I left. I believe I heard a "thank you" and "God bless you too." I certainly heard Brenda's powerful voice say, "Thank you, Ricky. We needed that."

I was nearly around the corner with my unmatched power walk when I heard Don yell, "Thank you! Thank you so much, Ricky! When are you coming back!? Come back and see us!" (No doubt he got my name right because Brenda had just said it.) I was already out the front door when Don finished his last sentence. Despite my distress, I admired Don. He was very family oriented. He didn't say, "Come back and see *me*." His family consisted of his comrades at the nursing home, and he looked out for them.

As I exited the building, I wondered where that "God bless you" came from. I wasn't sure if I really meant that. I had tried so hard not to say His name or to think about Him. I failed continually but, oh, how I tried. Was I just being polite, was I a creature of habit, or did I really mean it? That's what I often said to them in the past just before I'd leave. After quick contemplation, I concluded that it came out naturally, but I really meant it. Just because I was suffering and angry didn't mean that I wished that on others.

My emotions continued to build with every step as I trudged on toward my vehicle, I didn't quite make it to my car before the tears started. My mind was a complete cyclone. I sat there for a while with my head on the steering wheel as I gently wept–much different that my previous tearful sessions. I experienced several blasts of pain around the back of my neck and head that felt like shocks of electricity. During the pauses in between the surges of pain, I produced an accurate modification of Jason Mraz's lyrics to the song "If It Kills Me," regarding my relationship with God. While I rested my head on the wheel, I imagined God singing in Jason's voice, "And I will find a way to you if it kills *you*...if it kills *you*. It *might* kill you." I glanced over at the ball cap that was on the passenger's seat. I felt weak from being out of control emotionally, so I reached for it as if I had a ten-pound weight on my arm. I held it on my lap for a while with my head still on the wheel. Moments later, I mustered up enough energy to lift my head and put my cap on as tight as I could tolerate. I was grateful for the pressure that distracted me a bit from the ruthless headache. I reached for my purse to get some ibuprofen. After about ten minutes of trying to get myself good enough to safely drive, I took off for home.

It was a weekend, so when I got home, Ben was there and waiting for me. "How'd it go?" he asked as I walked straight past him to the bedroom.

"I'm going to sleep," I said in a monotone voice. I didn't even make eye contact with him. I dropped my coat on the floor and kicked my shoes off in the walkway. Ben followed me in.

"I made you lunch. Are you hungry?"

"No," I replied. I crawled into bed with my clothes and hat still on.

"Can I stay and cuddle with you?" He saw my pain and knew the power of his healing hands.

"Yes please," I said in a flat tone. His warm body and hands were so soothing. Whenever he touched me, innocently or passionately, I always felt better. He lay down behind me and spooned me. This position felt good, but I decided it would feel better if I faced him. I rolled over and put my head on his chest, my arm around his waist, and my leg between his legs. My hat fell off in the process. Ben put his arm around my upper back and gently ran his fingers through my hair. I became completely comatose.

My alarm sounded, and I awoke more refreshed than I anticipated. Ben wasn't by my side, but I didn't figure he would be. His hours were different than mine. I slept around six hours. Now that was in addition to the five hours I got before I went to the nursing home.

I feebly got up and shuffled to the shower. I stumbled along past Ben and caught a glimpse of him dozing off on the couch in front of the TV. Well, rightfully so; it was late. I had given myself only forty-five minutes to get ready for work. I regretted that. When I got out of the shower, I saw that Ben had my work clothes lying out on the bed. I got dressed slowly because my body just didn't want to go. I headed toward the kitchen where he had coffee and a sandwich waiting for me. He also had packed my lunch. "Here, sit down," he said as he pulled out the chair. "You're just barely going to make it."

"Thank you, Ben. I mean it. Thank you so much," I said tiredly. "It seems like it's been stormy almost every day, and every day you are my rainbow." I sipped on my coffee.

"That's one of the corniest and most romantic things you've ever said to me," he said with a huge grin. He leaned over and kissed my cheek. I didn't think his perception of my statement was accurate on either account. I've said way cornier and more romantic things. But by the look on his face, I knew that's what he really believed. Well, regardless of whether he meant it or whether he was trying to cheer me up was inconsequential. I was grateful for his kind words nonetheless.

It was a fairly emotionless day. I was drained. Sure, I was gentle with assisting my patients into painful positions on the X-ray table as usual, but I didn't have the compassion that was the inner core of me. Fatigue from anxiety and anger had siphoned it all out of me. I couldn't even fake a smile that day. I had enough coffee in me to keep a team of doctors alert on a fourteen-hour shift. It wasn't doing me any good though. I was still emotionless, but I had the jitters something awful.

My workmate, Ryan, noticed and mentioned it to me. "That's a lot of coffee, even for you," he said. I just told him that I was tired. "You look like a zombie, and I don't think the coffee is doing you any favors. Maybe you should try to eat something and have some water." He wasn't a real personable guy, so the fact that he even noticed *anything* about me and then decided to say something was quite thoughtful for him.

My mind wondered in my fatigued state: "Am I really acting different today? Maybe this is how I always act, but I just feel different day to day. I mean, as if I wore a mask daily. Could I be presenting contrary to what I feel daily, or do I just wear my emotions on my sleeve *all* the time. I was medicated there for a while. Some days I feel great, knowing Ben will be by my side forever. Some days I struggle with trying to keep God out of my life. And even though it's been almost a year now, the loss of Evie still has me staggering."

I always thought I was good at assessments, even self-assessments. I decided that I was a roller coaster that currently was spiraling low to the ground and going through a dark tunnel. I stared off into space as I thought about how far away I was from God, and how I was still so out of control.

"Fuck that shit!" I said to myself, snapping out of it. "Fuck all that shit in my head." I was back to being logical. I don't think straight when I'm fatigued. I dismissed that stupid train of thoughts and decided that I didn't know anything anymore except: Ben and I were deeply in love, Dad and Mom loved me and prayed for me continually, God is real, and Jesus is Lord–even though I was mad at Him for not healing Evie. The latter fact left a hole in my heart the size of a double-barrel shot gun. Those were the facts.

The day was grueling.

I wasn't quite sure if I was going to see Ben in the morning before he headed to work. Sometimes he went in earlier than others, depending on what was on the docket for the day. I was glad to see his car when I pulled in. Even just a hug and kiss good-bye sounded great.

Boom met me at the door. It was a charming ritual that he started, but it was hard for him to keep up with my frequent schedule changes. I was exhausted, but I picked up my furry friend anyway and gently rubbed his back as I walked up to Ben. I was surprised that Ben wasn't dressed for work yet.

"Are you going in today?" I asked.

"Yeah, I have something for you first." He motioned for me to put Boomerang down.

Right after I stood back up from lowering my fur-baby to the floor, Ben grabbed my neck and face and started kissing me. I was so exhausted that it wasn't doing anything for me. He was making such a great effort. Normally this would get me hot quickly, but it just wasn't happening. My lips were clumsy and ungrateful.

I stopped him for a second. "I appreciate your thoughtfulness, but I'm not into this right now. And you know what a white peacock that is. So you can just go to work with a clean conscience and not worry about me today."

"What about me? What about what *I* want?" he asked as he gently rubbed his thumb across my bottom lip.

I paused for a moment. "Oh, I didn't think of that," I replied, embarrassed at my selfishness. "Of course. Let's go. I just thought that you were…" I didn't know how to finish my sentence for a second because I was still embarrassed. "…trying to, make me feel better."

He kissed me again. "That's exactly what I'm *going* to do." He picked me up, wrapped my legs around him, and carried me off to the spare bedroom where I used to sleep when we were just friends. Weird. We'd never had sex in the spare bedroom before. We'd done it on the living room floor, the bedroom floor, the couch, the kitchen chair, the kitchen table, the shower, the computer chair, and even in the Impreza, but never in the spare bedroom. Those areas just mentioned were incredibly erotic but spontaneous, whereas this was clearly planned.

Ben pressed me up against the wall and kissed and groped me as he slowly lowered my feet to the floor. There was a small two-and-a-half inch shelf built into the wall, which rounded the entire room and was pressing into my tailbone. It was uncomfortable, but I was more worried about knocking over the knickknacks that were placed all along the small shelf. As Ben kissed my neck, I noticed that all of the knickknacks were crammed onto the nightstand.

Ben was being really aggressive. He practically ripped my clothes off, and then he continued pressing me up against the shelf hard as he groped and kissed me.

"Ben, this is a little uncomfortable." I said.

"You have *no* idea," he said, not letting up. I had no idea what that meant exactly. He slid his hand down to my vagina to see that I meant what I said earlier. I was completely dry. "Oh, that's just not gonna do," he whispered in my ear as he worked his fingers in and out of me.

I held onto his arms and leaned forward on his shoulder, helpless from fatigue. It was working. I was slowly getting wet and breathless, and I starting to moan softly. I kissed his shoulder in an oafish manner, as if I were completely intoxicated.

Ben wasn't pleased at my slow rate of progression, so he whispered to me using his sexy voice, "Rick, I'm gonna split you in half."

"What?" I piped up. What did he have planned exactly? My heart rate skyrocketed.

"I'm gonna pin you up against this wall and fuck you in half," he said more assertively. The hairs stood up on the back of my neck. Anxiety fired through my body, and I started gushing feminine juices–a paradox, I know.

I squeezed his shoulders tight and said in surprise, "Oh my God!"

He still had his hand below, assessing and facilitating my readiness. "Perfect," he said.

He lifted me up and put my ass on that two-and-a-half-inch ledge and bulldozed himself inside of me. He gave one slow, long, deep, hard thrust. I squealed and frantically moved my hands from his body to the shelf, then back to his body, not knowing what to do.

He grabbed my hands and placed them on the ledge. "Keep your hands here, baby," he instructed. That effectively took some of my body weight off of him, letting him move more freely. That was the hardest thing he'd asked me to do in a while. I wanted to push him away or somehow block some of his force, but I couldn't do that with my hands on the ledge. Ben had his forearms under my thighs and started fucking me hard.

"No! I can't. I can't!" I shrieked.

"You can do this, baby. I'm fucking the sexiest woman alive," he said breathlessly. I was pretty loud during this intercourse, and Ben didn't blast his music like he had done in the past. "Besides," he went on, "this is just a warm up."

"No, no. No. Uh! I know, I know you're joking," I voiced desperately as he drilled me against the wall.

"Rick, don't doubt me. Ah! You just *wish* I was joking." He gave me an extra hard thrust when he said "wish." I screamed a little louder, which made him laugh a little. After several more powerful thrusts, he said, "Here we go." He moved his hands from under my thighs to around my bent legs, forcing them as far apart as they would go.

"Oh my God! No! Oh my God! Ben, no!!" I was frantic. I thought hard about if I was going to have to use my safeword.

Ben slowed down to gentle but deep penetration. "You can do this, Rick. You can do this for me," he said soothingly. He leaned forward to give me a deep, sexy kiss. He really put some time into it too. He had his tongue in my mouth, and he sucked on my lips. I felt my body start to relax. After I relaxed considerably, he stopped kissing me and started gently moving again, but only for a couple thrusts. "And if you can't, you know what to say," he added. Then he seemed to increase his power exponentially. He was so strong, and apparently, this ledge was the perfect height for optimal leverage for him. I tensed up again, and soon, I was screaming louder than I had ever done before. He clearly gave me an out, but he also said how much he wanted this.

"I can...do this...for you. I can do...anything...for you," I expelled in between deep blows. I told this to Ben while trying to convince myself. A tear escaped my eye as a result of pain and high anxiety. His penetration actually hurt more when I was tense, so I had to maximally concentrate on relaxing my insides.

This was even more sadistic than the sex we had after my Thanksgiving fiasco. At least he gave me one hand to brace myself on the bed then. Bracing myself on the bed with one hand was entirely different than having to keep both my hands on the shelf so that he could move freely and fuck me harder.

I tried so hard not to say "no" and certainly not "stop." Instead, obscenities came pouring out of me. Eventually, my screaming died down to deep moans as he continued to drive his shaft deep inside of me while he forced my legs wide open. My face got warm, and I started to perspire. My body became completely relaxed in his arms. (I was definitely his play-toy at that moment.) This caused Ben to morph into a sex-maniac.

"Oh my God!" he cried. "Oh hell yeah! Oh *fuck* yeah!" he said with a clenched jaw without missing a blow. And yes, it felt like he was splitting me in two.

My sounds continued to drop to an incapacitated state of groans. Several times in the past, I felt like I might pass out during ravenous sex. But this day, I was sure it was going to happen. According to Ben, I went completely limp and quiet right before he came. He frantically carried me over to the bed and lay me down. He tapped my face several times and said my name. He even took my heart rate. Finally, I awoke to pretty aggressive slapping.

"Oh, thank God!" he said.

"I'm okay," I whispered after several moments. I didn't really feel okay, and I was unable to fully open my eyes.

Somehow, Ben got me cleaned up and into my pajamas. He also set up my fan and heavy blankets in that same spare bed room.

After Ben showered, he came out to check on me one more time. I was sleeping already. He kissed my cheek and whispered, "My beautiful angel." His kiss aroused me a little, but I still was unable to open my eyes.

"I love you too," I mumbled.

Chapter 50: Yes, Police Officer?

I slept hard after Ben left for work that morning. I dreamt that God was knocking at my door. He knocked gently at first. I furrowed my brow and tried to ignore Him by keeping really busy with cleaning the house. He firmly knocked again. "I told You to go away!" I yelled. I went back to cleaning. He knocked even louder than before. I threw a chair across the room and yelled, "Noooo!" I grabbed my head, which was now searing in pain. He knocked again, more gently this time. I cried and collapsed to the floor. "You hurt me. You hurt me so bad," I sobbed. I lay on the floor on my stomach and continued to cry. "I don't think we can work this out. How can I ever trust You again?"

After a few moments, He began to knock continuously. Anger ensued inside of me and quickly multiplied because of His persistence. I became infuriated. I pushed myself up off of the floor and marched over to the door, intending to open it, yell obscenities at Him, and then slam the door shut in His face. I flung the door open and was momentarily paralyzed by a bright, warm light. I held my arm up to shade my eyes because it was so blinding, yet the warmth was very comforting. The refreshing smell of spring flowers was carried on a gentle breeze my way. I leaned up against the door frame for support as if an inevitable slumber was about to blanket me. I began to slide down to the floor. My body grazed the floor gently, and I heard a loud "crack!" I sat up in bed abruptly and gasped. There was still knocking at my door. This dream surfaced because someone was really knocking on my door, but I was too out of it to know.

It sounded urgent. I flung the covers on the floor and staggered toward the door. My mind darted wildly. I hoped everything was all right with my family: my parents, my grandma, with Ben. I opened the door to see a police officer standing there. My heart sank to the bottom of the ocean. I was in complete dismay.

The cop could see the terror in my eyes, so he was quick and concise. "Ma'am, we've had a noise complaint, and I'm here to investigate." I closed my eyes and started to breathe again. I gulped hard and successfully fought back the tears. The cop could see the terror in my eyes dissipate. I'd never had a cop show up on my doorstep before.

After a couple seconds of composing myself, I said, "Please, come in."

The officer walked in and politely stood near the door way. "I work midnights," I said, explaining my disheveled appearance and why I was in my PJs. "Just give me a minute. I can't look like this in front of you." He nodded and I headed to the bedroom. I came back in a minute, like promised, wearing proper attire with my hair brushed. "Would you like to sit down?" I asked him. Our home was clean, very clean, so he politely thanked me for my offer and took a seat.

"Can you give me your name ma'am?" I looked at his name tag as he questioned me.

"Erika Blake," I replied.

"Do you live alone, Ms. Blake?"

"I live with my husband, Benjamin Blake."

"Are you having trouble with domestic abuse?"

"No sir."

"A concerned citizen reported that there was screaming coming from your house about an hour ago. Can you tell me about this?"

I didn't even hesitate. I wasn't even embarrassed. I was just exhausted. "Well, to be quite frank with you, Officer Taylor, my husband and I were having wild sex," I said emotionless.

He was so professional. This didn't even faze him. After he gathered that I was being serious, he asked, "Was this consensual?"

"Yes sir."

"I'm going to have to ask you to keep the noise down so you don't disturb your neighbors."

I snarked at him with, "We're newlyweds. Where's the fun in that?"

"All the same, Mrs. Blake, I need you to keep it down." He gave me the faintest smile.

"Well, I guess we can go back to turning on the radio really loud. No one's complained about that yet."

"No, not yet," he said, cautioning me.

"So, what happens now?" I asked, motioning to his notepad that he was writing on.

"You get a verbal warning."

"Is that all?" I asked with a smile. "Nothing in writing for me to frame that says 'noise disturbance due to *wild sex*' on it?" I laughed. I was very amused with myself.

"Not this time," he said as he smiled back. Apparently, he was a little amused too.

"Aw-WAH! How disappointing for my husband," I whined. I smiled even bigger.

He mirrored my smile and said, "I'm sure he wasn't disappointed at all."

"No, he wasn't." I laughed generously. I was taken with his candidness. He smiled even bigger, almost to the point of losing his composure. "Well, I'm sure you've seen it all," I added as I finished laughing.

"I've certainly seen too much," he replied a little more seriously. We stood up, and he headed toward the door. I politely followed behind to see him out.

"I hope this is the most eventful part of your day," I said, indicating that I knew what a difficult job he had enforcing the law.

He walked out the front door and turned around toward me. "Not likely," he replied with a smirk.

"All the same, be safe, Officer Taylor."

He nodded and said, "Yes ma'am."

As crazy as that was, I went right back to sleep.

Chapter 51: Sex Class, Anyone?

Ben came home that evening and said to me gleefully, "Man, my legs are just stupid from that Olympic feat we conquered this morning." He had a beautiful grin on his face and a gleam in his eyes.

"Oh, yeah? How do you think my pussy feels?" I replied snidely.

He came up behind me and playfully grabbed my breast and said, "Like the luckiest pussy in the world?" I turned around and pushed him away.

"No. Like the sorest pussy in the world." He laughed at my reaction. I couldn't camouflage my smirk at how cute he was, but I had to try. "Oh, by the way, a police officer showed up at our door this morning due a noise complaint from our wild sex." His mood morphed to a heavy one because, despite my sarcastic tone, he just knew that I wasn't joking. I assured him it was a lighthearted conversation, but he started to pace the house as he worried about what the neighbors might think. Maybe *they* thought he was abusive.

"Well, if they ask, I have no problem vouching that you are a sex master, and I am your humble and willing slave."

"You're not helping, *Ericka,*" he said, completely annoyed at me.

"What? You don't want the neighbors to know that we are having the best sex out of all of them in this damn little town?" I was not being compassionate toward his concerns at all. Then I went off on a tangent like a light bulb went off in my head. "Ya know, I should start a sex class for the women of this town. It could be a second income. I mean third, of course. It'd be the most lucrative one at that." Now *I* was pacing back and forth as I contemplated this scenario. "I'll teach them how to make their men happy in order to secure whatever it is they think they need to thrive in life, whether that's *amazing* sex..." I gestured to Ben as if to say "like what we have." I continued on with, "...gifts, status, or just appreciation!" I was seriously mulling it over as I continued to pace.

Ben grabbed me by the front of my shirt as I walked by and scared me half to death. He dragged me close to his face and said, "I'm gonna fuck that stupid idea right out of your head." Then he kissed me. My heart raced from his abrupt change in mood and his manhandling me.

After the initial shock of it all, I laughed at him. "You could try, but that's not going to work." I gave him a look like *he* was the stupid one because pleasuring me for such an idea would be positive reinforcement, and counterproductive if he really did want me to abandon my *genius* idea.

He bent over and threw me over his shoulder, knocking my breath out of me. I heard him firmly open and close a drawer in the kitchen. Then we were off to the bedroom. He threw me down on the bed and aggressively stripped me. When I tried to help him, he'd push me back down on the bed to stop me. He definitely let me know that he was in a dominating mood. My anxiety was building. I was still so sore from that morning, and I could tell this was going savage sex. I should've known better than to mock him like that. Doing that has only ever caused him to "burn [my] wicked garden down." STP was really on to something there.

After I was stripped of my clothes, Ben started tearing off strips of duct tape. "Ben, I'm really sore from this morning," I said as my apprehension hit the ceiling.

"Aw, that's too bad. Maybe you could add this to the class you are going to teach," Ben said mockingly. "This would be under the part where the wife does something to make the husband happy so she can be appreciated." He just finished duct taping my wrists together and then leaned forward to secure my arms over my head by taping them around the headboard. I didn't get a word in edgewise when he said, "Or you could add a section under types of possible punishments for cynical behavior towards your man." He paused for a moment and looked me in the eyes before he said, "You made your cake, now you have to lie in it." I'm not gonna lie, that was a pretty awesome—Ben messing up that expression on purpose to make fun of me due to my history of destroying expressions. He made yet another perfect opportunity to mock me. He reached over to turn his music on. Then he ripped off another piece of tape and attempted to put it on my mouth.

"What about my safeword!?" I yelled frantically as I rotated my head away from him best I could so that I could be heard.

"There is no safeword today," he said as he fought to tape my mouth shut. "Don't worry, baby," he said calmly. "I'm gonna use a lot of lubricant to make it easier on you, but I'm pretty sure you're not going to be able to make it to work tonight." After he grabbed the lubricant, he said, "When I call in for you tonight, I'll tell them that you can't walk because I fucked you senseless repeatedly today. And if they don't believe me, I'll tell them to read the local newspaper under 'Noise Violations.'"

Believe it or not, he started off gently for just a few thrusts. That's better than what I expected. Quickly he morphed into a psycho sex-machine. I was so grateful that he didn't force my legs apart like he did in the morning because my groin muscles were massively sore. He did, however, play around with holding my legs in different positions. Having my hands disabled gave him enough leeway to move anyway he wanted, so he didn't need to push my leg range of motion to the extreme. He was really having a good time. I could vividly hear his groans, for my sounds were suppressed by the duct tape.

This encounter was so conflicting for me. I *hated* having my arms restrained and my mouth taped, not to mention I was incredibly sore, but I *loved* to watch and hear Ben have so much fun. I had to concentrate on his sounds to avoid having an anxiety attack from being restrained. Ben moved flawlessly inside of me. I concentrated very hard on relaxing my body. He could feel the difference when I'd get like that. His moans changed, indicating that he noticed. He usually gets more barbaric, too, but he kept it just 10% subsavage. I think this was because, even though I fought hard to not have and anxiety attack, he could see the struggle in my eyes and breathing.

At one point, Ben removed the duct tape from my mouth for a couple seconds. I breathed deeply trying to catch my breath. I didn't realize why he had done that.

"No safeword?" he asked breathlessly, giving me only a couple of seconds to reply. I said nothing because I didn't have time to think! And I was concentrating on trying to catch my breath. It's kind of hard to breathe with your mouth taped. He readily reapplied the tape and then continued his fierce thrusts. I decided not to let him think he'd gotten the best of me, so I wrapped my ankles around his neck. He slowed down a bit and let out a crazy laugh, just like the one he did when we were in his car, drifting around the trees. I slid the top of my one foot down the back of his neck, gently pulling him forward. I pushed back with my other foot that was positioned on his collar bone, effectively holding him in place. I just showed him that I still had a little control. He stopped for a second and gave me a look of disbelief mixed with desire. It changed the tone of our intimacy. He grabbed my foot and kissed the top of it several times. Then he slowed down for deep, slow penetration until completion. He was so beautiful to watch. When he was done taking off the duct tape, he whispered in my ear, "I appreciate you." Then he put my ear in his mouth and sucked on it obnoxiously.

I weakly punched him off of me and said, "You're such a Smurf-hole."

"What!? You want it in the Smurf-hole!?" He lunged forward and grabbed me, forcing me onto my stomach.

"Nooo!" I yelled. He laughed heartily as he held me down. Then he grabbed my butt cheeks and spread them apart. I shrieked.

Totally ignoring my screams, he went on, "Well, okay, but first you gotta give me an hour." I wiggled and yelled some more. He laughed again and wrestled me until I stopped fighting him. "Normally, I'd say 'that's a bit forward,' but since you *are* Mrs. Blake, you can have it anywhere you want." He slid his hand between my butt cheeks.

"Ah! No! Nooo!" I insisted. He stopped and laughed some more. I was laughing too by then. "Get off me!" I demanded.

"What? You mean, right meow?" I laughed heartily at this. I thought he had a slip of the tongue.

"Whaa," I tried to ask, but my laughs interrupted me. "What did you just say?" I laughed some more. Ben let me roll from my stomach to my side to hear him better, but he still had me pinned down with his body weight.

"Right meow? You want me to get off of you right meow?" He smiled at how amused I was at his silliness. "I suppose you want a whambulance too." I burst into laughter that could've shattered the windows. My laugh quickly transitioned to a hard, silent laugh.

Finally, I composed myself enough to say, "Exsqueeze me? Baking soda? You're not making any sense." Now it was *his* turn to burst into laughter.

"You are super sexy when you *try* to quote *Wayne's World,*" he said with full gleam in his eyes.

He got off of me and let me roll over onto my back. Then he lovingly kissed me on my lips over and over. Finally, he got up and pulled me out of bed. He dragged me to the bathroom so we could shower together.

Once we were lathered up in the shower, I slid my hands down Ben's chest and said to him, "I don't know. It *could* be fun." I gave him a naughty look. Ben somehow knew exactly what I was referring to, and he was in disbelief at what he had just heard. "I mean, I wouldn't know unless I tried it," I delivered.

He looked at me lustfully and said with his sexy voice, "Mrs. Blake, you *are* a vixen."

"You make me want to do bad things, Mr. Blake," I replied in *my* sexy voice. "You are an amazing lover, and I am your humble servant."

He laughed giddily about that. As he continued to hold me, he said, "Ya know, I wasn't like this before we met." I didn't know what he meant, and I listened intently. He laughed again and went on, "I mean, you called me a 'sex master.'" He rolled his eyes at the thought of it. "I wasn't like that until I met you."

"Really?" I said doubtfully.

"Yes!" he said with another eye roll. "You make me wild and crazy with desire." He gave me a lavish grin and finished with, "You…have awoken…the dragon."

I laughed with delight. "Is *that* what you're calling it!?"

He laughed too. "No, no. That's what I'm calling *me*."

"Uh! I just had a great idea," I said as I squeezed his low back closer to me while looking up at him. "We should get matching dragon tattoos!"

He laughed and crinkled his nose. "What!?"

"Yeah! They could be smaller ones, and maybe on the shoulder blade. Orange, purple, green, and black! But how would the dragon be positioned?" I pondered. "Not flying. Should there be fire coming out of his mouth? There's so many options!"

"Ooh, that *would* be cool. Maybe we could get a dragon coming in for a landing."

"Yeah! Or maybe they could do a front view of the dragon walking towards you, wings up, mouth open, with fire in the throat but not coming out yet!"

"That does sound pretty cool." He looked into my eyes and gathered that I was serious about this. "You're absolutely insane," he said with a smile. And then he kissed me.

Chapter 52: Addicted.

I continued to struggle with how much I needed Ben. I didn't feel anywhere close to being okay when he wasn't around. Fortunately, our physical relationship was still an inferno, but I knew that couldn't last forever. I worried about how I would cope when the honeymoon phase came to an end. For now, he was giving me all I could handle and more. All I needed to do was look at him lustfully, and he'd climb right on top of me. Our physical relationship varied so greatly: playful, romantic, intense, wild, sweet, and it even had some elements of S & M.

One lazy afternoon, I straddled Ben while he sat on the couch, and I began kissing him. I watched his beautiful face and lips work magically. I'd occasionally get lost in the moment and close my eyes, only to open them seconds later to marvel at the masterpiece before me. Our kissing was passionate, but sweet this time. It wasn't hot and heavy at all, rather it was therapeutic and relaxing.

Ben opened his eyes and saw me watching him. I nonchalantly closed my eyes and continued pressing my lips against his. I waited a while before I opened them again. Not long after I did this, Ben opened his eyes again too.

He pushed me off of his lips and said accusingly, "Are you *watching* me!?"

"So what if I am?" It seemed harmless enough.

"You're kind of a creeper," he said in jest.

"I hardly call wanting to see your beautiful face as you kiss me *creepy*. It's hopelessly romantic," I insisted.

Ben raised his eyebrows and reinforced, "Creeper." I slapped him on the shoulder and he laughed. I smiled too.

"This time, kiss me with your eyes closed," he instructed.

"Shut up for a second, and maybe I will," I snarked. He smiled and then pulled me close for another kiss. I held my eyes closed as we kissed as long as I could. It was hard, and it felt unnatural. Ben moved his hand to the back of my neck, and I jumped ever so slightly. I couldn't anticipate his caress with my eyes closed. I didn't realize that I was so dependent on my vision.

I thought I just loved to watch him. Well, that's obvious, but it was definitely both elements. I opened my eyes and noticed Ben was watching me.

He pulled away from me and said, "You didn't even last thirty seconds! How long has this been going on!?"

"It's not a big deal, Ben!"

"So, since the beginning," he determined. I let out an exasperated noise, confirming his suspicion. He tossed me off of him onto the couch, and I bounced on the springs as he got up. I knew him well enough to know that he wasn't *mad*, and that he'd be right back. What I didn't know was what he was up to.

Ben returned shortly and reached for my hand. "Let's go to the bedroom," he said in a serious tone. I hesitantly took his hand and slowly stood up. He gave me unwavering eye contact as I did so. This was either going to be really good or really bad. I was starting to get wet in anticipation. We walked to the bedroom hand in hand.

Because Ben disrobed casually, I gathered that this wasn't going to be savage sex. Ben could tell that I knew something was up by the way I cautiously removed my clothes. I was too slow for his liking, so he helped me along. Ben turned his music on but not too loud, so that was a good sign.

He lay me down gently with his kisses and with his eyes fully open. He intently watched me watch him kiss me for a while. It was a little weird, but I refused to close my eyes. He started to smile as he watched and kissed me.

"Oh, this is gonna be good," he said after removing his lips from mine. "I can't believe I didn't see this before," he said joyfully to himself as he reached over the bed and grabbed something off of the floor.

"What are you doing?" I asked with growing concern.

"You'll see," he replied. This answer upset me.

He turned to me and started to put a bandanna around my eyes. I stopped him by grabbing his wrist. "What are you doing?" I persisted with a troubled expression.

"I'm going to blindfold you and make love to you."

I thought about this while I held his wrist. I did *not* like the idea of being blindfolded, but he did use the words "make love," so maybe he intended to be gentle. Sometimes what starts off as gentle with him can quickly escalate into something rough and wild.

I must've had my hand around his wrist too long because he said, "Rick, let go of my wrist, or I'm going to do this, *and* I'm going to tie you to the bed." I gasped at his harsh words and quickly let go of his wrist. My face was a train wreck. Ben tied the bandanna around my eyes, and I began breathing rapidly. He started off with gently kissing my body. I flinched with each soft kiss and touch.

He stopped for a minute and said, "Let's establish some ground rules."

"Ground rules!? What are you talking about!?" I screeched.

"Rule number one: You have to leave the bandanna on until I cum, no exceptions. If you remove it, I'll make you regret it."

"I don't like this. I don't like this," I said anxiously as my breathing worsened.

"Just breathe," he replied. His motivating words did nothing to help me relax. After a few moments of hesitation, he continued on. "Rule number two: Your safeword still applies, but I know you won't need it," he reassured.

"And you won't duct tape my mouth!?" I asked panic-stricken.

He laughed a little. "Rule number three: I won't duct tape your mouth." He inserted himself into me before I even agreed upon the terms. I squealed in surprise. Ben moved at a medium aggressive pace. Normally, that's what I love, but so far I was completely distraught. I flinched with every kiss and touch, and I fought and blocked his moves best I could at every chance. After several minutes, he took my hand and kissed it, and then he raised it above my head and held it there.

"No," I whispered. "No," I repeated louder.

"Relax, baby. Relax. You got this." He stopped moving for a moment, put his free hand behind my neck and kissed my mouth deeply. I relaxed completely. "Now move your hips with mine," he prescribed. I did what he said and gradually became delirious from pleasure. He stopped kissing and touching me in different places, so I stopped flinching. After a while, he interlocked his fingers with my free hand as he continued pleasuring me. I moaned freely and was completely saturated, saturating him in the process. He let me have this just a little longer before he slid my other hand above my head, with our fingers still interlocked.

"No," I whispered. "No," I repeated louder. He held both of my arms above my head with one hand, freeing him to touch my body with his other hand and not be hindered in any way. I was losing my composure because of this new position. First, he slid his hand along my forearm, down my arm, and to my side. I screamed loudly and tried to flail, but he was too strong to be displaced. I had *no* control! Then he grabbed my breast and pulled the top of it toward him and kissed it. I shrieked again. "Oh my God! No! No!!" My OCD combined with a little claustrophobia and visual dependency sent me spirally. I realized that my reaction wasn't normal under the circumstances. He wasn't pinning me up against the wall, forcing my legs apart as far as possible; and he wasn't pulling my hair, clawing, or biting me. Regardless, he knew what he was doing. He knew when he said, "This is gonna be good." I started to realize that he had acquired a taste for a little sadism back when we were dating, and now he was addicted. Mind you, what is sadistic to one may not be to another.

Ben stopped and said, "Rick, let's start over." He stopped moving and just held my arms above my head. My breathing was frantic, and my lips quivered as I tried not to cry. "Give me your lips, baby," he said calmly. He kissed me deeply, and I started to melt like butter. It took a good while for me to completely relax because of all that he had put me through and because I knew there was more to come. After I totally relaxed, he said to me, "I need you to do something for me, angel. Can you do something for me?" I hesitated a long time before I answered. I pressed my lips together as I thought about what he could possibly want. Finally, I nodded with my lips still pressed. "That's my girl," he said. I gasped lightly from what he said, and that flow of sweet nectar from my pussy increased. I loved it when he said that. It was a play on our age difference and our different sexual experiences.

"Uh," he replied, and then he started moving again. "I need to hear you say 'yes' for a change. Can you do that?" Don't get me wrong, I've said and yelled "yes" plenty of times during sex, but he wanted to hear me say it under conflicting circumstances.

"Yes," I whispered. He put his free hand on my hip, causing me to gasp loudly.

"I love you, baby. Do you love me?"

"Yes," I replied in between my irregular breaths. He slid his hand up from my hip to my breast. "Ah, ah, ah!" I said as if I'd just put my foot in cold water.

"I'm yours forever, aren't I, Rick?" He was still moving at a medium pace, holding my hands above my head with one hand and caressing my breast with his other hand.

"Yes!" I yelled exasperated. He put my nipple in his mouth. "Ah! Ah! Ahhh!" I yelled hoarsely.

After several moments, he took his lips off of my breast and said, "Does this feel good, Rick?" He wanted me to say yes, but I wouldn't. He knew I was going to fold because of my hesitation. He stopped what he was doing and went straight to my lips with his. When he removed his lips from mine, he whispered, "Do you remember what I need from you?"

I fought the quiver in my lips. A tear escaped from my bandanna. "Yes," I whispered back. He started moving again.

"You know I love you, don't you, baby?"

"Yes," I said. I started my breathing techniques. He grabbed my breast with his hand and kissed the inside of it. I flinched, but I was handling myself better.

"You know that you're the best thing that ever happened to me."

"Yes," I replied. He slid his hand down my side and under my butt. I took three deep breaths in a row. I was maintaining a mildly discomposed state at this point. He started pounding me harder. "Ah, ah, ah!"

"That's my girl," he said breathlessly. Another flood came. "Uh, ah!" he said. The flood continued. "Uh! Does this feel good, Rick!?"

"Yes!" I replied as he rocked my body.

After a couple of minutes, he slowed his thrusts down and said, "Rick, do you want me to duct tape your wrists, so that I can free both of my hands to touch your body?" I gasped deeply several times. "Not your mouth, your hands," he added. "And your safeword, that you won't need, still applies."

I let him rock me several more thrusts before I whispered, "Yes." I swallowed hard and debated the possibility of me having a full-blown panic attack. He reached for the duct tape, which was apparently stored in the night stand, and he started pulling at it with his teeth. He made sure not to let go of my arms above my head because he had worked so hard to get them there. I was still doing my deep breathing techniques. As he finished taping my wrists, I whispered, "Start slow."

"Yes ma'am," he replied. He put one hand behind my neck and kissed me and put his other hand behind my back while he thrusted inside of me. This felt heavenly. Then he slid both of his hands down to my butt and pulled my cheeks apart and kissed my collar bone. I squealed as he did so.

"Yes, Ben, yes!" That's what he wanted to hear, but I wasn't so sure I was being honest when I said those words. He was now teetering on being out of control. He grabbed my sides and slid his hands down to my hips. "Ahhh! Ah!" I screamed. Then he lunged for my breast with his mouth and began sucking hard on my nipple as he pounded me. "Fuck!" I screamed in place of "no." I put my feet on his hips and thrust down hard as I pulled my body up toward the head board. I didn't pull him out of me completely, but it was enough to pull him off of my breast. He was surprised that I was capable of this maneuver. I had the look of a cornered wild animal on what you could see of my face. He grabbed my hips and pulled me back down toward him. Without a second's hesitation, he was back to pounding me, but this time he left my breast alone.

"Are you ready for the grand finale, baby?"

"Yes," I said breathlessly. Ben sat up and grabbed a pillow. He lifted my hips and put them on top of the pillow. Then he leaned back and pulled my pelvis down as he thrusted upward into me. This deep grind felt so wrong and so amazing, but very soon, I realized what he was doing. He was going to make me cum and make me yell "yes" while I did so! My pussy soon got hot, and I felt like I was going to be incontinent. "Oh no," I whispered.

"Rick, do you remember what I need from you!?" Ben asked breathlessly as he ravaged me.

"Yes, yes, yes." I said in between deep thrusts.

"Aw! Uh! Ah!" he said in a deep groan as he sporadically changed his rhythm and depth. He reached up for my breasts to change things up and I squealed at the surprise of it. He continued to violate me deeply as he ruggedly raked his nails down my sides to my pelvis. He started to lean back again.

"Fuck me, you monster!" I said to him in between blows. Ben slowed down almost to a halt. Yeah, that was a gamble: me calling him the thing he felt the most ashamed about. "Own it, Ben," I added. "I love you just the way you are. Now fuck me, my monster," I demanded. He remained silent. After another second's hesitation, he turned fierce. He was brutal. He was unrestrained, unashamed, and monstrous. I expelled blood-curdling screams combined with a bit of crying as he continued to tear up my insides and touch me in places that I couldn't anticipate with the blindfold in place. Yeah, I guess you could call that a panic attack, but I was able to say and yell "yes" several times in between screaming and crying. During his Mr. Hyde moment, he came to enough to realize what he had to do to make me cum. He leaned his torso back again and did a deep grind with me. After several minutes of this, I blared, "Ben, I'm gonna cum! I'm gonna cum!"

"Do it," he said daringly. I tried to relax my body and just let go. It was hard, and it never gets easier.

"Yes! Oh yeah! Yes, yes, yes!" I roared as our bodies squished together. That's not really what I wanted to say. Again, having an orgasm felt wrong. The last thing I wanted to do is yell "yes" when something felt so wrong, but I did it anyway because Ben said that he needed me to.

"Ah! That's my girl! Ah!" Ben proclaimed just before he came. "That was fuckin' awesome!" he said, completely out of breath. When he removed my blindfold and duct tape, he saw my tear-stained face and had no remorse. From a guy's point of view, why would he? He just made me cum. He kissed my lips and said, "*You're* fuckin' awesome."

Chapter 53: Stranger at the Bar.

Finally, I was back to days at work. The journey through rotating from first, to second, and then to third shift was a turbulent one, so much so that I was considering making massage therapy my full-time job. I had Ben's support either way. I had several months to figure this out, and I wasn't taking the decision lightly.

On this particular day, Ben had to work a little late. Evie's birthday was approaching and I was feeling depressed. Instead of stopping to get some drinks at the liquor mart, I decided to hit the local bar. I had only been there once with Ben. I didn't fancy going to a bar by myself, but I decided to make an exception that day.

It was early, so there weren't many customers. Just a few guys playing darts and pool, blowing off some steam from their day at work. I was the only one sitting on a bar stool, and I didn't know anyone there. I was thankful for that because I could drink in peace. Ben and I lived ten or so blocks down the road from the bar, so I decided that I would walk home instead of driving if it came to that.

I determined that a Bulleit Rye neat was the answer for my ailment. The bartender was generous with his servings. I sipped the whiskey, pacing myself as I reminisced about what happened the last time I had too much of the Bulleit. I had one and a half glasses before I felt much of anything. And by then it was too late for me. Against my better judgment, I went ahead and finished that second glass anyway. I couldn't focus, and I fell into the wall several times as I tried to walk. I ended up vomiting, partly because I decided not to eat anything while drinking. That was before I smartened up, and before I built up a tolerance to whiskey. Even so, I wasn't about to embarrass Ben in his hometown with my poor drinking choices.

I just started my second glass when a young, black man entered the bar and sat down on the stool right next to me. It was nice to see someone who wasn't white in this town. As a matter of fact, I hadn't seen any Latinos or African-Americans in this town at all. My old church, in Fostoria, was quite diverse in ethnicity. The town itself was about one-third Hispanic, one-third Black, and one-third White from what I could tell. Since I wasn't going to church anymore, I had lost a great many friends–I mean family–of all ethnicities. I still worked in "Fo-town" at the hospital, so I got to experience different ethnic groups there as well. It seemed like people of all races were doing stupid things or were involved in unfortunate accidents that required the use of X-rays. I felt particularly sympathetic toward those who were there to rule out masses. Ruling them in was sad, and, unfortunately, common.

The man on the bar stool next to me wore a flat-brim cap that was turned partly sideways. I collected ball caps myself, but I always hated flat-brim hats. I preferred traditional rounded-brim caps. He had a black leather jacket with shoes to match and wore dark denim jeans. I could tell he was fit despite his loose-fitting clothing. He leaned forward and rested his elbows on the counter, and judging by his face, he was visibly upset. He fidgeted in his chair for a moment before he spoke.

"Zat killin' yo pain?" he asked, motioning with his head toward my drink.

"Nope, but it helps me forget about it for a while."

"Fair nuf, fair nuf," he said with a nod. He sniffed in deeply and then rubbed his nose. "Hey, yo, I'll have what she's havin'!" he hollered to the bartender, who responded quickly.

I've always been a compassionate person, to the point of fault, according to some. Many have expressed to me that I was a target for being conned, manipulated, robbed, assaulted, or worse because of my compassion for others. I always believed that my compassion was one of my greatest strengths. What better way to cause you to pray for someone or to help one in need, than to feel their pain? Jesus was compassionate. One of the commandments even instructs us to love our neighbors as we love ourselves. I had no idea what the origin of this guy's pain was, but I sympathized with him nonetheless. Pain is pain. And pain sucks.

He took a large drink of his Bulleit Rye. "My boy..." The stranger started and then abruptly stopped. I gave him my full attention as he looked down at the counter while he tried to speak. He choked on his emotions and tried again. "My boy done kilt himself," he said to me. He raised his eyebrows, pressed his lips together, nodded, and then turned his head away from me for a moment.

"That's horrible," I said. "I'm so sorry for your loss." I put my one hand on his arm and my other hand on his back and rubbed it to comfort him. I didn't care what other people thought about my forwardness. I only did what came naturally. The stranger didn't misinterpret anything.

"He jus, he jus uh, took uh gun, and uh, blew hiz head off," he said, still looking down. He took another big gulp of his drink. He seemed like a hard-core drinker by the way he handled those gulps.

"That's so tragic," I said empathetically. I removed my hands from him and there was a brief period of silence.

I assumed that this man was talking about a home-boy, or friend, and not his son. I assumed he would've said "kid" if he meant his child, according to the local dialect that I was familiar with.

"I don't know nothin' bout dis, but uh," he paused as he tried to keep composed while talking. "I hear dat chu don't git to heaven if you kilt yourself." He clenched his jaw to suppress the pain. My heart bled for him. What a horrible thought. I've learned this too. What could I say to help him? I had to say something.

"I've heard that too, but I know that God is merciful. If your friend had a moment of repentance and acceptance of God before he died, I know God would honor that."

He looked at me for the first time with skepticism in his eyes. "Don't you gotsta be baptized or summin' to git to heaven?"

"It's recommended that you do according to the Bible, but not being baptized doesn't mean that you can't get to heaven." I looked around the room. No one was paying us any mind, so I went on freely. "Like the thief on the cross next to Jesus when He was crucified. All he said was, 'Lord, remember me when You come into Your kingdom.' The thief essentially admitted that he deserved to die, but he acknowledged that Jesus didn't deserve to share his fate. He called Jesus 'Lord,' meaning he accepted Him as his Lord. And he certainly didn't get baptized. Accepting Jesus doesn't have to be so formal. You may have heard those preachers who say 'Repeat after me. Lord Jesus, I'm a sinner. Please forgive me of my sins. I acknowledge You as my Savior.' Blah, blah, blah. I mean, that's good and all. They're just leading people to salvation who don't know what to say or do. My point is that the thief on the cross didn't know what to say, but Jesus knew what he meant in his heart. Then Jesus promised him, 'Today you'll be with me in Paradise.'"

"What chu some Bible freak or summin'?" he said with tension in his forehead.

"I know enough," I said. I took another drink.

"Hm," he said with a quick exhale. "My granny tole me bout God uh lituh for she passed." He took another drink.

I was near the end of my second glass and was feeling the full effect. I motioned for the bartender to get my acquaintance another drink. "My treat. What's your name?"

"Damion," he replied.

"Rick," I said introducing myself.

"Rick, huh?" he asked with some snark, as if it were a stupid name.

"Short for Ericka," I explained.

"Thanks, man," he said as the bartender sat his drink down.

"So you think dat God, Jesus, or whoevah, knows what we thinkin' for we say it?"

"Yeah."

"Yeah but how you *know* dat?"

"I've got personal experience regarding the matter," I said. In fact, I hadn't told too many people about my personal experience. It was just *too personal*. And it makes me sound a bit crazy.

"You got personal experience regarding the matter," he said mockingly in a monotone voice. He bobbled his head side-to-side slightly as he did so, as if I was being too proper with my conversation for his taste. He let out one short laugh, "Huh! Like, what?" he said daringly.

I sighed. "I don't tell this story often because it's *personal* and people tend to think I'm crazy when I say stuff like this."

"Whachiz! Now you gotsta tell me!" he said, not being able to disguise his excitement.

I rolled my eyes. I wasn't here to entertain him, but at least he was temporarily distracted from the loss of his friend. I started my story with a sigh. "I was at home one day outside doing chores. It was raining. And I asked God a question in my head. But after I asked Him, I got scared and I didn't want to know the answer. I said out loud, 'Never mind. It's stupid, it's stupid, it's stupid.' Two weeks later when I was at church, the Assistant Pastor asked me to come up front, and I did. He said to me, 'You asked God a question, and here is your answer.' And then he told me the answer to my question. I was *blown away*. I didn't even ask it out loud."

"Well, shoot! What was yo question!?" he asked me, beaming with intrigue.

I was a little annoyed because I had just said that it was *personal*. I'd told only one or two other people that story and my reply to them, and to Damion, was, "It doesn't matter what the question was. It was stupid. But God decided to reach out to me and answer this little girl's stupid question just so that I'd know how real and almighty He is." I looked outside and noticed that it was snowing steadily. It was early March, so that wasn't entirely uncommon.

"Dat's uh mite fine story," he said. "Know what'd make it bettuh? If you told da whole thang."

I sighed again and paused several long seconds. Finally, I revealed this: "I told God that I know that I'm a good daughter, a good student, a good friend (when I had them), a good worker, and I was trying to be a good sister. But I wanted to know what *He* thought about me as a child of God. I got scared. I didn't want to hear that I was a disappointment. I didn't know if I could take an answer like that. So I pretty much told him that I didn't want an answer at all."

"What was His answer?" he pressed.

I paused in total disbelief that I was really going to go through this–that I was really going to tell a stranger this, this personal thing. "He said that I was 'brilliant.'" I choked on those words. It sounded so pompous, but that's what He said.

"Wow. You right. Dat does sound crazy."

I took my last gulp, not handling my Bulleits as well as Damion. "I may have been brilliant at one time, but that candle barely flickers now."

Damion was quiet for several thoughtful moments. Then he broke the silence with, "If He's so *merciful* like you say, den wouldn't He help you get dat candle burning brilliant again?"

"Yeah," I said without hesitation. "But I won't let Him."

"Dat's messed up," he said with his brow raised, rubbing his forehead.

"I've lost someone, too, and I'm still mad. God and I aren't speaking right now."

"But He hears your heart so dares uh line communication open least one way."

"Yeah," I said, marveling at how well he listened to me. After another silence, I directed the attention back to Damion. "I know what you're thinking. Did your friend have time to repent, or did he even want forgiveness? My Dad told me once that 'You never know what happens to someone just before they die. Someone who is not saved can become saved in an instant at their moment of death. So no one should presume someone went to hell based on whatever they think they know about a person.' You just gotta think like that and not dwell on it, otherwise you'll never find peace."

"Findin' peace, huh? Sound like you got yo own advice tuh folluh." I politely nodded. He chugged the last of his whiskey and said, "Best be goin' naw."

"You safe to drive?" I asked, as I watched him walk flawlessly toward the back door.

"Nah, Imma walk. I don't live far. Nice chat, Rick."

"You too, Damion."

I watched his unblemished ambulation as he headed out the door and turned right on the snow-covered sidewalk. I ordered a cup of coffee and some cheese sticks after he left because I wasn't in good shape like he was after two Bulleit Rye. I thought about which direction he turned out the door. The bar was on the edge of town. There weren't any houses in the direction he was walking. I didn't want him be unsafe with a long walk in the snow, so I headed toward the door to catch up with him. Surely, I could give him a ride once I sobered up.

I opened the door and turned to the right, but he was nowhere in sight. I walked down to the edge of the building and peered around the corner, looking for him in all directions. He couldn't have gotten far. I was dumbfounded because he was just gone! I walked farther into the parking lot. After scanning in all directions, I turned around to look back at the bar. I didn't see any foot prints except my own. I carefully tried to reassess the situation. Nope, those were my footprints only, but there wasn't enough snow falling to cover his tracks within the forty-five seconds that it took me to head out the door behind him. I looked around for him again, and then at my footprints again. I was so confused. Did I just entertain an angel unaware? There was no other explanation. I walked back to the door and stopped. I know that he turned right, but there were no footprints to the right or left save my own, meaning there was no room for an error in judgment in my drunken state.

I went back inside and drank my coffee and ate my cheese sticks. I couldn't get my mind off it or even wrap my head around it. So what if he were an angel in disguise? Why would he come see me? There are so many people in this world. Surely, there are more deserving people, or people in more need. How many occurrences like this happen daily? Maybe it wasn't such an anomaly. Maybe other people just don't figure it out when they've met an angel. Somewhere in Hebrews, the Bible talks about how we should be nice to strangers because we might be "entertaining angels unaware."

I drove home and was absent minded all evening. I prepared Ben a microwavable meal, which was something we referred to as the "emergency stash" of food, only to be used when we were completely exhausted or otherwise out of food.

I contemplated more about my angel friend. I was convinced that's what he was. (The lack of footprints in the snow... He completely vanished less than sixty seconds.) What I didn't understand was why. I ran things over in my head. Was that a test to see if I was going to do the right thing and help someone out who was in spiritual need? If it was a test, I passed. I did what I was supposed to do for the greater good of humanity, even though God and I were on the outs. What if it wasn't a test? Maybe the encounter was necessary to facilitate my healing. Maybe I couldn't heal until I started talking about God and Jesus to another, letting that person know what He has done for us and reminding myself in the process. Even so, an angel wasn't necessary for that. God could've easily caused someone in need to cross my path instead of sending and angel.

Ben commented on my absent-mindedness that evening. "Did something happen to you today?" he asked as he munched on his microwavable meal. I had decided that I didn't need any more food, so I just politely sat with him at the dinner table.

"I went to the bar after work. I had two glasses of Bulleit Rye, cheese sticks, and a coffee. I met someone interesting. I just can't stop thinking about him is all."

"He must've been quite the enigma." I think I noticed a hint of jealousy there.

"He was Black. He was the first Black person I've seen in this town. He said he lost someone. He was sad and I was able to cheer him up."

"Oh," he said in between bites. "Well, that's good," he added reassuringly.

Chapter 54: A Sickness and a Death.

Shortly after my visit from an angel, Mom came down with a terrible case of pneumonia and had to be hospitalized. It really took her strength away. She spent a week in the hospital, and then she went to the skilled nursing wing of the nursing home that we often performed at. After Physical and Occupational Therapy did their evaluations, they estimated that she would need two to three weeks of strengthening in order to get back home. She had lots of prayers, visitors, and love while she was recovering.

I visited her daily, since she was just a couple of miles away from where I worked. She had several church members in and out during the times that I visited. It was hard to see so many people that I had instantly cut out of my life after Evie passed, and who were once as dear to me as family. Most of them graciously tried to make it as easy on me as possible by being so kind and nonjudgmental. Mom would have had it no other way. I wondered if their behavior would've been different without her there supervising them. It was tiresome to have the same exact conversation with each person. "Hi, Ricky. How are you? You still working at the hospital? I hear you got married." The few who were much more annoying asked two more questions: "Are you going to church anywhere?" and "Are you still playing the piano?"

Miss Bertha didn't like my answers to the last two questions. She shook her head and said, "Mmm, Lord have mercy. I'm still prayin' for you."

"Thank you, Miss Bertha," I muttered angrily.

Don came up to me in complete dismay one day as I walked through the nursing home door. "You're here! You're here! Jacky isn't doing good! They say she's *dying!*" He threw his hands up and then put them on top of his head. Then he shifted side to side anxiously. His eyes looked like they could pop out of his head.

"I'm so sorry, Don," I replied.

Jacky was a regular attendee to my family's music services. She'd come in, sit down, and fall asleep immediately. Her hair always looked like she had stuck her finger in a light socket, and she always wore those large red-framed sunglasses with the dark shades. She wore loud clothes and thick, plastic hoop earrings, like she was stuck in the eighties. She walked around the nursing home expressionless, and she only walked when she had to get somewhere. Don, on the other hand, shot around that place, like a bullet, all day long, talking to whoever would listen to him.

"Come with me! Come with me!" Don led me to her room where she lay in bed. She was surrounded by several of her friends, who were in their wheelchairs or with their walkers. Some of their faces depicted pain, some confusion, and some interest.

The nurse, Katelyn, came in after she saw the commotion of Don dragging me down the hallway. She said to me, "Jacky requested not to go to the hospital. She's a DNR. We are just keeping her comfortable. It won't be long now." She stayed in the room with us.

I looked around at the distraught crowd, then back to Jacky. Jacky only ever came alive when we'd sing "The Old Rugged Cross" and "Mansion Over the Hilltop." I sat beside her bed, put her hand in mine, and started to sing.

"On a hill far away, stood an old rugged Cross
The emblem of suff'ring and shame.
And I love that old Cross where the dearest and best
For a world of lost sinners was slain."
When I got to the chorus, the entire room joined in.
"So I'll cherish the old rugged Cross
Till my trophies at last I lay down.
I will cling to the old rugged Cross
And exchange it some day for a crown."
We also sang to her "Mansion Over the Hilltop." When we finished with that song, Jacky took in a deep, choppy breath and exhaled one last time. Katelyn walked over and palpated for a pulse. She shook her head no, indicating that Jacky had at last passed. The room was solemn.

After a while, Don broke the silence. I was stunned by how normal he sounded when he said, "Do you think she heard that?" I turned to him with my mouth hanging wide open. Don tends to talk loud and breathlessly all the time because he's always running around the building excitedly. "I think she heard that, and she liked it," he continued in a normal tone. "She's with Jesus now and there's no better place to be. I hope that when it's my time to go, you will all sing to me."

"Me too," Tony said. Others agreed with murmurs and nodding. "We will," I heard along with, "Yes, that's a good idea."

After we exited her room one at a time, Katelyn grabbed me and hugged me tight. "That was the most amazing thing I've seen in a long time. Jacky didn't have any blood family, but her adopted family were all here for her. I'm sure that meant the world to her." I mirrored her tearfulness.

"I'm thankful that I got here when I did," I said to her.

"We all are," she said. She hugged me one more time before she quickly departed. I'm sure she had several arrangements to make.

Don stopped me on the way out the door. "You got your voice back! You got your voice back! Hahahaha! That means you can come sing for us again! When will you sing for us!?" He was back to his normal self.

"After my mom gets well and goes home." He was satisfied with that answer and let me leave peacefully. I reflected on the importance of what just happened. I was stunned at how I was able to sing. I didn't think about it when I was doing it. I just felt like it was what I was supposed to do. I wasn't so sure that I could sing again under different circumstances.

I came home to see Ben in the garage working on the same dresser that he had been for a while now. He was finally finished with the structure and now doing detailed carvings.

"It's beautiful," I said as I walked up behind him.

"I was hoping to get it done for your wedding present, but it just didn't happen."

"Well, I am kind of a handful," I said sheepishly, implying that our wild love life was reason that he couldn't finish his project in time.

"That you are," he said, smiling at me. "After all this hard work, this is the fun part," he said, redirecting his attention back to his art project. He carved more designs as I watched.

"Yeah! It's like...licking the icing off of a cake you just baked!" I said boisterously.

"It's not *at all* like that," Ben said with a confused look on his face. "Baking a cake isn't hard, and licking the icing first? That's gotta be the worst metaphor I've *ever* heard." He peered at me out of the corner of his eye when he said that, so he couldn't see that I was trying not to laugh. He directed his attention back to his work. I loved the upset look he gave me when he explained that to me, so I decided to pester him some more.

"Well! It's like...eating your ice cream sundae first and saving the cherry for last!"

"That's even dumber than your first one!" Ben said horrified. I fought harder to restrain my smile. I didn't want him to know that I was just messin' with him, but I just knew that my eyes were soon going to me away if my smirk didn't first. "It's nothing at all like eating *anything*," he persisted.

"Well then, it's gotta be like when you do something really hard, and then you get to do something easier and fun in the end, like a reward!" I said as sprightly as a child.

"That's *exactly* what it *is!* Stop being stupid!" he said. I burst into laughter. Ben turned around quickly in surprise and finally realized that I was joking. He cracked a smile.

"Well, maybe, maybe..." I laughed hard as I tried to come up with something else stupid to say. Ben cut me off by grabbing the back of my head and putting his other hand over my mouth, essentially sandwiching my face, and then jerking me forward closer to him. I instinctively grabbed his forearm. He actually lifted me off of the ground a little when he pulled me forward. This triggered a lustful response in me. Ben only manhandled me like that when we were about to get hot and heavy. I was like Pavlov's dog, only I wasn't salivating. Ben looked into my eyes, fully recognizing the transition that occurred.

I don't know what he was *going* to say, but here's what he said after he noticed my response, "Do you need something from me, love? All this talk about cake, sundaes, and cherries makes me think you need something from me." He held me close to his lips with his hands still sandwiching my face, and he used his *sexiest* voice when he said that. I nodded because that's all I could do under the circumstances. He leaned forward and whispered in my ear, "Say no more."

He forced me to walk backward over to my table that we kept in the garage–the one that I flipped over in a fit of rage before I moved in with Ben. He guided me by my face and neck, for I was still in his subdued lock.

When we reached the table, he removed his hands from my face and went straight for my pants. After he wrenched my pants down to my thighs, he lifted me up and sat me down hard on the table. Then he zealously knocked me down onto my back and forcefully pulled one of my legs out of my jeans. He decided that was good enough. He then pulled his pants down only as far as he needed to and positioned my ankles around his neck. He grabbed my waist and pulled me down the table closer to him. Finally, he moved my underwear off to the side and thrust himself inside of me. He moved so quickly with peeling our clothes off and getting me in the right position that all of this happened within a couple of seconds! It was wild; it was fun; it felt so good. I tried to keep my noises in check since we were in the garage. I'd frequently look at the garage door, knowing that it was unlocked and that someone could just walk right in at any time. Ben decided that my underwear was hindering his performance, so he tore them along the seam and ripped them out of the way. Then he grabbed my shirt and bra and shoved them both upward. My breasts bounced down out of my bra after he did so. He made crazy, light groans and beastily groped my breasts. I had to put both of my hands over my mouth to keep in a relatively quiet state. I could tell by his vigor that he liked how hard I was working to keep from making too much noise. That actually made him wilder.

After he came, he said, "Sorry that was so short."

"Don't be sorry about *any* of that," I replied. "I'm a fan of fast and furious." He smiled lavishly at me. "Now what are we going to do?" I asked because we were bound to have a mess as soon as he removed himself from me.

"Well, these are no good anymore," he said, holding my torn underwear in his hand. "We'll use these." He gave me a spirited look, and I gave him a crinkle-nose smile.

Chapter 55: Evie's Birthday.

Evie's birthday didn't sneak up on me by any means. I had been dreading it. I took the day off work and planned to take flowers to her grave with Dad and Mom. After that, I planned to drink the rest of the day.

Ben was upset that I didn't tell him it was Evie's birthday or that I took the day off. I made him breakfast as he got ready for work that day. He came up behind me in the kitchen and rubbed my shoulders up and down. "I would've happily taken today off to spend the day with you."

I turned to him and said, "I'm being kind of selfish today. Aside from spending a little time with Mom and Dad at the grave site, I want to be left alone."

"I understand," he said as he touched my face with his hand. "But you still should've told me." I nodded.

It was nice to eat breakfast with him before he left. We didn't talk much because nothing seemed to be bigger than *Evie's first birthday in heaven.* Odd. That's not the way I had intended to think about it. I expected that I was going to think, "Nothing seemed bigger than being without Evie on her 26th birthday." I contemplated this change in my thought process while I sipped my coffee and watched Ben eat.

"If you need anything today, just give me a call," he said, followed by a good-bye peck on the lips.

It was a sad day for us all, but I could tell that Dad and Mom were better off than I was with regards to healing from their loss. They made much of the day about trying to help me heal. It was kind but wearisome. Dad talked about heaven a lot: how there was no more suffering or tears, just joy unspeakable, and how it radiates Jesus' glory. Despite his kind words, it seemed like I could've drowned the entire town in my sad, tired tears.

When I went home, I drank…whiskey mostly: whiskey neat, on the rocks, and with hot apple cider. I stumbled through the videos looking for something to distract me from the pain. I came across *Heaven* by Pat Robertson. I held that video in one hand and my whiskey in the other. I stared at it several long moments. I had already watched it once as a promise to Dad, but I was thinking about watching it again. And that's what I did. I watched it and cried, and drank, and cried. There was so much good information on it, but the bulk of what I had taken away from it was that everyone who died and went to heaven didn't want to come back, save one lady who had a baby.

After I turned off the TV, I was drained from my vortex of emotions. I sat down on the couch with Boom and remembered the conversation Evie and I had just before she passed. "If I do die," I reminisced, "I want you to know that I know I'll go to heaven." She also said, "You know, some people don't get the chance that I got: knowing when the end is near. I've had time to prepare my heart. If I had died suddenly in a car accident or something, I don't know if I would've gone to heaven."

I collapsed onto the couch and cried. It felt as if my body was being lifted and lowered on a symphony of pain and peace. I'm sure that at least some of this was due to my intoxication. The painful low was like having my body dragged through the ground with my skin being thrashed by weeds, dirt, and stones. The high was like being lifted out of the ground and into a bright, warm, and comforting light that healed all of my bloody wounds instantly. Then back into the ground I'd go. That was a rough and real feeling experience. I didn't really know how much of it was from my drunkenness, but I knew that I never wanted to be drunk again.

Ben was able to get off work a little early. He just knew, and he was usually right. I was passed out on the couch like a hot mess when he got home. When he woke me up, I puked on myself. Ben ran to get the trash can just in time for me to heave once more. He took my barf-ridden shirt and pants off and tossed them into the can. So there I was, lying on the couch practically naked and smelling of vomit. I heard Ben running the bath water for me as I fell in and out of a stupor. He carried me to the bath tub and helped clean me, as if I were an infant.

"I don't want to get drunk ever again," I muttered as I fought back the last urp. Ben ran a soapy washcloth across my body.

"I can't say that I'm entirely opposed to that right now," he replied.

I was silent for a spell. Then I said anxiously, "I'm hot. I'm too hot!" Panic had stricken me. Ben ran and grabbed a small fan. He put the cool air on me while I sat in the hot water.

After a moment, I said, "That feels good. That feels real good." My eyes got heavy.

"Oh, no you don't," Ben said as he shook my body. He startled me and I gasped. "You're going to stay awake until you eat something," he demanded.

When he got me out of the bath, my legs barely supported me. He sat me down onto a chair where he could dry me off. I was slumped over, mumbling things. I had no idea what I was saying. I do know that at one point, Ben stopped drying me for several seconds. My body started to get cold. I looked at him to see that he was staring at me as if he'd just seen a ghost. I placed my arms across my chest to warm myself as we looked at each other. After a few more moments, he seemed to snap out of it and started drying and dressing me again. I think I went on talking.

After I was clean and dressed, Ben partly carried me to the kitchen with my one arm around his shoulder. He put me in a chair and scooted me real close to the table. He also surrounded me with the backs of other chairs so that I wouldn't fall over. He made me chicken noodle soup and spoon fed me. I felt him harshly grab my hair to hold my head up several times. It *felt* harsh anyway, but who knows, my perception was quite distorted.

When he was done feeding me, I clumsily pawed at him and asked him if we could go to the bedroom. "No, I don't think that's a good idea," he said. "You're pretty messed up." I whined for a bit. Then he said, "Tell you what, if you can hold your head up straight for sixty seconds then I'll take you to the bedroom and give you whatever you want." Needless to say, I couldn't do that for more than fifteen seconds. "I didn't think so," Ben said as my head bobbled down and then back up again.

"That shouldn't count," I mumbled.

"*You're* going to bed," he said. He scooted my chair out and held my hands. "Can you stand up?" I tried, but immediately deviated to the side and almost fell. He caught me and then sighed. He put my arm around his neck once again and helped me into bed. "Thank God tomorrow is Saturday," he said. He tucked me in, kissed my cheek and then left the room.

I went to bed around 5:30, so getting up around the same time that Ben did the next day wasn't hard. I walked into the kitchen using the wall for support. Ben was, of course, up and making breakfast. I grabbed my cap off of the table and tightly fastened it around my head. I dispelled a relieved sigh.

"Coffee smells good," I mumbled as I sat down.

He set down a full glass of water in front of me and said, "You have to drink two full glasses of water before you get a cup of coffee." Once I gathered that he wasn't joking, I was in complete dismay, as if he had just hurled a terrible insult at me.

"One," I tried to negotiate.

"Two," he said firmly. Then he sat another glass of water down next to the first one along with 200 milligrams of ibuprofen. He could've just filled the one glass after I drank it, but he was proving a point, I'm sure. He placed a plate of scrambled eggs and toast in front of me.

"Thank you," I muttered. I started with drinking as much water at a time as I could. That amounted to just a half of a glass. I sighed and then slowly started on my eggs. We sat there silently while we ate. After I finished my first glass of water, I hopelessly looked at the coffee pot. Ben saw my pitiful look and then got up, so naturally I expected that he was going to reconsider my renegotiation. Instead, he got me a straw out of the drawer and put it in the second glass of water.

"This will make it go down faster," he said. I sighed again. This time I sucked and sucked until I was finished. I wanted coffee so bad.

"I'm impressed," Ben said after finishing a fork full of eggs. He got up and brought me some coffee.

"Thank you," I said in anticipation.

As I took my first sip, Ben said to me, "So you met a Black angel at the bar, huh?" I spit out some of my coffee and choked on the other part of it. I coughed a few times and gasped for air. After I stopped coughing, I was dumbfounded and at a loss for words. I held my cup tight in my hands, even though it was resting on the table, and my mouth hung wide open. He smiled because, obviously, I didn't know how he knew that. I hadn't told *anyone* that. "You told me last night when you were drunk." I still sat there frozen with my mouth hanging open. I didn't know what to say. "You weren't going to tell me, were you?"

"I, uh, hadn't decided yet," I stammered. "You can't argue with how crazy that sounds."

He laughed, "No, I can't. So tell me the whole story."

And that's what I did. I told him about the scripture in the Hebrews, about how there were no footprints in the snow, and how Damion seemed to just vanish. When I was finished with my story, I anxiously waited for a reply.

Ben raised and lowered his eyebrows quickly, and then took a deep breath. "That's incredible," he said, followed by a full exhale. He was silent for a couple moments. I took another sip of my coffee. "You shouldn't keep secrets from me. No matter how crazy they may sound. We're married now." He smirked before his next remark. "And I just might be crazy enough to believe you." I smiled back at him. I certainly wasn't expecting that kind of reply. "So, can you hold your head up for sixty seconds?" he asked me, with his eyes fully gleaming. I did remember that conversation from the previous night. His aggressive handling of my hair ensured that I did. I giggled and smiled wider still. "In that case, I just may have something for you." And just like that, my whole morning turned around.

Chapter 56: Reflection.

After reflecting on the encounter with my angel and his words about my need to find peace, I stopped fighting God and actively sought out peace. It was an arduous process because of the way I approached it–because of my analytical personality. In retrospect, it would've been easier if I would've just surrendered all my pain and anguish to God, but that's not what I did.

First, I reintroduced Christian things back into my life that caused me the least amount of sorrow. I started with listening to Christian music on the radio again. My tolerance as to how long I could listen at one time depended on the message being delivered and how tearful I was feeling. Some songs were still too painful to listen to, like "Thy Will" by Hilary Scott. Then I added listening to various preachers on the radio. Lastly, I began playing my piano once a week. Despite all of this, I just wasn't able to talk about religion or even pray, and I was fathoms away from being able to sing about the goodness of God. Even thinking about singing was like a punch in the stomach.

It confounded me that I was able to talk to Damion about God and that I was able to sing to Jacky as she was passing, but I believed that I couldn't do either of those two things again if another situation presented itself. I concluded that I was only able to do what I *had* to do. I had to help Damion. I thought he needed me. I had to sing to Jacky. It's what she would've wanted. At the time, it didn't matter what I was going through. I just knew that I needed to help them. Well, that's what I thought, when really, I needed to help them–to help me. Those things I said to Damion were actually spoken to remind myself. In essence, Damion was part of an extraction team. Acts of love needed to be extracted from my heart in order for me to heal.

At times, I'd try to rationalize what happened the day I met Damion, or pretty much try to talk myself out of the truth. "You did have two drinks, Rick." I laughed at the thought that two used to knock my socks off, but not so much anymore. I saved the receipt so that I couldn't talk myself out of what happened. I paid for his drinks. There was proof on my bill, and that was just more confirmation to the other parts of the equation.

One morning, while Ben and I were getting breakfast around, I asked him, "What do you think about coming to church with me? Finding a new church together?" It was the first time I'd brought up anything to Ben that indicated I was actively trying to heal since Evie passed. It was a very hard thing for me to ask him. I'm not sure why. Maybe I was afraid of his answer. I asked him this question with my back to him as I stood at the counter preparing breakfast. Somehow, this avoidance was supposed to make it easier on me. He stopped what he was doing, walked over to me, and stood beside me. I didn't want to turn and face him, but I had to. It was the polite thing to do. I gulped hard as I turned around slowly to face him. He cradled my face with his hands and looked deep into my eyes. I gasped as he touched my skin. I was trying so hard to control my emotions, and his touch made it all the more difficult.

"Whatever you need," he said. Then he kissed my forehead. I had told myself that I was going to be strong when I asked him this, but he made that impossible. I looked down and tried to gulp back my tears. I tensed my brow and nodded as he held my head and caressed my face. "Always, whatever you need," he reaffirmed. He hugged me, which caused my tears to slide. He held me tight until I was done sniffling.

Chapter 57: Rick's back?

Over the weekend, I talked Ben into going to Lowe's with me to buy bird feeders for our backyard. I thought it was a lavish back yard, especially for it being in town, and that birds singing to me at sunrise and sunset would be the perfect addition. The backyard was surrounded by a tall, white picket fence that sheltered the beautiful plants and flowers that Ben cared for. I took that job over when we married. There was a stone walkway to the center of the yard where a bench and an old water fountain rested.

I didn't realize picking out bird feeders was going to be such a big deal. I hated shopping, and Ben loved to linger in Lowe's. I tried not to get upset at him, but my frequent, deep sighs gave me away.

"You're the one who wanted to come here," he said with snark.

"Yeah, but I didn't want to pitch a tent here," I replied snarkier with a head tilt and an eyebrow raise. "Here, this one," I said as I grabbed the tall, thin metal post designed to sink into the ground and hold bird feeders. I held the pole longways and took off with it toward the bird feeders. I started marching and making trumpet-kazoo sounds with my mouth as I did so. When I passed the outdoor potted trees, I took a quick 90-degree right face, just missing all the outdoor items around me with the metal pole. Then I continued marching on. I did this intending to make Ben nervous, and that it did.

"Oh, geez," he mumbled. He was slightly irritated–or amused–I wasn't sure which. I continued to march on with my trumpet-kazoo noises until I got to the bird feeders. I stopped and put the pole up at attention with the stem resting on the ground. Ben finally caught up to me and began inspecting each bird feeder in the most serious manner. He did this over and over, starting from the beginning of the shelf, as if it were the first time through. I already told him several times which one I liked, and I became totally irritated with him when he started examining them from the beginning of the shelf the fourth time through. It wasn't that I thought he should just get the one I told him to. It was the fact that he couldn't make a decision in a timely manner, even with my input. Instead of barking at him in my huffy state, I decided to get him back.

"I like this one," I said, pointing to the one I liked. Several seconds later, I said, "I like this one," as I pointed to the same one. "I like this one." I went on pointing. "I like this one," I said in the same tone. During the last time I said it, I had let the metal post slip in my hand slightly toward the bird feeders. It didn't even come close to hitting them, but Ben relieved me of it, nonetheless.

"Give me that," he said harshly.

I looked at him holding the metal post and smiled because it reminded me of King Triton's trident. I started singing to Ben. "Ah, we are the daughters of Triton. Great father who loves us and named us well. Aquata. Ha ha ha, ha ha ha, ha ha haaa! Andrina. Ha ha ha, ha ha ha, haha ha haaa! Arista. Haha ha, ha, ha! Atina. Haha ha, ha, ha! Adella. Haha ha, ha, ha! Allana. Haha ha, ha, ha!" As I sang, I walked circles around Ben and made sure that my ha ha ha was as annoying and as close to his face as I could get, considering our height difference. He did not look amused, but he did have a decent poker face at times. "And then there is the youngest in her musical debut. Ha ha ha ha! Our seventh little sister, we're presenting her to you. Ha ha ha ha! To sing a song Sebastian wrote, her 'voice is like a bell.'" Ben had turned away from me and put the trident down. I continued with, "She's our sister—" but before I could finish, Ben turned back toward me and put his hand on my mouth.

"Shut up!" he whispered intensely. He looked at me with those beautiful brown eyes. I smiled with his hand over my mouth. After several seconds, he let go of my mouth and turned around to retrieve the trident and the bird feeder that I picked out. There were a couple of shoppers who had caught my debut and were smirking at us from across the plants as they walked by. Fortunately, Ben didn't notice them or he would've been horrified.

"Did you do that on purpose!?" I asked Ben energetically.

"Do what?" he asked annoyed.

"The song ended there! Did you know that!? Did you do that on purpose!? The only difference was that you didn't let me say 'Ari.'"

"I've never seen *The Little Mermaid,*" he replied tiredly.

"A-ha! I never said it was *The Little Mermaid,*" I said accusingly.

"Let's go," he said, even more annoyed. Ben walked right past the bird feed toward the checkout line. I quickly grabbed a bag and followed behind him. He must've been really upset to forget about the bird feed. I thought I was being cute. I sadly traced Ben's steps the checkout, carrying the big bag of bird feed that was as heavy as my heart. That was how I used to act before Evie died, and he didn't seem to be into that.

Once we got to the car, I tried to continue on with my carefree mood. "Well, now that we're out of that Lowe's labyrinth, we'll have more time for sex today," I chirped. Then I turned my head away to hide that my heart hurt. On the way home, I continued to softly sing *The Little Mermaid* songs, such as "Part of Your World" and "Under the Sea." Ben's mood seemed to lighten a little.

We pulled in the garage, and Ben turned off the car. I started to open the door, but Ben stopped me by putting his hand on my knee. "I'm sorry, Rick."

"What for?" I asked, still trying to hide my hurt.

"You know what for. I haven't seen you that goofy in a while, and I screwed it up."

"It's okay. I suppose a store wasn't really the place for that."

He leaned over and gave me a kiss on the cheek. Then he got out of the car and hustled around to meet me at my door. He grabbed me by my hand, dragging me behind him and up the garage stairs. We tore through the living room toward the bedroom.

"Are you going to show me your portal to a different dimension that you've been hiding from me!?" I questioned with a giggle as he pulled me along.

"Something like that," he said, smiling, and then he tossed me onto the bed.

Later that afternoon, we hung the bird feeders. Boom was outside with us as we worked. He was safe within the privacy fence and with us present. At first, he tentatively marched in place on the grass, letting it massage his toes, but soon he turned as spry as a kitten as he mastered this new sensation. I laughed and scruffed his little head as he bounced by me several times.

"He probably thinks he's camping," Ben said with a smirk. I laughed heartily at that. Ben always said the funniest things.

"Is you campin?" I said to Boom in my girlie pet voice. "Is you campin', Boom Boom?" Ben smiled at the way we played together.

The day ended up being amazing with a lot of horse-play. After one of our sessions of wrestling and laughing in the living room came to an end, Ben held me in his arms and said to me, "I've got you back. I've got my Rick back, don't I." It was more of a statement than a question. I just smiled at him. "I claim it, in Jesus' name," he said. My mouth dropped.

"Where did you learn that?" I asked in astonishment. What he just said was a statement of faith, and that type of thing is beyond beginner Christian practice.

"Your dad." He laughed. "When I asked him if I could marry you, the answer was yes, as long as I listened to a three-hour lecture on God, Jesus, the Bible, and the Holy Spirit, or whatever." I still stood there with my mouth still hanging open. Ben went on, "You know, he knew that I was going to ask to marry you. I made no indication that I was going to ask, and we hadn't even been together that long, but he knew anyway. He had coffee ready and his Bible out on the table and everything!" Ben chuckled with his arms still around me.

"That doesn't surprise me. I'm sure God told him," I said blandly.

"Yeah, I know," Ben said gleefully.

I was silent for quite a spell. Finally, I closed my mouth. "I thought we weren't keeping secrets," I said to him.

"That wasn't a secret. It just never came up."

"That was quite a while ago, and it just never came up?"

"What? So you're mad at me?" he asked.

"No. I'm just confused." I paused, consumed by thought. Finally, I added, "I guess I'm a little upset at realizing how selfish I've been." Now Ben looked confused. "If you wanted to go to church, you could've asked me. I would've went with you."

"Naw," he said as he rocked me side to side in his arms. "I knew you'd come around. I wasn't in a big hurry."

I let him hold me for a bit. Then I smiled and playfully pushed him away. "It's quiz time," I said.

"Shoot," he replied, knowing exactly what I meant.

"So, who is Jesus?"

"He's God's son, who was sent to earth through the virgin Mary to die for our sins, so that we can go to heaven."

"Wow. That was very concise. Well done. So, was Jesus murdered?" I asked, thinking I was being sneaky.

"No. He gave his life willingly. He could've opted out at any time if He would've just said the word." I nodded and marveled at his answer.

"How do we earn our way into heaven?" Again, I was being tricky.

He laughed like my questions were child's play. "You don't."

"How *do* you get into heaven?"

"You have to be saved," he replied.

"How do you do that?" I asked as if I really didn't know. Now I was playing the part well.

"You..." He hesitated. Maybe I stumped him. He continued with, "...ask..." He paused again. "...Jesus to forgive you of your sins, and accept Him as Lord."

I walked up to him, put my hands on his chest, and asked him softly, "Are *you* saved?"

"I, I don't know," he replied.

"Did *you* ask Jesus to forgive you of your sins, and did you accept Him as Lord?"

"I did."

"Then are you saved?" I asked him again.

He smiled at me, knowing that I already knew the answer to that question. I just needed to hear him say it. He needed to hear himself say it as well.

"Yes." He smiled. I smiled too.

"It's as easy as that," I said. I leaned forward to kiss his lips. "One more question," I said. "Who wrote the Bible!?"

Ben's eyes got so bright. "The Holy Spirit through men's hands!"

"Wow!" I said. "You are quite the knowledgeable one! That was a hard one!"

"Did I pass?" he asked with a hearty chuckle as he held his hand on his stomach.

"With perfection," I replied.

I was so amazed by his answers. But I shouldn't have been surprised, knowing that Dad pinned him down for three hours. I would expect nothing less than excellent teaching from Dad.

So, I didn't marry a Christian. I married the man that I loved, but somehow, he became the Christian man that I dreamt I was saving myself for. Even if that weren't exact, I knew that he was well on his way. And I claimed it in Jesus' name.

Chapter 58: Finding a Church.

Ben and I decided to find a church together. I wasn't interested in going back to my previous church because it would be too painful with all those memories of Evie there. Instead, we tried four new churches around our area. He basically let me call the shots as far as what type of churches to attend. I searched for non-denominational churches that taught the Bible–very basic. We attended a different one each week for four weeks. Ben let me choose where to sit, which ended up being in the back so that we could come in last and leave first. This way we wouldn't run into much in the way of conversation. I didn't want to introduce myself repeatedly. I didn't want to tell them where I was from or what I did for a living, or how I'm a newlywed with no children yet, or that I play the piano, or how I haven't been to church in a while. And I didn't want to hear about them either. It sounds coarse, but I was protecting myself.

It was all I could do to keep from crying each service. I wore the lightest tinted sunglasses I could find, so that folks would think that they were prescription glasses. I didn't want to draw any attention to myself by wearing dark shades, but I needed the obscurity that they provided by limiting how well others could see my eyes.

True, each service was painful, but I felt the sting just a little less each time I went. I still couldn't sing though. I just couldn't sing to save my life, but I mouthed the words to avoid drawing attention to myself. And I clutched onto Ben's hand the entire sermon, as if he were my life-preserver, when God should've been the one I was clinging to.

My sweetest Ben, who looks deep into my soul, said to me one day after church, "It's getting easier, isn't it?"

"Yeah," I said with a tired smile.

He smiled back with one much larger than mine. "I'm so glad."

At the end of two months, I asked Ben if he thought it was time to make a decision on which church we should go to, or if we should keep alternating a little while longer.

"Are *you* ready to make a decision?" he asked.

"I think so," I replied. "How about you?"

"Yes. Whatever you decide is fine."

"Actually, I think *you* should pick."

"Yeah?" he asked with surprise.

"Yeah," I said confidently.

"Well, I'm sure we can come to a decision together," he said. I could see his wheels turning. He must've actually thought that I wasn't going to consider what he wanted. He eagerly pulled out pen and paper, intending to break it down pros and cons style. He wrote out the names of the churches and made a chart. He was taking this very seriously. I had a much simpler plan, which involved music versus the sermon: which was more important? Each place we went to was lacking in either area, in my opinion, but not in both. His plan was much more detailed. Yes, he considered the sermon and the Praise and Worship, but he also charted on how friendly and annoying the church members were. He noted which churches had more complainers than others. I was so focused on keeping myself together that I hadn't paid that any mind. He even added a category for age of congregation. I was completely content with going to a church with mostly an older congregation, but Ben valued seeing people his own age at church. The only input that I gave was that I preferred a topic style sermon instead of verse-by-verse sermon. That's what Bible study was for.

Finally, we came to a decision. We picked the church that had a friendly, younger, non-complaining congregation. They lacked a bit in the Praise and Worship department, but the pastor made up for that nicely with the topical sermon.

"I see what You're doing." I was having an unspoken conference with God. "You think that I'm going to help out with the Praise and Worship service. Well, we'll just see about that."

Ben actually interrupted my thought with, "Besides, they could use a little help with the music, if you decide that's something you're interested in, in the future." Kismet. Strange and unexpected happenings like this didn't tend to surprise me anymore. I was used to all sorts of unexplained coincidences growing up in my home. It was just a "huh" moment for me. I marveled for a minute about it. Then my mind wandered back to the fact that I didn't say "no" to God. I just said, "We'll see about that." God loves to throw things back in your lap when you tell Him no.

Ben became quite outgoing at church with meeting new people. He loved to introduce me as his wife and liked the polite attention we would get regarding our age difference. He started buying me beautiful dresses to wear to church. I hung on his arm like a gem. I didn't mind the way he was acting at all. He wasn't overdoing it, and so what if he was. He was happy. Happy to finally have true love, happy to have me love him so completely, happy to have a fiery physical relationship, and happy to show me off. And he deserved all of that! He was quite remarkable. I would give no other man my time, and I sought after him like a lost treasure.

During this time, Ben was growing quickly as a Christian. I felt like he was stepping past me in a way. And that was okay, right? I should be so lucky to have a Christian man stronger in the faith than myself. I learned from my parents that I should pursue a Christian man so that we may be "evenly yoked together," but somehow, I was extremely blessed to get the perfect man for me who became a Christian after we married–no thanks to me. That was God's plan with lots of prayers sent up by my parents.

Dad and Mom hid their disappointment well when we announced that we were going to start attending another church. They were just happy that we were going to church at all, I supposed. We continued the tradition of having a family lunch after church. Dad and Ben would exchange information on what the sermons were about. Mom, Grandma, and I would sip our coffee and either listen to them, engage in conversation with them, or have our own discussions. It was nice to see Ben so excited to talk with Dad about Christianity. Ben was in a sponge phase, and he just soaked up everything Dad said.

There was still a cigarette burn on my heart with Evie's name on it, but I recognized how far I had come. I only hoped that I would keep on healing. After all, it had only been just over a year. I closed my eyes and listened to Dad and Ben talk about

God. As they did so, I imagined Ben, Dad, and Mom standing in front of me on a large rock. Ben was on his hand and knees, with his other hand extended down, reaching for mine. Dad and Mom stood behind Ben, eager to help in any way they could. They all had big, stupid smiles on their faces and were ready to help me climb the next boulder.

Chapter 59: To My Evie.

I'm still struggling, but I'm getting better little by little. I still have difficulty singing praise and worship songs, and I nearly choke every time I pray out loud. But I *am* trying. That's more than I was doing before. Before I was sliding backward. Now I crawl forward. Someday, I'll walk and maybe even jog on. But for now, moving forward is moving forward.

Since my motorcycle adventure, I ride more than ever: to and from work until the winter weather keeps me from my machine. I use that time to try to pray. And when I choke, I stop, take a deep breath, and try to meditate on the lyrics from "Just Say Jesus" by 7eventh Time Down. There's something very real and powerful about the lyrics "When you don't know what to say, just say 'Jesus.' There is power in the name, the name of Jesus." So often, I just don't know what to say to Him anymore. Have I forgotten how to pray, or is it just that it's still so painful?

I'm so sorry that I lost you when I did, just when we were getting close, but I don't really know if we would've gotten as close as we did under different circumstances. We should've been best friends, and we are both at fault for not trying harder. I like to think we'll be best friends in heaven, but I don't know if that's possible. I imagine that we'll *all* be best friends, and in a weird way that makes me sad. Somehow it feels less special that way. It's a stupid thought, so I just do a quick head jolt and change the channel. Regardless, it'll be perfect there, and I'm glad I'll get to share it with you.

It makes me sad that you didn't find your true love on earth. This may sound corny, or crazy, or impossible to know, but Ben and I are soulmates, and we'll be happy forever. It's an amazing feeling. I realize that we are still in the honeymoon phase. Geez, we've only known each other just over a year now! But I also know that nothing will ever come between us. I can't imagine a fight that we'd have that couldn't readily be resolved. We can't afford to push each other away. Neither one of us would survive that. I wish you could've known that amazing feeling. I know that you don't worry about such things now–now that you are wrapped in Jesus' perfect love.

Speaking of us lovebirds, we've cleaned up our language since we started going to church, and Ben's helping me cut down on drinking. He wants me to quit altogether. He's quit for the most part, except for special occasions, to lead by example. I'm holding onto it though because I don't see the harm in having one or two a day. He insists that I need to be able to go without it for a while to prove that I don't need it anymore. I say that I don't need it, I *want it*. But isn't that what alcoholics say? I suppose that I need to rise up.

Ya know, I wonder if Ben noticed that we are thirteen years apart in age *and* that I'm "number 13." I bet he noticed and thinks there's something special to that. I know that we were meant to be, and I don't need such coincidences to solidify that. But if he needed that initially to get the ball rolling with our relationship, then I'm good with supporting that idea. I might ask him if he considered this coincidence in the future on one of our anniversaries, if it doesn't come up before then.

I've seen Johnny a couple of times since I doubled him over. Sadly, I still have trouble not smiling when I think about how good it felt that day. I'm still so mad at him, but I don't hate him anymore. Progress.

I read through all the poems I wrote as a kid, and I didn't think much of them. I definitely went through a preachy teenage phase of poem writing. LOL. Reading through those again was very amusing. I never did finish that book of poems that we talked about, partly because they just weren't as good as I remembered. Instead, I wrote this book, hoping it would help me heal. Just maybe it will help someone else like me, who was fighting peace, to find peace instead. Don't be upset at me because, since I have a captive audience, one who has made it with me this far in my journey, I thought I'd leave one more chapter in loving memory of you.

Chapter 60: Book of Poems for Evie.

"The Land of Clod"

My little world is so weird and so odd.
I think I'll name it the Land of Clod.
Angels have scales, bunnies have long tales,
A giraffe can fly up in the sky.
Don't look now, my hero arrived:
A blue and purple tree with a squirrel beside.
There's a wolf with four ears and a hump on his back,
No grass–just a little–only a stack.
There's a mermaid in the sky
Who just figured out how to fly.
Her head is all hair. You better beware,
For this is the end of my little scare.

"Flower"

The lonely little wondering flower
Rustled in the whistling rain.
The wind blew the poor little lonely flower
And it withered without pain.

"Just Do It"

Don't think positive.
Don't think negative.
Don't think at all,
And just do it.

"Hey Snoopy"–with a clap your hands.

Hey Snoopy (Clap-clap, Clap). You're the man.
No one, (Clap-clap, Clap) can do what you can.
Getting', (Clap-clap, Clap) all the girls.
Got Lucy, (Clap-clap, Clap) there go her curls.
Now Charlie, (Clap-clap, Clap) is a worry,

But you'll fix that, (Clap, Clap) in a hurry,
Lucy, (Clap-clap, Clap) is a nut.
(Clap, Clap) Let her go. (Clap, Clap) So what.
Linus, (Clap-clap, Clap) is a gag. He's always with that little rag.
Hey Snoopy, (Clap-clap, Clap). You're the man.
No one, (Clap-clap, Clap) can do what you can.

"What is a Friend?"

What is a friend?
Someone who cares
When you're in need and in pain somewhere.
Someone whose presence brings joy to your heart.
You think to yourself, "We will never part."
Friends will never let you down.
Through the thick, through the thin
They're always around.
Friends always share their loss and their gain.
They stick together through pride and through pain.
I'm going to tell you just what I'll do.
I promise to stick with you,
My dear friend, true blue.

"The Pitiful Tree on Christmas Eve"

Alone I'm growing here
And in my eyes are tears,
And in my heart are fears,
For being firewood.
'Cause no one will have me
With one day til Christmas Eve.
I say a prayer before I rest
For someone to rescue me.
Then a child looked at me
To see a grubby tree.
She felt me calling in her heart
To come and rescue me.
Her parents looked me up,

And then they looked me down.
Then they said with a frown.
"Let's take it home for Shelly Lee."
My heart was filled with glee.
The comfort of their fireplace
Made me snug and warm.
No more snowfall on my leaves.
And no more winter storms.
As you can plainly see,
I've got a home on Christmas Eve
Because of this beautiful family.

"A Puppy's Point of View"

People pass me by,
Looking in their wallet.
I just don't understand why
No one will cast their ballot.
The mall opens at noon.
Some people come to look and see.
I pray, "Oh please don't go too soon,
Just for this little puppy!"
Then I give them my big brown eyes,
And scratch, and sniff and paw.
They say their hellos and good-byes,
But seemed to like what they saw.
Then more people would arrive.
I'd promise to be true.
My price is only 95.
Am I worth it to you?
I just spotted my new target.
A kid walked by the wall.
This time I didn't start to fret.
I just chomped on my red ball.
The child said, "Hey look you guys!"
The parents looked so pale.
But then they saw my big brown eyes,
And fished me out by bail.

I bet you know the rest.
They named me Little Chew.
I knew that *I* was the best.
From a puppy's point of view.

"Lost Dog"

The dog runs away, away!
Away to find a stray,
And in the wind his tongue.
O little one, your heart is fright
In the middle of the night.
Where doth thou run?
You're as lost as a needle in the hay.
You heard a sound and you were found.
Their happy home is where you'll stay.

"My Magical Mystical Pony"

My magical mystical pony
Meets me at the forest every day.
I'm always so happy to see her.
I bring for her apples and hay.
In return, she gives me rides on her back,
And we go soaring through the blue sky.
I miss that sweet magical pony.
It makes me sad when we say good bye.
But that's okay, the sun will still shine,
And I can always see her again.
I love that sweet pony with all of my heart,
And we'll always be best-est of friends."

"Favorite Pastimes"

Hurdles and high-jump, jumping over bleachers
Swimming and ice skating, tormenting band teachers.
Jumping off haylofts, pretending I have wings.
Racing my friends for maximal height on swings.

Running out back, like a mad dog been freed.
Blazing trails with my bike o'er the weeds.
Hanging upside down from the high maple tree.
Wondering what the neighbors really think of me.

"Ted"

There once was a man named Ted.
Who went to the courthouse and said,
I will testify.
That killer will fry.
And that's how Ted ended up dead.

"Crazy Am I?"

Crazy Am I? 'Cuz I don't wanna see
What's become of the world?
It's a shame, a pity.
I'll never stop trying to make you happy again.
I love to see smiles. Is that such a sin?
Crazy Am I? I just wanna cry
When I watch the news—statistics on suicide.
I love to watch the waves crash on the sea,
And view the snowcapped mountains, enjoying the beauty.
Crazy *you are*! You think you're job's done.
When nobody cares, the devil has won!

"The Impossible Mission"

Whatever happened to warm hospitality?
He's not the same color? Face the reality.
Love thy neighbor as thyself.
"Not good enough for me. I've got more wealth."
Let's start with domestic. You know—home life.
Stop child abuse, and abuse to your wife.
How about foreign? Please stop the wars.
Give pollution our attention and open new doors.
Lend people a hand. Fight crime on the streets.

Our impossible Mission: establishing world peace.

"The Captives"

I came to you in quiet pain with nothing left to lose of gain.
The battle is lost. Our tears, they fall.
Has it been worth it? All in all?
Being enslaved for the rest of my life.
What has become of my children and wife?
The bruises, the beatings… Be brave and stand tall.
I hear death's whisper. Should I answer the call?
A missing life for each and every sigh.
Please God, one more glimpse of that pale, blue sky.
Heartaches come with the silent pain.
Never knowing peace or laughter again.

"The Unwanted"

I'll paint you a picture of my short life.
They cut Mommy open with a blade and a knife.
A gasp for air. The struggle begins.
But in the end, we know who wins.
Who knows, I could've been a doctor or a president.
But you went ahead without your parent's consent.
The truth is I'm being hunted.
Just a piece of trash, unloved, and especially unwanted.

"Behind the Mask"

Behind the Mask.
It's scary you know.
When you first discover,
That you're your worst foe.
You've just found out
What's at the pit of your soul?
To gain sanity back
That'll be your goal.
The ringing in my ears.

I'm bound by tight chains.
Agony of defeat.
Pleasure in pain.
Behind the Mask,
I ask how to correct.
Is this insanity temporary?
Or has it a chronic effect?

"Thoughts Unspoken"

The things I think but cannot say–dare not say.
They light me like a fire within.
The glow illuminates from my eyes, my mouth, my fingertips.
Brighter with fury until I'm motionless,
Powerless to move.

My head tipped back with my mouth open slightly,
Looking to the sky.
My arms extended at my sides
As if chained to the floor.
I burn brighter with fury.
My body trembles.
I fall to my knees.

The angels that camp about me
Are standing at attention, first in wonderment.

An eruption of sound occurs and a horrible cry is birthed,
Heard throughout the heavens.
The animals join in this sad song of agony
Because, truly, it is a beastly resonance
Unrecognized by man.

The angels, now alarmed by these beastly sounds,
Stand with their backs to me.
They are ready to fight on my behalf,
But there is no foe in sight.
They look around sharply, perplexed,

As the wail continues
With no signs of wavering,
Still exhaling.

The light now radiates through my entire body
With nearly no visible signs of me left.
The earth now shakes beneath my feet
Until the light explodes from me.
Too bright to see.

Silence.

There on my hands and knees,
I breathe heavily,
Dripping sweat, naked,
Arms and legs trembling.
I collapse further to my chest and face, still breathing heavily.
Too weak to move, to numb to care.

Sleep comes, warranted.
My face covered in tears.
Each tear named:
Anger, Hate, Despise, Sorrow, Vengeance, Malice,
Injustice! Injustice!! Injustice!!!

No man heard this inaudible cry
That discharged from all of my pores
And stained all that it touched.
No man, just beasts, angels, and God.

Alarm clock sounds, another day.
A better day?
Absurd.
Still these thoughts remain…
Unspoken.

And finally,

"Finding Peace"

I have no more poems deep inside my soul.
I search for positive things to say, but wind up feeling unwhole.
When I think about you, I feel a tear rip through my heart.
I cringe from the punch in my stomach that is:
"Why did we have to part?"
Since you've passed, I been fathoms short of a saint.
If Mom knew what I've said and done,
I'm quite sure that she'd faint.
I feel God's hands tugging at the strings of my heart.
The fact that I'm not pulling back on them is surely a good start.
I *am* trying, which is more than I can say about my past.
I use visualization and positive self-talk,
So my suffering's not so vast.
Without Ben, Dad and Mom,
I would've fallen and surely remained down,
And continued on in my sinful path,
Ignoring God's plea to turn around.
This is an unfinished journey. Of that I am sure.
I can do all things through Christ Jesus, who helps me endure.
I meditate on "I'm a conqueror"
And "This pain will eventually cease."
Finally–*I've stopped fighting*–now I'm on my way to...
Finding peace.

Disclaimer: This book is a work of fiction. All of the names, characters, businesses, places, events, and incidents are either the products of the author's imagination or used in a fictitious manner. Any resemblance to actual persons, living or dead, or actual events is purely coincidental.

www.ingramcontent.com/pod-product-compliance
Lightning Source LLC
Chambersburg PA
CBHW021846010726
47493CB00005B/1580